The drumming [...] there was a v[...] soft and crooning, sing-song, almost chanting. I strained my ears to hear more clearly – it had become vital that I hear it distinctly for the voice, I knew, was an echo from my childhood, the source of all my newly found security.

The voice was everything.

It was a summer voice: a droning of flies behind hot windows, a wood pigeon's hollow call, a warm murmur of content. Scent of honeysuckle and new-mown lawns hung on the air. Deck chairs and sandalled feet and orange squash to drink at tea-time. Through every bliss the voice was weaving and every nerve in my body was caressed by those crooning tones.

I looked up, half expecting to see beyond the window pane a swag of full-blown roses and a sky of hazy summer blue . . .

Nothing.

Just the leaden grey of winter rain. Cold. Bleak. The voice was fading. In something approaching panic I looked down once more at the fabric of the window-seat but the pattern too was growing dim, bleached, lifeless, ordinary once again.

The voice had vanished. The golden globe of safety shattered and splintered all around me and I was vulnerable and cold. A man's voice, Archie's, I knew from the fear that flushed through my body, was being poured on my discomfort like oily black smoke.

"Fern, do you remember your cousin Gerald?"

About the author

Joanna Hines was born in London. She went to Oxford and the LSE. For the past eighteen years she has lived and worked on the Lizard, Cornwall with her Canadian husband. She has a step-daughter, a daughter and a son. This is her first novel and she is currently writing a second.

JOANNA HINES

Dora's Room

CORONET BOOKS
Hodder and Stoughton

Copyright © Joanna Hines 1993

First published in Great Britain in 1993

Simultaneous Hodder and Stoughton hardback edition 1993

Coronet edition 1993

The right of Joanna Hines to be identified as the author of this work has been asserted by her in accordance with the Copyright, Designs and Patents Act 1988.

Printed and bound in Great Britain for Hodder and Stoughton Paperbacks, a division of Hodder and Stoughton Ltd., Mill Road, Dunton Green, Sevenoaks, Kent TN13 2YA (Editorial Office: 47 Bedford Square, London WC1B 3DP) by Clays Ltd., St Ives plc. Typeset by Hewer Text Composition Services, Edinburgh.

British Library C.I.P.

Hines, Joanna
Dora's room.
I. Title
823.914[F]

ISBN 0 340 58399 1

For my parents

Prologue

Swift winter twilight blurred the gaunt outline of the house on the hill: a white tide of mist was stealing up from the valley below and the night would bring frost. The cold evening air was so still that the inhabitants of the house, had they listened, could have heard the faint stirring of the trees that bordered the orchard. And in the copse at the far end of the garden an owl called to his mate before starting off to hunt along the hedgerows. A single beam of light shone from the house across the darkening lawn: it came from an upstairs room where, surrounded by his family, an old man lay dying.

It was to be a surprisingly peaceful death, a quiet releasing of the life on which he had maintained such a grim and determined grip. It had long been expected, and there was no one who would mourn his going, but even so, the formalities must be observed.

The nurse had called them in, and now they stood ranged about his bed in awkward, shifting silence: his second wife, his son and his grandson, each one a prisoner of their own memories as they regarded that face, bleached and humiliated now by long illness, and yet still displaying that granite egotism which had held them captive for so long. In each one the hope now flared that as his tyranny was ending so each would gain their share of his long-awaited fortune.

Archie, his son, had borne the shackles of the dependent son into middle age. Too weak to stay and fight the old man, too greedy to turn away, he had seen his self-esteem eroded by a lifetime of petty tyrannies and humiliations; but now, at last, he saw the coming of his manhood.

Tillie, the dying man's second wife, watched and waited

patiently by his bedside as she had done through the days and months and weary eternity of her marriage, her expression impassive, betraying nothing. She had endured the boredom of sickroom routine, the fretful nagging of sleepless nights down all the years that had seen her fragile charm eroded by bitter lines and twisted hopes, but today, at last, the reward of freedom was within her grasp.

Gerald, the grandson, watched confidently; he was still young enough to be certain of his share simply because he had been a favourite, and spoiled. Fascinated and revolted by the mechanics of death, the lonely intimacy of dying.

The harsh breath of lungs that will soon be stilled for ever filled the room and the emptiness of death gathered around the old man in his huge bed. But still he was to be granted one last shaft of clarity: without opening his eyes he could see the scene around him and he knew what each was thinking. He had always known.

His grey lips twisted into a smile. There had been a child, a small dark-haired girl who had played for a short while on the big lawns about the house and brought daisy chains to his chair, before disappearing for ever from his sight. The vision faded. He could feel the insistent pulse of the three gannets about his bed, but even now, as he died, he would not let go his mastery over them. He had cheated them.

Surrounded by his family, and a smile stretching his lips, the old man drifted finally into oblivion. The nurse, a sentimental lady who had not known the family many days, declared, with a tear in her eye, that it had been a beautiful death.

A few months before, there had been another death; white, sterilised and impersonal. In a hospital within a hospital the two nurses watched occasionally for the end, the second death in a life which had been broken many years before. The face on the pillow was that of an old woman, although she was not yet fifty. Her former beauty, like her youth, obliterated by years of insanity.

"She won't last the night," said the staff nurse.

"Poor thing. It'll be a release anyway."

It was past midnight and the ward for once was quiet.

"I didn't expect her to go so fast," said the staff nurse, "I should have informed the next of kin."

"Her daughter? She can hardly have known her, poor girl."

The two nurses went away to look at the rest of their patients. In the stillness of the darkened room the woman, so long silent, stretched out for speech. "Fern . . ." she murmured, "Fern . . ."

When the nurses looked in again the woman was dead. And the room was filled with moonlight.

Chapter 1

Paula rolled down the car window and stuck her head out into the icy cold. "Hey, mister! You over there!"

She always did have a sweet way with words and the dulcet accent of Illinois sounded more out of place than ever in the museum elegance of this honey-yellow village. "Which way is Long Chatton?"

"This *is* Long Chatton." The elderly man she had just yelled at looked peeved by her North American informality.

"Oh hell!" Paula drew her head back in and turned to me accusingly. "I thought you said— "

"Chatton Heights," I explained. "The village is called Long Chatton but the house we want is Chatton Heights."

"Then why the hell didn't you say so in the first place?" She stuck her head out of the car window and "hey"ed even louder than before. The elderly man had already turned to walk away but he stopped at once, rooted to the spot by her magpie screech. "My friend Mary says the house we want is called Chatton Heights. Know it?"

"Damned tourists," he muttered. "Of course I know it. Everybody knows it. But it's not open to the public, you know. You can't go inside."

This was too good an opportunity for Paula to miss. "Oh yes we can," she gloated. "You see, my friend Mary here, she's— "

"Paula, shut UP!" I spoke through gritted teeth and for once in her life Paula actually did as I asked.

Reluctantly the man came back to the car and stooped so that his head was nearly on a level with ours. He had a beaky face with white tufty eyebrows and his features were pinched with the cold. The temperature must have

1

been hovering around zero, there was a stiffish breeze and it looked as though it might rain, so I could understand his reluctance to loiter.

"You've come too far," he said briskly, as though such stupidity was all one could expect from a pair of female tourists. "You'll have to go back through the main street, then turn left at the post office – that's the building at the end with the sign on it saying Post Office – follow the road up the hill for about three-quarters of a mile and then you'll see the turning on the left. It's just behind all those trees on the side of the hill."

"Thanks," said Paula and she began to roll up her window when suddenly the man put his hand on the glass, stopping her.

"Wait a moment," he said. His expression had changed. With his tufted eyebrows and his thin face and hooked nose he had looked like some rather dyspeptic bird, a vulture perhaps, or an eagle, peering down from a craggy height. Now his eyes sparkled as though the bird had just caught sight of something extremely interesting and quite possibly edible as well. He was no longer looking at Paula, but past her at me and his expression changed rapidly from bewilderment to triumph. "Surely," he said, still clutching the windowpane with arthritic fingers, "it must be . . . it's Fern, isn't it? Fern Miller."

"Sorry." Paula rolled her eyes at me as though to imply it was just our luck to have targeted the local Long Chatton loony. "You must be mixing her up with a cousin. Or something. Thanks all the same, we must— "

But I interrupted her. "Yes," I said, "I'm Fern."

And that was the beginning of it, somehow.

Not the solicitor's letter or the phone calls, not even my grandfather dying, but that moment on the edge of Long Chatton where the overgrown Cotswold village fades into country and the road divides and one way goes past the pond with the horsechestnut tree over it and the other way goes out by the new estate of smart little houses towards Chipping Campden; the moment when Ted Bury looked at me for the first time in my life and knew exactly who

2

I was. There was a drip on the end of his nose and I tried to think of something I could laugh about afterwards with Paula but just then I couldn't think of anything. He was peering at me in a curiously proprietary way and saying, "Well, well, who'd have thought it, Fern Miller," and it was uncanny and homely and frightening all at once. Like in those games of hide and seek when you're a child and you try to keep hidden but want to be found at the same time. I didn't really know what to make of it. Not then. Not for a long time.

Paula was staring at me as though I'd just confessed to being the last of the Romanovs, but the old man was delighted. "I knew it," he said, "I knew it the moment I saw you. It couldn't be anyone else. You're your father to the life."

That was it. I released the handbrake and drove off without saying a word. At that precise moment I couldn't think of anything worth saying.

"Fern? *Fern!* Is that a name? Or what?" Paula hurled the word back in my face. "Who the hell is Fern? Whatever happened to my old friend Mary? I thought you were— "

"Don't shout, Paula. I'm barely a foot away from you."

"But *Fern!*"

"It's my first name. There's nothing so odd in that. Plenty of people use their middle names. Fern Mary. I suppose my family used to call me Fern but Dring always preferred to call me Mary and when I started school I dropped Fern and kept Mary. It was simpler, somehow."

"I should say. Why did your family lumber you with a name like Fern, for God's sake?"

"I never asked. But I was born in hippy time, remember. All that flower power and peace and love. Loads of parents chose odd names for their children."

"Yours sure as hell did. I mean, I could understand Flora, or Rosy or something like that. But *Fern*, that's not even a flower. Just some kind of leaf, isn't it?"

3

I hesitated. Paula is vastly knowledgeable about a great many things but botany is not one of them. I thought of trying to explain the significance of ferns but baulked at the thought of all those spores and sexless reproduction. "Think of Twiggy," I offered instead.

"I guess it could have been worse. Who was that old guy anyway?"

"I haven't the faintest idea."

"He sure as hell knew you. What a dark horse you are, Miss Mary Fern Miller."

"Fern Mary."

"Fern. I don't believe it. Hey! Left here, remember. By the post office with the sign over it saying Post Office like the old man said. What's the matter? Why are you stopping?"

I pulled my Renault over to the side of the road and switched off the ignition. Across the street was a row of sturdy Tudor houses; they had been built with the wealth of wool merchants and clothiers and now they were antique shops and small hotels. For a moment I had the impression that their dark windows were impassive eyes, watching me, waiting to see how I would next act.

Paula said, "We don't need to ask again. It's left here. I remember perfectly."

"It's not that."

"What, then? That old guy didn't upset you, did he? You've gone all weird-looking."

It wasn't cold in the car but suddenly it was hard to speak because my teeth were chattering so much. The sensation that, all morning, had felt like the unexpected flutterings of excitement in the pit of my stomach, now seemed to be curdling into a cold swell of sickness and fear. "I simply don't know if I can go through with this," I said.

"Of course you can, Mary. Fern. Hell, what am I supposed to call you now?"

"Mary will do."

"Don't be such an abject coward, Mary. You can't chicken out now."

I didn't say anything. I had no objection to chickening

4

out, none at all. The only thing in the world that I wanted to do at that moment was to start the car up and drive straight back to Bristol and never come here again.

"Look." Paula changed the subject – to give me time to gather up some courage, I suppose. "That nosy old cow in the post office is looking at us."

It was true. A grey-haired woman with spectacles and a blue overall was peering through the glass window between an announcement of a coffee morning in aid of Cancer Relief and a pile of Postman Pat stationery.

Paula mused, "Maybe *she* knows who you are."

"No," I said with certainty, "it's you she's staring at."

It was usually the way. People stared first at Paula and then glanced briefly at me, if at all, as an afterthought.

Paula can only be described as arresting. With high heels and her hair piled up she is nearly six foot tall and skinny as a rail. Her hair is that dark red colour that looks almost painful and her skin is milky pale. Her features are awkward, clumsy: she has a bulgy nose and a square chin but you never notice those sort of details on her. She is definitely not pretty and has never shown any desire to be so. Just so long as she attracts maximum attention she's satisfied. Today she was wearing black wool trousers and a black top that was halfway between a cloak and a jacket, and an enormous scarf in a shade of magenta that clashed wonderfully with her hair. Huge hoop earrings and a mass of necklaces and bangles that looked as though they had been stolen from the Sutton Hoo burial. The total effect was stunning.

If Paula's aim was to be the centre of attention then mine has always been to melt quietly into the background. People turn to look at me when they want to rest their throbbing eyes after too much of Paula's vivid contrasts. Not that there's anything wrong with my looks – I have perfectly adequate features and plenty of dark hair and people have occasionally told me, in an encouraging sort of way, that I have beautiful eyes, but the whole thing never quite adds up. I look safe and dependable and maybe just a little bit boring. Usually I wear jeans and an old jersey, uniform of the under-twenty-fives, but on that particular day I was wearing my good skirt, navy and just below the knee, a cream jumper and a blue anorak. As I said, I aim to pass unnoticed.

"Look," Paula, more used to bullying, was doing her best to sound persuasive, "the whole thing will be over before you know it and we'll be on our way again. There's nothing to get in a flap about."

"I can't think why I came."

"To meet the solicitor, stupid. And to see the house. You know you've been longing to look round it again."

"But Paula, consider for a moment." I was pleading with her. "Can't you imagine how awkward it will be? I haven't been there or seen any of them since I was six years old and now, suddenly . . ."

"Sure. Okay. It will be a bit embarrassing to begin with, but that doesn't mean— "

"Embarrassing? Paula, they're going to loathe me. And you can't blame them either."

"Why not? It's not your fault if your grandad left everything to you."

"They can still hate me for it."

"But they're your family."

"That doesn't mean a thing. Not to me. Dring's the only family I ever had and she's all I ever want. It's too late for any hypocritical family reunion stuff now. I should have arranged to see the solicitor at his office. It's all wrong like this."

"You'll have to go over the house some time. Okay, maybe they're not going to greet you with open arms like some long-lost prodigal son or daughter or niece or whatever. But give them time. Your charm and personality are sure to win them over eventually. Don't laugh, Mary, I'm serious. People always like you if you just give them a chance to get to know you. And even if they don't end up eating out of your hand, what's the worst they can do? They may resent you, act unfriendly, and maybe it won't exactly be a day at the beach, but that's not the end of the world, is it? If they can't handle

6

your good fortune then I reckon that's their problem, not yours."

"You could be right."

"I'm always right and you know it. You'll have to face them some time. Best to get it over with."

That's what decided me, really. Although one part of me, a pretty big part, wanted to run away and never come back to this place ever again, there was another part of me that I knew would never be satisfied until I had come face to face with my relatives, examined my strange inheritance. The solicitor's letter had stirred my curiosity, so long dormant, into life. I might try to ignore it, but deep down I knew I would never be able to escape. So I started up the car again and began to climb the hill towards Chatton Heights.

After all, as Paula said, the worst they could do was to carry on resenting me.

Or so I thought then.

By the time we had left the honey-coloured charm of the village and turned off the road for Chatton Heights, some of my nervousness seemed to have rubbed off on Paula. Perhaps it was the gate-posts on either side of the entrance to the drive that did it. They were topped with stone birds, wings out as though ready for flight, which looked only slightly less aquiline than the old man we had spoken to in the village. And the driveway itself was fairly impressive, twisting through a mass of dark green shrubbery with no sign of the house itself.

As Paula's fears grew, so mine vanished. Quite suddenly, the whole episode had become totally unreal, the last and most ludicrous event in a whole series of fantasies beginning with the solicitor's letter the week before. Ever since reading it I had been agitated and confused but now, all at once, I was completely detached from what was happening. Not that I felt it was happening to someone else, as people usually say: more as though the me who was driving towards Chatton Heights through a dark green sea of laurel was a different me from the Mary

Miller who did normal everyday things. It was a most peculiar sensation, but a good deal less uncomfortable than that hideous moment of panic I had experienced in the village.

"Your family certainly went in for greenery in a big way," said Paula, and I noticed that her mid-west tones had become unusually subdued.

In fact she sounded both awed and disappointed at the same time and I knew the reason. Such a long driveway should have been imposing, or mysterious, or even, on an overcast winter's morning like this one, a little bit frightening. The driveway to Chatton Heights was none of these things. It went on for a long way but it was solid and monotonous – almost, but not quite, claustrophobic.

I was driving slowly. The driveway contained its fair share of potholes. It seemed to go on for ever.

"There are some fine trees," I said.

It had begun to rain, and that, somehow, was appropriate – raindrops bouncing on big shiny leaves. We both lapsed into an oppressed silence when suddenly, as much to my surprise as to Paula's, I exclaimed, "Look, d'you see that tree over there?" I was pointing to a single large tree, an evergreen than towered above all the rest. "There's the holm oak! It's the oldest tree in the garden. Do you see the one I mean?"

Paula looked, but I could see she was hardly delirious with enthusiasm. "What's so special about some dumb old tree?"

"Oh, I don't know. I just . . . it's not important."

I was confused. I sank back into silence and was glad when Paula did not bother to question me further. I hadn't known, until that moment, that I even knew what a holm oak looked like, much less that there was one at Chatton Heights, or that it was the oldest tree in the garden. But the moment I set eyes on it, that massive bulk of greeny-black leaves, the information was there, whole and complete, right in the centre of my brain. And I would have staked my life that I was right. Still, as Paula said, what was so special about some old tree?

"Who are these people anyway?" she asked. "Who lives here?"

"I think my grandfather remarried, so I suppose his widow must live here still. And of course there's my uncle."

"Is he married?"

"His wife died some time ago." I didn't elaborate. I didn't like to admit that most of my knowledge concerning the household was gleaned from magazine articles about my uncle.

"Any children?"

"There was a boy about my age."

Before Paula could plumb the full depths of my ignorance concerning my relatives, a sudden twist in the driveway brought us to the front of the house.

Paula caught her breath. "Je – esus!" she murmured.

I said nothing. Only stared. The house distorted scale, diminishing the viewer. My Renault became tiny, a rowboat dwarfed by the shadow of a mile-long supertanker.

On that first sight of Chatton Heights I was struck with the amazement that has always come back to me whenever I see the house again after an absence: amazement that so much money and time and labour was ever squandered on constructing something so totally devoid of merit. It was big and it was ugly. To recognise the full extent of the architect's achievement you have to remember that Long Chatton lay in the heart of the Cotswolds and that the Heights, like all the houses round about, was built of the mellow gold local stone. A beautiful stone – anywhere but here.

Here the honey-gold colour appeared to have soured into something resembling jaundice. Perhaps it was the fault of all those fussy additions: red brick round the doorways, irritating patches of stained glass. "More is better" – the message of a rich man's house. I suppose the style of architecture could charitably be called late Victorian Gothic but it has always seemed to me to bear more resemblance to one of those huge Victorian prisons than to any cathedral I can think of. Almost as though

9

the architect had known instinctively that many of the future inhabitants of the house would have been more at home in some kind of penitentiary or asylum than in an ordinary house.

In fact, as I later discovered, when my great-great-grandfather built the place his intention was to use it to house the incomparable art collection he one day hoped to acquire, and the architect was given strict instructions to make it as burglar-proof as possible. Hence the air of fortification, the high narrow windows and the massively thick doors. Since I have never been able to imagine anyone in their right mind trying to force their way *into* Chatton Heights, the building's fortifications have always seemed designed to prevent escape. My burglar-fearing ancestor, by the way, died in a characteristic fit of apoplectic rage before he had the chance to spend the money he had worked so hard to accrue, so the art collection never materialised. There were a couple of Tintorettos, I believe, and a few other items, but they were sold just after the First World War, to pay death duties.

"Jesus," Paula said again, "it sure is big."

"Yes." There was no denying it.

She looked at me sideways. "Are you sure all this belongs to you?" Like most North Americans she was constantly baffled by the English class structure but she understood and was impressed by money. And Chatton Heights breathed money. Look at me, it boomed, I am the biggest house for miles around. I am Money. I can afford to be ugly. Prettiness is for the poor and the mediocre.

And now this monument to Victorian mercantile certainties had been passed to me, the least certain person of all.

"Apparently," I answered, wavering.

"So what do we do now?"

It was a reasonable question. I had parked the car before the largest front door I could ever remember having seen (the kind of heavy wooden door with iron bar and studs that it takes six Nubian slaves to open in the films) but it remained resolutely shut. I knew that I should go and knock on the door, or try to find another door that showed some signs of having been opened during the past fifty years or so, but I didn't.

Paula drummed on the dashboard, her orange fingernails dancing. "Come on, Mary," she said, "we can't just . . . oh look, someone's coming."

From round the far corner of the building, a huge distance away, a weird figure was hurrying towards us. Hurrying, scurrying, dancing sideways like an insect caught by a draught. Coat flapping, head bowed against the wind.

"Who in hell is this?" Paula asked incredulously.

Since I had not the faintest idea I didn't answer, but climbed out of the car.

The windblown insect-woman almost collided with me and there was an overpowering scent of mothballs, lavender and stale wardrobes, like the bundles of old clothes in an Oxfam shop. A smell of rejection and lack of care.

"Of course," she gasped, "certainly . . . so sorry."

It was hard to tell her age. She had huge, china-blue eyes which protruded rather as though her thyroids were out of tune. The skin on her face was baby-smooth, unnaturally smooth for a woman already past middle age, with the exception of the area around her mouth where the skin was puckered and furrowed in a mass of tiny wrinkles, almost as though someone had thrown a hairnet over her chin. Or as if once, long ago, she had dipped the lower part of her face in cobwebs and they had remained glued there ever since. The contrast between the wax-doll smoothness of her upper face, with its staring blue eyes, and that tiny mouth trapped in cobwebs below was most disconcerting. I consoled myself with the thought that she was probably some dotty old retainer, kept on by the family as a gesture of benevolence.

"Good morning," I said, "I'm Mary – I mean, Fern. Mr Miller's grand-daughter."

"This door is never . . . you must have thought . . . we so glad at last . . . *family*!" This last word was emphasised with a heavier breath that was almost a groan and then this strange woman suddenly flung her arms around my neck

11

and her puckered mouth landed a kiss on my cheek. My immediate response was one of intense physical revulsion and it was all I could do to stop myself from pushing her away. It was a reaction, I was to discover, that the poor woman produced in almost everyone.

Paula had got out of the car too and she was rubbing her hands together to revive her circulation. Ignoring Paula completely, the woman darted off and ran up the five broad steps to the front door and began to turn the enormous handle backwards and forwards with great energy. Thinking she was going to let us in we began to follow her but she turned to us, shaking her head and smiling. "This is the main . . . but never since I can . . . if we go round the . . ." And, having demonstrated the unshakeable shutness of that particular door, she scuttled down the steps and back the way she had come. We followed, walking briskly. It was very cold. Big, isolated drops of rain were splashing on the gravel.

At the side of the house, towards the back, we entered through what must, in a different era, have been intended as a garden room. There was a glass roof and a tiled floor but no sign that it had ever contained any plants. Wellington boots and mackintoshes, an old dog-bed, a few bundles of yellowing newspapers, a dead Christmas tree, a rusting washing machine.

The first impression, on entering the house itself, was that there was no appreciable improvement in temperature from the icy cold outdoors. In fact, the mausoleum chill of the long passageway in which we found ourselves and the damp stone flags of the floor combined to create an impression of subterranean gloom.

The insect-woman scurried ahead of us, occasionally turning to interject odd little phrases, but her speech was so disjointed and her voice so light and breathy, the kind of voice a dragonfly might have if it could speak, that it was almost impossible to make out what she was saying. I caught the words "solicitor" and "apple crumble" and "summer" but couldn't work out any connection between them.

We emerged into a huge hallway with a wide flight of stairs leading up to a first-floor landing domed with a glass skylight. There were some pictures on the walls, most of them landscapes that looked as though they had been painted at dusk, though that might have been the effect of several layers of varnish, and a massive fireplace of black marble. Amid all this reproduction baronial bleakness the spindly modern table which held telephone and directories was ridiculously out of place, especially as the wall above it was graced with a pair of murderous-looking pikestaffs on one of which was impaled a local bus timetable. And there, facing the stairs, was the door through which we had failed to enter: inside the house we had followed a route parallel to the one we had taken outside.

Now that we had reached the hall the woman suddenly appeared to be uncertain how to proceed. She pirouetted slowly as though suspended from the ceiling by a long thread. Then she darted forward suddenly as though to open one of the doors leading from the hall, but, changing her mind, turned again and came back to the centre, glancing first at Paula, then at me, with increasing agitation.

"Mr Markham is . . . not the keep waiting . . . perhaps after lunch?"

Paula was quicker than I was to interpret the jumbled phrases. She was hugging her black cape around her and her cheeks were turning a delicate shade of blue but, "That's okay," she said soothingly, "I realise Mary – I mean Fern – has family stuff to deal with. Just park me by a fire some place and I'll be happy to wait."

Relief touched those strangely expressionless blue eyes and the tiny mouth puckered for speech, a thousand wrinkles radiating outwards like the spokes of a wheel. "Yes, yes . . . I'll just . . . the solicitor first."

Just before the woman grabbed my hand to lead me off to see the waiting Mr Markham, I heard Paula's voice, low and confidential, just above my ear. "I hope, Mary dear," she was saying, "I do hope most sincerely, that you are in no way linked *genetically* to this female freak."

It was the very thought that had just been troubling me.

Mr Markham, my grandfather's solicitor, was a robust man. He breathed an air of masculine common sense and certainty. He was not a man one could ever imagine being assailed by any kind of doubts or fears: to him the whole business of living was as straightforward as a legal document – no room for grey areas there. Since in Mr Markham's view money and position are the goals people strive for, it followed that I must be delighted by the terms of my grandfather's will; it would have taken far more confidence than I then possessed to attempt his disillusion.

I don't remember all that much about that meeting. Mr Markham used a good many words that were new to me then, words like probate and residual beneficiary – though heaven knows they became only too familiar later on – and although I'm sure he explained them to me as we went along I think I was too much absorbed in trying to take in the strangeness, the unreality of the whole thing, to focus on legal terminology.

We sat on either side of the fireplace. A coal fire burned in the grate but did little to warm the room. My knees grew hot as my back continued to freeze and I was glad the woman who let us in had not taken our coats.

Mr Markham informed me that this had been my grandfather's study. I tried to imagine a man of wealth choosing to spend his time in a workplace of such relentless gloom – tried, and failed. He must have been a man utterly oblivious to his surroundings. How else could he have endured these sombre greys and browns, such hideous furniture? My grandfather's study had all the charm and warmth of an old-fashioned station waiting room.

I sat on the rim of my chair – nothing in this room encouraged relaxation. Mr Markham sat facing me, brisk and confident and quite unaffected by the atmosphere of over-furnished austerity. He had dark hair, going white above the ears, and his complexion was florid, his build corpulent. He reminded me of one of those eighteenth-century squires you see in old portraits, the ones who had a quart of sherry for breakfast and ate huge amounts of game pie and boiled mutton for lunch. I could tell that he was trying to put me at my ease, but the more confident and reassuring he tried to be, the more I felt like a junior schoolgirl who has been called in to see the headmaster. When I told Paula this later she said that was ridiculous because I was paying him for chrissake and who did he think he was anyway? But at the time that thought never even occurred to me and, to be honest, I don't think it would have made much difference if it had.

A few things I did learn: that affairs were now in a kind of limbo and would remain so for some time, at least until my twenty-first birthday in August when I was free to inherit; that the woman who had shown us in was, in fact, Tillie, my grandfather's widow – not my grandmother, for she had died before I was born, but his second wife whom he had married about ten years before he died – and that by the terms of the will she was entitled to remain in the house until her death. She also received a legacy, an income of about eight thousand pounds a year, which seemed like a lot to me when he mentioned it first . . . but not for long. Just as in America you keep crossing different time zones, I had the impression, during that interview with Mr Markham, that I was passing through different money zones. Very soon he began talking in tens and hundreds of thousands of pounds and I lost all control of the noughts so that when he said to me, "You will, of course, require an interim payment while probate is going through. Will ten thousand be enough?" he must have interpreted my blank stare as disappointment because when I replied vaguely, "I suppose so," he gave me a quick look and said, "We'd better make it fifteen, then," and made a note on a piece of paper. It was all I could do not to burst out laughing.

The whole thing might have been funny if it hadn't

been scary as well. At one point I had the impression
he was almost apologising because my grandfather had,
apparently, speculated unwisely and as a result there
would be "only" about seven hundred thousand pounds
in investments after death duties had been paid. By that
time my head was swimming with noughts and I even
wondered if that made me a millionaire.

I said I thought I might be able to make ends meet
somehow but he merely looked puzzled.

I think Mr Markham was as relieved as I was when we
got to the end of what he called "this little preliminary
chat". Obviously I was a disappointing heiress, sitting
there on the edge of my chair in a cheap navy skirt
and shivering in my pale blue anorak. I gave no sign
of anything much except a polite interest in words I was
only half listening to – but then he wasn't to know that
Fern Mary Miller had trained herself long ago, back in
the days before Fern became Mary, never to show any
but the most superficial emotions.

But what, really, did he expect? Looking back, odd
though it may seem, I think he expected me to be grateful.
Just as bearers of bad tidings used to have their heads cut
off, or whatever, I think Mr Markham expected me to
be grateful to *him* for telling me the good news of my
grandfather's bequest. It wasn't his fault that gratitude
was the last thing on my mind, just then.

"Well, Miss Miller, unless you have any questions,
I think that's enough for the time being. You must
be eager to see the rest of the family. But if you
do have any questions, things that need clearing up,
feel free to give me a ring, either at my office or at
home. Any time, any time at all. It's no trouble. This
has been a surprise for you, quite a lot to absorb,
but remember, I'm always available to answer your
questions."

I smiled politely and thanked him for his offer of help
– but doubted I would ever take him up on it. He was
so positive, such a stranger to doubt and muddle, he
could never comprehend the labyrinthine workings of

my family. He could never answer the only question, just then, in which I was interested.

What whim of malice or misplaced generosity had caused my grandfather to single me out for special attention, when, perhaps alone of all his relatives, I asked nothing more than to be left in peace?

I found Paula seated in lone splendour in an enormous sitting-room – the drawing-room as it was called at Chatton Heights. And, to my amazement, this room was almost warm. A log fire was burning in the hearth and there were radiators that gave off a faint heat.

Apart from the welcome difference in temperature this room was as gloomy as the one that had been my grandfather's study. Three tall windows looked out on to the garden at the front: rain-soaked gravel and beyond that lawns and the endless army of laurels. There was a very old carpet with some kind of maroon paisley pattern on it and flocked wallpaper of urns and scrolls in the same colour. Paula was seated on an enormous sofa which was covered in some kind of buttoned leather and there was a good deal too much furniture in stained oak protruding from the walls.

Two large oil paintings hung on either side of the fireplace (black marble again like the one in the hall). To the right of the fire there was a rather sooty Turneresque representation of a ship going down in huge seas of what looked like black treacle, while in the picture to the left a stag, his throat torn and bleeding, was being dragged to the ground by three slavering hounds. The stag's eyes were rolling heavenwards with an expression reminiscent of that worn by some of the early martyrs. Death accidental and death intended: the subjects seemed suitably morbid for Chatton Heights and I wondered if nowadays my relatives would choose to hang pictures of air disasters or seal clubbing on the walls of their homes. Like my grandfather's study, this room made not the slightest gesture towards comfort or colour or elegance. I think I must have been in urban underpasses that seemed more welcoming.

17

Paula, reclining on the leather sofa with a schooner of sherry in her hand, seemed to have arrived at a different verdict. "I could learn to live like this," she said. "Over there, look, help yourself to a drink, that's what the lady said. On the sideboard."

I poured myself a tonic water and said, "That lady, by the way, is my grandfather's widow. My step-grandmother, I suppose – but no genetic link."

"Thank God for that, eh? Come and sit over here and tell me how things went with the solicitor."

"Oh, just a lot of legal stuff." I sat down beside her but left my answer purposefully vague. Some instinct warned me not to discuss the details of my inheritance.

It's strange how people's appearance changes against different backdrops. Paula had erupted into my quiet Bristol home with all the glamour and force of a professional actor in a small-town dramatic society. But here, in the drawing-room at Chatton Heights with its disdain of ornament and its timeless ugliness she was too transient, too stylish to fit in. This was a room that belonged to stout women wearing sensible tweed skirts, women whose hands were roughened by grappling with the suckers in their rose beds or tightening the girths on their hunters. Paula's orange-painted nails and her high-heeled boots belonged in city streets and apartments, not here. But, selfishly, I relied on her gaudy reassurance, and was more than glad she had come.

From the hallway beyond the drawing-room came the sound of men's voices raised in hearty greeting. One was Mr Markham's but the other, sardonic, drawling, was new to me – new, and yet strangely familiar. I didn't recognise it but I knew in my bones I had heard that voice before.

Paula was still talking – I think she was describing how she would redecorate the room if it was hers – but I could no longer focus on her words. The voice in the hallway both fascinated and terrified. It was a voice evocative of port and Havana cigars, the fruity accents of an old-fashioned radio announcer.

And, as the door opened, even before he came into the room, I knew without question the identity of its owner.

My uncle. My father's elder brother. Archie.

Of course I would have recognised him anyway, just as Paula did, from the interviews and profiles that appeared on him from time to time in magazines. I saw her jaw drop, literally, and a flush touch her cheek before she clamped her mouth shut firmly and darted me a look which said, as plainly as only Paula's looks can, Why the hell didn't you tell me before?

But Paula's surprise was nothing compared with my own.

As my uncle stepped into the room and paused for a moment, a genial and smiling figure, in the doorway, a flash of pure terror surged through me powerful as an electric shock. Terror as real and vivid as it was unreasoning.

Imagine that all your life you have suffered occasionally from a recurring dream, a dream which varies each time in its detail but which revolves around a single figure, a man. That man is tall, with good-looking if rather heavy, almost Levantine features. He has very black eyebrows, dark eyes with somewhat drooping lids and a full, sensual mouth. Nothing particularly remarkable about him at all except for the fact that whenever he appears your dream self is paralysed with fear. The instinctive fear of nightmare. The terror of a small child who screams in the empty darkness for a comfort that is gone for ever.

And then imagine that one day, all unexpectedly, this dream figure walks into your waking, everyday world. A curtain is shifted briefly, and the dark terrors of the dream world pour in, stifling, choking, blinding . . .

Fear so powerful it almost knocks you down.

And then evaporates.

One moment cold hands of panic were clutching, clasping, paralysing me . . . and the next I felt myself breaking free, like a helium balloon detaching from the string that restrains it, breaking away, floating into the clear blue

19

air where there is no room for fear, no room for any emotion at all.

Detached, floating above the little group of people, I took part in the civilised chirrups of introduction: Paula, my Uncle Archie, Mr Markham, Paula Grove . . . My uncle joined in: Fern, my dear, how little you have changed . . . can I pour you a drink? Ah yes, I see you have one – and another for your friend? It seems like only yesterday . . .

If I had feared the first meeting with my relatives was going to be embarrassing in the extreme then I had reckoned without my uncle's urbane charm. His voice purred like the engine of an expensive car.

How was your journey? No difficulty in finding the place again after so long? Few changes since you saw it last . . . garden has declined, lack of staff, usual problem, kitchen wing has a new roof – your grandfather always disliked change.

Paula, having recovered from her shock, was laying herself out to charm my uncle. She wasn't quite doing the wide-eyed American *ingénue* routine, that wouldn't have been her style, but she was definitely stretching her American accent until it was in danger of snapping and she brought out her full array of witty comments on the transatlantic comedy of manners.

Soon she and Archie were deep in conversation and I was free to examine him more closely. The dream figure had been firmly returned to whatever closed corners of the mind he had inhabited until now and I could no longer imagine what, in the appearance of this attractive and pleasant-seeming middle-aged man – whose face at least should have been familiar enough from photographs – could have triggered such a shockwave of panic.

In his youth he must have been conventionally good-looking – tall, dark and definitely handsome – but in recent years his features had weathered to an appearance no less attractive but altogether more interesting. His eyes, hooded and dark, seemed to withhold as much as they revealed; his lips were full and fleshy, their smile a downward droop of the corners. Looking at my uncle for the first time one would assume he was a man who had found pleasure and suffering in equal generous measure, a man whose instinctive reserve was only partially disguised by an air of practised *bonhomie*. And his hands, I noticed, were baby-pink and beautifully manicured, the oval tips of his nails gleaming white. The hands of an undertaker or dentist. It was a younger, more finely textured Archie who had somehow insinuated his way into my childhood dreams.

Tillie came to the door. "Ready when you now . . ." she began. "Lunch is . . . though perhaps not Gerald yet."

Archie smiled, a smile of indulgent teasing. "Tillie is not, unfortunately, gifted with clarity of speech." He spoke in a low aside to me and Paula. Tillie herself made no sign that she knew she was being discussed, except perhaps for the nervous twisting of her hands. She stared blankly somewhere in the direction of the middle distance and her mouth moved as though she were sucking an imaginary peppermint.

"You'll learn to decode her messages in due course," he went on. "She has just informed us a) that lunch is now ready and b) that we are to begin anyway and not wait for my most unpunctual son. Isn't that right, Tillie?"

She glanced up at him almost gratefully and nodded. Still smiling, my uncle laid his hand on her shoulder and together they went out of the room, closely followed by Mr Markham.

In the hallway Archie lingered to see the solicitor out, while Tillie, trailing her forlorn aroma of mothballs and stale clothes, led us down a wide and dimly lit passageway towards the dining-room.

Just as we were about to enter the dining-room Paula dug her orange fingernails into my shoulder and hissed in my ear, "Why did you never tell me it was your goddam uncle who wrote *Dora's Room*?"

Dora's Room. It had caused a minor sensation when it was published. Only a minor sensation, however. It was beautifully written . . . broke new ground . . . crossed the boundary between poetry and prose . . . a myth for our time . . . but critics say those kind of things regularly and, praise notwithstanding, the books they describe tend to sink into rapid and well-deserved obscurity.

Not so *Dora's Room*. Within a few years it had become what is often described as a cult book and it inspired passionate devotion in its readers. This much I knew, this much everyone knew. What I had not known, but realised now, was that Paula was one of the book's most ardent admirers.

She was watching Archie closely as he came in a little later, having said goodbye to Mr Markham, and took his place at the head of the table in a dining room that was as huge and bleak as all the other rooms I had seen at Chatton Heights.

The windows were overhung with the leaves of an evergreen magnolia so that what light did filter through was dark green, aquatic. The huge dining table would have seated twelve comfortably, twenty without a squash. The five table settings that had been laid in readiness for the meal were lonely flotsam in a sea of polished wood.

Looking around me for the first time I realised that the depressing atmosphere of this room was crucially different from that of the drawing-room and the study, for here someone (who?) had actually tried to make some impact on the bleak proportions and sombre lighting of the house. Tried . . . and failed. There were glazed chintz curtains in a cheerful design of irises and lilies, but they could not disguise the fact that the windows were too narrow, that they shut out the light, rather than letting it in. And the paintings, jolly seaside scenes in soft pastels (a boy with sunhat and shrimping net, another child waving a foot with a crab clinging to it, fishing boats and gulls) were too small, too far apart, to look anything but ridiculous in the huge desert of dust-coloured wall. Only the sideboard, a monstrous construction of dark oak, heavily decorated, was strong enough to hold its own in that room. And the collection of pewter jugs, platters and tankards which stood there seemed more suitable than the household china and glass which was laid on the table. I had the feeling that in a room such as this, one should tear one's meat with knife and hands and throw the surplus to waiting dogs.

But there were no waiting dogs, no jolly minstrels to break the silence, which was my silence, my failure to speak out . . .

As we began the meal I was wondering how I could bring up the subject of my inheritance – but it was hard to find a chink in the banal lunchtime conversation – Would you care for more soup? Yes, and I'd like you to know that my grandfather's will was as big a surprise to me as it must have been to you. I think we should discuss it. Now? Yes, now. I daresay Paula would have grasped the nettle thus firmly but to do so required reserves of social poise that I had never even dreamed of. Someone who has spent their life trying to remain invisible has a fairly rudimentary grasp of social poise. I drank the soup – which was remarkably good, did Tillie possess hidden talents? – and said nothing. Hoping that after lunch a more suitable opportunity would arise.

It soon transpired that my uncle had other plans for the afternoon.

"A journalist is visiting us after lunch. I thought you might be interested. There is to be a new edition of *Dora's Room* in the summer. After all this time it is obviously difficult to find anything new to say or write about the book but as luck would have it the cleaner found some old photographs when my father's room was cleared out. There are some shots of Clancy among them."

"Oh," I said, "are there?"

My lack of interest was so obvious it was painful. But what was I supposed to say?

Clancy. Clarence. Who was he?

Archie was watching me kindly. "I thought you might be interested to see them."

I squeezed my hands into tight fists. Was I interested? I found on examination that, no, I wasn't. Not particularly.

23

Not at all. My father died when I was five. Dead and gone for ever. I could not remember ever having heard his Christian name before. Clarence. Clancy for short. Why should I be expected to be interested in examining his image in old photographs? I fought down the first stirrings of curiosity, of unease. My father was no longer anything to do with me; he was a stranger, an irrelevance from the past. Let the dead bury the dead . . . it has always seemed to me to be excellent advice.

So I just said, "Oh," and stared wooden-faced with embarrassment into my now empty soup bowl while Paula brayed her enthusiasm. "I've admired your book ever since I first read it in junior year of high school, Mr Miller. I felt it was speaking directly to me. Now I can see how amazing that was, because your world, growing up here in this house, must have been so different. Yet somehow you cut straight through the superficial differences that divide young people, right into the universal truths that unite them – and it takes real genius to do that."

I actually blushed for Paula. Surely this was laying it on with a trowel, even by her standards, and I was half hoping, half dreading, that Archie would make some snubbing remark, introduce a sense of proportion, but to my surprise his wide mouth tucked upwards at the corners in a positively feline grin of self-satisfaction and he murmured, "Dear girl, do call me Archie."

His eyes slid round to meet mine. "And how about you, little niece, do you also consider your clever uncle to have produced, in *Dora's Room*, a work of genius?"

I met his eyes briefly, then looked away. "I don't know," I mumbled, "I've never read it."

Silence. A baffled silence. Now it was Paula's turn to be embarrassed by me. But Archie was quick to smooth over any awkwardness. "Heavens above, why should you have read it? There are plenty of other books more deserving of your attention."

Paula said, "Oh, but M— Fern, you must. You don't know what you've missed."

"I'd like to . . . somehow I just never . . ."

24

"There's plenty of time," Archie laughed, "and I even have a few spare copies in the house. Hardbacks. If you like, I'd be only too happy to make you a present of one."

"Of course . . . thank you."

"Not at all. And consider yourself lucky that I am hardly verbose. No great corpus of literature to be broached, only a single slim volume. You should be grateful that my muse is a slim-hipped beggarly woman; that is, if she hasn't vanished altogether. I rather think she has."

Paula asked eagerly, "Are you working on anything now, Archie?"

"And you shall have a copy too, my dear."

I noticed that he had avoided her question. Paula was profuse in her gratitude and the conversation flowed pleasantly between them. I told myself that I was being churlish, but still, there was something that jarred, something in my uncle's most genial manner that filled me with unease.

The fifth place that had been laid on the table remained empty throughout the meal.

It was after lunch that the strangeness began.

Or rather, that was when the strangeness grew so strong that I could no longer ignore it, for the truth was that ever since the solicitor's letter had arrived with Randolf & Miles franked across the top in place of a stamp, and I had opened it and read the baffling information that I was named as main beneficiary of my grandfather's estate, weird changes had begun to take place that I fought hard to ignore. Nothing outward, nothing tangible. Daily life had gone on as usual: I looked after Dring, went to my classes at college, attended my part-time job at the estate agent's office, but inside, deep inside my brain, there was a kind of stirring, as if things – what things? I had no idea – that had lain dormant for years were waking, stretching, preparing to move. I could almost feel their tickling beneath my scalp, as though these unnameable, waking "things" were moths, secret brown moths, the

25

kind with furry bodies and powdery wings, which were emerging from their chrysalises in the dark recesses of my skull and were fluttering their impatience to emerge into the light of day.

It was nonsense, of course, complete nonsense. A letter had come, that was all. A letter that presaged great changes, it was true, but a letter that belonged firmly to the real world of probate and dividends and cash in the bank. A letter that had less than nothing to do with moths emerging from chrysalises under my skull. I told no one of these feelings, tried not even to acknowledge them to myself. I could imagine Paula telling me, if I had confided in her (which I had absolutely no intention of doing) to cut down on my caffeine intake and eat a proper breakfast for a change. So I followed her imagined advice.

For days I had managed to ignore these weird and uncomfortable sensations, but suddenly, after lunch on the day of that first visit to Chatton Heights, I was powerless any longer to resist them.

I had refused Tillie's offer of coffee (still trying to cut down on caffeine). Archie was telling an enraptured Paula about his most recent lecture tour of the States and the motel in Milwaukee that wanted his advice on the decor in their *Dora's Room* cocktail lounge. Paula was lapping it up but for some reason, perhaps because of my embarrassment at never having read the book, his benign story-telling grated on my nerves and I went over to the window and stared out at the wet gravel and the wet laurels and the sky that was heavy with ever more wetness to come.

I was just wondering how I could bring up the subject that must surely be uppermost in Archie's and Tillie's minds as well as my own, that of my grandfather's eccentric will, when there was a creaking, crunching sound to the right of the window and an old man, looking extraordinarily like Peter Rabbit's Mr McGregor, came into view pushing a wheelbarrow. Although the wheelbarrow was empty he appeared to be pushing it

with some difficulty. His thin jacket provided hardly any
protection against the rain that was still falling steadily
and his scrawny body was hunched against the cold. He
passed quite close to the window – creak crunch creak
– but, head bowed with concentration, he never saw me
watching him and he creaked and crunched his way past
the front door and out of sight. I watched the emptiness
while the channel cut by the wheel in the gravel filled
with rainwater.

Who was he? Why was he there? Archie could have
told me – but that wasn't the point. The old man with
his wheelbarrow suddenly represented all the complex
workings of this house which I now owned but of which
I knew nothing. Perhaps that was *my* wheelbarrow he was
pushing. It was certainly *my* gravel. Probably he was *my*
gardener. Mr Markham had said something that morning
about an estate manager, wages and rents – and I hadn't
listened. The simple fact was that the stubborn-looking old
man, head bowed against the rain, knew what his role was
within the household, he knew where he was pushing the
wheelbarrow and why and, if he had looked up and seen
me, I had no doubt that he would have known exactly
who I was, just as the man in the village had known.

I sat down on the window-seat. Like the other ground-
floor windows at Chatton Heights this one was a tribute
to my ancestor's paranoia. It was tall and narrow and
the recess in which it was set bulged outwards like the
hull of a canoe. The window-seat was a good deal larger
than the actual width of the window since it took up the
whole of the recess – when the curtains were drawn the
window-seat recess would be completely cut off from the
rest of the room.

I resisted the temptation to draw the curtains and shut
off the sight of Paula's and Archie's animated conversation, of Tillie staring blankly over the coffee trolley, her
cobweb-imprisoned mouth moving constantly, like some
ruminant chewing imaginary cud. It was chilly here, away
from the fireplace; coldness and damp seeped through
the ill-fitting windowframe. Beyond the streaming glass,

the rain fell continuously and the sound of its patter was soothing, blurring the sound of voices.

The fabric of the window-seat was rough beneath my fingers – rough, but with the smoothness of long use. Heavy linen with a faded pattern of leaves and flowers, twisted and contorted like vines.

I traced the curving shape of a tendril with my fingers. It was then that the strange tingling in my mind, quite unlike anything I had ever experienced before, grew stronger. The sensation was so new, so impossible to explain, that I suppose I should have been afraid, except that in that moment I was launched into a place where fear no longer existed: I was warm and protected, cresting a high wave of happiness.

With the coming of the sudden miraculous sense of haven another change took place. The fabric beneath my fingers gradually transformed, the bleached colours were growing stronger, clearer, becoming focused, brighter, like the image on a photograph as it passes through the developing fluid – a leaf emerged in succulent, juicy green, its veins deepest indigo and the jungle flower beside it was a vibrant, blood-stained red, a fantastic gaudy lily. My fingers traced the patterns with an almost drunken pleasure as if the fabric contained another, magic world and with just the slightest effort of will one could step inside . . .

The drumming of the rain grew faint and instead there was a voice, a voice soft and crooning, sing-song, almost chanting. I strained my ears to hear more clearly – it had become vital that I hear it distinctly for the voice, I knew, was the source of all my newly found security.

The voice was everything.

It was a summer voice: a droning of flies behind hot windows, a wood pigeon's hollow call, a warm murmur of content. Scent of honeysuckle and new-mown lawns hung on the air. Deck chairs and sandalled feet and orange squash to drink at tea-time. Through every bliss the voice was weaving and every nerve in my body was caressed by those crooning tones.

I looked up, half expecting to see beyond the window-pane a swag of full-blown roses and a sky of hazy summer blue . . .

Nothing.

Just the leaden grey of winter rain. Cold. Bleak. The voice was fading. In something approaching panic I looked down once more at the fabric of the window-seat but the pattern too was growing dim, bleached, lifeless, ordinary once again.

The voice had vanished. The golden globe of safety shattered and splintered all around me and I was vulnerable and cold and a man's voice, Archie's, I knew from the fear that flushed through my body, was being poured on my discomfort like an oily black smoke.

"Fern, do you remember your cousin Gerald?"

It wasn't his fault that his arrival had been so grotesquely ill-timed. As I looked up and saw his unsmiling face, I tried not to loathe him for shattering the almost-dream.

"Hello, Gerald."

He did not smile and I noticed, as we shook hands briefly, that his palm was damp and trembling.

"Hello, Fern. Long time no see."

"Yes."

I could think of nothing further that was suitable to say to a cousin whom I had last seen fifteen years previously (My, how you've grown!). And while I was casting around for a topic that was fairly neutral without being totally banal he said, "You've got a bloody nerve, coming back here now," and with that he turned on his heel and strode over to the trolley with the coffee on it and poured himself a cup. I guessed his hands must still be shaking because a good deal of the coffee slopped into his saucer.

Archie remained at my side and, with no scruples about banality, he said, "It looks as though it will rain for the rest of the afternoon. Ah, the joys of an English winter."

I should have been grateful that he was at least trying to smooth over a hazardous moment, but his efforts were too

29

late: the time for hollow politeness had vanished. Gerald's abrupt statement had broken the spell of silence we had all maintained until now as surely as his arrival had broken whatever spell had woven itself around me while I sat on the window-seat. I knew I had to seize this chance.

Yet still I wavered; reluctant to admit that my mirage of summer bliss had vanished. And in the meantime, while Archie spouted mellifluous and utterly meaningless remarks about Candlemas and Lent, I took this opportunity for an oblique study of my cousin Gerald.

He was of medium height – the same height, I saw now, as his father, though under the influence of childhood memory I had until now seen Archie as huge, a towering giant almost. Like his father, Gerald had full lips, but there all similarity ended. Archie's mouth was sensual, self-satisfied as a cat's, whereas Gerald's lips, which glistened slightly, seemed more inclined to pout or sulk. Archie's colouring was dark, Mediterranean even, but Gerald's was all English: hair the colour of summer straw which flopped loosely over his forehead; cheeks the colour of ripe red apples, eyes of a pale and watery blue. A faint memory of tantrums echoed in my mind and, for all his expensive clothes and polished brogues, Gerald reminded me, even then, of an overgrown child who might, at the least provocation, stamp his foot or throw his food across the room. He had square, workmanlike hands and his nails, I noticed, were bitten until the skin on his fingertips bled.

You've got a bloody nerve, Fern, coming back here now . . . Dread dragged at the pit of my stomach – and yet, surprisingly, there was also a kind of relief. No alternative, now, but to confront the topic of my grandfather's will.

I needed courage. As I stood up and went over towards the fire I strained to hear the voice that had come to me while I sat on the window-seat, to remember that fleeting vision of safety, as though the memory of it might give me courage, as a talisman does. Perhaps it did. Perhaps I was braver than I knew, and the burden of silence had become intolerable.

I stood in front of the fire.

"I'm sure this is difficult for all of you as well," I began, "but I think we should start to talk about . . . I know we're all thinking . . . I don't know how it happened but . . . I mean, my grandfather's will."

It wasn't a very good start. Actually it was a fairly dismal one but at least it was a start. And for someone like me who had always been paralysed by shyness, it almost merited a medal for valour in the field.

There was a silence. I had hoped that once the subject had been broached one of the others might take it up but no one spoke. All I could hear was the hiss of logs in the grate and, beyond the windows, the drumbeat of rain on gravel.

It was a waiting silence. All eyes were fixed on me: Archie's dark, humorous; Tillie's blue and empty as chips of coloured glass; Gerald's slightly close-set and narrowed now to watery slits beneath his thatch of hair as he watched me carefully. Even Paula looked as though she had temporarily forgotten to breathe.

There was nothing for it but to struggle on. "Mr Markham's letter was as much a surprise to me as it must have been to all of you. I never imagined . . . I mean, I don't know why he decided to leave so much to me, the house and everything. I didn't particularly want . . . I never tried . . ."

I was no longer even sure exactly what it was I wanted so desperately to say. I suppose I had some vague idea of bringing it all into the open, of clearing the air. It no longer seemed such a good idea. The air remained most definitely uncleared and what, after all, could I say? I never wanted him to leave it all to me. I really don't want the house and the money – in fact I'd much rather it went to one of you? Fine words *now*, now that it was too late to do anything about it. And they weren't to know that it was true, that I really didn't want his wretched money or his hideous monstrosity of a house.

Silence again. Broken only by the noise of Gerald's cup rattling in its saucer. An ominous sound.

This time Archie's voice was a welcome intrusion. "My dear girl," he said smoothly, "no one is accusing you of unfairly worming your way into the old man's affections – if, indeed, he ever had any, which is highly improbable. We are well aware that we were the ones who were on hand to do the worming. Unless, of course, you have hitherto undisclosed skills in telepathy."

"But now it's all so unfair."

Archie merely shrugged. "Fairness is a concept I have never really understood. Not very English of me, but there it is, I never took to cricket either. Life is a gamble, a lottery, a throw of the dice and you have just thrown a double six while we— "

"For Christ's sake, Pa, shut up, can't you!" Gerald was twitching with fury. "No one wants a bloody lecture on gambling!" And in his rage he jerked so vehemently that his coffee cup shot off its saucer and crashed to the floor. His cheeks flushed a darker shade of red as he fell to his knees and began mopping at the mess with a large handkerchief. Only swift action on Tillie's part stopped him from knocking over the entire coffee trolley as well.

"Clumsy as ever, Gerald," was his father's comment. "When you've finished spreading your usual mayhem, perhaps you'd like to offer some pearls of wisdom to your unfortunate cousin."

"Unfortunate – hell! You know bloody well what I think. Your damned father cracked up and the will is invalid, it must be. We need to find a lawyer with the guts to say so in court."

"Hm. I see. I want, ergo I must have. That's always been your motto, hasn't it, Gerald? But on this occasion the real world has thwarted you by presenting actual immutable facts. No lawyer would waste his time contesting my father's will. His time or your money."

Gerald stood up and stuffed the coffee-soaked handkerchief back in his pocket. "I don't see why not."

"That, dear boy," Archie assumed an air of exaggerated patience, "is because you are congenitally blinded by stupidity. You knew your grandfather. Did you ever know him to make a mistake of detail? When he checked the milkman's bill and found it was a penny out did we ever for an instant think the milkman could have been correct? Of course not. It was unthinkable. And legal documents were his forte. He devoted the final years of his life to that massive document which is called his will. He spent hours on it, months. To a legal eye it is probably a work of art, a monument to— "

"It's not a monument to anything except his idiocy. He must have gone senile."

Archie regarded his son with mock compassion. "Poor Gerald. Do you honestly believe that only senility could have caused him to leave you out of his will?"

"But surely," I broke in, "Mr Markham said that you had both been left legacies. I never thought you had nothing."

Gerald spun round as though I had just jabbed him with a cattle prod. "A legacy!" He spat the words out like nails. "Call that a damn legacy! A hundred bloody thousand pounds! And that not till I'm twenty-five. And there's death duties too. By the time all that's paid up there wouldn't even be enough for a bloody bedsit in Knightsbridge. And what do you expect me to do? Get a mortgage? Get some piddling little job? You must be out of your tiny mind if you think I'm going to scrabble around paying off some stupid crumby mortgage."

"Most people do," I said, relieved that Gerald seemed to have been left a fairly sizeable chunk of money after all.

"Well, not me, thank you *very* much."

"But there's no need, Gerald," I went on, "after all, you live here, you've always lived here, and nothing needs to change just because our grandfather has died. You don't need to move out or anything."

I thought Gerald had been angry before but at this he became positively apoplectic. "Oh, and very generous I'm sure! So good of you to let me stay in *your* bloody house. Do you expect me to grovel with gratitude? If you think

I'm going to ask your permission to live here just because my grandfather went off his head and the damned lawyers don't have the balls to do anything about it, then you're out of luck!"

Gerald's face was turning the colour of cooked beetroot and his full lips were glistening with spittle. I clenched my fists by my side and willed myself not to cave in before his fury. "I only meant you don't have to move out," I said.

"You're bloody right I don't. I'd like to see you try to kick me out. Just you try – see where it gets you, just— "

I was shaking so much that I could think of no way to dam the flood of his rage. Archie was watching his son with a detached air of amusement. Tillie, as so often, was nowhere, gazing beyond us all to a blank patch of wall beside the martyred stag. To my relief it was Paula, whom everyone seemed to have forgotten, who cut in.

"Get a grip on yourself, Gerald," she said, in a voice that was more than a match for a mere disinherited youth. "Stop acting like a complete asshole. It's not Mary, I mean Fern's, fault that you messed it up with your grandfather and if you've come out with a hundred grand then I can't see what you're bawling like a spoilt kid for. Leave her alone."

Gerald turned to look at her slowly. His shoulders were twitching as if he was in the grip of a violent spasm. For a moment I was afraid he might lash out and hit her – but then I remembered that Paula had been learning tai chi for years and would probably break his arm if he tried. During the long silence, while Gerald stared down at Paula, his face like a gargoyle's in his rage, and she returned his stare as coolly as if he was a room service valet and she had just ordered a tray of tea, there was a sound of a bell ringing, far away. Almost unnoticed, Tillie rose and left the room.

At last Gerald spoke, though his voice was so tight he could barely squeeze the words out. "Who – is – this?"

"She's my fr— "

"Paula Grove," said Paula easily, "I'm Mary Fern's friend and I came along with her today to make sure she gets a nice warm welcome from her family."

"Sod off," said Gerald.

"No."

I was just wondering whether, there and then, I could grab Paula by the arm and make a dash for the car, when the door of the drawing-room opened and a man came in, Tillie following.

"Adam Bury," she said.

"Oh hell," said Gerald, and stalked out.

Chapter 2

Gerald's outburst had left me so shaken that I barely
managed to mumble a "hello" to the newcomer. I had
a vague impression that his face was somehow familiar
– but that was all.

I was too stunned even to envy Paula her ability to
deal with conflict. I suppose my life with Dring had
always been so quiet ("Unreal," Paula called it, "you
and that old woman cooped up alone together," but it
had always seemed real enough to me) and I simply had
no experience of rows, no notion how to cope with such
a situation. As usual I had become completely paralysed,
with a sort of appalled numbness, by what had happened.
Goodness knows how I would have managed if Paula
hadn't intervened when she did, if Gerald had not left
the room. As it was I was able to mumble "hello" and to
thank Paula for the lighted cigarette she passed to me.

The newcomer, Adam Bury, looked at Paula and me
(down at me, across at Paula) with interest. "I shall con-
gratulate my father on the accuracy of his descriptions,"
he said.

"Your father?" It was Paula who asked.

"You stopped him in the village this morning and he
gave you directions."

"Of course, remember him, Mary Fern? I see the family
resemblance now."

It was true, there was a similarity. The man in the
village had been taller, certainly, and his strong features
had been made more dramatic and hawklike by the
thinning of his flesh and the tufted eyebrows. Adam
had something of his father's air of impatience about
him, but his features were rounder, less exaggerated.

I guessed him to be about thirty. He had thick brown hair, grey eyes and an attractively lop-sided smile. An intelligent face, I thought . . . and it could well be that the easy-going air was deceptive.

By the time Paula had told Adam how like his father he was and Adam had said his father thought I looked just like my father, and Tillie had drifted out with the coffee trolley, and Archie had suggested he and Adam go to his study to collect the box of photographs so we could all look through them together, and Paula and I were at last left alone together, the frozen sense of numbness was beginning to thaw.

I went over to the window-seat. I suppose I was half hoping to recover the almost-memory that had possessed me when I sat there first, but if so I was disappointed. It was just an ordinary window-seat with a faded linen cover and beyond the glass the dreary rain was making puddles on the gravel.

Paula came and joined me. "Are you okay?"

"Mm. I could have done without Gerald's temper tantrum."

"Don't waste time over that. It's better now it's out in the open. And anyway, Mary, what the hell is he squawking about? A hundred grand? You wouldn't catch me complaining if my grandfather left me a half of that. I'll lay odds your cousin starts to come round after this."

"I hope so."

"Sure he will. And I bet it's not so much the money side of things he's upset about, more the rejection."

"What do you mean?"

"It's a classic. By withholding the money your grandfather has posthumously withheld his love, his approval. And he's given them both to you. For some reason your grandfather wanted to punish Gerald – and so now of course Gerald wants to punish you."

I groaned: "That's all I need."

"Don't worry. I reckon he'll ease up now he's said his piece. And you have to admire him for being so forthright. And as for the other two – Tillie is so spaced out I don't

37

suppose she even understands what's happening, and your uncle, well, it's easy to see he's too absorbed in his writing to care much about material things."

"Do you really think so?"

"I'm sure of it."

I wasn't altogether convinced – but I fervently hoped she was right. "We could leave now," I suggested, "I'm not interested in a stupid box of old photographs."

"Oh no you don't, Mary, you're not chickening out now. You don't want your cousin to think he's scared you off, do you?"

At that stage I didn't care much what Gerald thought but I was in no condition to persuade Paula to do anything against her will. So we stayed.

The box turned out to be a whole drawer full of albums and packets of photographs. My heart sank. It would take hours to look through all these, but then Archie said that he had already selected most of the ones that he thought might interest Adam. We settled around the fireplace in a fair imitation of a cosy family gathering: Paula had manoeuvred herself to a position next to Archie on the sofa, Adam and I sat in armchairs on either side. He smiled at me briefly as we sat down. I realised my face was too frozen with tension to do anything but stare back at him bleakly.

It was Archie who began. "Most of these are new to me. It is an interesting sidelight on my venerable papa's character, this, hoarding all these touching pics beneath his bed. Do you suppose he unhooked himself from his oxygen tank when no one was looking and shed a tear for his sons' lost innocence? Ah well, we'll never know – thank Christ. But it's lucky they've surfaced in time for the new edition."

Paula was curious. "A new edition?" she asked.

"Large format paperback with introduction by impressive literary celebrity – *and* six pages of photographs."

"My paper is running a feature on Archie to coincide with publication," said Adam, "hence the need for photographs."

"But I don't understand," I said, "surely *Dora's Room* is a work of fiction. Why should they want six pages of photos of the author?"

Archie smiled, the corners of his mouth just whiskering upwards in that catlike way of his. "Perhaps I should explain," he was speaking to Adam, "my niece has so far been clever enough to escape the lure of *Dora's Room* and has never read my little book. Even the inflated public accolade has not been sufficient to tempt her."

Adam directed his gaze towards me once again. His eyes were so intense (with what? curiosity? amusement? I had no idea) it was a bit like being caught in the headlights of a powerful car. "You should read it," he said simply, "it's good."

"I intend— "

"This very day," Archie continued with a wide gesture of his arm to denote the bearer of gifts, "I propose making Fern a present of my work to enable her to remedy her deficiency."

"The reason for the photographs," explained Adam, who was the only one who had not lost sight of my original question, "is that although *Dora's Room* is strictly speaking a work of fiction, there are such strong parallels between it and your uncle's own childhood and adolescence here, at Chatton Heights, that it is verging on autobiography. Thus the photographs are highly relevant."

"Thank you," I said, and now, perhaps soothed by his general air of steadiness and calm, I was able to return his smile, "I understand now."

"Ah, here we are," Archie's voice motored on, "I found this one the other day, Fern, and I thought you'd like to have it. Look, the devoted parents with their baby. Most charming."

This time my curiosity was stronger than my reluctance. I took the photograph from his outstretched hand. It was large, about eight inches by twelve, the kind of portrait that is sent to proud grandparents at Christmas time: a young man and his wife both with long and untidy dark hair, both smiling with that kind of doting soppiness peculiar to baby pictures – and between them a pudgy blob of infant flesh with an open-mouthed and toothless grin. I discovered they might just as well have been three Martians. Nothing whatsoever to do with me.

"How – nice." I squeezed the words out.

"Crack a smile, Mary." Paula actually appeared to be embarrassed by my lack of enthusiasm. "It's a great picture. They both look so young and – and— "

"Thank you." I pushed the picture into my bag.

Archie beamed at Paula. "My niece is clearly a shining example of the great British talent for burying emotion. Doubtless beneath that frosty exterior there yet beats a human heart. Now, Adam, to business. I thought this one might be useful to you: there weren't many taken during my adolescence."

Adam took another photograph and examined it closely. "This one is fine," he said, "it's easy to recognise you, Mr Miller; and the other boy, he must be your brother."

"That's right. Clarence."

"The one who died?"

"He was killed in a plane crash in South America. Fern's father – a great tragedy."

I winced. For some reason the way Archie said "a great tragedy" jarred on my senses, though I couldn't, just then, have explained why . . .

Adam passed the photograph to me. "You'd probably like to see it, Fern," he said, and once again I was aware of his slate-grey eyes appraising me carefully. "And now I see what my father meant by family resemblance."

I took the photograph, gazed down at it. Two boys standing on the steps in front of the enormous front door which Tillie had so theatrically failed to open that morning. Both the boys were in their best clothes, carnations in their buttonholes as though setting out for a wedding. Archie, handsome, swaggering, was already a young man and he smiled into the camera with easy self-confidence.

The younger boy, my father, was still a child. He looked about ten or eleven. He was small, much smaller than Archie, with a thin, pointed face and huge eyes. For all his expensive suit and the flower in his buttonhole there was something wistful and waif-like in his appearance. A casting director might have chosen him for an Oliver Twist, clutching his empty bowl of gruel, or one of the pathetic inmates of Dotheboys Hall – but never for the young son at "the big house". Unlike Archie he looked as though he had forgotten he was having his photograph taken and his large black eyes were staring vaguely at some point beyond the person holding the camera. It was the face of a dreamer, of a boy who is always late and can never find his games kit when required. The face of a boy whose carelessness is more readily forgiven than that of other boys.

Paula, looking over my shoulder, had seen the same thing. "Just look at that," she said, "the extrovert and the introvert. They look like illustrations from a manual of psychology – what a contrast, eh, Mary Fern?"

"You look as though you were off to a wedding," said Adam.

"I expect we were. Keep it if you want, Adam. None of these are needed for the book. You can return them all later. Ah, look, Fern, this is a good one of your father on his own. It must have been taken about the same time. Here— "

This photograph was in black and white which made the overall effect even more waiflike, if that were possible. He was wearing those dreadful baggy shorts that always make boys' legs look impossibly thin, like chicken drumsticks. He was frowning.

"Poor kid," said Paula, "he looks miserable."

Archie glanced at the picture. "Clancy's habitual expression," he commented drily.

"I bet you used to bully him."

"As a matter of fact, no. Hardly ever. I don't think anyone did much, not even at school. For all that he was a skinny little bugger he wasn't that sort of child."

A note of tenderness had crept into his voice, a tenderness all the more remarkable because in such contrast to his previous air of detached amusement. It took me by surprise and I looked at the picture again.

"This must have been taken at the front of the house," I said. "Is this the drawing-room window?"

"One of them," said Archie.

Recognition like a shock of warm water against my face. "But the roses have all gone!" I said.

They were there in the photograph, those huge swags of roses I had half expected to see when the memories lapped around me on the window-seat: huge and pink and blowzy they were, I was sure of it – although of course in the photograph they were varying shades of grey. There was a sudden excitement in realising that the roses I had looked for just now had once been real.

"What roses? Oh yes, those— " I could hardly expect Archie to share my enthusiasm.

"I didn't see— "

"They were grubbed up some years back when the gravel was extended to the walls of the house. To save on maintenance."

"How long ago?"

"Lord knows. Ten years, maybe fifteen."

Adam was still examining the photograph of my father in his baggy shorts. "Mr Miller, did your younger brother ever play with dolls?"

"Dolls? Christ, no. Our father would have had a fit. Boys were boys in our family – guns and trains and soldiers, all that sort of thing. Even pets were frowned on as too girlish. Our upbringing was strictly sexist."

"Then I wonder what he's holding here. It looks like some sort of doll."

I looked again. Just what he was holding it was impossible to say with any certainty but it was the attitude of his hands, the cradling gesture of his arms, that suggested some kind of doll.

"A bear, perhaps?" I volunteered.

But Archie was adamant. "Definitely not," he said.

"No bears, no dolls, no pets. Instant sissydom lay in wait for the unfortunate boy who was so indulged. And becoming a sissy was a disaster of the first magnitude."

Paula opened her mouth to speak. I was afraid she was about to offer an interpretation that encompassed latent homosexuality and Freudian fixations (she was forever ferreting out anything latent or fixated) but on this occasion she restrained herself to asking merely, "And your mother?"

"Dead. By then anyway. If Clancy was eleven when that picture was taken then she'd been dead for about a year."

"Poor little mite," said Paula, "no wonder he looks so wretched."

"She was my mother too," said Archie. A strange remark, it seemed to me then.

In spite of my initial reluctance to look at the photographs I found myself increasingly absorbed. There were so many – it would have taken a whole day to look through them all. There was my grandmother, looking young and pretty in her wide-swinging new-look skirts, her two sons beside her. Even a few of my grandfather playing cricket on the lawn with his sons – though there was something grim about his enjoyment, as if he was a man to whom "play" was an alien concept and he smiled for the camera with all the gruesome levity of a Victorian Presbyterian minister making his annual joke to the congregation.

Archie was beginning to enjoy what he insisted on calling this "trip down memory lane". "Christ, I was a good-looking bugger, wasn't I? How about this one, the young author clutching a book to his bosom? The torment of the young scribbler trapped in a philistine household," he chuckled. "What do you think, Adam?"

"I'll take it anyway." Adam seemed to know exactly what he was looking for and quite soon he had amassed a neat pile of photographs. "These are just what we need," he said, sliding them into a reinforced envelope. "And now to the interview proper. It won't take long."

"You sound like a damned detective," grumbled Archie

wryly, "or a dentist. Your father led me to understand you were only interested in the photographs." He went to the sideboard. "Anyone care to join me? No?" And he poured himself a large whisky.

"Even a colour supplement has to have some text," said Adam.

"If you must." And Archie sat down again. "Still, if you weren't Ted's son— "

"Point taken," said Adam with a brisk smile. "Your reluctance to be interviewed is well known. Of course, the best thing, from our point of view, would be to know what you are working on at the moment; if indeed you are— "

"Thank you for that 'if', Adam." Archie treated his interviewer to the kind of smile some politicians reserve for the question they intend particularly to avoid. "Yes, yes, I work. How could I do otherwise? Writing is in my blood, it has been all my life. But— " He broke off, as though that single "but" contained all the information anyone could want.

"But?"

Archie looked pensive. "There have been too many buts in my life. Too many . . ." He broke off once more and stared into his glass, in which only a little whisky remained. "Yet I still have hopes that one day . . ." His voice drifted into silence.

Adam waited for a moment or two before asking, "Are you then working on another novel?"

"You could call it that."

"Then shall I say— "

"Say what you want."

Adam was frowning, as though trying to untangle a puzzle. "I'm only harping on about this," he said, "because *Dora's Room* has always struck me as a book of such energy, of such vitality, the work of someone who had a huge amount to say, was barely able to contain it all. And yet, in the thirteen or more years since publication— "

"There was *Maiden Voyage*," Archie interrupted, "for God's sake don't forget poor old *Maiden Voyage*."

44

Adam's frown only deepened. "You have yourself acknowledged on many occasions, Mr Miller, that your second book hardly bears comparison with the first. At the time, as I remember, there was a good deal of speculation that it was in fact an earlier, perhaps even a juvenile work and that you were wrongly pressured into allowing it to be published. Was that in fact the case?"

"My dear Adam, these bothersome questions of chronology are so irrelevant to the fundamental process of creativity. As a writer – of sorts – yourself, you are surely aware than every artist always has more than one project, more than a single theme, in his mind at any given moment. Which of these projects comes to fruition at a particular time is, if not completely a matter of chance, then certainly beyond one's absolute control."

"Then there is no definite date for any further publication?"

Archie beamed at him as though he were really a very clever pupil after all. "And maybe there never will be, Adam, maybe there never will be. Inspiration, if not precisely like lightning, is definitely a fickle benefactress. Forster wrote half a dozen novels of recognised genius but after the age of thirty-five – nothing. Rossini ceased his opera writing while still a young man and— "

"And became hugely fat eating Italian sausage," Adam grinned.

"Your interests extend to opera, then?"

"Those same facts have been mentioned in your previous three interviews." Archie looked momentarily annoyed, but Adam said swiftly, "I don't suppose you have any such weaknesses?"

Archie waved his glass amicably. "My vices are of a more liquid nature."

"Perhaps," said Adam, "we should turn our attention to *Dora's Room* itself. The article is after all intended to coincide with the new edition."

"By all means, though after so long I can't imagine

that there can be anything new to say. Of course, I will try . . ."

"Thank you. The central conundrum, as always, has to be the identity of Dora herself." Archie was about to interrupt but Adam went on swiftly, "I know you've repeatedly denied that there was such a person— "

"And I do so again now. And even if there was . . . all that you, or any other person needs to know about Dora, or anything else to do with my life, is in the book itself. Who was it who said, 'Let the man who wants to find out about me read my books'? Or words to that effect. Whoever did say it certainly knew what he was talking about. It's all there, Adam, read the book, it's there."

"But so ambiguous, Mr Miller. The identity of Dora remains open to so many interpretations."

"*All* in the book!" Archie repeated with some satisfaction. "All, everything. Tutti. Alles. And that is why, you see, on my so-called lecture tours, I confine myself simply to the reading of selections, often random selections. Let the academics and the burrowers and the – yes, Adam, the hacks – let them root around and attempt to reduce my creation to a dry assemblage of footnotes and explanations. *Dora's Room* stands alone. I will not add to it, I will not subtract from it. Not a sentence, not a word, not the dot of an 'i'."

He stood up and poured himself another drink.

"But still the puzzle remains." Adam was certainly persistent.

"Yes?"

"If there was no such person as Dora, why was the first edition of the book dedicated to her?"

Did I imagine it or did the merest shadow of some unwelcome emotion, anger or grief perhaps, ripple across Archie's face as he raised his hand to touch the silk cravat at his throat? And was his reply, "It was a mistake, Adam, a trivial mistake," just a touch too swift, too dismissive?

Though I had never read the book, had no idea who this unknown Dora might be, I found suddenly that I was intrigued. Adam put me in mind of a skilful prosecutor questioning the defence: his manner implied that he had some hunches concerning the answers to his apparently innocent questions, that the truth, were it ever revealed, would be quite different from the official version, perhaps even that he had guessed the identity of Dora – and I longed to ask him about it myself.

Adam said, "Some critics have suggested the Dora figure might represent some kind of bird, others perhaps a mythical figure— "

Archie shrugged in mock exasperation. "Is it a bird? Is it a plane? No, it's Dora— "

"Perhaps I'm being particularly obtuse," (Adam did not, however, sound in the least bit apologetic) "but I've never been able to see the need for the mystery. She could of course be the older woman who initiates the young boy into manhood, but that particular theory has never made much sense to me. Unless, of course, there is a real person you were trying to protect. I must say, the secrecy, and the controversy it has created, strikes me as nothing more than a gimmick, albeit a very successful one."

It was obvious to me that Adam was deliberately trying to provoke my uncle, to annoy him into making a less carefully guarded statement. A shiver of fear ran down my spine. I wanted to beg him to stop. That earlier, irrational terror that had gripped me when I first heard Archie's voice in the hallway must have distorted my judgement, for there was Archie, still smiling, still unruffled, saying, "It wasn't a gimmick," and now here was Paula, unable to contain her impatience any longer.

"Hey, Adam, hang on. You've headed way off course here. Don't you see, you've missed the whole beauty of the central concept. Dora is a symbol, the expression of an archetype, and as such she has a far deeper meaning than if she was confined to a single physical reality."

"So there's no mileage in the suggestion that Dora might be a phoenix, for instance?"

The question was addressed to Archie, but once again it was Paula who answered. "Of course, Adam, as far as it goes, that's a perfectly valid interpretation. Dora can be a phoenix, a symbol of regeneration and rebirth – after all, one of the many themes that run through the book is the allegory of the birth of manhood or, conversely, the death of the boy, the child within us all. But Dora is different for each one of us. Archie's genius has created something clear enough to be concrete and recognisable but which each person can interpret in their own way, a way which is uniquely relevant to them alone."

Adam looked depressed. "People always say that but it's never rung true, not to me. That's why I thought there must be a far simpler explanation— "

"Simpler?" Paula was moving rapidly through the gears to top. "Why should you expect the truth to be simple? As it says in the book, truth has to be unclear. Dora can be seen as an anima figure, the archetypal mother/lover/daughter/priestess and then, of course, it can hardly have escaped your observation that Dora is an anagram of Road, the sacred path, the Way, enlightenment . . ."

She carried on in this vein for a while longer but I had stopped listening. One of the reasons I had always avoided *Dora's Room* was the calamitous effect it so often produced in its readers. And now here was Paula who, for all that she had majored in literature at Illinois State, usually maintained a fairly robust attitude to contemporary fiction, babbling on like a fully paid-up habituée of Pseud's Corner.

If I had been Archie I'd have been squirming with embarrassment before she was even half finished and I expected him to cut her short with a few succinct words, but no, he was positively lapping it up.

"Very eloquently put, my dear girl," he beamed when she had finished, or at any rate had run out of breath, "it's gratifying for us humble scribblers to know that there are at least some readers out there who have the wit to see what's under their damned noses."

"Don't misunderstand me, Mr Miller," Adam's voice was almost weary, "I've always loved *Dora's Room* and not only because of its connection with Long Chatton.

48

But the aspect I've always admired most is its essential simplicity. I hate to see it snowed under with such a mountain of theorising. In the beginning, when the idea for Dora first came to you, surely it was a simple one, a single image, a— "

"Simple bullshit."

The obscenity was all the more shocking because unexpected. As soon as the words were spoken Archie's anger vanished as quickly as it had appeared and he reverted to his previous air of urbane calm, but the message was clear enough: his tolerance of questions, and of his questioner, was over.

Adam was equally unruffled. "May I quote you on that?"

"Say what you bloody well like, dear boy. It's all lies anyway. What you people print," he added quickly, "all lies. And as for this lot," and here he knocked the drawer of photographs to the floor, scattering packets and envelopes and loose pictures all over the carpet, "they're the biggest bloody lies of all. Tea in the summer house, cricket on the lawn, smiling bloody Mummy – it makes me sick. Pie in the sky, fairy tale . . . God's in his heaven and all's right with the . . . don't look at me like that, Fern, you don't have to worry, your dad was okay. He was all right, Clancy was, nothing wrong with him . . ."

He stood up and went to pour himself another drink. I was beginning to think longingly of my little Renault and the journey back to Bristol. My knowledge of drunkenness was almost entirely gleaned from books and films but I guessed that Archie had passed through anger and was rapidly becoming maudlin. He was launched into the mood where the dead are seen in a sunset glow of perfection and the last thing I wanted was to hear him maunder on about my father.

I switched on the standard lamp that stood behind the sofa, then began tidying the photographs and albums back in the drawer. Paula helped.

"We really should think about getting back," I said,

my voice tinkling with inappropriate politeness, and this time, to my relief, she did not contradict me.

Then, "Nonsense!" Archie boomed. "You can't leave now, not yet. You haven't looked round the house yet. You must see what is yours, my dear, lord of all you survey . . . and we mustn't disappoint Gerald either, poor sod's been bursting his buttons with excitement for days. Gerald!"

"Perhaps another time— "

"GERALD!"

Although Archie shouted quite loudly I hoped Gerald would not hear him. Chatton Heights was such a large house it would have needed an intercom system to cover it – but he must have been lurking in the hallway because, to my chagrin, he came in almost at once. Archie waved his glass towards us. "Sunshine tours of the stately home, please, Gerald."

"With pleasure."

Gerald, to my surprise, seemed almost good-humoured. A bit hot and bothered, perhaps, but still, he smiled affably enough at Paula as though she had not, less than an hour earlier, called him an asshole and he had not told her to sod off.

Although he did not smile directly at me there was a definite softening in his pale eyes as he said, "Just the house today. It's getting too dark to see much else," and I began to hope that perhaps Paula was right and that Gerald's animosity towards me was waning.

"Do you mind if I join you?" Adam asked. "It could be useful for the article."

"Christ, man, haven't I given you all the copy you need?" Archie laughed as he asked the question, but I sensed genuine annoyance beneath the smile.

"It's Mary Fern's house now," said Paula, and I would gladly have throttled her, "she's the one you should ask if you want to look around."

"Don't be ridiculous," I said, "let's all go."

The reason for Gerald's eagerness to show us around

the house that had just been left to me soon became apparent: he was able to act out the part of the young squire, showing the parvenues the house in which he alone had been brought up. At every turn he demonstrated his natural rights to the place: he was the one who knew the house, who belonged there – we were mere tourists, intruders.

The main impression gained, on that first viewing, was one of vast size and penetrating cold: shadows of a winter's dusk, long slate-floored corridors and a huge and empty silence. Since that January afternoon, of course, I have come to know the house well, but though I've seen it since on sunny days and on summer days I still think of it as it appeared then, while we trooped along behind Gerald's polished brogues – a dwelling place as dark and cheerless as the bottom of a well.

Only the central portion of the house at the front was in use. The two wings that formed a kind of three-sided courtyard at the back were entirely closed off and so bitterly cold that we whizzed around them as quickly as we could, stamping our feet and hugging ourselves to keep warm.

The names of the rooms were a litany to a bygone age: the cider room, the honey store, the butler's pantry, the buttery, the boot-boy's room, the nursery suite (with rooms for both night and day nurses and a housemaid and tutor) the gun room, a billiard room, the morning room . . . an age that must have vanished soon after the house was built towards the end of the nineteenth century. The family business had suffered a decline between the wars, so Gerald informed us as we stood in the housekeeper's sitting-room and watched water drip from an ominous bulge in the ceiling; the manufacturing business had been sold off and even the import–export side of things had declined and there was less and less money to maintain the formidable array of staff required to tend the proper upkeep of the house.

Whole sections of society were, in Gerald's view, responsible for this lamentable state of affairs – almost everyone, in fact, except the Miller family itself. "Bloody socialist governments have tried to squeeze people like us out of existence, they won't be happy until everyone is on the dole. And there's no one who'll do a decent day's work any more. Even a bloody gardener expects a car and a colour TV; no wonder the country's falling apart."

Considering that only a short time before, Gerald had stated his own determination never to find a job, I was amazed by his diatribe. I noticed with relief that Adam too had been listening and there was an expression of incredulity on his face. "Would you agree," he asked mildly, "that the rot really began with the abolition of child labour?"

Gerald peered at him uncertainly. "Children used to enjoy working," he said, "better than watching bloody videos all day anyway," and, without waiting for Adam's reply (which seemed to take the form of a poorly muffled snort of laughter), Gerald hurried from the room, almost tripping on the shallow stair as he did so.

My house, Gerald called it, *my* ancestor's business. It was the theme of the tour, as though, by leading us around, he was reclaiming the house as his own rightful property. "This is where *we* always entertain the tenants at Christmas," he said and, "This was *my* nurse's room," and "*my* grandfather". Even, when we reached a small sitting-room (the smoking-room, Gerald called it) which was dominated by a pair of double portraits, "Those two are *my* parents – and those are *my* uncle and aunt."

I found that I had no wish, just at that moment, to examine a portrait of my parents and I was about to leave the room when I heard Adam say in correction, "You mean these are *Fern's* parents."

"I suppose they must be." Gerald was chewing the skin around his thumbnail. "I never thought of them as being hers, somehow." But then he brightened at a thought. "Poor old Aunt Louise was a nutter, you know."

I flinched. Adam's arm brushed against my sleeve. It could have been an accident, but I thought: he's on my side. Paula said, "Look, Mary Fern, your mother was real pretty."

For a moment a twinge of curiosity caused me to hesitate. But then I shrugged. "Come on," I said, "it's freezing in here. And I've had enough ancestor worship for one day."

Adam was studying the two double portraits with interest. "Have you seen these before, Fern? I wonder who the artist was. They're much better than the usual run of modern portraits."

Gerald glanced surreptitiously at the signature at the bottom of one of the paintings. "D. Brewster," he said, as if he had known all along, "his work is pretty sought after these days."

"Is he still alive?" Adam asked, but Gerald pretended not to hear. "I'm sure I recognise that name," Adam said, half to himself, as we left the room.

We all trooped upstairs.

In a small back bedroom we came across Tillie who was crouched in an armchair in front of a television set. She was watching a wrestling match and grunting in sympathy with the two blubbery men who writhed on the screen. In contrast to all the other rooms in the house this one was furnace warm, but Tillie was still wrapped in the two shapeless handknitted cardigans she had worn earlier. The whole room was filled with that slightly acrid and depressing smell that boxes of old clothes give off at jumble sales. A smell of neglect and despair. Only in Tillie's room did I feel myself to be an intruder.

Most of the bedrooms, like the smoking-room, the billiard room, the library and all the other downstairs rooms, were huge and impersonal and old-fashioned – walnut wardrobes and high beds and gloomy Chinese carpets on the floor and a predictable succession of heavily varnished landscapes interspersed with jolly huntsmen being borne over five-barred gates. The accumulated effect of so much grandeur and so little taste and so few signs of life was a distinct lowering of the spirits.

I realised I was not the only one to be so affected when

Adam remarked, "Don't you ever miss something a little more intimate? It all seems pretty bleak to me."

"Do you really think so?" Gerald had to tilt his head back in order to look down his nose at Adam but he seemed to consider the effort worthwhile. "It rather depends on what one is used to," he said, speaking with slow emphasis, as though to an audience of mental defectives. "If one has been brought up in a place of a certain size, anything else is horribly claustrophobic. One does acquire certain standards."

Adam was unable to suppress a grin which made his face look suddenly boyish. "One wouldn't know about that," he said with deceptive mildness – and for the first and only time that horrible day I felt a sudden urge to laugh bubble up inside me.

Gerald frowned, hesitated, then, muttering to himself about standards, he led the way down yet another cold and empty passageway.

He had been saving his biggest treat until last.

"This was my grandfather's room." He threw the door open on a bedroom larger and more oppressively gloomy than all the others. "Quite a fine room, don't you think?"

We stood in silence.

What, I wondered, had induced the anonymous someone to cover those high walls in a dark brown paper which was ornamented only by a collection of cold grey urns? Did they consider it imposing? Impressive? Baronial? The chocolate and grey walls enclosed a random assemblage of objects; the bed was covered in a quilt of heavy maroon brocade; a mahogany tallboy glowered in a dark corner next to a pathetic collection of modern storage units and a trolley that might have been used for medicines. At the foot of the high bed stood a massive bow-fronted chest, black lacquered and covered with a pattern of birds that could have been herons, or egrets, perhaps. In any other setting it would have been a handsome piece of furniture; in the context of my grandfather's bedroom it merely added to the funereal darkness.

Gerald said, "He was pretty well bed-ridden for the last few months. Of course, he should have gone into hospital but Pa and I understood his wish to remain here. We had nurses, all did our bit. One pulled together, you know." Adam made a muffled choking sound but Gerald carried on, oblivious. "Pa and I were with him when he died and I can tell you, it was a moving experience, the whole family together at a time like that."

It was a fairly obvious snub, except that I don't think Gerald meant it that way. Paula said, "Sounds as though you missed a real treat, Mary Fern," but Gerald never even noticed. Just carried on chewing his mangled thumb.

Rain was falling beyond the stone-mullioned windows. The overhead light was dim and the room itself looked dark and old. An old man's room, a room to die in.

I went to the window and looked out. We were at the front of the house, almost directly over the main hallway. Light from the drawing-room was falling on the rain-shiny gravel and beyond that the laurels and trees that bordered the drive moved silently in the windy darkness. Far off there were a few lights which must have been Long Chatton, but blocking most of the village was a larger, darker shadow: the holm oak.

I knew that it could be seen from this window just as, when we were approaching, I had known its name and that it was the oldest tree in the garden. Just as I had known there had been roses beyond the window. The house, implacable and sure, gave off its own truths, like the perfume from within a sandalwood box.

I turned away, longing for light and the sound of voices chattering. Then I stopped. Gerald was gazing at the huge maroon-glazed bed and his pale, close-set eyes were as fierce as needles, fixed on an unmoving point, just as if someone was lying there, just as if our grandfather had not yet died.

And his expression was not in the least that of someone who has helped nurse a much-loved relative through a tragic illness. His expression was terrifying.

"This room gives me the creeps," said Paula.

We all trooped out.

The tour was over. Our visit to Chatton Heights was over too and as far as I was concerned not a moment too soon. I was seized with a sudden irrational fear that we might somehow be prevented from leaving and have to stay overnight, even sleep in one of those echoing lonely bedrooms. I began to make fevered plans for escape, just in case my car, for some reason, refused to start. There must be a taxi service in Long Chatton, I thought. Or else Adam could give us a lift to the nearest station. I did not consider asking Archie or Gerald.

My cousin was distracted, hardly speaking to us while he fetched our coats: Paula's black cape and my pale anorak. I realised with dismay that Adam was leaving ahead of us and I began to follow him down the corridor, as though to see him out.

"Maybe I'll see you again," he said. "Your cousin's quite a charmer. If the socialists used him in their advertising campaign the revolution would come overnight."

And then he was gone. In the hallway Gerald held our coats. "Say goodbye to Tillie for us, won't you," I said hastily, "and your father too."

He was helping Paula with her cape. "You'll come again, I suppose," he said bleakly.

Paula and I both spoke at once.

"You bet your life," she said.

"There's really no need," I said but he wasn't listening anyway.

I had that fluttery feeling in my stomach that you get when you know you're going to be late for a train. I would willingly have run down the corridor and through the garden room and on to the gravel. Never has cold wet air felt so welcome on my cheeks and in my lungs as it did on escaping from the stifling grip of Chatton Heights.

"Wait! You can't go yet. Wait!" Archie's voice boomed out like a tannoy. For one wild moment I thought my fear of being trapped at the Heights was justified and that Archie was trying to prevent our departure. I hurried on across the gravel towards the small shadow that was my car.

"Hang on, Mary Fern," Paula remonstrated, "your uncle only wants to say goodbye."

I forced myself to slow down. Archie was pounding towards us, breathing heavily. "Just wanted . . . my dear . . . the book . . . and one for . . . your friend."

"Well, isn't that fine." Paula's response was a good deal more spontaneous than mine. "I sure hope you've written in it, Archie."

"Just look inside. And I hope you'll visit us with Fern again. Come for a real stay next time, Fern. Inevitably it will be something of an ordeal to begin with but that will wear off with time, and anyway, there's a certain justice in your good fortune, you know. Funny, I never thought I cared much for justice, but I find this instance most" – he searched for the word – "most absorbing."

He sounded perfectly sincere – and yet for some reason that I had no wish to analyse his words only increased my discomfort.

I wrenched my car door open. "Thank you for the book," I said, "I promise I'll read it now."

"You do that. I'd be fascinated to learn your reaction."

I thought "fascinated" was overdoing it a bit. "And thanks for the photographs," I added politely.

"Oh them. They're probably yours anyway."

In my eagerness to leave I pulled out the choke too far and nearly flooded the engine. A warm sweat of relief covered my back when it finally started. I swung the car round in a huge arc and for a brief moment the headlights shone on Archie and he raised his hand in farewell. Behind him the façade of Chatton Heights rose up tall and grim as a Norman keep.

I put my foot on the accelerator and we roared off down the drive.

"Hang on," said Paula as we bounced over the potholes, "what's all the hurry?"

On the way home I wanted nothing more than to be left in silence with my thoughts. But Paula was in a talkative mood.

"Some family you've been hiding! You let me think you were some poor little Orphan Annie and all the time you've had a whole pile of relatives stashed away!"

I resented the Orphan Annie slur. I said, "Both my parents are dead, that's all."

"But you never told me about your uncle and all the rest of them. You're a real dark horse, Mary Fern. What other surprises do you have hidden away around the countryside, huh?"

"I wish you wouldn't call me Mary Fern. Either Mary *or* Fern but not both."

"Why so edgy? You need to decide who you are, Mary or Fern. Two names sounds like a recipe for a major identity crisis."

"Don't be ridiculous."

"I just can't believe you never told me about your uncle. I've lived in your house for nearly six months and you never even mentioned it. Archie Miller of all people . . . and I could have gone back home without ever knowing how close I was to meeting him if your grandfather hadn't thoughtfully died."

"I never knew you were interested."

"And wasn't he good about the will and everything? I told you not to worry about it all and I was right. Why do you think he said all that stuff about justice?"

"I've no idea."

"Most probably because you had such a rough deal as a kid, what with your father dying and your mother going crazy and all the rest. He must have figured you deserved a break. But then, if they knew how bad it was for you, why did they never invite you to Chatton Heights before? That place must be great in the summer."

"I doubt it."

"Oh, you're just bitter and twisted. Your uncle was real welcoming and I'm sure your cousin is okay underneath."

"Gerald?"

"Who else? He's pretty good-looking too, you know. A bit like the hero in *Brideshead*, the blond one."

"Oh Paula, he's nothing like that at all. Just because they live in a big house that doesn't make them a bunch of aristocrats. As a matter of fact the family money began with a new design of some kind of plumbing valve about a hundred and fifty years ago. Then they started trading overseas. There's nothing remotely Brideshead about export or plumbing valves. Definitely Trade."

"Why are you so down on them all?"

"Okay then, what about Tillie?"

"Oh her, wasn't she terrific? No proper country house is complete without the dotty old maiden aunt batting around in the attic. Or in your case the dotty old step-grandmother. I'll bet she communes with spirits on moonlit nights or goes in for table turning or has Siamese cats that talk to her in Greek."

I gave up. The hugeness of the house coupled with my uncle's fame had quite unravelled Paula's powers of critical perception. To her Chatton Heights represented a glimpse of the England she had read about as a misfit teenager in an Illinois suburb and which she had so far been unable to track down in the student bedsits and pubs and cafés of Bristol. Nothing I said would convince her that the pseudo-Gothic monstrosity built by my paranoid ancestor was not the genuine aristocratic article complete with priest-holes and loyal retainers and probably the odd ghost or two as well.

She glanced at me sideways. "Does Gerald's wife get to live there too?"

"Paula! You surely don't fancy him?"

"I might do. I loved the way he talked. Shouted."

"You only want to add him to your collection of great British types. You've had the working-class hero and

59

the alcoholic poet and now you want to notch up the young laird."

"Sometimes, Mary, these things just happen."

"I thought he was affected and rude."

"Why? Because he let you see that he was hurt and upset by the terms of his grandfather's will? But he was just being honest about his feelings, Mary, and that's a good thing. Not everyone is so uptight about showing their emotions as you are. And once he said his piece he was okay – and I thought he was real interesting when he showed us round."

I remembered the way Gerald's face had changed as he stared at the empty bed: the way his pink lips had twisted into an expression far more sinister than his habitual pout, and his pale eyes glinted with hatred. Interesting? Maybe . . .

Paula went on blithely. "You mustn't let people like that get to you," she said, "you're so stiff and awkward sometimes, Mary, that you only make it harder for yourself. You have to let go sometimes, act up to them a bit."

"I can't." My words came out hard and cold as pebbles. "I've been acting all my life. I can't do it any more."

"You what?"

If I could have padlocked my mouth shut at that moment I'm sure I would have done so. Acting all my life – whatever had made me come out with such a wildly untrue statement? I backtracked rapidly. "I was only joking."

"Yeah?" Paula looked at me oddly but to my relief she didn't press on with her suspicions. My hands slipped on the steering wheel and I realised I was sweating. I've been acting all my life. Again, I asked myself, what on earth had induced me to make such a ludicrous remark? Bad enough that it was blatantly untrue: no one was ever worse at acting than I was. At school I'd always had a horror of being asked to perform. Even when safely stowed away inside a stuffy sheep costume at the back of the infants' nativity tableau with nothing more taxing than an occasional pious bleat to remember I'd be reduced to a tangle of stage-fright. So that to say I'd been acting all my life was obviously false. But worse, much worse, than the fiction, was the fact that the statement seemed to have arrived on its own. My mouth spoke the words without my brain having thought them. For a few moments I felt like one of those people in horror films who find themselves possessed by an alien power, almost as though the voice that I was going to produce wasn't mine at all.

No wonder sweat was making my hands slip on the steering wheel.

"Well," I said brightly, "I can't wait to see Dring and tell her what we've done." And it was less for the sake of the words themselves than to hear my voice and reassure myself that it was still *my* voice, my own mouth, projecting words which I had chosen to speak.

"Yeah," said Paula again, but without much interest.

We had left the motorway at the junction for Clifton and the zoo. I had been looking forward to seeing familiar streets and road junctions all day long but if I had been hoping that the city would welcome me back and tell me that the day's events had been nothing more than an irrelevant blip in my routine then I was disappointed.

The neighbourhood in which I had always lived seemed to have grown shabbier during our absence, as though the houses themselves had shrunk. So that I knew at once what Paula meant when she said suddenly, "It all looks different, now, doesn't it? All a bit dingy and small and close-packed and – " she hesitated – "different."

"Looks pretty much the same to me," I lied. "Oh good, there's a parking space right outside the house."

In the orange glow of the streetlights I could tell Paula was watching me as I parked the car. "Maybe you weren't joking," she said.

"What?"

"When you said that about acting all your life. Maybe that was the truth."

"Oh, for heaven's sake, Paula, spare me the amateur psychology, please. It's been enough of a day without that too."

And she must have agreed because she said nothing, merely followed me into the house.

The tatty streets that led to Alderly Drive had not produced the reassurance of the familiar that I had been hoping for. Dring did. Just as I had known she would.

As soon as I pushed open the door from the hall into our front room and saw her sitting solid as a lump of dough in the same chair in which I had left her that morning, I felt that I had come home, that everything after all was going to be all right. She was scowling at the figures on the television screen and the only concession to our arrival that she made was to say, "Idiots! Prancing around like that. And they expect me to watch!"

I went over and pressed the off switch. "You could have done that yourself," I said.

"I didn't feel like getting up," was her grumpy reply, "the leg's been bad again today and I've been that giddy . . ."

"Why do you think I got you the remote control? That's the whole point. You just sit in your chair and— "

"I was looking for it." Her crumpled face looked up at me in a fair imitation of a pathetic old woman. "I couldn't find it. You must have hidden it somewhere."

"No. You just put your ashtray down on it. Here. Look."

She didn't look. "Well, I don't need it now, do I? You're back."

I brushed the cigarette ash off the baby-pink garment that was stretched across her enormous bosom and emptied the ashtray and tidied the leaf litter of sweet papers and matches and the knitting thrown down in disgust and the newspaper that seemed to have exploded into something that resembled a kite at her feet. The simple chaos that always accompanied Dring was blissful after the gloomy ostentation of Chatton Heights.

She watched impassively while I restored some kind of order to her corner of the room. Then she lit a cigarette and shifted to a more comfortable position in her chair. A fine spray of ash began to fall once more on the pink plateau of her bosom.

"Use an ashtray, for God's sake," I said.

Paula had been watching from the doorway. "You two carry on like an old married couple," she said. "I'm off to the pub for some light relief."

"Okay," I said, barely attending to her. I guessed she wanted to find someone willing to listen to a highly coloured telling of her "day with my landlady the heiress". ("It was just like Brideshead, really it was. Even an old woman who's half ghost already. And my friend Archie Miller, you know, the famous writer . . ." By morning all her friends would think I had inherited Chatsworth.) If she was eager to inflate the day then I couldn't wait to reduce it to insignificance – and for that I needed Dring and her stoical common sense.

The front door slammed shut and we were alone. I made a pot of tea and cut some slices of bread and butter and carried a tray through into the sitting-room and then, for a while, it was enough simply to sit by the fire with Dring and listen to the hiss of her wheezing breath and smell the stale cigarette smoke and lavender water that had surrounded me since the day I was five years old and she first arrived out of nowhere like some stout and ailing Mary Poppins to take care of my mother and me. And now I felt the tension begin to ease a little, ebb away. That feeling of relaxation when you take off the hard high shoes that have pinched your feet all day and put on a pair of old and kitten-soft slippers. I wriggled my toes, luxuriating.

I remember once hearing someone say – it might have been one of the teachers at school or perhaps a neighbour – that my father would never have chosen Madame de Rhin (Dring was a five-year-old's adaptation of her puzzling name) if he had known that the ugly lady with the purple hat was to be my guardian, not merely for a few weeks but for the whole of my young life. She wasn't in the least the image of the motherly comfortable nanny, all starched bosom and clockwork routine. Quite the contrary, she had always had a penchant for squalor and now that she was over eighty her habits tended to be odious. She was grumpy and untidy and a fearful hypochondriac, the scourge of every outpatient's department and doctor's receptionist in Bristol. She was frequently rude and surly and grumbled endlessly about trivia. She had a face like a mongrel dog and wiry, grizzled, terrierlike hair.

Yet despite her manifest shortcomings she possessed a formidable strength that I had somehow recognised at once. A strength I clung to through the horrendous weeks that followed my father's departure for South America and his death in a plane crash. Not so much a rough diamond, was Dring, more untidy granite: an appearance of disorder masking the immovable stone beneath. That, at any rate, was how I chose to see her.

And apart from occasional stomach-churning embarrassments (the school concert when she erupted into the hall looking like a character on a poster publicising the plight of the homeless and demanded a seat in the already full front row on account of her – totally fictional – deafness) I had always been comfortable with Dring and never, or hardly ever, felt my lack of orthodox family to be a disadvantage. Quite the opposite: as my childhood progressed through adolescence I came to the belief that I was luckier than many of my friends. While their parents quarrelled, divorced, chose new and unsuitable partners and battled with each other and with their children, Dring and I pondered the medical advice in women's magazines, grumbled over the quick crossword in the evening paper, cut out recipes and wound skeins of wool into balls for her knitting.

Was I lonely? I suppose I must have been, but I don't remember it ever troubling me. And my loneliness was not as complete as it must have seemed to outsiders: unknown to other people I had Tom, Lucy and Alexander for company; not exactly playmates, since I never met them, not yet family, as we weren't related, but still they were close, real and very much alive to me. They were the three children of the Poulter family, whose nanny Dring had been from the early thirties, when Master Tom was less than a year old, until after the end of the war when Alexander finally put on long trousers and was packed off to Harrow. If I ever met any of them now, those middle-aged, never-seen siblings, they would be amazed at how much I knew about them. Does Tom remember the day he threw a cricket ball through the dining-room window and it fell in a bowl of trifle, splattering the chests of his mother's guests? Can Lucy recall the dress she was wearing that Christmas Eve when her first period began? (Butter-yellow lawn with puff sleeves and the red stain had nearly ruined it by the time it was noticed.) But Tom was a bit of a prig and had a cruel streak and I was too much in awe of Lucy who was considered beautiful and had a hard, cold face and married a banker soon after her nineteenth birthday. Alexander was my favourite. Alexander the reckless, the perpetual baby of the family. Alexander was the one I liked to hear of most. And, since Dring had left the family while he was still a child, he remained for us always a child, twelve years old, proud owner of a lop-eared rabbit called Suza and two bantams who between them laid one egg a week.

I often thought about Tom, Lucy and Alexander and wondered what they were like now, where they lived, what they were doing. I hardly ever thought about my relatives – not until that letter arrived from Randolf & Miles and changed everything.

Dring was rubbing her painful left knee and watching me closely. I began tentatively, "At least it's over now."

Dring waited.

"They weren't too bad, I suppose. Gerald made a fuss— "

"Always was a spoilt brat."

"He calmed down after a bit. Even showed us around."

"What about that woman your grandfather married?"

"Tillie? She was most peculiar. I couldn't make out if she's always been like that or if she's grown that way slowly. Or perhaps she's temporarily unhinged by grief at being left a widow."

A contemptuous grunt from Dring.

"My uncle was there too. Archie. It was all pretty awkward but he seemed to be prepared to make an effort to smooth things over."

"A nasty piece of work, your uncle. You want to be careful of him."

"What do you mean?"

"Just that."

"He was friendly enough. He gave me a copy of his book even though he was naturally put out that I'd never read it."

"I'd never want to read anything by him. He's a cruel man, that one, cruel and unreliable. Dangerous too."

"Why do you say that?"

"I have my reasons." A veiled expression clouded her eyes, her maddening Sphinx look, and I knew better than to waste time trying to probe her thoughts. Since Dring often took an irrational dislike to someone she hardly knew, I wondered if her adamant refusal to like my uncle might, when I was still a child, have caused me to fear him, if perhaps that had been the unreasoning terror that had surfaced when I first heard his voice.

"At least I don't need to go there again." Was I hoping to reassure myself? "I made it clear to the solicitor that I wanted to have as little as possible to do with the running of the place – you know, don't you, that it can't be sold until after Tillie dies but the agent seems happy enough to keep it going as it is."

"There'll be things to do."

"Letters and telephone. I don't have to be directly involved."

Dring shrugged.

"It's funny," I was half talking to myself, "but even though I can't have been there since I was, what – five years old? – I kept remembering things quite clearly, knowing exactly how they were going to be."

"Yes you did."

"What?"

"Went there. After your father died. Just once, for a visit. While your Aunt Frances was still alive."

"Archie's wife?"

A nodded affirmative. "She was all right. The only one. Spoiled that brat of hers terribly but she meant well. Kind enough to you, anyway. All the same, the visit upset you, stirred things up. Nightmares and that sort of thing. I decided it was best to stop here. Some things are best forgotten. Better to forget . . ."

"I see. I hadn't realised that."

It could have been Dring's motto.

Forget. When bad things happen, forget them. Pretend they never were. When you wake from a bad dream, quiet now, don't talk of it, forget. It's over. The present is hard enough to deal with, don't stir in the past as well. Forget the past. Forget the bad things.

And so I had. Always. Forgotten.

Until today.

Today when I discovered that memories, like old soldiers, never die – they merely bide their time and wait until the moment when you are all unprepared and defenceless against them and not expecting anything at all. Then they tease you with a half memory, startle you with something totally out of context, trip you into saying something you never even thought of.

Like that moment on the window-seat when I seemed to be plunging into a warm sea of contentment and the sound of the sea was that voice, the voice of journey's end and safe harbour; like that moment when I looked up expecting to see the swathes of roses that used to swarm around the window but which had long ago been grubbed up in the cause of efficiency. It was a memory that flirted with me, peeping out from behind a curtain, refusing to reveal itself completely.

And then that other moment when we were in the driveway and I had looked at the tall tree and known that it was the holm oak and the oldest tree in the garden.

Funny, I thought, how often it's the trivia that stick longest in the brain.

"A penny for them," said Dring.

And I replied, "Oh, it's nothing important. Just a few silly details I keep remembering. Nothing worth bothering with."

And at the time we neither of us guessed the irony of my words.

When I was a child Dring always used to linger in my room in the evenings. She never read me stories or anything like that. Sometimes we'd chat a bit, sometimes she'd potter around, sometimes she'd just sit. There must have been a time, as I grew older and before she became infirm, when we both went our separate ways in the evenings but if there was I can't remember it. For the past eighteen months, since her ulcerated legs and all her other ailments had made movement so difficult for her, I had been the one to help her get settled for the night and I usually lingered for a while, chatting and pottering about.

With Paula's arrival on the scene this time together was often skipped, but the evening of my first visit to Chatton Heights I had a sense of the fleeting preciousness of the old woman's company.

By then the rain had stopped but I could still hear cars swishing through the wet streets. Somehow that only made Dring's room seem all the cosier, a contrast to the dismal January night outside, above all a contrast to the monstrously gloomy bedrooms at Chatton Heights. The solidity of the room was Dring's doing: she favoured furniture that required three people to lift and which in our tiny rooms left barely any space to move around. The details were left to me. On the mantelpiece over the hissing gas fire were photographs of Tom, Lucy and Alexander Poulter, all smiling in that brightly confident way that is usually reserved for much older people, politicians and other public figures. There were a couple of vases that I'd made in pottery class and a shell box which I'd brought back from a school trip to Burnham-on-Sea and various home-made cards. Over the chest of drawers was an oil painting of an orchard full of apple blossom. I loved that picture: the frothy pink paint conjured up an eternal May morning. Even on a cold wet evening like this I could almost hear the birds singing and the bees humming as I looked at it.

Most of the other surfaces in the room were occupied by bottles of pills and jars of ointment, cotton wool, bandages, paper handkerchiefs and ashtrays.

Dring herself always looked her most monstrous, even I had to admit that, when she was prepared for bed. She had a passion for the kind of nightwear that might have been suitable for a Paris courtesan of the grand epoch but which did nothing at all for an old woman with grizzled hair and rumpled features. Yet I never felt fonder of her than I did on that evening, her tired eyes peering out over a frenzy of lilac frills – and I regretted my recent neglect.

"Is there anything else I can get you?"

"A new leg," was her automatic reply.

"Not available on the National Health." It was what I always said. So many of our conversations had developed into a kind of shorthand, like the responses in church. It was ages since we had said anything new to each other.

I was irritated that we had to do so now.

"I *wish* he hadn't," I said.

"Who?" asked Dring. "What?"

"Left me all his money and the house and all the rest of it. My grandfather. Everett Miller. It's going to spoil everything and we were perfectly all right as we were. We didn't need anything. Certainly not all that money."

"Money never hurt anyone." Dring closed her eyes wearily. "And it can come in useful."

"But we don't *need* it. We've got all we want here. It's just going to complicate things and change them and I don't want anything to change."

"What you want has nothing to do with it." She spoke with a certain relish. "Never does. Things change soon enough whether you want them to or not. We can't go on like this much longer."

"Why on earth not? We've always managed well enough until now."

"Not any more. I'm old. I can't keep on for ever. I'm getting too ill, too much for you. You'll have to put me in a home."

"Don't talk nonsense. You've been saying that for as long as I can remember. You're just tired, that's all."

"I wake up tired. It's too much of a struggle now. I'm old, useless. I'd be better off in a home and you can afford it now."

I scolded her, but my scolding barely hid my panic. I had come back from Chatton Heights to the security she had always provided only to find it slipping away, escaping. Like trying to catch smoke between your fingers, hopeless. Impossible.

I didn't want to leave her that evening. I wanted only to stay in that unbearably stuffy room for as long as it took for her to be well and strong again. I needed her – needed her more than ever.

We argued a bit, then slid into silence. I leaned my head on the overpadded back of the bedroom chair and closed my eyes and tried to pretend that nothing had changed. ("I'd have thought you'd be glad not to have the responsibility any more," said Paula later, when I told her. "You don't understand," I said. Which was true.) Tyres sprayed the rainy tarmac, the cheap alarm clock ticked methodically, the gas flame was steady . . . to pretend that all was just as it had always been.

I began to relax, and as I did so I slid into a strange intermediate state, neither waking nor sleeping, half conscious, half dreaming – and then to my delight I heard the voice again, that gentle summer voice and a warm safety billowed around me like silk. It was the voice I had heard on the window-seat (a man's voice? I could not be sure) only this time it was different. There was a rocking as though in an old-fashioned cradle, or a boat at anchor on a gentle sea. The motion was a caress, just as the voice was. Gentle, lulling, rocking . . . swinging.

The sound of the front door. Paula's return.

I opened my eyes and saw above the chest of drawers the picture of the orchard massed with apple blossom. Pinkness and light.

"Dring," I said, "do you know if there was a swing at the Heights?"

"A swing? God only knows. Bugger off with your questions. I was almost asleep."

"Good night then."

I switched off the lights and crept out. And all the while I moved in a shower of golden light. Sunshine and summer content.

Chapter 3

Paula was determined that I should return to Chatton Heights – and I was equally determined to avoid it.

"You've hardly even seen the place. What about all the outbuildings and the gardens and the tenants' cottages?"

"The agent will tell me all I need to know."

"But aren't you even curious?"

"No. And you only want me to return because of Gerald."

"Have I been talking in my sleep? It's not only his aristocratic charm that makes me want to go back there – I am thinking of your welfare as well, you know."

"Thanks."

"You can't keep running away for ever. You have to face it some time."

"I'm not running away for heaven's sake. I've been there once, haven't I? Isn't that enough?"

Plainly, Paula did not think it was. I couldn't blame her for her impatience, her curiosity . . . but then neither could I share it. To her it was all a game, an intriguing game, something to write about in letters home, but to me it was all chillingly serious. Excitement and intrigue were precisely what I had always striven to avoid. Paula had no way of knowing how diligently I had worked to create for myself a life of security, how fiercely I still clung to that precious routine in spite of all that was happening.

Just because I was heir to what still seemed an unreal amount of money I saw no reason why my life must change. I continued to turn up for my part-time job at the estate agent's, still attended my business studies course three times a week. I scorned Paula's suggestion that I might employ someone to help care for Dring.

Yet despite all my efforts to act as though nothing was changed, I often felt that I was performing a difficult balancing act and, since Chatton Heights seemed to be the cause of my unease, I had no reason to risk a second visit.

My determination was sufficient to withstand Paula's nagging, but I had reckoned without Adam Bury.

At first I didn't recognise him. I was just emerging, one cold dank evening, from the neon-lit warmth of the college when a man's voice called out, "Fern! What a surprise!"

I turned, startled. No one at the college had ever called me anything but Mary and when I caught sight of Adam I had that sense of dislocation that occurs when a familiar face bobs up in unfamiliar surroundings: that broad, lop-sided smile and those questioning slate-grey eyes belonged in the drawing-room at the Heights, not here on the steps of the college.

"Adam, whatever are you doing here?"

He grinned. "I could say looking for you but it wouldn't be true. I'm due at the hospital in an hour or so but I thought I'd look up a couple of old friends first."

"You're not ill, are you?"

"My interest in the hospital is professional, not personal. I'm researching a piece on rising violence and underfunding in an inner city casualty ward."

"Sounds like fun."

"I'm hoping for something memorable. You don't by any chance feel like assaulting a student nurse, do you? Running amok with a bed-pan?"

I laughed. "Sorry. I'd be glad to help out but I do have a prior engagement. Anyway, that sounds more like Dring's line of country than mine."

"Dring? Oh yes, I remember, the eccentric old dear who fostered you."

I was just wondering how he knew about Dring when he added helpfully, "My father told me."

"Oh."

What else had his oh-so-informative father told him?

73

Mindreader that he was Adam said, "He told me quite a bit about your family, actually."

"Oh," again. More bleakly.

The new owner of the biggest house in the village is a fair target for gossip, I knew, but all the same I found Adam's omniscience far from comfortable. In fact it made me feel like one of those butterflies you see stretched out in a collector's case for all to peer at: public property, nowhere to hide.

I turned away. "I'd best be going. Dring will wonder— "

"Hey, don't race off like that. Look, why don't we go somewhere for a drink, or a coffee? There's a café down the road I used to go to a lot. Let's see if it's still the same."

"What about your nurses?"

"Polishing their scalpels at this time of day. Mayhem isn't scheduled to break out until after seven. They promised."

I wavered. "I don't know. I ought to . . ."

It was hard to tell whether he had heard me but decided to ignore my indecision, or whether he genuinely did interpret my mumbled protest as acquiescence. From what I later learned of Adam's character I guessed he had simply decided to ignore me but at the time I was inclined to be more charitable.

There was a warm fug in Pierre's Patisserie and Coffee Lounge, a smell of damp raincoats and strong tea. Adam chose a table near the window and fetched a menu. "How about something to eat?" he asked. "Chocolate fudge brownie? Submarine sandwich? Stuffed baked potato? Steak and chips with a side order of— "

"A cup of tea will be fine."

He peered at me critically over the top of the menu. Some eyes just look at you, others seem to be trying to drill a hole into your thoughts and Adam's, at that moment, were definitely of the drilling kind.

I explained, "I don't really have much time."

"So you keep saying. But why not allow yourself the wicked luxury of a small something to eat? Wait, don't

74

refuse. My guess, speaking strictly as an investigative journalist, you understand, is that since your old lady with the odd name fell ill you haven't had the first idea how to look after yourself. I'll bet you haven't had a decent meal in weeks. You look horribly undernourished."

"Thanks for the compliment. I only hope that theory isn't typical of your professional skills. I happen to be an excellent cook, much better than Dring ever was. And anyway, *I've* been looking after *her* for years."

"Oh well, so much for investigative journalism. I'm going to have some sandwiches. Never contemplate the dying agonies of the National Health on an empty stomach."

"No sandwiches for me, thanks." When the waitress had taken our order I added, "Nurse-bashing sounds woefully sensational. I imagined your tastes were more literary."

"My tastes have nothing to do with it. When you're at the bottom of the heap you do as you're told. While I was doing my stint in the provinces I spent months penning wickedly clever book reviews which raised not a single eyebrow – not a hair of a single eyebrow. My big break only came when I unveiled a Boys' Church Group Sex Camp Scandal. Perhaps you remember it?" he ended hopefully.

I shook my head.

"A pity. I had a wonderful interview with the farmer whose meadow was the unlikely stage for the orgy. He claimed his Friesians were so outraged their milk yield dropped by a third."

"I never saw cows as especially puritanical."

"That just shows how important it is to read the papers carefully; if you did you'd be an expert on bovine moral attitudes by now. But after that first article it all got pretty tacky: hordes of irate parents claiming they'd never had any idea . . . etc. etc. Three of the camp leaders ended up doing time. The story was taken up by the nationals— "

"Fame and success for the local reporter."

"Just so." He looked glum.

"Don't you find it disheartening having to do that kind of sensational stuff?"

"Not in the least. I mean, I don't go in for extremes. I don't shove a microphone into someone's face and say, 'How do you feel now that your husband has just died and you've lost both your legs?' or anything like that."

"I'm delighted to hear it."

"But I do enjoy talking to people, listening to their stories. Oh good, here are the sandwiches . . . and our tea. If you change your mind about the food, help yourself. So what about you, what were you doing at the college?"

"I'm doing a part-time business studies course."

"So that you can handle your inheritance wisely?"

"You know all about my grandfather's will, then?"

He nodded.

"I suppose I ought to have realised that in a place like Long Chatton news travels fast."

"As a general rule of thumb you can reckon that a quarter of the village will have detailed knowledge of any event at least twenty-four hours *before* it actually takes place."

"How do you know the village so well? Has your father always lived there?"

"Didn't you know? Ted was rector of Long Chatton when I was small and he stayed a long time. That's why the place has always been so important for me, first memories, all that sort of thing. And that's the reason I'm so devoted to your uncle's book – it positively reeks of the place. If he'd grown up anywhere else he'd have had to write a different book. Don't you agree?"

"I haven't read it, remember. Archie did give me a copy but – I somehow haven't got around to it yet."

"You really should. You'd love it."

"Maybe . . . so your family has always lived in Long Chatton?"

"Oh no, my father was moved on eventually, or promoted or whatever they call it in the Church. We went to Portsmouth and for a few months I hated the place, never really settled there. I don't think any of us did.

76

There's a magic at Long Chatton, despite all the ghastly antique shops and olde worlde tea rooms, a magic you can never quite escape from. You must have felt it."

I ventured a non-committal, "Mm," and asked, "So what does your father do there now?"

"He retired. And then at about the same time the rectory came on the market: all part of the Church's mania for selling off their old properties and rehousing their unfortunate clergy on modern estates – a policy my father heartily disapproves of, I might add. However, on this occasion he managed to swallow his principles and seize the opportunity. In fact I think the whole affair has bolstered his somewhat flagging respect for the Almighty."

"I thought the clergy couldn't afford grand houses."

"No, the money was on my mother's side, enough to buy the rectory at any rate. But she died eighteen months ago so she never enjoyed the pleasures of retirement."

"I'm sorry."

"Yes." He was silent for a few moments, apparently absorbed in contemplation of his thumbnail. "But she'd had a full life and achieved most of what – I mean, it must be much harder for you."

"Me?"

"The fact that your mother died without, from what I've heard, ever really knowing what it was to live. That must be so . . . but stop me if it upsets you to talk about it."

I sat very still. From the street outside I could hear the urgent wail of a police car. At the table behind me two women were discussing their teenage offspring in tones of shocked fascination. I stared at the orange surface of my tea. "Why should it bother me? I hardly even remember her. It's just like talking about a stranger, nothing personal at all."

"Are you sure? Ted reckons you must have been about five or six when your father died and she was admitted to hospital. I'd have thought you'd remember them both."

"No I don't," I said firmly. Too firmly. I hesitated, and then, with the caution of one who feels herself to be venturing into uncharted waters I began, "Or at least, not until recently. I never thought about them at all, there just wasn't much point, somehow. I stopped visiting my mother years ago – it was just too painful. But now . . . since all this happened . . . it's not so simple any more."

"You find you keep remembering things?"

"How do you know?" I looked up sharply, met his eyes for a moment, turned away. "No, not remembering exactly. More . . . it's hard to explain."

"Maybe now is the time you need to know about them."

"Why? What's the point?"

"Instinct, I suppose. It's only natural to want to know who your parents were. Most people take it for granted, but if you don't grow up with the knowledge then sooner or later I should think you'd want to find out."

I was impressed by the way Adam made my messy tangle of emotions sound quite reasonable and only to be expected. "You seem very well informed on this."

"I should be. I did a piece last year on people who'd been adopted as small children or babies and who only traced their natural parents once they were adult. It was amazing the emotional pull these total strangers had on each other. Almost uncanny."

"What amazes me is that anyone will allow such personal stories to be published."

"That's one of the aspects of the job that took some getting used to. The majority believed their story might help others who were going through the same struggle. And they found the actual process of explaining what had happened, what their emotions had been, to be somehow satisfying in itself. A kind of unburdening. Most people are only too glad to find someone who'll listen to them."

He beamed at me. Just as I was noticing that his slatey-grey eyes had tiny flecks of gold in them and that when he smiled, as he was doing now, his whole face smiled and tiny creases spread out from his eyes, just

as I noticed all this my stomach clenched with sudden
fear. It was the way he said it. "People are only too
glad to have someone to talk to," and then the way he
smiled encouragingly, as much as to say, "So now it is
your turn, Fern Miller. Step into the limelight and let
me hear your story." And I thought, of course, he's still
trying to get material for his article on Archie. He didn't
get much from his visit to Chatton Heights on Sunday
and so he thought he'd try me. Suddenly it was all so
obviously contrived, the way he "just happened" to be
passing my college when I was leaving, his "sudden"
decision to pause for coffee. No doubt he would also,
accidentally of course, bump into Tillie and Gerald and
others whom I didn't know before his wretched article
was finished. Or maybe, even worse, he's thinking of
doing a new piece on the trauma of inheritance: Special
Revelation by Fern, reluctant beneficiary of the Miller
Millions.

In that instance his grey eyes with the gold flecks in them
looked not in the least bit attractive – cold and calculating
they were, like a hungry wolf checking through the day's
lunch menu. And that wide, apparently generous smile
was nothing but a trap to snare the unwary. "All the
better to eat you with, my dear."

I pushed my cup away.

"Is anything wrong?" Adam was all concern.

"I'm not going to be much help as an informant,
that's all."

He betrayed no sign of disappointment. "I didn't have
you marked out as a chatterbox, somehow. Apparently
your father was the same, the kind of person who watches
all that goes on but says very little."

I felt hopelessly confused. Part of me longed to trust
him but another part of me feared the risk was too great.
I decided that on balance the enigma of Adam Bury was
more than I could cope with. I said, "Good heavens,
look at the time. I really must get back. Dring will be
wondering where I've got to."

"Oh yes, I'd forgotten the mysterious old housekeeper."

"She's not a housekeeper."

"What then? A nanny?"

"No, she's just . . . oh, it doesn't matter. But I must get back."

"I'll pay, then. Can I give you a lift?"

"My car is just around the corner."

It was wretchedly cold outside, far too cold for lengthy goodbyes. "Thanks for the tea," I said, zipping a dollop of freezing air into my anorak.

"Don't rush off. Look, it's great we bumped into each other like this." (Coincidence? You're getting paranoid, I told myself, of course it's just a coincidence.) "I'll be going down to Long Chatton again soon. Why don't you come with me? I know Ted would love to meet you properly. And it might be interesting for you too – a chance to find out more about your father, I mean."

Why was everyone so convinced I wanted to know about my father? He was dead, wasn't he? What else was there to know about him? "I don't really think so. I must be going."

But Adam, as I was learning, had the persistence of a bull terrier when he got hold of a good idea. "I'll let you know when I'm going down. I've got your telephone number."

I'll bet you have, I thought as I hurried away to find my car. Name, number, address . . . Age, blood group, hobbies, favourite TV programmes, zodiac sign . . . his father had known who I was the moment he set eyes on me. Small wonder if the son decided to fill in the missing details. An heiress was news after all, especially if she was the niece of Archie Miller. A reporter from the local paper had been round a few days earlier. "What does it feel like to be suddenly rich, Miss Miller?" "Not much different." "Have you planned how to spend your money?" "Not really." If my answers are boring enough, I thought, they might not bother to run the story at all.

I couldn't decide about Adam. Why should he want me to go to Long Chatton with him anyway? Was he hoping for another, impromptu meeting with Archie? "I thought we might just pop in at the Heights. I mentioned to your uncle that you were coming down and he said of course we must go to lunch." More material for his article? But maybe the article was finished, maybe I was being paranoid and he had simply thought a duty visit to his father might be more enjoyable with me along. Maybe he had been smitten with a violent passion for me over the photograph drawer and was crazed with impatience to see me again. I had to admit there was a distinct flutter of the spirits at the thought of that particular scenario but common sense soon reasserted itself. Even in my best navy skirt and my fiendishly seductive pale blue anorak I had never knowingly inspired a violent passion in anyone – not anyone that mattered, anyway.

I had just read the final page when the phone rang.

For a few moments the sound jangled on the edge of my mind, so filled was I with the magic of the story, so entangled in the rich skein of words. Like a dreamer reluctant to leave the magic of sleep for the alarm clock's call.

A sense of satisfaction, completeness. Something whole and perfect to be surveyed and absorbed slowly.

So that was *Dora's Room*. Just that . . . No wonder. Short, not quite a novel. More, much more than a short story. It read with an effortless ease. A flavour lingered. A richness, an airy lightness. Strong vivid characters – were they based on real people? The crescent wave between childhood and adolescence, the timelessness of youth, the tension and the pain.

And always, a shadowy companion, real yet undefined, the figure of Dora. Mysterious Dora, ally and friend and . . . what else besides?

As I put the book down and stood up to answer the phone I had that slightly breathless sensation occasionally produced by the discovery of something new and fresh and wonderful. Breath taken quite literally away.

"Hello?"

81

"Fern? Adam here." My brain swivelled with difficulty to confront the real world.

I said, "I've just this moment finished reading *Dora's Room*."

"How did you like it?"

"Very much." To say more was to risk drowning its simplicity in a sea of interpretation, as Paula had done.

"So now you see what everyone has been raving about all this time. Look, I'm in Bristol at the weekend and I thought I'd drive down to see Ted on Sunday for the day. Why don't you come with me?"

I almost laughed. What a stupid question. Hard to think of anything I'd be more reluctant to do with a free Sunday. The very nerve of the idea.

"Yes, I'd like that," I heard myself say.

There was relief in his voice as he said, "That's great. I'll aim to pick you up around eleven and Ted can give us lunch. I never thought I'd get you to agree so easily."

As I replaced the receiver in its cradle I couldn't help smiling at his admission that he had been prepared to overcome any initial resistance I might have to the idea.

But his surprise was nothing to my own. I could have said no. I thought I had wanted to say no, but my agreement had popped out anyway.

With unsteady fingers I lit a cigarette. Perhaps I did want to go, after all, and only thought I didn't. Perhaps the real truth was that I longed to go back to Long Chatton, hear strangers talk about my family, learn more about my newfound kingdom. But why should I want one thing and only think I wanted the other? It didn't make sense. At least, not any kind of sense that I could understand.

I blamed the book: *Dora's Room*. There it lay on the side table where I had left it, singing its siren song of green leaves and wide spaces and a tall grim house on a hill . . . a place that was menacing but which nevertheless drew you back, time after time. The book was coloured with Chatton Heights like sunlight through stained glass. No wonder they wanted photographs for the new edition. No book was ever more truly rooted in one place.

A place which now belonged to me and which I had believed I never wanted to see again – so why had I just now agreed to return, and with hardly any persuasion at all?

Perhaps the attraction was Adam himself, and not the house. I didn't know. I only knew that events seemed to be slipping beyond my control, and that I was afraid.

Only let me stay here, I thought, within these four small walls and the unchanging pattern of my days.

Outside, I noticed, the sky was sombre with cloud. It might snow, I thought, clutching at meteorological straws.

Roads blocked, snowdrifts, sheet ice . . . inadvisable to travel . . . motorists are strongly recommended to stay . . . "Oh, Adam, what a shame – and I was so looking forward – perhaps some other time . . ."

The possibility was distinctly cheering. I was quite sure I didn't want to go.

Punctually at five minutes to eleven on a morning most perversely free of even a whiff of snow, Adam pulled his battered estate car to a halt in front of our gate.

Paula peered through the net curtains of the living-room (an English habit I'm sure but one which she had adapted to with remarkable speed).

"Lover boy is here."

"Don't call him that."

"Why not? He's quite good-looking. And maybe an older man is what you need, more of a father figure. But I still believe you can aim higher than him, now that you've all this money. His car is a disgrace."

"I wish you wouldn't say those things."

"Wasps around the honey jar."

I was so annoyed with Paula that for the next ten minutes I forgot to be annoyed with Adam. She was right about one thing, though, his car *was* a wreck and the heating system was on the verge of collapse. Either furnace-hot air blasted out, or nothing at all.

"Sorry about the temperature," Adam grinned, "the

heating system isn't perfect," (an understatement). "This particular trick only developed yesterday and I haven't had a chance to get it fixed yet. There's a rug on the back seat if you need it."

I did. Then I didn't. Alternately we froze or roasted. "Perhaps it's good for you," Adam suggested hopefully, but without any real conviction. "Like those Swedish bath-houses which provide steam and then chuck you out in the snow. Maybe all we need now is birch twigs."

It didn't feel healthy, more like externally induced fever as we shivered and sweated our way along the motorway, turning off to follow the smaller roads that led to Long Chatton.

When I came this way with Paula I had been too absorbed in following the route and controlling my nervousness to notice the changing countryside. But Adam knew this road well, his conversation was easy and reassuring and I found myself enjoying the journey. We passed through an area of market gardens, orchards and huge greenhouses; there seemed to be farm shops every half mile or so. And then it was as if we crossed an invisible boundary; from now on all the houses were built of yellow Cotswold stone and the landscape became more austere – cold sheep-cropped hillsides and few trees.

The road became narrow and twisting, forcing us to reduce our speed; Adam said this was an old sheep-drovers' route. As we rounded a tight bend we had a brief but panoramic view of Long Chatton, an oasis of picture-postcard charm even at the dead of winter, nestling, as such villages ought always to nestle, in the fold of a hill. But even at this distance the effect was distorted by the pseudo-Gothic extravaganza of the Heights, its razor-slit windows glowering down at the village over the tops of the sheltering swathe of trees.

Adam said, "When I was a child I always imagined Jack and the Beanstalk taking place here. I could just about imagine a runner-bean plant stretching all the way from our garden to the Heights – and it seemed entirely possible that a giant might live there; it was obviously too big for ordinary-sized people anyway."

Silently, I agreed.

The Old Rectory, as it was called so as not to be confused with the present rector's house, was everything an old rectory ought to be: square and welcoming and cluttered with books and papers and with pictures that were waiting to be hung stacked against the walls. The rooms did not look as if they had been decorated since the house was purchased – but the furniture and all the random assortment of objects awaiting final placement had an air of being worn and threadbare with much use and loving.

Ted Bury greeted us in his somewhat fierce, aquiline way. "Come in, Fern, I'm delighted to meet you properly." The angle of his eyebrows could have been a scowl but was, I saw at once, his version of a welcoming smile. He must have been an impressive vicar, I thought. I could just imagine him in his dark robes looming over the congregation like some prophetic bat and warning of hellfire and judgement.

"Hello, Ted." Adam shook his father by the hand and they eyed each other warily for a few seconds before Ted made a non-committal "hrmph"ing sort of noise and led the way into the sitting-room, sweeping books and papers off the chairs to make room for us.

While he poured us each a sherry a rather dim-looking woman in a flowered overall poked her head round the door and stared at me with the open-eyed curiosity of a child.

Ted scowled at her. "Come in and say hello if you must, Elsa. I'd have thought it could wait. Elsa's sister is housekeeper at the Heights and she cleans there two or three times a week," he explained to me as I said hello. "She's been dying to meet you for days. Now, run along, Elsa, or lunch will be spoiled. Sorry about that," he said as she retreated towards the kitchen, "but you're bound to be an object of curiosity in a small place like this. You might as well get used to it."

"So I'm learning."

"Adam tells me you regard your inheritance as a mixed blessing – though as the vast majority of blessings *are* mixed, I can never understand why people are so surprised by the fact. Talking of mixed blessings, Adam, how is Ben?"

"Fine." The statement was a shade too positive.

Ted "hrmph"ed again.

In spite of her eagerness to spend as much time as possible staring at me, Elsa prepared a competent lunch. Conversation remained neutral, desultory even, until Elsa had brought in a steaming apple charlotte and the dining-room door was firmly closed behind her, when Ted began abruptly, "I was sorry to hear of your mother's death last year."

"She died a long time ago."

He nodded. "In a sense, of course, you are right. But still, one always hopes . . . and there had been such promise."

I didn't want to hear about it. "Did you know her well?" My voice tinkled on like a clockwork toy.

"I don't believe anyone could really have claimed to know her well," he answered thoughtfully. "I did try to get to know her and I think, to a degree, she trusted me, even though, as a middle-aged vicar, I was rather regarded as a representative of an alien life form."

"Did you always think her unstable?" (Of course she was! Why ask?)

Again the considered pause before answering. "Highly strung, yes, unhappy too, often. And difficult. But I never expected . . . I blamed the drugs. All that experimentation was fine for most people, for your father for instance, we discussed it once or twice – but there were others, like your mother, who could have survived, I'm sure, but not with those kinds of pressures, those distortions of reality. She didn't, as they say, need that at all. Perhaps if she had had different treatment, or treatment sooner . . . I often wonder if I could have helped her in time if I'd only been aware of the inner demons she was fighting."

"I thought you told me," said Adam, "that it was only when Fern's father died that she broke down."

It was odd, this admission that my family was considered locally to be a valid topic of conversation. For the first time I knew what it was to belong to the "big house". Well, if it was soap opera the locals wanted, the Millers had always provided plenty of that.

"Eventually," Ted replied, "not right away. I went to see her a couple of times after his death. I never saw you, Fern, you were always at school or out with that old lady who looked after you. I was amazed on both occasions by how well she was coping. The next I heard . . . it was too late. I went to see her in the hospital but there was nothing . . . I do wonder occasionally if the drugs she was given by the hospital didn't do her nearly as much harm as the drugs she had taken for fun – or experience or whatever. I didn't go again."

"No. There never seemed much point in visiting."

I saw Adam glance at my hands and I looked down. The cloth napkin in my lap had been scrunched up into a little ball. I smoothed it out carefully.

"Fern," Adam's voice was gentle, "if you don't want to talk about this— "

They were both watching me carefully.

"It doesn't bother me," I said, "I hardly remember them."

"More's the pity." Ted's compassion, like all his emotions, was tinged with impatience. "Such a wretched waste. Perhaps that is what makes it so important to try to find out about them now."

I remained silent. Not so much important, I thought – inevitable, that was more like it. I had to get to know them both. Now.

"Did you know that I married them?" Ted asked suddenly.

"No, I didn't know that."

"It was here at Long Chatton. I can't say it was the most joyous wedding I've ever attended. Your grandfather disapproved as only he *could* disapprove and he threatened to stay away. There was an uneasy mixture of guests with flowers in their hair and those with flowers in their buttonholes. Not really a proper mix at all. I was only glad fighting didn't break out between the opposing camps."

Adam asked, "Which side was Archie on?"

"Buttonholes, definitely. Not that he bore the hairies any ill-will. In fact, apart from myself he was the main agent for harmony until he eventually passed out behind the marquee."

"Drink?"

"Drunk as a lord. Always immoderate, Archie. But he was decent enough – in those days."

"But not now?"

"I hardly know the man any more. I used to think I did but now – no, not now."

I thought of *Dora's Room*, those pages airy as thistle-down, innocent as a spring dawn, and then I thought of my uncle and his easy charm, that voice sumptuous as a rich brocade.

"Has he changed so radically?" asked Adam. Material for his article, I supposed, but it no longer bothered me. Good luck to him if he could make a good story out of Archie.

"Radically? From the root up. Yes, I really believe he has. More than the usual process of ageing, changing. Either that or else the Archie I used to think I knew was not the real man, was only a façade. Looking back I can see that Clancy's, your father's, death must have devastated him – more than anyone at the time realised. The brothers never appeared to be particularly close but that must have been a superficial reading. Your grandfather was so opposed to any display of feeling that it could be Archie had no way of showing his emotion. And then when his wife died so soon afterwards . . ."

"Aunt Frances," I broke in eagerly, "you know, I *do* remember her. She used to read us stories at bedtime. Wretched stories about trains with faces because they were the only ones Gerald liked." (Could that be the voice, I wondered, the voice that had come to me on the window-seat, that voice of pollen-heavy summer air?) "She used to read for hours. Was she ill for long before she died?"

"Ill?" Ted looked startled. "Of course not. Didn't you know?"

My blank expression must have been answer enough.

"Oh dear, well then . . . she killed herself."

"You can't be sure, you know you can't." Adam was quick to correct his father. "The inquest found a verdict of accidental death. It could have been an accident."

"Oh nonsense, Adam. It was obviously suicide. The verdict was just to spare the feelings of the family and because any evidence for suicide was missing. Did you really not know about this, Fern? It was in all the papers. They were on holiday in Cornwall, she and Archie. Gerald stayed here, I believe, though by that time I was in Portsmouth so I only heard it all secondhand. She went out sailing, one of those little dinghy things. The dinghy was picked up later that day but her body wasn't recovered for nearly a month. Perhaps it was the waiting, the uncertainty, that scarred Archie so horribly. The next time I met him, a few years later, he was . . . different."

"But a sailing accident, why assume it was suicide?"

Ted dismissed his son's question with an impatient wave of the hand. "Because she wrote her sister a note, a letter. One of those 'by the time you get this I shall be dead' variety. It wasn't produced at the inquest."

"Why not?"

"Family solidarity, it's the usual reason. Better for Gerald after all. To grow up knowing your mother chose to abandon you in such a brutal manner creates an intolerable burden of rejection for a child. I didn't approve. You can't lie to children like that, they always know, they always suspect. It only adds muddle to the tragedy. And muddle is frightening, however well intentioned. But the note was missing, so – accidental verdict."

I thought of Aunt Frances and the way her brown hair

fell across her forehead as she read those stories. "Why do you think she did it? What kind of woman was she?"

"Pleasant enough. Open, friendly – no great brains or beauty but she did have tremendous warmth. A simple girl in lots of ways, that was the impression I had. Perhaps she never learned to deal with the intrigue and the hostility at Chatton Heights."

I said, "That still doesn't add up to suicide."

"No. You're right. I had the impression, each time I saw her and Archie together towards the end – at your father's memorial, for instance – that she was drowning long before the final accident."

I closed my eyes. Aunt Frances' gentle face, her brown hair brushing her cheek as she held the train book in her hand. Green-cold seawater closing over her head.

Adam stood up and his chair leg scraped on the tiled floor. "Let's get some fresh air, Fern," he said. "After that meal I could do with a walk. Don't worry about clearing away, Elsa will do that. And Ted always likes a period of contemplation with his eyes closed on a Sunday afternoon."

As I thanked Ted for the meal Adam's hand touched my elbow briefly, an unspoken reassurance. Ted frowned up at us from under white eyebrows and ordered us sternly to enjoy our walk.

It was good to be outside in the soft winter sunshine. The sky was bright after the morning's rain and the whole village sparkled. We walked across the churchyard where, away from the quaintly olde antique shops and the cafés of the main street, it was still possible to see the sinews of the genuinely old Cotswold village; almost all the cottages had been transformed into bijou retirement homes but here and there a few remained that seemed to have maintained a connection with their past; in the back lanes there were lichen-covered branches of plum trees reaching out over high walls; long-legged underwear on the washing lines; potting sheds and neat rows of cabbages and leeks.

"This lane goes right up to the Heights," Adam explained. "This used to be one of my favourite trespass routes; high fences and Keep Out notices have always held an irresistible attraction."

"Even for the rector's son?"

He grinned. "*Especially* for the rector's son; especially when he has two well-behaved older sisters; especially when the rector in question thoroughly disapproves of everything his son does anyway." He walked for a while in silence; then, no longer smiling, he said, "I hope that wasn't too difficult for you back there. My father loves to play the part of village elder and pontificate about his years here, the people he knew well. I think it was the best time for him, for all of us in a way. I knew you were interested in your family and . . . well, I thought if you came along he and I would be less likely to rub each other up the wrong way. Since he's been on his own I've tried to visit more often . . . but he's never been easy."

I told him not to worry about me, that I was far more resilient than I appeared, and he smiled again and murmured, "I've been wondering about that," before continuing up the hill.

The lane we were following had become narrow, only just room for two people to walk side by side. There was the damp brown smell of winter hedgerows. The path led upwards for about a quarter of a mile, then we stopped by a small gate.

"Here we are," said Adam.

Beyond the gate a field sloped steeply upwards, rows of bare trees, winter-pale grass. "I thought you said this brought us to the house," I said. There was no sign of Chatton Heights anywhere ahead.

"Don't you recognise this? It's your orchard. Look, there's the beginning of the shrubbery at the far end, and the house is beyond that."

"Oh yes!" Suddenly I was excited. "The old holm oak is blocking off the view of the house!"

The mass of dull green leaves overshadowed the orchard; it was a cloud, a curtain, screening off the house. Adam was watching me, half curious, half amused. I wanted him to share my excitement.

"I've been here before, Adam, I know I have, this very spot. But it was different, somehow, more . . . I can't remember. I must have been smaller . . ." My voice trailed away, suddenly my enthusiasm seemed faintly ridiculous. "That's hardly surprising, though, is it, under the circumstances."

"How much *do* you remember?"

"Hardly anything." I stopped, tried again. "It's true that I have very few memories of that time, and even those are fragmented, trivial, and yet . . . sometimes I feel as though there is a whole mass of memories, just below the surface, just out of reach."

"And now you want to uncover them?"

"I don't know if wanting has much to do with it."

He laughed gently. "Poor Fern, don't look so downcast about it all. Do you want to go on and have a proper look at your mansion? You can hardly have seen the outside when you came before."

"Yes . . . no . . . I'd like to, but not like this."

"Why not?"

"I can't simply turn up without telling anyone."

"It's your house, surely you can do as you wish."

"No, just the opposite. If it *wasn't* my house I could turn up any time. Now that it's mine everything is infinitely more difficult. They'd think I was snooping, or checking up on them or something."

"Are you sure you're not making this more complicated than it really is?"

"Money complicates things. And possessions. I'm only just beginning to realise how much." I thought of Paula's remark that morning: wasps around the honey jar. Would Adam be spending his Sunday afternoon with me now if it was just me here, just Fern Miller with no famous uncle or Cotswold mansion or huge fortune? Not that I suspected him of being mercenary, or anything like that, just that the things that probably made me interesting to him weren't really to do with me at all, not the me inside my skin.

"Let's go back," I said. As we walked back towards the

92

village I felt bleak and empty, loneliness washing over me in waves. Would I feel so alone, I wondered, if he were to put his arm around me?

But he walked beside me in silence, absorbed in his own thoughts.

Back at the Old Rectory my sense of unease was increasing. And the loneliness. If I had known Adam better I might have been able to reach out to him, but he had become absorbed in his own thoughts, as if he had somehow removed himself, leaving me more isolated than ever.

And now I regretted that I had ever agreed to come. The visit had been unsettling. To come so close to my grandfather's house – my house, now – and yet not to see or visit it; to have to feign detachment while two men I barely knew discussed my family's tragedies, to learn of my aunt's death by drowning – all these had left me feeling vulnerable and unsure. As if all my life until now I had been a tightrope walker, carefully placing one foot after the other on a narrow thread of security; and now a wind was blowing, a hurricane, and I must concentrate with every ounce of strength to save myself from losing my balance and falling for ever . . . Control. I must stay in control.

I tried to focus on ordinary, outward things: shaking hands with Ted: "Thank you for a lovely day. Yes, I hope to see you again soon"; a winter evening; people walking; Adam's profile beside me in the car. Would he come to look more like his father? Thin the cheeks, brush the eyebrows into tufts, paint them white – yes, the bones were there, not quite so fierce perhaps, a gentler eagle. Farm shops at the roadside, signs for the motorway, the slip road, cars in the dusk.

Adam talking, mouth moving, words coming out. What words? Chatton Heights, the place, atmosphere so strong. *Dora's Room*. "When he wrote *Dora's Room*— "

Dora's room.

His voice faded to a murmur and blurred with the hum of the car's engine. And then he was gone, and the car,

93

and the grey Sunday evening had vanished too, and I was standing in a white corridor. A door at the end of the corridor blew open suddenly and beyond it was a long room.

A huge room: pale, sunny, with high windows along both walls. Something not right about the windows – bars? There were chairs in the room, random chairs. A cluster of chairs around the television, others scattered, meaningless. People sitting, some talking. Some talking but no one listening.

And then the smell. I knew that smell in my bones, could never forget. Piss and disinfectant and hopes ripped out. It filled my nostrils, my lungs. No air in my lungs, only stench.

Slippers shuffling over polished floors. Feet moving, going nowhere. Back and forth. Back and nowhere, nowhere and back.

A figure detaches from the rest, is led forward. A woman's face floats like a pale balloon before my eyes. I recognise her face yet at the same time it is utterly alien. I've seen that nose before, that mouth, those cheeks, I have always known them – but not that puffy whiteness, those green eyes lifeless as pebbles, dulled and blank, all the expression washed out of them, rinsed away by the ruthless care of strangers.

My mother.

A limp puppet with no hand to move her strings. The shell of my mother. My real mother had long since gone, flown away, blown away. Left me.

I had snowdrops in my hand. A bunch of flowers picked for Mummy. I hold them up.

"We brought you some flowers." "We" is safer. Dring is here, too, watching, knitting, keep an eye on Dring.

The ghostly balloon face makes no sign, does not choose to see. Those dulled green eyes are staring, but beyond me. Fear thunders at my feet, rises through me like a tide. The snowdrops tremble in my grasp; my arms ache with the effort of holding them outstretched: take them, please take them. See me, Mummy. Have I become invisible?

94

I'm here, over here, look at me. Now the eyes focus, see me. And scare me with their power.

That shapeless mouth mumbles, forming words. Dora's Room.

"Flowers, Mummy, please."

"*Dora's Room*. The devil . . . Lucifer and Satan . . ." Her silence had been awesome but this leaden speech is even worse. I want to back away but my legs are ankle deep in terror and refuse to move.

"I brought you flowers— "

"Remember the devil, always remember . . . he wrote it, he did— "

The snowdrops fall to the floor; tender scraps of white and softest green that I had brought from their safe corner of the garden to be crushed on this floor by unthinking feet. And it was my fault.

My balloon mother's lips are so white it is hard to see the line where they become skin. Something damp is oozing on to her chin as her voice chants its mantra of accusation.

"The devil wrote *Dora's Room* – Lucifer, the Prince of Darkness, master of all evil, he wrote it, remember that— "

There is a burning pain in my chest and I want her to stop. Please make her stop, make her go away. Dring's shoes, brown lace-ups with splashes of mud. Other feet running, hands steer me away.

Breathless voices: "Come along now, Mummy, say goodbye nicely. Be a good mummy, perhaps another day— "

Dring wheezing and cross. The moaning stench follows. The stench clings to my clothes. The moan and the stench will never go away. Hurry, hurry away. Want to wash, scrub away the stink and fear. Dring's voice, "Over now. Forget about it. No need to dwell on what can't be helped. Think of something nice instead. We'll get an ice cream, shall we? Chocolate flake? Forget, forget . . ."

A voice that did not fit. "Fern, are you all right? Fern?"

A voice dragging me from a deep river of memory. Adam's voice. It must be. And his hand was stroking my forehead, pushing back my hair.

The hospital terror receded slowly, like a mist rolling away. My eyes looked and saw not the tumbled bunch of snowdrops, not the hurrying feet of anxious nurses, but the interior of a car. There were a couple of tattered paperbacks in the glove compartment and steam on the windows. Gradually I became aware that the car had stopped and that we must therefore have pulled over on to the hard shoulder. I discovered also that I was hot – and yet shivering as if with cold.

Adam's face was very close and somehow gaunt with concern. Slate-grey eyes searching my face. Shame flooded through me, chasing away the last vestiges of fear.

"Fern, what is it? What's the matter?"

Leave me alone, I wanted to say, let me hide, run away . . . But, oh my God, why was he so anxious? What had I said or done or— ? What had happened to me on the outside while the memory had control? He must think I was . . . No, not that. Never that.

"It's nothing, Adam, really." A normal-sounding voice, thank heavens. "I must have dropped off for a moment – some kind of nightmare – but it's over now."

"Are you sure? You seemed to be hallucinating, mentioned your mother."

"Did I? It was . . . I was just remembering something that happened when I was little. Or at least I think it happened. Or else I dreamed it. Sorry about that. Anyway, it's not important."

"No? You looked terrified, Fern. It might help to talk about it."

"Not at all," I laughed lightly. Tinkle Tinkle. "You sound just like an agony aunt."

"That wasn't quite how I saw myself." His arm was around my shoulders still. Very gently he pushed a strand of hair from my forehead. His face moved fractionally closer to mine and I thought: he's going to kiss me. And then I thought what a fool I'd been

96

even to imagine such a thing for he pulled back and asked, "Just what did you . . . remember? About your mother?"

"I . . . she . . ." I wavered. The temptation was so very strong: to share the truth of my crazy mother, the sheer terror of looking up into the dearest eyes in all the world and seeing green nothingness there, a hideous worse-than-stranger, the whole edifice of safety wrenched loose and crumbling away into the void. "She just said . . ." And then I stopped. What had she said? That Archie Miller was Satan, the Prince of Darkness. Oh yes, very interesting. Adam was waiting, his grey eyes searching my face. Waiting. For what? Why should he be so interested in my waking nightmare anyway? What was it to do with him? Unless . . .

"Motorway Panic of Crazed Heiress. Archie Miller Accused of Devil Worship. Exclusive." It was just a thought, a fleeting thought, probably a paranoid thought, but it was enough. Even a whisper of paranoia is sufficient to strangle confessions in their infancy.

"No," I said coldly, "there's really nothing to talk about. I tell you, it was just some kind of dream but it's over now. It doesn't matter."

He frowned. "You don't trust me."

"Maybe not. Look, don't you think you'd better get the car off the hard shoulder? I'm sure it's illegal and the motorway is always crawling with police cars."

"Let me worry about that. Maybe your dream, hallucination, whatever you want to call it, was triggered by all that talk of your parents at lunch. Have you ever had – " he hesitated, choosing the word carefully – "experiences like that before?"

"Everybody dreams, Adam."

"Yes, but not like— "

"I'd much rather not talk about it, if you don't mind. And I do want to get home. This isn't the most comfortable car in the world, you know."

"Okay." He turned the ignition key and the car rumbled appreciatively, depositing icy cold air on my knees. "I can't help thinking it must be my fault you're upset like this, that I should have been more careful."

"But I keep telling you, I'm not in the least bit upset."

"Hrmph," he said, a sudden echo of his father's disapproval.

It was a strain, keeping up the bright and breezy chatter all the way home. Adam seemed preoccupied but perhaps that was simply because these roads can get pretty congested on a Sunday evening. I kept thinking how wonderful it would be when he went away and I could drop my phoney "whatever made you think there was anything the matter with me" smile – but when we pulled up in front of the little house in Alderly Drive I suddenly didn't want him to go.

"Would you like to come in?"

He considered. "Is that a genuine question or are you just being polite?"

"Genuine."

So he came in, but not for long. It had been foolish, really, to ask him. Dring was at her most petulant and churlish, ignoring Adam completely and demanding that I run round and fetch and carry for her. ("She's jealous," Paula said later. "Nonsense," I replied. "Yes she is, Mary. She needs more and more of your time and she's terrified of anyone who might take you away from her. That's why she plays the bloody-minded geriatric in front of your friends.")

So it was, after all, a relief when he left.

"Goodbye. I did enjoy meeting your father." (Polite to the end.)

"I hope so. But I'm afraid it was a bit— "

"Oh no, not at all."

"I'm often in Bristol at the weekend. You can usually get in touch with me at this number." He was scribbling on a scrap of paper. From inside the house I could hear Dring scolding the animals on a nature programme for their messy eating habits. I took the paper, intending to throw it away.

98

Still he hovered on the doorstep. Like an encyclopaedia salesman, I thought in desperation.

"I must go now," I said, "Dring needs me."

His grey eyes were fixed on me very intently. "Ah yes," he said, with just the glimmer of a smile and more than a glimmer of irritation, "Dring the human moat. I'll be in touch, then, Fern." And with that at last he was gone and I barely had time to think how odd it was to refer to Dring, solid, ailing and immovable, as any kind of moat, before I went back into the kitchen to prepare some soup for her evening meal.

I was asking Dring about my memory.

"Sounds like nonsense to me," she said. She was sitting up in bed, her old old face rising from a whirl of pastel nylon. "They always had special rooms for visitors and I don't remember that you ever went to the hospital at all. There wouldn't have been much point."

"Perhaps they thought it might help her."

"Bloody stupid doctors. I wouldn't put it past them. But I can't remember any row."

"Then perhaps you forgot. You were always telling me to forget stuff. Almost everything that happened."

"So? No good dwelling on what can't be changed. Best just to get up and on with life."

"Yes. But . . ." Something had been worrying me ever since I came into the room and now, all at once, I knew what it was. The image had been tugging at the corner of my brain: "Look at me, here I am. Up here, over the chest of drawers. Can't you see?"

And now I saw.

It was the orchard picture that I knew so well I had long since ceased to see it. Sunlight dappling the creamy blossoms, a brief May moment of froth and colour. But now it was different. Now I knew what it looked like in the winter months as well, when the trees were stripped of leaves and the grass was pale with winter stillness. I had seen that orchard today in winter drabness.

"That picture was painted at Chatton Heights," I said, "that's where I was today with Adam."

The painter must have set up his easel just inside the gate where we had stopped. Turned back.

"So what?" said Dring.

I went and looked at the picture more closely; at the painter's signature. Why had I never noticed it before? D. Brewster. A familiar name.

Of course. D. Brewster was the man who had painted the two double portraits at Chatton Heights. Now that I realised where I had seen the name before the connection seemed inevitable.

It was as though I had been treading all my life on a fine mosaic floor, seeing only the random pieces, each individual shape and colour, but never even aware that there was an underlying pattern, that the patterns made up a picture.

And the picture was a story, waiting to be told.

Now I was beginning, only beginning, not so much to see the pattern or the picture but just that there *was* a pattern, if I could somehow sweep away the dust and confusion and see it plainly.

Dring smiled, a rare event at the best of times.

"That picture always gives me a warm sort of feeling," she said. "Happy. Like being young again."

Exhausted by the day's events and the jumbled emotions they had aroused, I went early to bed. I thought I was tired but my eyes remained obstinately open, staring at the patch of orange light on the ceiling. Now I realise that what I feared was the loss of control that accompanies sleep, afraid of the dreams that lay in wait for me, afraid of unwanted images like that memory of my mother – memory? But if it had never happened, if it wasn't a memory then how come I had suddenly conjured it up out of nothing?

I called it fear of losing control but even then, lying in the darkness of the only bedroom I had ever known, I think I must have known what the real fear was. My mother was mad, a schizophrenic, signed sealed and delivered to a mental hospital for ever. And madness ran in families, everyone knew that, it was hereditary, don't ask how but it was. Some little speck of madness passes through the placenta to the unborn child and lodges there. Waiting. For years. In the car that afternoon I had freaked out, hallucinated, lost track of reality. Wasn't that one of the hallmarks of a crazy person?

I pleaded with my fate. I don't mind being physically ill. I can put up with that somehow. Just leave my mind alone, let my mind be strong. Let it answer to my will. Please, oh please.

Some time, just before dawn, I couldn't fight it any more and I drifted into sleep.

And there, instead of the demons I had so dreaded, I entered a haven of tranquillity and content, a summer world of warmth and birdsong. Something precious, more precious than anything I had known before in a long long time, was there, almost within my grasp, just waiting for me to reach out and catch hold of it.

When I awoke the knowledge was clear in my brain: I wasn't the child of a crazy mother alone, I also had a father. Clancy. The young man in the photograph who had gone to South America and hurtled out of the sky to his death. He was all right, Archie had said so. And to be "all right", to be normal and not mad, was my deepest wish. All my life I had carried the burden of being my mother's child, but I was also Clancy's. I might be heir to his sanity, not her madness, but I had no memory of him to cling to. I needed to discover and grasp hold of his wisdom, his ordinariness. I had to return to Chatton Heights. If I could find him anywhere, this man on whom it seemed my confidence of sanity depended, I would find him there.

This conviction was so satisfying, so obviously true, that I fell asleep again, comfortable and dreamless.

I awoke for the second time soon after nine and, in the sober light of morning, I dismissed the certainties of the night. I told myself that I had become overwrought

101

as a result of the visit to Long Chatton and that it would be ridiculous to prescribe more of the same dangerous medicine.

So I delayed my return to the house in which my father had grown up. I busied myself in "ordinary" life and shut my mind to the changes that were taking place all around me.

Chapter 4

Paula had been telling me for days but I refused to listen.

"You have to call a doctor for her, Mary. It's not fair. Her leg is giving her a whole load of pain and she needs proper treatment."

"Don't worry about Dring, Paula. You don't know her like I do." I was working my way through a pile of ironing. I loved the way the smooth metal slid over the fabric, the neatness of carefully folded pillow cases and the crisp clean smell of ordinary things. "She was just talking in her sleep," I went on, "she often does that. And she's always had trouble with her leg, it's nothing new and Dr Phelps looked at it only a month ago. It gets worse and then it gets better again. It's her cast-iron excuse for getting out of anything she doesn't want to do – a most useful leg in lots of ways."

"She isn't faking this time, Mary. The only place for her right now is hospital."

I was ironing the cuffs of my white shirt with meticulous precision. "I'm sure you mean well, Paula, but you really know nothing about it. Dring loathes hospitals more than anything else. The nurses all call her 'love' and patronise her and won't let her smoke. She'd do anything to stay out of hospital."

"Like lose a leg, maybe? You could be done for neglect if you don't have a doctor call on her now."

"She hates hospitals."

"Who does? Her or you? Okay, I'm sorry, don't go all tight-lipped and silent on me, I know that old bundle of fun up there means a lot to you and I know this is difficult for you right now but do you realise she hasn't been downstairs in over a week?"

"Paula, please. Stay out of it. I've looked after Dring for years without any help from you. Now, do you want me to iron these shirts for you?"

"No, leave them. You only make me guilty when you do that."

And she did stay out of it, I guess, for as long as she could. I don't really blame her for what she did next. Obviously I can't blame her at all since she only did what she thought was right and everyone agreed it was for the best. And yet I couldn't quite forgive her for it either. It felt too much like treachery. The first of Paula's treacheries.

Maybe I was over-sensitive but I'd never really had a friend before, not a proper friend like Paula. There had been casual friends, of course, girls I'd met at school who had invited me back to their homes or to join them on holiday, people to go out with and gossip with but never anyone that I trusted as I trusted Paula. I suppose that when I saw the advertisement in the newsagent's window requesting a room for a female graduate student I must have been unconsciously casting around for someone to fill an empty space in my life. I had often thought what fun it would have been to have had sisters and for a while Paula became the older sister I had never had.

But only for a while. In the early months it was the differences between us that brought us so close – Paula once exclaimed that she had never believed anyone like me existed outside of a nineteenth-century novel, that I should have been born in Barchester, not Bristol, and for me it was like having a continuous American film playing in my home – but recently there had been growing room for misunderstanding. Beginning with my reaction to my inheritance. Paula could not understand why I wasn't delirious with joy at the fortune my grandfather had bestowed on me. Not that she didn't try to understand: "I can see how it's awkward for you, difficult. A shock. Well, it must take some getting used to. I suppose." But then she'd fall silent and I could almost hear her mentally spending the money for me until she could bear it no longer and she'd burst out with, "I hear the weather's terrific in southern Portugal at this time of year and you can buy an old villa there dirt cheap," or "Did you see those new convertibles at the garage on the corner?" or even, once, "Have you ever thought what fun it would be to own a racehorse?"

No. I hadn't. And now that I did I couldn't say that the suggestion had much appeal.

It wasn't that I minded Paula wanting to spend my money for me. As far as I was concerned she could have the lot and spend it herself; I didn't even mind her occasional suggestions that I was showing symptoms of miserliness – "Are you coming to the film tonight or do you want to stay home and count piles of gold?" – what I found intolerable was the unspoken implication that my lack of enthusiasm was somehow weird, that any normal person would be off their head with rapture to share my fate.

So I wasn't normal.

It was ironic, I suppose, when you consider that all I wanted was to put the clock back to the beginning of the year when I had been an ordinary girl, not an heiress. Now it was my very longing to be just like everybody else that was laying me open to a charge of abnormality.

There were other, subtler barriers growing up between us. I think I was more aware of them than Paula.

There was an awkward moment when she presented me with the monthly rent cheque. In the moment of my hesitation, when I was on the verge of saying, "Keep it, Paula, you don't have to give me this," she said curtly, "Go on, then, take it. I'm not a goddam charity case, you know."

"But I don't need it and you do. It doesn't make sense."

"Then give it to a worthy cause. Just take it."

I think it must have been around then that she started making occasional extravagant gestures and buying grocery items like walnut oil and ready-prepared Chicken Kiev which I knew, from the happy days of our shared anxieties over money, that she couldn't afford. I tried to keep to the things we had always bought for the house but I was afraid she put it down to meanness.

One Saturday towards the end of February, when the sky was overcast and that kind of flat grey colour which inspires strangers to chat knowingly to each other in shops about the likelihood of snow, I drove the car to the supermarket and filled it with provisions enough for a month's siege. My plan was to tell Paula that we had to be stocked up in case of snow and hoped that would put a stop to her reckless spending.

I was well armed with replies to all her arguments – "Mary, there's a store right at the corner of the street." "Panic-buying at the first flake of snow. It's an English tradition."

But none of my carefully prepared conversations equipped me to deal with what was waiting for me on my return.

Paula was hovering in the hallway and showed not the slightest interest in my mammoth shopping spree. Instead she was anxious, half apologetic, even a little defensive.

"Mary, promise me you won't be cross. I only did . . . I mean, hell, Mary, I had to. You couldn't stand by and let a dog suffer like that and not do anything. I was going to tell you before but you went out so early I didn't get the chance."

I stared at her stupidly, knowing, yet not registering the fact. I said, "I was here at breakfast."

"Dr Phelps said he'd come right round. He said it was quite right to phone him and there was probably nothing to worry about and he'd just check up to be on the safe side. Don't look at me like I'm some kind of worm, Mary. I expect he'll just give her something for the pain, something to help her sleep at night. That's all. No big deal."

I was so flabbergasted that Paula had taken it on herself to interfere between me and Dring that I couldn't, just at that moment, say anything. I must have been staring at her. I can remember thinking that I had never noticed, before, how very unattractive she was. All that red hair the colour of a fake fur coat and eyes that were really rather small, piggy almost. The pale and pudgy nose of a street fighter in an old film. The chin jutting forward in defiance.

"You were crazy not to call a doctor before," she said.

My knees almost buckled. Don't call me crazy. Dear God, don't call me crazy. Anything but that.

"It's okay, Paula. Of course I don't mind."

The doorbell rang.

My legs were stiff as stilts as I went to open the door. Let in Dr Phelps. Smiled. Showed him up the stairs to Dring's room. Went back downstairs. Waited.

Dr Phelps had always wanted me to like him; that much I had known, even as a small child. He was kind and conscientious and good at his job. He smiled a lot. He had a shiny face that looked as though it had been carved out of candlewax and now that he was growing old his chin seemed to be melting into drops and folds. I had always disliked him intensely.

As soon as he arrived Paula retreated to her own room. Dr Phelps was up with Dring for some time and when he came down to the front room his smile for once was gone and the candlewax face was rigid with anger.

"Mary," he said, "why in heaven's name didn't you call me earlier?"

Something deep within me froze. "It's only the same old trouble," I said lightly, "I didn't think . . ."

"Just ten times worse, that's all. That leg is so bad we'll be lucky if it doesn't . . . Heavens above, girl, no one in their right mind would let it get as bad as that. You should be grateful your American friend had the sense to ring me. Really, if I didn't know you better . . ."

"But Dring never asked me to call you."

"She's been taking large amounts of pain killers without telling you. Didn't you even think to check the bottles? The drugs have fogged her brain."

I sat down. It felt more as though the chair had lifted itself to catch me.

"Can I use your phone?" I heard him ask. "I need to call an ambulance. Hospital is the only place for her now."

The frozen feeling deep within me was spreading; a kind of icy numbness travelling through the bloodstream, creeping into every part, arms, hands, face. Especially the face. I concentrated all my will to make my mouth shape itself round normal words. "You don't need to call an ambulance, Dr Phelps, I can easily drive her there myself. I'm sure she'd rather . . ."

"My dear girl, you couldn't even get her down the stairs in her present state. The ambulance men do this sort of thing every day." He was already dialling.

"Then I'd better go and pack her things." Thank heavens my voice at least is normal, ordinary. Stick to practical details. "She'll want to be home again as soon as possible. I can make whatever adjustments are necessary. There's space for a little bathroom at the end of the hall and if she needed any kind of professional nursing then I can always hire someone— "

"Mary." Dr Phelps put down the receiver, came and sat opposite me, leaning forward slightly. The waxy face rearranged itself into an appropriately compassionate smile. "Don't build up your hopes, my dear, she's an old lady and she's very, very ill. She's going to need hospital treatment for a long time and after that a nursing home might well be more suitable."

"No! I will not allow her to be looked after by strangers. She'd hate that!"

"She might not have any choice."

"After all she's done for me the least I can do is care for her now."

"Mary, listen." His hands twitched and for one dreadful moment I thought he was going to reach across and try to take my hand in his. Instead he placed his large palms on his knees. His smile oozed understanding. "You've done such a lot for her already. More, much more, than most young women do for their grandmothers – or mothers even. There's no reason at all for you to reproach yourself. I think you might try to look on this as a blessing in disguise because, in so many ways, it *is* a blessing. You're young. You have your own life to lead. The last thing you want is to be burdened with an elderly invalid."

"She's not a burden, Dr Phelps."

"Not now, maybe, but in time . . . and now you don't need to worry about her. She's off your hands. You can relax a bit, enjoy yourself."

I sat absolutely still. He was talking about some other pair, surely, not Dring and me.

He leaned imperceptibly forward and I could almost smell the loathsome syrupy compassion on his breath. "This is a difficult time for you now, Mary, I do realise that. What with your mother dying and now Madame de Rhin going into hospital . . . and I read about your grandfather's will in the papers. A lot of changes. A lot of adjustments to be made."

"I can manage, Dr Phelps. You don't need to worry about me."

"No?"

"I've always managed perfectly well in the past."

"Hm. I sometimes wonder . . . certainly you've always been very independent, very reserved. Perhaps too much so. It doesn't do to bottle up emotions, you know, not the powerful ones like grief and anger. There's no reason to be ashamed to show these ordinary human feelings which we all share. I'm putting this awkwardly I know but . . ."

I sat very still, not moving, not speaking. I know what you want, Dr Phelps, awkward or not. You want me to break down. You want the gift of my tears. That would make you feel good, wouldn't it? You could put your arms around me and comfort me and then *you'd* feel better, not me. That's what you've wanted all along. "Do you miss Mummy?" "Have the nightmares been troubling you still?" "Daddy's not coming back, is he, Mary? How does that make you feel?" Like a stone, Dr Phelps, like ice. And you'll never know any of it. Never never never for as long as I have the strength to be silent.

"Do you find it easy to cry, Mary?"

You prying fool, I thought. My tears dried up on the day they told me I no longer had a father. No tears for me. Certainly no tears for you and your thick treacle smile.

I said, "Thank you for all your help, Dr Phelps. I must go now and pack the things Dring needs."

I pushed myself forward on the chair, pushed my weight on to my feet. Thank God my legs supported me with only the slightest sway, one after the other they carried me to the front door.

"Thank you again." My tinsel politeness reflected back his phoney compassion. His back retreating down the path. His final "You know I'm always here when you need me" smile. The door closed.

The empty hall. Silence.

And in the silence a single thought: they were going to take Dring away.

The catastrophe I had dreaded more than any other for as long as I could remember.

Dring leaving.

All the safety I had ever known being cut from under me at a single savage stroke.

Remain calm.

No reason to panic. No normal girl would panic. No? Then what would she do? A normal girl would go upstairs, pack Dring's case, get her ready for the ambulance. Stay calm. Be a normal girl.

It wasn't impossible, after all. The numbness that had been creeping through my limbs was complete now. My body felt oddly detached as I walked up the stairs, almost as though it belonged to someone else and the real me was floating somewhere just ahead of me. As though this other person's assembly of flesh was merely obeying the commands that I gave it, automatically, as a robot might do. There was no sensation at all, just an eerie floating calm.

But when I pushed open the bedroom door and saw Dring, the calmness shivered, almost broke. She looked so old and frightened and ugly in her lilac nightgown. She smiled up at me, half apologetically, and blinked.

110

"Oh Dring, why didn't you tell me how bad it was?"

"I didn't want to worry you, dear. I thought it would get better on its own."

"But you made such a fuss about all the little things and then something like this comes along and you say nothing." There was a sharp pain at the base of my throat. She was all I had in the world and I hadn't even realised when she needed help. The gap between us yawned, an uncrossable chasm.

She turned away. "This was different."

I began to understand. To Dring life was an endless battle against ill health. She might enjoy the minor skirmishes, relish the brief victories over her body's weakness, but in the ultimate fight she knew she could only lose. She turned away from the real battles. Forget, don't think about the unpleasant things. It had always been our watchword, after all.

"We'd better get you packed and ready. And if we forget anything I can bring it in later."

My voice sounded so steady, matter-of-fact. No hint of the weird disembodied me who floated somewhere above us.

I looked around the room. "What else will you need?"

"I'd better take these." She nodded in the direction of the three photographs on the mantelpiece: Tom, Lucy and Alexander. I placed them in the suitcase on top of her angora bed-jacket. Their faces smiled up at me with stupid confidence and for a moment I felt my childhood was being erased.

The ambulance men arrived like a well-rehearsed comedy duo, one tall and thin, one short and fat, both equally cheery and efficient.

They bypassed me, ignoring my offers of help.

"How lucky you are to have such a kind young helper!" Mr Short-and-Fat shouted into Dring's ear. Already she was being treated as though she was not only ill but deaf and stupid as well. If it hadn't been for the blessed numbness that cushioned me from all emotion it would have been almost unbearably painful to see how Dring

111

gasped and struggled to maintain her dignity as she was manhandled, awkward as a butcher's carcass, down the narrow stairs to the hall.

I picked up her suitcase and went to stand at the top of the stairs.

The two men had paused for a moment in the hallway "to give everyone a breather". And as I watched from the landing my skin grew tight with horror as the memories flooded through my skull like sunlight in a forgotten attic.

I had stood here before, long years ago, a small child with bare feet and a nightdress that reached to my ankles. The carpet was rough under my bare feet and the cotton fabric (sprigs of little flowers on white) brushed against my legs.

Long ago I had stood here, looking down. Noise and confusion in the hallway, then, and men in uniform with kind faces and cruel hands, but it was not Dring they took away that time.

It was my mother, struggling like a trapped animal, crashing into the telephone table, her fingers clutching at the mirror. Her dark hair was dishevelled and she looked unwashed and she was lunging to free herself from the hands that held her. And then my mother twisted her face round to look up at me and all at once I was staring into eyes that were huge and green, deep green holes filled to the brim and overflowing with terror and misery. My mother was trying to call out but the words were incoherent and I never knew what she wanted to say. Then the men looked up, saw me, and were angry. I wanted to run away but I couldn't move. "Who the hell let that child stay here?" said one, and the other one swore. Dr Phelps was there, and a woman in a suit, but it was another man, a man not in uniform but who seemed to be organising them, who detached himself from the group and came up the stairs towards me.

And then my bones turned to ice as I saw the face of the man who was coming to drag me back to my room. I saw a dark face, handsome, with hooded eyes and a full, sensual mouth.

Archie.

"Miss! I'll take her bag out now. She'll be wanting that."

"Oh yes. Of course. I'll— "

It took a massive effort of will to focus on the face of Mr Tall-and-Thin and to force my legs to move slowly down the stairs and follow him out to the ambulance.

Dring lay on the stretcher like a medieval knight secure on his tomb; already she was beginning to enjoy the attention.

"I'll be along to see you this evening," my normal voice said. "Let me know if you've forgotten anything."

I suppose she heard. "Just you make sure you drive carefully," she said to Mr Short-and-Fat, "I'm not an emergency case. None of that putting the siren on and racing like a maniac just to get back in time for your dinner."

Short-and-Fat winked at me. I pulled my frozen lips back into an apology for a smile.

And then they were gone.

I went into the house and the emptiness echoed all around me like the boom of a fog-horn in an estuary at dusk. All the loneliness of the world seemed packed between these few walls.

I walked slowly around the living-room, the kitchen, the hall. Empty as withered husks. I remembered that Paula was still upstairs but somehow that didn't make any difference. She was a lodger, a novelty, a bird of passage. Dring was the lifeblood of the house, its pulse, its heartbeat. With her gone it was home no longer.

So what do I do now?

I found a pack of Dring's cigarettes on the mantelpiece and shook one free. It took a long time to light because the match seemed to waver, to miss the mark. My hands were shaking. At last it was lit and I inhaled deeply.

Do I exist, I wondered, am I here, when there is no one here to see me?

The thought had materialised from out of nothing, one of those gypsy thoughts that had a life independent of my brain and which arrived, fully formed and uninvited, right in the middle of my skull.

"Are you okay?" Paula, red hair piled up like a crest of flame, stood in the doorway.

"Yes, I guess so. Just a bit shaken."

"I'll fix you some lunch."

"I'm not hungry."

"Christ, I'm sorry, Mary. I didn't know it would hit you like this."

"You did the right thing. I wish I had known how bad . . ." My voice trailed away. What was it Dr Phelps had said? No one in their right mind would let it get as bad as this. What did that mean? Was I in my wrong mind? And what was a wrong mind anyway?

"Mary, you're shaking."

"I'm all right." And then, because some kind of explanation seemed necessary, "It reminded me . . . they took my mother away, you see. Just like that. In an ambulance . . ."

And Archie, what had he been doing there? Where was Dring? She had been left to look after us both, my mother and me. Why hadn't she been there when we both needed her so badly?

"You poor old thing." Paula came and put her arm around me. "This hasn't been much fun for you, has it?"

The pain at the base of my throat had grown so fierce it was almost unbearable. "Paula, just tell me, what am I supposed to do now?"

"Why not sit back and let Aunty Lodger take care of you for a change."

"I don't know what . . . Dr Phelps said I ought to go out and enjoy myself. He said I had my own life to lead. Maybe he's right. But how do I start? I've never been able to go out much because of Dring and now she's not here I don't know how . . ."

"Look. I'm supposed to be going round to the Prof's

this afternoon but I'll ring and cancel and then you and I can do something together. How about that? We can go to a film, or have a spending spree. Shop until you drop – that's a fine way to get rid of the blues."

I'd forgotten the money. "I suppose I could get some stuff Dring will need in hospital."

Paula grimaced. "Learn to think big, Mary."

"No. Don't ring the Prof. No need to mess up your love life just because Dring is in hospital." Since Paula's Brideshead fantasy with Gerald had failed to materialise she had become involved with her tutor at the university. Married – but conveniently misunderstood by his wife.

She could barely hide her relief. "Mrs Prof is visiting her sister this weekend." His wife away? Until then I had not realised the magnitude of the sacrifice she had been offering to make.

"I'll need to visit Dring. And I thought I might give Adam a ring." I hadn't actually thought of any such thing but it sounded like the sort of normal, everyday action I was supposed to make.

"Great idea. But I thought he lived in London."

"He often comes to Bristol at the weekend. He gave me the phone number of the friend's house he stays in."

"Male or female?"

"I don't know."

"Right. You give him a ring and I'll fix you some lunch. Tuna sandwiches? And don't start shaking your head at me. It's not going to do Dring any good if you become anorexic."

I discovered, as I went in search of Adam's telephone number, that the floating sensation was beginning to dissipate. The texture of the banisters was firm beneath my palm; my legs still felt somewhat rubbery, rather like the first day up after 'flu, but they were *my* legs, connected, solid.

Adam, when I got through, sounded harassed, and a television was chattering in the background.

"Fern, yes, I'd love to see you. Why don't you come

over here? I'm a bit tied up at the moment, babysitting, but . . ."

"I'm sorry. I didn't realise it was awkward."

"Hell, Fern, don't back off like that. I'd love to see you. I've been meaning to get in touch – " here he put his hand over the phone and talked to someone, obviously a child – "it's just easier if you come over here. I'll give you the address. It's easy to find."

"Any luck?" asked Paula when I joined her in the kitchen.

"I suppose so. I'm going round to his place. His friend's place, after I see Dring. It turns out he's babysitting."

Suddenly Paula began to laugh. "What do you bet he's minding the Prof's kids? There'd be a fine bloody irony there!" And she laughed so much she inhaled a scrap of tuna and I had to thump her on the back until we both felt better.

By the time I found the address Adam had given me my nerves were jangling. It had taken a monumental effort of will to force myself to visit Dring at the hospital. I recognised that my hospital fears originated with those horrendous visits (how many had there been?) to my mother. But this is different, I told myself, this is Dring and it's physical and she's going to get better. Nothing stopped the rising panic; everything increased it. The ghastly jollity of the staff, the sick with their skin the colour of cardboard, the primitive fear of the visiting relatives. And Dring, in her hospital bed, looking so ill, so frail, so helpless. So infinitely far away.

As I was leaving, a rosy-cheeked nurse asked, "Is she you grandmother?"

"Not exactly but . . . we are very close."

"She'll be fine now, never worry. Now that she's being *properly* looked after."

Her reproach was all the worse for being justified. I knew that now. I fled.

Fled through the cold streets to the address Adam had given me . . . and then, as I leaned against the doorpost and heard the sound of footsteps on the stairs within, wondered what on earth I was doing there anyway.

"Fern, come in. I'd been about to call you anyway. What's up? You look dreadful."

"I'm fine." I tried to smile brightly but the smile teetered precariously.

"That sounds hopelessly brave. Never mind, come and meet Ben."

A small child appeared at the head of the stairs and squinted down at me suspiciously.

"You said you were babysitting."

"In a manner of speaking." Adam shut the door behind me.

Ben was a far from cherubic boy of three with a mass of brown curls and a storm-force scowl to which he treated me before stalking off to commiserate with the cat. Not the Prof's child, as it turned out, but Adam's.

I began to wish I hadn't come. Adam must be married. Where was Ben's mother? For a while Adam was too absorbed with Ben to pay much attention to me and I looked at children's books and tried not to see those other, more powerful images: Dring in the ambulance, the terror in my mother's eyes, Archie walking up the stairs towards me . . . I wanted to leave. I ought to leave, this was all hopelessly embarrassing – but where could I run to now?

I realised Adam was watching me. "You never look robust, Fern," he said thoughtfully, "but today you're more wraithlike than ever."

I tried to shrug off his concern. "Just a bit of a headache," I lied.

"I'll make you some tea. Or would you rather have something stronger? Jane usually keeps a bottle of brandy for emergencies."

"Tea will be fine."

While Ben was absorbed with a huge alphabet puzzle, Adam and I retired to the kitchen. Like the rest of the flat it was sparsely furnished but with a strong sense of design. The elusive Jane, it turned out, was a teacher of textiles.

117

"She's gone to a wedding in Frome this morning," he explained, "an old childhood friend. She said she'd be back by four o'clock so we can go out and get a meal later. Mr Right has just lurched into her life, apparently, and this wedding must have seemed the ideal opportunity to show him off to her friends."

An edge had entered his voice as he talked of Ben's mother, but I was not sure of the cause. Bitterness? Regret? Jealousy?

"I didn't realise you'd been married," I said, and even as I spoke I saw the photograph that Archie had given me, the one of my parents with their new baby – and then suddenly my mother's face was transformed from happy laughter to the terror of that trapped creature I had remembered thrashing to free herself in our narrow hallway . . . I frowned and shook my head, as though to shake off a troublesome insect.

"Here, drink this." Adam pressed a mug of tea into my hand. "We were never married. We hardly lived together much. It was the kind of relationship that is usually described as stormy, though heaven knows it dragged on long enough. By the time Ben appeared on the scene the whole thing was way past its expiry date – but Jane had just turned thirty and decided she wanted a child. And she's always been adept at getting her own way."

It was bitterness, then, a lingering anger. While Adam escorted Ben to the bathroom I sipped my tea and tried to focus on the companionable murmur of their voices, to drive out those other voices that crowded in my brain: no one in their right mind . . . you must be crazy . . . now she's looked after *properly* . . .

When Adam came back he said, "Ben's arrival has made my life incredibly complicated, but he's a great little character." He grinned. "I can't imagine life without him now."

From the nextdoor bathroom the great little character could be heard singing tunelessly.

"So that's why you do West Country articles whenever

you can?" I asked, and he nodded. "How were the nurses?"

"Disappointing. A whole night and not a single respectable piece of violence. I had to be content with angels in uniform instead."

I clenched my fists. Don't think about the nurses. Don't think about ambulance men, hospital orderlies, warders, armed prison guards . . . I said, "And the piece on Archie?"

"All finished and put away ready to coincide with publication of the new edition. Only . . . somehow I'm still not satisfied with it. It just doesn't feel finished."

"He didn't give you all that much to go on."

"As much as I expected. He's notoriously difficult. He's given no interviews at all for five years, not since he was given such a hard time after *Maiden Voyage*. My father persuaded him to let me see him by promising I'd be as meek as butter. It went against the grain. There's a story there, a real story, if I could only dig it out . . ."

"You make it sound a mystery."

"And yet the book itself is so very simple. Even though the identity of Dora is ambiguous, I feel sure the explanation, if only one could find the right key to it, would be quite straightforward."

I agreed. "I can't stand the pompous way people always go on about archetypes and anagrams. And yet when Paula started on about all that he seemed positively to lap it up."

"That whole conversation made me angry. As though he was using words to create a barrier to hide the truth. Something about his wife – or Dora – that made him uncomfortable, that he didn't want us to know."

"Then perhaps your father is right and he covered up the real story of Aunt Frances' death."

"If he hasn't then I don't— " He broke off. "Heavens above, Ben, you look like someone from the Golden Temple at Amritsar."

Ben glared up at us defiantly. "Why not!" he said, a declaration of purpose rather than a question. An entire roll of white lavatory paper was wound, turban style, around his head.

"Why not indeed?" Adam was prepared to be philosophical about his son's taste in millinery. He cocked his head on one side and surveyed the child critically, as though he were a piece of sculpture at auction. "How do you propose to keep it in place? You realise, don't you, that the really *clever* trick is winding it all back on the roll so no one can tell."

"Why not!" declared Ben once more, but less certainly. He was squinting with the effort of trying to see the concoction he had erected on his head.

"Here," I said, "let me help."

"Why not?" And this time the two syllables were almost friendly.

"Are you sure you don't mind?" Adam asked a little later, when Ben and I were struggling to distinguish "n" from "u" in the huge floor puzzle. "Jane should be back soon."

"I'm enjoying myself," I said. And it was true. Somewhere between the turban unwinding and the alphabet puzzle I had forgotten about Dring and the hospital and the tide of panic which had threatened to sweep me away.

If you ever find yourself in need of an instant cure for the trauma of seeing the person who has always been your life's anchor taken away in an ambulance then I can recommend nothing more therapeutic than a couple of hours with a boisterous three-year-old. Curiously enough it was Ben's truly awesome selfishness that was so refreshing. All day I'd been treated as something vulnerable – Dr Phelps with his "This has been a difficult time for you," and Paula offering to forgo her entire weekend with the Prof for my sake, even Adam describing me as wraithlike – and I'd begun to think I *was* frail, might fall to pieces at any moment. Ben's robust cheating at Wildlife Lotto and his determination to crash his big train into my little one whenever he could as we chuffed over the threadbare carpet made me feel sturdier than I had done in weeks.

Once Adam was assured that I wasn't going to wilt under the onslaught of Ben's personality he went into the back bedroom to mend a sash window, but his good intentions were not enough to see the task through and I found him there half an hour later, reading old magazines.

"It's gone six o'clock," he muttered, looking at his watch, "I can't think where Jane has got to. Bath time for Ben, anyway."

When Jane finally returned, some time after eight, I was reading Ben the same horrid books about trains with faces that my cousin Gerald had so enjoyed as a child – only I was pleased to note that Ben had the good sense to alter their faces; most had moustaches or glasses and some even had rather odd-looking genitals.

"What the hell kept you so long? You said four o'clock," I heard Adam say in the hall.

"It was a *wedding*, Adam." The woman's voice was scornful.

"You could at least have telephoned."

Ben stopped listening to the story and looked towards the door with a blank face as his mother launched into a stream of invective: Adam always complained at not seeing enough of his son and now a whole day was too much, was she supposed to be accountable to him for every moment of her day? Resented her having fun, judgemental, everyone else always in the wrong.

I heard Adam say, "Jane, be quiet. I'm leaving," as he strode into the room. "Time to go, Fern, here's your coat."

Jane was examining me curiously as I lifted Ben off my knees and closed the book. She was dark-haired, attractive, with a strong and vibrant face. "I hope Ben hasn't worn you out," she said, although she didn't look as though she cared much either way.

"I've enjoyed playing with him," I said.

Her expression was sceptical. "*Chacun à son goût*," she

said – but this remark, I knew, was for Adam's benefit, as he said goodbye to Ben and promised he would see him again the next day.

As we went into the hall Jane said in a low voice to Adam, "And next time you might have the decency to check with me before entertaining your girlfriends in my flat."

He had taken my arm and I felt the pressure of his fingers dig into my flesh. He paused, obviously on the verge of a stinging retort, then closed his mouth firmly and a muscle of annoyance twitched in his cheek. "Let's go," he said.

"Enjoy yourselves," Jane said mockingly. In his anger Adam walked so rapidly down the street that I could barely keep up.

"Damn her!" he said. "She knows I won't say anything in front of Ben." Then, after a brief silence, "Sorry about all that. A film, don't you think?" And, without waiting for my reply, he put his arm around my waist and set off in the direction of the cinema, his stride still long, and angry.

Adam had seen the film, a comedy, before but he declared that it was well worth a second viewing. It struck me that he didn't seem to be enjoying it much, but when I glanced at his face, I saw he had fallen asleep almost at once.

I can't remember much about that film. The rest of the audience seemed to be laughing a good deal. From time to time I turned to look at Adam's sleeping face: there was a slight frown between his eyebrows and occasionally his eyelids flickered as though he was dreaming. He had told me he drove down from London late the night before and that Ben had woken him after only a brief sleep. I tried to focus on the film but, released from Ben's welcome tyranny, I was unable to prevent the images from earlier in the day from superimposing themselves on my thoughts. I was relieved when Adam awoke and, his anger apparently forgotten, said with a grin, "Didn't I tell you it was worth seeing twice?"

"How do you know? You've been asleep the whole time."

He denied this vigorously. We shuffled with the crowd out into the freezing city night. He put his arm loosely across my shoulders and explained all the details in the comic sequences that could only be appreciated fully the second time round.

"Then you must have transparent eyelids," I protested.

He maintained that, of course, transparent eyelids were the primary qualifications of an investigative journalist, enabling him to keep watch while apparently sleeping. I laughed, but it was no longer the easy laughter I had shared with Ben. The evening was nearly over and quite suddenly I was afraid, afraid of the empty house I had left earlier, and the silence, and the moment when Adam would say goodbye and I would be left alone to face the fear and the half-remembered past.

"What now?" he asked. "I could do with something to eat."

I tried to read the message behind the words. Was he simply being polite? "I don't know," I wavered, "it's getting late."

"Italian, I think. One needs robust fare after an afternoon with Ben, don't you agree?"

Was that boredom in his voice? "I should be getting home."

We had been walking down the hill that led from the cinema but now he stopped, turned to face me and said, "For pity's sake, Fern, every time I suggest something you say you have to go home. It's like going out with a homing pigeon. Surely your old dragon nanny is safely tucked up in bed by now?"

"She's not there."

"What?"

"She had to go to hospital."

"Why didn't you tell me before?"

"Did I not? It must have slipped my mind. It's not important, nothing to worry about, just a routine visit."

I couldn't bear the way his eyes were searching my face.

"When did this happen?"

"This morning. An ambulance came." Block out the images in my mind.

He was looking thoughtful. "I see," he said. I sincerely hoped he didn't.

I rattled on quickly, "She's quite all right, nothing serious. And I'd known about it for some time. It's almost a relief . . . she's been a lot to look after recently." Why was I lying to him? Why was I so afraid to let him see my fear? Was it simply that the thought of his pity was dreadful, unbearable – or was it something more?

"Is your friend Paula at home?"

"She's . . . busy this weekend."

"I'll bet she is. Poor old Fern. This must have been rotten for you."

I said, "Look, why don't we go back to my place now? I could find us something to eat."

"Is that what you want?"

"I wouldn't ask you otherwise."

"No? Sometimes I wonder if one doesn't need experience as a code breaker to know just what you do mean. Okay, let's go back to your place."

As I had expected, there was no sign of Paula at Alderly Drive; her weekend with the Prof must be turning out well. I put on all the lights, lit the gas fire in the sitting-room, ignored the empty chair where Dring always sat . . .

In the kitchen I was startled to find the fridge and cupboards crammed with booty from my morning's shopping trip designed to prevent Paula spending more than she could afford. The day seemed to have stretched so it was hard to believe that mundane activity had taken place just a few brief hours before.

I contemplated the packed fridge. "You've come on the right evening, at least. There's even some wine."

"I'm impressed. You weren't by any chance expecting me, were you? Or an entire football team, perhaps."

124

Adam watched me while I found the corkscrew, opened a bottle, poured the wine, handed him a glass.

"Thanks. Tell me about Dring. Has she always lived here?"

"Why do you want to know about her?"

"Because it affects you, of course."

I tried to ignore this. "Oh. It's hard to know where to begin. She's been here about fifteen years – but it seems like for ever. She was only meant to stay for a month or two, while my father was away, but then . . . he died and my mother became ill . . . so she just stayed. It all worked out quite well, really."

He smiled. "I love the way you describe the events of your early life. Death and disaster and total catastrophe all around and you murmur 'it all turned out quite well really' as if it was all perfectly normal. The story of your early years was about as normal as the last act of *Hamlet*."

"Maybe I simply arrived too late to be affected by any of it. Like Fortinbras."

"He's not the character who springs immediately to mind. But tell me, this Dring lady must mean a good deal to you."

I stared at him. A good deal? It was like describing the rock on which your life has been built as a handy little accessory.

"I'm used to having her around."

"Has she ever been away before?"

"I don't think so . . . no, never." Even though I was watching my finger trace the rim of the wine glass I was painfully aware of his scrutiny. "But I don't mind," I said swiftly, "in fact I quite like being alone. It gives me a chance to think things through."

"Does that mean you want me to go?"

"Oh no, not unless . . ."

"Unless what?"

I said nothing. Couldn't think what to say. I wanted him to think that I was strong and capable and independent, the kind of person he could admire, but everything I said

125

only made my position worse. He must be thinking me hopelessly young and pathetic – and maybe he was right. I shut my eyes, tried to think clearly . . . but instantly the image of my mother's distorted face filled my brain. White and huge and terrifying as a pumpkin at Hallowe'en.

Panic. Open my eyes. Be practical.

"Do you want something to eat? I could cook up some spaghetti or— " I went to the fridge, opened the door, began to sort through the packages.

"Not just yet."

"Perhaps some cheese and biscuits. I could make a salad."

"Fern, tell me. What is it you want? Do you know?"

I paused. There was exasperation in his voice, he was growing impatient. He might go . . . and then all the emptiness of the house would be mine alone. To drown in. To swallow me up.

I was staring at a package of oak-smoked ham – as though it might contain the answers to my confusion. "I want you to hold me," I said in a low voice, "I want you to stay here tonight."

I could hear him move towards me. I stood up, closed the fridge door.

"That's what I want too," he said. And he put his arms around me. For a long time we stood there, not kissing, not talking. Just holding each other.

If I had hoped for an instant panacea for all my fears then I was surely disappointed. I was still afraid to close my eyes in case I saw my mother's face; there were still flutterings of panic to be wary of – and yet the panic and the fear were infinitely more bearable with Adam's arms around me.

I found myself aware of every detail: the pressure of his hands against my back; the way my weight was pushed forward slightly on to my toes; the voices in the alley at the back of the house. Still I felt myself a separate person, lonely, vulnerable . . . and I longed to make the connection that would break down the shell of fear in which I was trapped.

126

I lifted my face and Adam stooped and kissed me slowly; and only then did I dare to close my eyes, knowing that I was moving towards a place where the old fears could not harm me, a place where I could be strong and whole because at that moment there existed a person to whom I was more real than anyone else in the world.

Adam pulled away after what could have been seconds, or hours . . . but time had been playing tricks on me all day. "You're full of surprises," he said, and smiled.

What did that mean? "Don't stop," I said, "I was just beginning to enjoy myself."

He was smiling in a puzzled sort of way as he leaned to kiss me again. Then he pushed me away gently. "Hmm . . . for some reason you make me feel I should come courting you in an old-fashioned way. With sonnets or a lute – armfuls of flowers."

"Why? Do you think I'm different?"

"Of course you are, foolish Fern, that's the whole point."

"Oh." I couldn't keep the disappointment from my voice. I turned away and put a lump of cheese on a plate, not because I was hungry, far from it, but I needed something to do.

Adam poured us both some more wine. "Besides," he said, "I have a confession to make."

I didn't want to hear it. He had a wife and triplets in London; he was gay; he was leaving tomorrow for four years in the Gobi desert; he and Jane had decided to marry after all, for Ben's sake.

"Oh really?"

"That time when I bumped into you outside the college, it wasn't an accident at all. I'd found out where you were studying and decided to see if I could find you there."

"Why? Did you need more material for your article on Archie?"

He was puzzled. "What on earth does Archie have to do with it? You know even less about him than I do. You hadn't even read his book, not then anyway."

"So why?"

"I wanted to see you again, obviously."

"But what about violence in the casualty ward?"

"That was genuine enough. I had a couple of hours to kill and Ben had gone to a birthday party so I thought I'd come to the college and see if I could find you there. Does that bother you for some reason?"

"Not at all."

"Come here. You disappear faster than a Cheshire cat's grin." He put his arms around me, kissed me again.

It was simpler, now, not to say anything, just to feel the warmth of his arms, the pressure of his mouth on mine. Words were so often dangerous, they could as easily separate as unite. Safer by far to rely on the silent communication of our skin.

No longer afraid of the images that had been haunting me all day, I began to relax, to allow myself the luxury of responding to his touch, to recognise that this was what I had been wanting since the moment I heard his voice answering the phone that morning, what I had wanted while I watched him attempt, with no success at all, to mend the back axle on Ben's tipper truck, what I had wanted as I watched his sleeping face in the flickering light from the cinema screen. It seemed to be that all I had ever wanted, the whole world and more besides was concentrated in the energy between us.

He pulled away. "Is this what you want, Fern?"

I smiled. It seemed incredible to me then that our little back kitchen with its Beautiful Britain calendar on the wall and the cupboard door which had been sagging on its hinges for months should be the stage for sensations so strong that for a few moments I was quite breathless, but, "Yes," I said, "I'm absolutely sure."

"Then I suggest we go upstairs. Kitchen tables don't do much for me, as a rule."

I walked up the narrow stairs ahead of him. My brain, which had been partially paralysed just now, began to race. I wondered if I was falling in love. But why falling? Leaping into love was more accurate. Was this, then, what it was like, this drunkenness which had nothing to do with

128

the wine? Suddenly my mind was full of all those clichés with which we are endlessly bombarded – heart racing, fire in the veins, melting kisses. Falling in love. You're my world. In love with love . . . and now it was me, and I knew that this was what all the stuff of teenage fantasy, all Paula's bawdy talk, all the paraphernalia of love so clumsily portrayed on film, was all about: this hunger, this greed, this vitality: being more alive, more fully aware, than ever in my life before.

On the landing I paused. The door to Dring's room was ajar and the bed, with its pink satin counterpane for once free of ashtrays and litter, stared at me blindly. Adam, watching my face, pulled the door closed.

In my own bedroom with its flowered wallpaper and posters of Impressionist paintings and my dressing-gown on its hook behind the door, it was bitterly cold. I knelt down and lit the gas fire. When I stood up Adam put his arms around my shoulders and kissed me gently.

He paused. "Fern, you're shivering."

"It's cold in here, that's all."

He hugged me tightly, stroked my hair. "Have you done this before?"

"Oh yes," I replied, swiftly. And, strictly speaking, it was true. While I was still at school, one by one all my friends had lost, or claimed to lose, their virginity: it was a normal part of growing up, a rite of passage on the way to adult life, and no teenager was ever more vulnerable to social pressure to conform than I was. The older brother of a friend obliged one Sunday afternoon when the others had gone to a charity swimming gala. Afterwards he was keen to repeat the exercise but I wanted only to obliterate the memory of an event which had left me feeling depressed, somehow diminished. From then on I preferred to read about sex and romance in books, or to watch it depicted on television, or listen to Paula's endless sagas of psychological conflict and sexual tensions, than to risk the disillusion of my earlier experiment. But now, with Adam, I was confident again. He was different – which meant, I suppose, that I believed myself to be falling in love with him. And that, as everybody knows, meant nothing could possibly go wrong. So I kissed him again and said, "It's only the cold, don't worry."

"I'll hold you," he said, "you won't be cold any more."

And just at that moment his words were a promise of so much more. Suddenly there was a stabbing pain at the base of my throat and all I wanted was for this moment, just like this, to last for ever.

He hesitated, frowned. "Fern, are you on the pill? No?" He swore softly. "And I'm not prepared either. Hell."

"Paula might have something. She usually does . . . unless she took all of them with her."

"You'd best go and look."

Paula's room was a riot of disorder. I had never helped myself to anything of hers before but I knew that on this occasion she would be wholehearted in her approval. Still, there's nothing quite like rummaging through odd socks and jars of moisturiser and used Kleenex to dampen the ardours of love. Or lust. Or whatever name one gives to the wondrous state in which I found myself. At last I found a packet of condoms poking out of her US passport like a bookmark.

"Found some." I took the packet back to Adam.

He grinned. "One will probably be enough. To be getting on with." And with a secretive gesture, as though he did not want me to see what he had been looking at, he replaced something on the chest of drawers. It was the photograph of my parents with their new baby which I had placed in a smart wooden frame.

"That's the one Archie gave me that day at Chatton Heights."

"I thought so. Your mother looks so happy, doesn't she?"

"Yes."

It was what Paula had said, too. "She looks real nice, Mary, not like a crazy person at all . . ."

So what had happened to transform those eyes, creased and sparkling with laughter, to the green pits of misery that had blazed up at me from the hallway on the day they took her away, the dull pebbles of nothingness that had looked past me at something no one else could see that day at the hospital when she spoke of the devil? Was it some outside force that had changed her? Or was the truth perhaps that she had always been a crazy lady, that when the picture was taken she was only acting like a normal person, putting on a good show, playing the part of the young wife and mother while the time-bomb of insanity ticked away to its inevitable catastrophic conclusion?

Was that what I was doing now?

Adam stooped and kissed me, but something had happened. A change had taken place between us. The magic ease was draining away. I could feel my spine, rigid with tension, shiver beneath his hand.

He pulled back. "Fern, where are you now?"

"I'm here. It's all right. I just . . . kiss me, Adam."

But it was too late. The surface of my skin, my lips, my cheeks, my hands, no longer conducted the energy that had run between us; it had become a shell to keep him out. And this time when he kissed me it was as if his mouth was pressing the air from my chest, there was a constriction in my lungs, my throat, I could not breathe.

"Please, Adam . . . wait."

He stroked my hair. "Easy," he said, "relax. Don't make it so difficult for yourself," and he moved to kiss me again.

His hand was huge, like the mauling paw of a bear. I twisted my head away. "No. It won't work. I can't explain. It's not the same any more."

His arm fell to his side and I took a step backwards, away from him.

"Are you serious?"

I nodded. "I'm sorry. I don't understand how – but I know I can't—"

"You don't have to look so anguished about it, Fern. There's plenty of time. Here . . ." His voice was travelling over a huge distance that had opened up between us. His face, the grey eyes and the wide mouth so quick to smile, looked unreal, like a photograph pinned to the wall of my room.

"No, Adam, please don't try. I know it's no use, not now."

"Maybe we should go more slowly."

"It's not that – but I can't explain. If you simply went away . . ."

"Jesus, Fern, what kind of game are you playing here? Are you going to explain or are you just going to escape again into one of your damned silences?"

"I'm sorry, Adam, I didn't mean— "

"Don't fob me off with apologies!" He stared at me for a few moments, then turned away, as though in contempt, or exasperation, and sat down on the edge of the bed. "Oh hell, Fern, I didn't mean to get angry with you. But your moods change so quickly, I don't see how you can be so fired up one moment and the next – you make me feel like something that's just crawled out from under a stone."

"I don't know." It was all I could say. Even speaking to him had become the most enormous effort. He had grown into a huge and unwelcome stranger. "It doesn't matter. Why don't we go downstairs and— "

"No!" All at once he was angry again. "It *does* matter. It matters to me and it sure as hell ought to matter to you too. You can't turn people's emotions on and off as if they're some kind of damn tap. Why can't you come out and say what you think for once in your life? What are you so afraid of?"

Silence. I said nothing. Willed him to stand up and walk downstairs, walk out of the house and away for ever.

He was frowning at me as though I was a mathematical puzzle chalked up on a board. "Maybe you have some kind of phobia about sex, or men in general. Maybe it's only men of thirty-one with three-year-old sons that you can't stand. There must be some reason that makes you pull this disappearing trick on me all the time."

Silence. No words to say.

"It's not the sex, Fern, that's not important – it can

wait at any rate. It's the way you keep shutting me out."

"I'm sorry," I said, "I can't— "

"If you could just try to explain, that might be some kind of a start."

I didn't speak. He was waiting for me to say something but all the words had died inside me, all the words had shrivelled into little empty balls of dust and drifted away into the void.

"Oh hell," he said, "I always thought it was men who were accused of not being able to express their feelings." He looked up at that moment and his expression was so forlorn that I wondered briefly if it would be better just to go through with it anyway, try to pretend things were as they had been ten minutes before. But I knew that would be worse, worse than nothing. "It's only words I'm asking for, Fern, nothing more than that."

He was watching me, waiting for me to speak, but I might as well have been born mute. How could I begin? Where were the words to tell him of the panic that was engulfing me, the terror of madness, the spectre of my mother, two-faced like Janus, the normal and the mad? And it's not a fair fight, the crazy always wins. Sanity was a knife-edge, I saw that now. One false move and you fall for ever into black chaos. Like she did. And he sat there so calm and self-assured and asked me how I felt.

I turned away. "I'm going downstairs," I said, "why don't— "

"Wait!" With sudden speed he was on his feet and had placed himself in front of the door, pushing it closed with his back. "Do you want me to decide for you? Why are you hurting yourself like this? If I didn't know you so well . . . You want to be careful, Fern, now that dragon-nanny's not here to look after you."

"Adam, it's no use." There was a sound in my ears as though I was standing under a waterfall.

"How can you be so sure?"

The roaring grew deafening. "Adam, please, I can't stand it."

He stood aside, let me pass. I went downstairs to the kitchen.

Adam stayed the night, but he slept on the sofa in the sitting-room. Or didn't sleep . . . I know I didn't, but since I was responsible for the whole shambles I didn't waste any pity on myself.

Another sleepless night. The same fears, the same pleading with my fate. Images of Archie, my mother, the hopeless terror of it every time I closed my eyes. I remembered that other night when waking nightmares had driven away sleep, that night after my first visit to Long Chatton with Adam. I remembered the calm that had enveloped me when I could shake off sleep no longer, the calm that was somehow connected with my grandfather's house and that half-heard voice on the window-seat. Perhaps this time too . . . but in the brief moment of sleep that came to me that night there were only disjointed fears, the wolf-howl terror of childhood.

Paula returned unexpectedly early next morning. "Fast work," she murmured when she saw Adam drinking black coffee in the kitchen.

"It's not what you think," I hissed.

Adam barely spoke to Paula and left soon after she arrived. He kissed me lightly on the cheek as we parted. "Forget about last night," he said, "that doesn't need to be important."

I wanted to find a reply that would begin to heal the gulf between us but no words came. For the first time, now that he was leaving, I realised with a pang of loss that I found Adam remarkably attractive.

"Take care, Fern. And get in touch if you want . . . if you need me. Goodbye now."

As I turned and closed the front door I noticed the wellington boots I had bought a week earlier. I'll need those at Chatton Heights, I thought.

And then I knew that I had to go back. It wasn't so much that I made a decision, more that I accepted the inevitable. There was nothing to keep me in Bristol any more. Paula could look after the house, an heiress had no need of a part-time job at an estate agent's office, nor a diploma in business studies – and if I was away from here I wouldn't be able to visit Dring so often. My visit to the hospital had revived all my deep-rooted fears of institutions where white-coated strangers wield power over helpless loved ones.

I wandered aimlessly into the sitting-room. Both at the hospital and here in this little house that had always been "home" but was so no longer there were too many reminders of my mother's madness. For days now I had been on my guard but the images, the memories, were too powerful. And now my efforts to reach out to Adam, to find an ally who would help me blot out the lonely fears, had ended in pathetic failure.

If a person could not help me, perhaps a place could; perhaps at Chatton Heights I would discover some inner core of certainty and wholeness, that mirage I had glimpsed when I heard the voice on the window-seat, some knowledge of my father, my mercifully sane father, to save me from my present hopeless blundering through the days like a sleep-walker, making a hash of even the simplest task. It was a possibility. It felt like my only hope, right now.

I was about to go to my room to start packing when Paula came down the stairs, a grin of triumph on her face. She said, "If it was all so bloody platonic between you and Adam, then why the hell d'you take my condoms?"

Chapter 5

At Chatton Heights, in the smoking-room which we had visited briefly on that first Gerald-conducted tour of the house with its smoke-cold walls and the incongruously elegant chaise longue, the portraits were waiting for me. Here you are, they seemed to say as they stared down from the high walls. At last.

One couple within each frame: Archie and Frances; Clancy and Louise. Two couples, four faces, eight eyes fixed on me as I sat perched on the chaise longue and hugged my knees to ward off the cold.

There was a marked difference between the two paintings, a difference of style. That of Archie and his wife had that static, almost closed look that finished oil paintings so often achieve. Each button, each eyelash, each fingernail in meticulous detail. The one of my parents was more of a sketch; it looked as though it had been painted in a hurry, or as if the artist had not taken the same trouble. Perhaps because of that it breathed a liveliness, a dash, that the other had not achieved.

I devoted much time to studying their faces, trying to know them.

Archie, in his youth, had been extremely handsome – as tall and dark as any stranger in a teenage magazine – and he looked as though he knew it, too. His chin was raised, head slightly turned so that his fine face showed to advantage. It must have been summertime: there was a haze of delphiniums and roses behind his shoulder and he was wearing a lightweight suit and a white shirt open at the collar. His hand rested on the back of his wife's chair. He was not smiling exactly, but he looked immensely pleased with himself.

There was no such self-assurance about his wife. Straight brown hair framed a face that would be forever condemned to the meagre praise of "niceness". In her flowered cotton dress she retained the manner of an English schoolgirl. She must have been popular at school, my Aunt Frances, a good sort; I was sure she would never let the side down, would be more baffled than outraged by double-dealing. She faced the painter, hands clasped in front of her; pale blue, slightly closely set eyes (that was the bit that most reminded me of Gerald) looked out and hoped to please. Anxious, wanting only to be liked.

Anyone who saw the painting would know they were a couple with money behind them, that they had a place in society they saw no reason to question. Had she lived, Aunt Frances would surely have become a pillar of local strength – meals on wheels, church fêtes, books for the blind. Not in a bossy way, not because she was from the big house, but drawn in because she wanted to help, was unable to say no. Thought one really should try to do one's bit.

An observer, contemplating the contrast between husband and wife, might wonder why someone as handsome as Archie should have chosen to marry such a mousy young woman. Was she clever? Did he recognise and need the security someone like her could offer? Or maybe she was pregnant when they married. One might guess he would be unfaithful – and that her forgiveness was almost inevitable. A woman born to smooth her husband's path. Then the accident at sea, water closing over her head, salt water filling her lungs . . .

Turn to the second portrait. My parents. And this one, for all its verve, was less easy to read. There was my father, gazing out of the frame with a strange intensity in his eyes, as if he had just thought of something vitally important he wanted to say. Although without his brother's swarthy good looks, my father's face was nonetheless attractive, his features thoughtful and expressive. His hair was long, unruly. He had not put on special clothes for the sitting, unless that flowered shirt was a favourite. He was wearing jeans.

Like Frances, my mother was seated on a chair; unlike Frances she did not look content to stay there long. Her heavily made-up eyes were almost obscured by a thick curtain of black hair; she wore a good deal of jewellery and scarves; her skirt was tiny, the sleeves of the blouse huge – icon of a vanished year. But the face was unreadable, muddy almost. As though the artist had tried and failed to capture her expression, tried and failed again, tried and failed and finally given up in despair, concentrating instead on the paisley pattern of her scarf, the detail of the Indian bells around her neck.

Speak to me, I begged the portraits, tell me who I am.

They were silent.

My decision to return to Chatton Heights threw the household briefly into turmoil. Not that they hadn't been expecting me, oh no, it was my house after all and therefore only natural that I should come back for a "proper" visit. No, it was my insistence on being given my father's old room that caused the trouble.

My father's old room. Why on earth should I want to sleep there? Tillie and Elsa, who helped with the cleaning, had spent days, so they told me, spring cleaning the best bedroom in readiness for my return. They had scrubbed and swept and dusted and polished until the huge bedroom glowed with a sombre opulence. Even worse, my father's old bedroom (or Gracie's room as it was called after some long-forgotten nanny who had once stayed there) was in one of the side wings of the house that had not been used in years and was never heated. It was cold and it was damp. There were jackdaws in the chimney, mice in the wainscot and spiders everywhere.

I was adamant. Having summoned all my courage to face my family again I was not to be thwarted over the choice of a bedroom. If it was cold, then I could heat it; if it was dirty I would clean it. I had my way.

Tillie and Elsa moved in with their brushes and dusters and the strange disjointed conversation they carried on between them. (Tillie: ". . . one must always be so careful with strangers . . ." Elsa: "Did you see that programme last night?" Tillie: "Always locked the house, my husband, never trusted . . ." Elsa: "They had some lovely prizes." Tillie: ". . . can be violent, murder even . . ." Elsa: "The couple that won got a holiday in the Bananas.")

Gracie's room was much smaller than the best bedroom and the job was completed in a couple of hours. It was in the kitchen wing, a portion of the house separated from the main landing by a green baize door; only a boy eager to distance himself from the prickly bosom of his family would have chosen it – and I liked it for the same reason, in spite of its manifest disadvantages. It had not benefited from the rewiring that had been carried out in the fifties, nor the installation of central heating in the sixties, so there were neither radiators nor modern power points. However, Archie, who alone at the house seemed genuinely pleased by my return, remembered having once seen a Calor gas heater in the coach house and Gerald was dispatched, muttering disagreeably, to find it and bring it in.

So the room was clean and it was warm.

It was also disappointing.

Just an ordinary room. Small, almost poky. Looking out to the back at the stables and the outbuildings which now held nothing more glamorous than the family cars, and beyond them the washing line where Mrs Viney hung her tea towels, and the remains of the old kitchen garden where nothing grew but a couple of rows of cabbages and a Brussels sprout or two. No trace in this room of my father, no trace even that this had been the room of a boy, a teenager, a young man. Had there once been pictures on these walls, books in the bookcase under the window? Had he sat at this table and done his schoolwork? Made models? Smoked his first illicit cigarette? It was unlikely I would ever know.

All in all it was about as impersonal as a room can be.

The walls were covered in woodchip paper and painted a dull cream; the curtains were a faded blue; the rug was a colour which might, once upon a time, have been beige. The furniture was an odd mismatched assortment: a dark Windsor chair in front of a modern pine desk, an old divan bed and a heavy oak wardrobe. It was a room hastily assembled for someone of small importance – for a servant, perhaps. Or a neglected son.

I did not try to make the room my own. I hadn't brought much with me. Although I had left my part-time job at the estate agent's I did not intend to stay here long.

The only ornament I had brought was the photograph of my parents which Archie had given me. Whenever I came into the room they smiled at me with misplaced confidence from behind the glass in their smart wooden frame.

I was no longer afraid of the house as I had been on my first visit, but I did not yet like it.

Sometimes, as I wandered through empty rooms, I felt like a child who has been sent back to boarding school early, before the holidays have really ended. The echoing rooms had that bare, impersonal air about them that you find in empty institutions. They were waiting to be filled. I could almost imagine that at any moment a coach would pull up on the gravel at the front and a horde of children weighed down with sports gear and gossip would tumble out and burst into the house like a wave, running up the stairs, pushing open all the doors, filling it with noise. Soaking up the emptiness.

But of course there was no coach, no children. No end to the solitude and the silence.

My relatives, I soon discovered, had established patterns that ensured their paths seldom crossed. Archie was generally to be found (or, more exactly, was not to be disturbed) in his study, a large room on the ground floor. Gerald made few appearances in the house: his little empire was the stable block and coach house where the cars were kept – most of them older models which he was restoring with scrupulous care – and where he had erected a pen to house a pair of recently acquired young labradors. Tillie flitted between the kitchen and her own room at the back of the house where her television was seldom silent. I made several attempts to ask her about my grandfather and about herself, but although I shaped the questions as tactfully as I could they threw her into a mild panic each time; her tiny mouth worked its imaginary peppermint back and forth as she struggled with the words: "Sometimes one feels . . . but not always of course . . . and even then, you see, not easy . . . one was much younger . . ." Her phrases fluttered past my ears like scraps of confetti and try though I might I could make no sense of them. After a while I gave up but continued to help her as much as I could with her tasks; perhaps when I had won her confidence she might talk more freely . . . her glossy blue eyes stared blankly at me and beyond and offered no hope of future intimacy. Sometimes I wondered what my grandfather could have done to drive her into such an inaccessible retreat – and the thought was enough to make the fine hairs on my spine shiver with apprehension.

On the whole my family seemed to accept my appearance in the house without much interest. There was no hostility, no open hostility at least, but no glimmer of friendliness either. It was as though, having decided to move back to Chatton Heights, even for a short time, I had forfeited my right to a separate existence.

Sometimes, not often, I heard the voice: that low summer murmur of forgotten ease, like a shell held to the ear, which had first come to me on the window-seat when I saw the gardener push his wheelbarrow over the gravel. Of course, I never told anyone about the voice since they would not have understood: they would have assumed that I "heard" the voice in the same way that I heard the wind that swept down from the bleak Cotswold hills one stormy night and howled around the cold stone walls of the house, rattling the windows in their frames. But it wasn't like that at all. More like a tune that gets lodged in your brain, one of those annoying little tunes that you can't shift. Persistent – yet elusive as a draught that slips around the corner of a passageway. I did not know how to conjure up the voice: it came and went in its own time like some will-o'-the-wisp on an empty moor. When my head was filled with ordinary silence, thoughts of the summer voice made me uneasy. Had my mother too heard voices? But then I heard it again . . . and longed only to know it better.

One afternoon when the sky was overcast with the threat of rain I retreated to the smoking-room to contemplate the portraits once more. This undistinguished smoke-coloured room was rapidly becoming my favourite downstairs retreat, not least because no one else seemed ever to use it. Compared with the other rooms at Chatton Heights this one was small, cosy almost, with leather-bound almanacs and old volumes of *Punch* in the bookshelves. At one time it must have lived up to its name since the carpet was pock-marked with cigarette burns and there was a large scorch mark on the back of the chaise longue. As I shivered and contemplated the double portraits which dominated the room I wondered if some previous visitor had been driven to set fire to the furniture in a desperate attempt to keep warm.

"So this is where you lurk all day." Gerald stood in the doorway, his watery eyes gazing at me contemptuously. "If you're going to hang around in here all the time you ought to get Elsa to light a fire for you. That is her job, after all."

"I only came in to look at the portraits."

"Pretty fine, aren't they?" He sat down on the arm of my chair and examined the paintings critically. I had expected him to back out of the room as soon as he saw me. On the somewhat distorted scale of friendliness that prevailed at Chatton Heights this encounter so far registered as an effusive outpouring of *bonhomie* and his moist lips were drawn back in a smile that could be interpreted as conciliatory. "It's a shame the painter made such a ghastly hash of your parents," he said although he sounded delighted at the botch-up, "the portrait of Pa and my mother does show what he was capable of when he really put his mind to it. You can tell he was inspired when he did the first one – and then dashed off the one of your parents in a frightful hurry and ballsed it up. Pity, don't you think?"

"How can you be so sure they were painted in that order?"

"Of course they were, older son and all that."

"Don't you think the second picture has an energy, a vitality, that is missing in— "

He interrupted. "I always did feel a bit sorry for poor old Uncle Clancy," he said cheerfully, "one of life's losers, poor sod. I mean, it can't have been easy for him having an older brother like Archie."

"Was your father so unkind?"

"I don't know about *unkind*. What I meant was, your poor father was always in Pa's shadow. Just look at them both: you can tell Pa was the successful one, the achiever, the one who did well at school and university and had heaps of friends and of course he was wildly attractive to females— " Here Gerald paused briefly to tear at the skin around his thumb. "While your poor dad . . . well, you can tell by looking at him that he wasn't any great shakes, just some kind of dreary hippy. And then, to cap it all, the poor bugger has to go and fall for a loony. Can't blame him for looking so bloody miserable. Typical younger brother syndrome, one saw quite a bit of it at school. I often think the reason he escaped to South America when he did was that he simply had to get out from under Pa's shadow."

"But he had business to do out there."

"Business, eh?" Gerald turned to look down at me. Somehow he contrived to appear both embarrassed and sneering at the same time. "I grant you, business was the public excuse but there must have been more to it than that. I mean, your dad was notoriously bad at business anyway and just about anyone in the firm could have closed down that office more efficiently. And by then everybody knew your ma was heading for the deep

143

end. You can see it in the picture, can't you? Maybe Uncle Clancy was desperate to escape from her, and South America was the most distant office the family had. That's a thought, eh?"

"You and I interpret the pictures quite differently."

He considered this possibility. "Hm. Eye of the beholder and all that. But ask anyone and they'll tell you the same story: your pa positively worshipped the ground his brother walked on – the poor bugger spent his whole life trying to emulate him. And that was before Pa became famous. It was probably a good thing Uncle Clancy died when he did."

"Are you serious, Gerald?"

Some more thumb-biting, then, "Well, not from your point of view, obviously, but then if he *had* stuck around I bet he'd have found it pretty bloody hellish coming to terms with big brother's fame and glory – not an easy act to follow, you have to admit that."

"Archie hasn't had much luck following *Dora's Room* either, has he?" I broke off. My daddy's stronger than yours! Well, my daddy's a policeman! I hadn't had a conversation like that since infant school and I had no intention of starting one now. "There's no point in arguing about it, Gerald," I said wearily.

He stood up. "Who's arguing?" And then, as he went towards the door, "I imagined you'd be grateful for a bit of enlightenment, that's all, only trying to help out. After all, you've never known much about them, have you?"

"That's why I'm trying to find out about them now," I said, more to the four grey walls and the eight staring eyes of the portraits than to Gerald, who had already left.

Alone once again, I found the room a bleaker, emptier, altogether colder place than it had been before. Gerald's words had sent a shiver of unease over the tranquil surface of my contemplation.

There were only two places at Chatton Heights where I did not feel myself to be an intruder – and neither had been included on that first tour with Gerald.

The first was the kitchen. A huge, high room with an Aga and a large scrubbed table and a good deal of kitchen equipment that was so old it was practically antique, this was the domain of Mrs Viney, the Long Chatton woman who came in each morning to prepare lunch for the family and who often stayed on into the afternoon, baking or making marmalade (or, now, chatting with me).

She was a tall, stout woman with skimpy curls and an expression of permanent disapproval. Her father was Tom Page, the old man whom I had first seen as he wheeled his empty barrow over the rain-soaked gravel at the front of the house. He had worked at Chatton Heights since boyhood and now that he was officially retired he continued to come in practically every day. Apart from a lad who mowed the lawns and trimmed the paths in summer, no one else now paid any attention to what had once been a fine garden, so that his efforts were all that kept the place from reverting to wilderness.

Though often dour, Mrs Viney was a fundamentally kind and straightforward woman. Once we had overcome the "My don't you look like your father and isn't it a tragedy he died" hurdle which I soon discovered to be the inescapable prelude to any kind of social contact in Long Chatton, I came to regard her as a potential ally, the only person in the house whose company I actually enjoyed. ("It comes of being reared by a domestic," I overheard Gerald remark to his father, "the girl is really only at home in the kitchen.") But she wasn't informative about my father: a shy child, a quiet young man, someone who had been translated to a kind of martyred uniqueness by his early death. That was all.

But surely there was more?

My determination to find out about my father drove me to that other part of the house where I also felt at home: the attics. There were several of these, running the whole length of the front of the house and piled high with generations of clutter: a totally different world which I loved immediately. There, under the eaves, I was remote, cut off from the rest of the household. I could hear sparrows scuffling under the slates and the distant chiming of the church clock, but the ordinary sounds of the house – the telephone, Elsa's hoover, tradesmen banging on the kitchen door – none of these penetrated my dusty eyrie. Wisps of pale sunlight filtered through the windows which were tiny and high up, giving only a view of clouds and sky. It was bitterly cold there, even on the mildest day, but for an hour or two I could become so absorbed in my search that I forgot my frozen bones and chilled fingers.

I quickly discovered that searching is hard when you don't even know what you're looking for. Or whether what you are looking for ever existed. Best of all would have been to discover something like a diary belonging to my father, so that I might hear him speak, could learn just a little of the kind of man or boy he had been. Failing that I would have been happy to discover letters he had written; even the formal letters a child writes to his parents from school would have been better than nothing.

After several mornings spent battling with the cold and the cobwebs and the dust I was forced to the reluctant conclusion that mine (with the single huge exception of Archie and *Dora's Room*) was definitely not a family of writers. Hoarders, yes. Amazing that huge mounds of cast-off possessions should yield up so little of interest or value: one trunk was crammed full of old mackintoshes white with mould; there was a collapsed heap of back numbers of *Country Life* which had been reduced almost to confetti by nesting mice; there were enough odd shoes to equip a one-legged army. Almost nothing had been thrown away: every butcher's bill and parish magazine, every seed catalogue and theatre programme, every charity appeal and holiday brochure had been tossed into the attic for some future generation to deal with. Perhaps one day a social historian would be delirious with gratitude at such a treasure trove of trivia – but not a diary, not a letter, not even an old school book or album of scraps. Nothing that was of any use to me at all.

146

Until I found the postcards.

A small bundle, twenty or so, in a brown envelope that had been jammed between a broken gramophone and a biscuit tin full of sea-shells. The corner of each card was missing where the stamp had been cut neatly away. They were all addressed to Archie and they were all signed with an exuberant "C". Clancy. My father.

It dawned on me that I had never seen his handwriting before, that I would not even have recognised his signature – though I knew at once that this was him, not some other "C". A huge semi-circular flourish and then a dot. That was all. My father's signature. A bit like a back-to-front bass clef.

I waited for some emotion.

Nothing.

I read the cards.

(It never occurred to me that I was spying on Archie's private correspondence. Postcards are not the place for secrets and, besides, the years had made these the property of spiders and the mice – no longer Archie's.)

Exotic locations with banal messages. "School French not holding up too well" (Arles). "Great architecture and even better wine" (Venice). "Wasted nearly a week waiting for the Land-Rover to be fixed" (southern Greece). "Thought I was dying but food poisoning only" (a view of an amazing gorge in eastern Turkey). "At last a chance to wash my underclothes" (Nepal). Arranging the European ones in date order – and cheating a bit with the blurred ones and the cutaway bits – I gathered that he had done the overland trip to India about five years before I was born.

Well, it was something to know that much, at least.

The last two were of a much later date and from a different continent. South America, in the year of his death.

Dear Archie, God, how I hate this place. I still can't believe all that has happened to us but don't worry, I won't come home until it has all blown over. Keep an eye on Lou and the Rat for me. Sorry has to be the most useless word in the language. C.

Dear Archie, the opposite of wish-you-were-here. Sheer hell, nothing but the heat and a bad conscience for company. I shall end up like one of those tortured creatures in a Graham Greene novel. Any luck with *Dora's Room*? I wonder where she got to. Paul Sobey might help. C.

I read them through quickly a couple of times, then slowly, then meticulously, picking their dry bones for information, but instead all I found was questions, unanswered questions, springing up thick as dragons' teeth.

Won't come home until all *what* has blown over? Why sorry? Why the bad conscience? Wonders where *who* got to? Dora? But if even my father knew who Dora was, why had Archie always made such an enormous mystery of her identity?

I searched through the rest of the postcards but they only yielded more of the "weather is good and so is the food" school of creative writing. Some crisis had driven my father to this uncharacteristic burst of rhetoric, the crisis that had driven him to abandon his wife and child and endure the misery of self-imposed exile in South America. But what crisis?

I sat back on my heels, the cold forgotten.

"Keep an eye on Lou and the Rat— " That was me, the Rat. Not a very flattering term of endearment. Had he called me that? No echo remained in my memory to tell me so if he had.

"I still can't believe all that has happened— "

"Sorry has to be the most useless word— " To whom was he apologising? Archie? Perhaps . . . but equally it could have been to my mother, my grandfather even. Or some other person I did not know. (Or Dora? My mind constructed a scenario where the two brothers had been in love with the same woman, the enigmatic and elusive Dora, who had rejected them both. Archie poured his loss into a magical work of prose; my father escaped with his pain to another continent, another hemisphere.)

I checked the date of the final postcard again: 5th April, one month before his death.

God I hate this place . . . sheer hell . . . some tortured character . . . Just how hellish had his exile been? How intolerable? All that I knew of my father's death was that he had been killed in a plane crash. I had always assumed he had been on a commercial flight, a helpless passenger. But now another possibility occurred to me: there was a young man, alone and far from home. Cut off from all those he loved and weighed down by a guilty conscience, had he perhaps found the hell to be quite simply unendurable?

An image flashed through my mind of a tiny plane, white above the Amazonian jungle, no one but the pilot on board. And the pilot, tortured by homesickness and remorse, can take no more . . . the plane nose-dives, hits the trees, bursts into flames. Yes, perhaps my father's death had happened that way.

I no longer wanted to be alone in the attic. Still clutching my bundle of postcards I went down the narrow steps and through the door which led on to the landing. The telephone was ringing and in the hallway Elsa was busy with her hoover.

I was glad that Paula was planning to visit at the weekend – though if I had been opposed to the idea I'm sure she would have come anyway. Now that I had "got smart" about my inheritance and returned to Chatton Heights, no argument of mine would have kept her away. A stately home, a famous author and an eligible bachelor, what more could a weekend in the country have to offer?

I tried to tell her about the postcards when I picked her up from the station that cold, wet Friday evening but she was far too busy pumping me for information about Gerald and Archie to pay much attention.

"Why spend your time buried in the attics? It's people who are interesting. Have you discovered if Gerald has a serious girlfriend?"

To my relief she was greeted with tolerable warmth

149

by my relatives – but after nearly a week at Chatton Heights I was learning that so little ever happened there that they were probably glad of any diversion. Gerald even condescended to eat supper with us, something he had not bothered to do since my arrival. Tillie had changed into one of those dresses that are properly called "frocks" and had spread lipstick like a fresh wound across her mouth.

Archie, sitting at the head of the table and pouring liberal quantities of my grandfather's claret, smiled at us all benignly. "What a delightful family gathering. Even Gerald, well well, what an honour . . . and Tillie looking as glamorous as a fairy on the Christmas tree. Such a pity we can't pack you away in a box on Twelfth Night. Ah well."

Paula laughed extravagantly. She was wearing a sweater with a huge collar in a shade of darkest purple and earrings as big as gongs and she looked magnificent. She even managed to appear animated while Gerald spoke to her of his cars, in particular of the vintage Daimler he was currently working on.

Archie's voice purred on. "A word of warning, Paula my dear. My son, for reasons only he can explain, uses words like camshaft and carburettor as a form of foreplay. Where more traditional youths come courting with flowers and music, Gerald favours sprockets and big-ends. Isn't that so, Gerald?"

At the mention of courting with music and flowers I thought briefly, painfully, of Adam and his wish for sonnets and a lute, but Gerald, as his father had surely intended, was discomforted. He laughed, then scowled. "Oh well . . ." was all he managed to say, then chobbled his thumb.

Archie murmured, so softly it was as though he was talking to himself alone, but loud enough for all to hear. "Always the master of the pithy phrase . . ." And for a while Gerald hardly spoke at all, until Paula restored his wounded pride with the admission that one of her teenage fantasies had always been to be driven around in a well-appointed Daimler.

Which she did the following morning. So that it wasn't until the afternoon that I managed to persuade her to walk with me to the village and was finally able to tell her about the postcards.

"Why don't you ask Archie?" she said, as soon as I had explained the mystery. "He's the only person now who can help you."

"I don't know if there's much point."

"You're not still nervous of him, are you? You said yourself he's been fine since you arrived."

"But he's not keen to talk about my father, not in any detail, at any rate. Just vague things like 'no problems with Clancy', that sort of thing. Never anything specific."

"Hmm." Paula was thoughtful. "Do you think he might be covering up for your dad in some way?"

"How do you mean?"

"Sounds to me like a classic case of over-compensation. Archie keeps affirming that your father was 'all right' as you say because just before he died something happened that was all wrong. I mean, all that bad conscience stuff doesn't sound too good, does it? Maybe your dad was caught embezzling his old man's funds or having sex with little boys or— "

"I did think it might be something to do with Dora. After all, the way he says it in the postcard – 'I wonder where she's got to' – that makes her sound like a real person, doesn't it? No one says that about some mythic bird or mysterious archetype."

Since Paula belonged firmly to the mysterious archetype school of Dora-appreciation she chose to ignore this. "I reckon it was a cover-up," she said firmly. "Little brother was caught with his hands in the till or something like that and big brother packed him off to South America until the storm blew over."

"You sound like Gerald. He told me my father went to South America simply to get out from under Archie's shadow."

"He could be right."

"But there must be more than that. The postcards

prove that there was a specific reason, some crisis that triggered the whole trip."

"You'll have to ask Archie. No one else can help you."

"Yes, maybe . . ."

We were walking back from the village, taking the route that Adam had showed me when we visited Long Chatton that Sunday. This was another cold, bleak day. The time of year when the turn of the seasons seems to have stopped and it feels as though winter will continue for ever.

When we came to the end of the lane we paused by the gate that led into the orchard.

"Do you recognise this?"

"Am I supposed to?"

"It's where that picture in Dring's room was painted, the one of all the blossom."

"Small world, eh? Talking of which, look who's coming towards us. The young laird of the glen himself. Hi, Gerald, how's dog school today?"

"Pretty good, pretty good, all things considered."

He was accompanied by the two young black labradors he had acquired ten days before, two dogs of quite unsurpassed vitality. I was convinced that their combined energy, if properly harnessed, could power the television sets and tumble dryers of Long Chatton for ever. As it was they had nothing more strenuous to achieve than the total exhaustion of their master which, judging by Gerald's purple cheeks and rasping breath, they had nearly accomplished already.

"Just a question of showing them who's boss," puffed Gerald while the puppies maypole-danced their long leashes around his legs. He wobbled dangerously, growing flustered. "Get back there, Tara. Philo, stop being so bloody stupid, damn you – oh, for Christ's sake . . ."

"As far as I can see it's still an open race," said Paula. She crouched down to caress one and was instantly the victim of a deluge of canine kisses, the dogs' tails and tongues all motoring wildly. "Hey, steady on, you sex maniacs," she laughed, "whoever taught you to kiss like that?"

Gerald was trying to haul them off. "They're not lap dogs, you know!"

Paula allowed the dogs to tumble her over on to the grass and her red hair fell around her shoulders. "No? This one sure thinks he is!"

I was enjoying the scene. Paula's sudden devotion to dogs was for Gerald's benefit entirely. She had gone to WEA classes with her working-class hero and AA meetings with her alcoholic poet, so a touch of hunting, shooting and fishing with Gerald posed no problems.

I did not enjoy what followed. Gerald landed one dog a massive kick in the stomach. It yelped and tried to leap away, only to be caught by the leash and fall back choking. Gerald whacked it across the nose with his fist twice.

"Gerald, stop it!" I shouted.

He had hold of the other dog by the collar and yanked it out of my reach. He struck it several times across the head and the young dog howled with pain.

"Let go of him!" I tried to grab Gerald by the arm but his elbow caught me a blow on the chin that almost knocked me to the ground.

Paula scrambled to her feet. "Are you crazy?" she yelled. "Stop that at once!"

"Mind – " (puff) "your own – " (whack) "bloody business!"

"You can't do that!"

"Gerald, for God's sake stop it!" Paula and I were both shouting at once.

"They have to learn." Both dogs were now whimpering and cringing at his feet and that at least seemed to satisfy him. "It's their own bloody fault after all. Come along, then, heel, damn you."

We both stared in shocked silence as he set off across the orchard. For a moment I thought I was going to be sick; my jaw was throbbing painfully. Both dogs were being hauled on such short leads they choked and struggled for breath.

"Sadistic bastard," said Paula. "What in hell had they done wrong anyway?"

I had a sudden memory of a small boy with yellow hair who smashed his train set against the nursery wall rather than share even one of his precious toys with his visiting cousin. "They made him look a fool," I said.

"What a jerk." Her voice was thick with disgust.

A fine rain was beginning to fall as we walked in silence up the hill towards the house.

"Fern has a mystery for you to explain," said Paula that evening at supper.

"How very intriguing." Archie raised one dark eyebrow and smiled encouragingly, as though unravelling mysteries was his favourite parlour game. "Whatever is it, my dear?"

I was standing at the huge baronial-looking sideboard, putting cold meat and salad on a plate. Supper was generally a simple meal, most often cold, that Mrs Viney assembled before she left in the afternoon. As usual Gerald was absent, no doubt consoling himself in the White Hart for his dogs' insubordination. Tillie was present, silent, apparently unseeing. Often, now, I forgot altogether that she was in the room.

For some reason I felt embarrassed as I resumed my seat. "Oh, it's probably very simple if you know, not really a mystery . . . I thought you might be able to help."

"At your service, my dear. You know you have only to ask."

Archie was the picture of a genial host that evening. He was wearing a loose jacket of faded burgundy velvet and at his throat he wore one of those extravagant silk cravats that seemed to be his favourite sartorial indulgence; this one was in opulent shades of russet and blue.

I hesitated. Paula shot me a glance that said: there you are, I told you he would be happy to help out. "Well," I began, "you know I've been trying to find out more about my father, what sort of man he was . . ."

"Ah yes. *A la recherche du papa perdu.*" It was his

154

favourite joke, repeated each time I ventured any interest in my father. "And you know, don't you, how eager I am to assist you. Your tenacity is quite touching. I can't help wondering if young Gerald would show the same devotion to my lingering ghost."

"But he knows you, so it's different."

"I shall assume the insult was not intended."

I persevered. "While I was in the attic a couple of days ago I found some postcards, ones he'd written to you. Most of them were ordinary enough, pretty boring in fact, but there were a couple from South America that I couldn't make out at all."

Archie's benevolent smile had faded abruptly. His dark eyes were fixed on my face. "Tell me, dear niece, is this pawing through other people's correspondence another of your endearing little foibles we must somehow learn to endure?"

"But they were only— "

"Hell, Archie, everyone reads postcards," said Paula bluntly, "even the postman. They're fair game."

"Is that so? I take it, Fern, that you still have these postcards?"

"They're in my room."

"Then might I humbly suggest you go and get them?"

His sudden coldness was so unexpected that it never occurred to me to refuse. By the time I returned to the dining-room with the postcards Archie had recovered his self-possession. He reached out his hand and, with only the briefest moment of hesitation, I gave him the package. He was smiling as he shuffled through the cards, barely glancing at the writing on the back.

"Ah yes, the famous overland trip to India. It all seems to be fairly straightforward. That was where he met your mother, you know, some louse-ridden Indian temple."

"But those last two, Archie, the ones he wrote from South America," already I was regretting having handed over the precious hoard of cards, "he must have written those about a month before he died."

Archie found the two I meant and frowned, holding

155

them first at arm's length and then close to his eyes as though he had trouble deciphering the words.

I said, "He talks about something happening. Something that drove him to go abroad at that particular time. What was it?"

"Heavens above, Fern, you surely don't expect me to remember that far back, do you? It's all of twenty years."

"Fifteen. But it must have been serious, Archie. He talks about having a bad conscience and being sorry for some reason. It looks as though he's apologising to you. You surely can remember why."

"I shall have to disappoint you after all." And he stowed the postcards back in their envelope. "Your father was always seeing dramas where none existed and this must have been one of those occasions. He was a long way from England, he was homesick, he may even have been running a fever – and he must have begun fretting about all sorts of trivia that everyone over here had quite sensibly forgotten about long before."

"But if it was all so trivial, why didn't he come home? If you read them carefully you can see that it was because of what had happened that he had to stay in South America until it all blew over. Read it and you'll see."

"Really?" Archie made no move to take the postcards from their packet which lay beneath the palm of his beautifully manicured hand. I knew instinctively that he would resist any attempt on my part to retrieve the package. He turned away from me. "Paula, my dear, would you care for more claret?"

I persisted. "He also mentioned *Dora's Room*."

"Ah." His hand, pouring the wine, barely faltered. "Did he now?"

"He asked how you were getting on, suggested a possible publisher."

"How very considerate of him."

"And he wondered where Dora had got to."

Archie glanced quickly at me, then at Paula. "Did you

see these postcards, my dear, these fascinating relics of my brother's?"

"No, but Fern has told me about them."

Archie fingered the rim of his glass. "I can't say that I remember any direct reference to Dora," he said.

"It is there. I can show you."

Quick as a cat Archie slid the postcards into his breast pocket. Recovered his poise. Smiled at me with avuncular benevolence. "It must have been some kind of joke," he said, "we were always having those kind of jokes, you know, playing with names. One forgets the details after so long."

"But I'm sure he meant more— "

Archie interrupted me. "Fern, my dear, I can't help thinking that you are in great danger of taking this preoccupation with my brother just a little too far. Of course, a certain amount of curiosity is quite natural and only to be expected but it seems to me that you are becoming somewhat obsessive. All this prowling around in attics, reading other people's correspondence, trying to construct a major drama about some trivial and long-forgotten incident mentioned on the back of an old postcard, it's not altogether natural, you know. Not really healthy. I'm sure you must be able to find better ways of spending your time."

"It has become important to me."

"And believe me, if I could help you, I would. Now, ladies, I regret that I must leave you."

"Are you keeping the postcards, then?"

"They are addressed to me. It is customary."

"But I thought . . . I don't have anything with his writing on it."

"Then in that case," he removed the packet from his breast pocket and for a moment my spirits soared, "which would you prefer, dysentery or engine failure? Why not have both and I'll throw in dirty underwear in Nepal for good measure. Never let it be said that I lack generosity – but I also like to have something to remember him by. He left few enough traces, God knows."

"Archie, wait. Before you go, there's one other thing I want to ask you."

"If you insist." The raised eyebrow no longer indicated amusement at solving mysteries; rather he was impatient, his anger barely restrained.

"It's about the plane crash in which he died. Was he . . . I mean, were there other people involved?"

"There was no other plane involved, if that's what concerns you. Some kind of engine failure, I believe, the aircraft lost control."

"But, were there other passengers or . . ." Once again I could see the plane, small and fragile as an insect against the dark green canopy of the rainforest and a single man, a man who had reached the limits of his endurance, alone in the cockpit . . .

"Now I catch your drift. It was a commercial flight, Fern. Not a large aircraft, fifteen, perhaps twenty on board. There were only three survivors, one of whom was the pilot. Somewhere I still have the newspaper report which appeared in England at the time. I'll give it to you if I find it. Or you might come across it if you continue your ferreting in the attic. Though on the whole I think it advisable that you endeavour to moderate this somewhat obsessive search. Good night, my dears, and do finish the claret."

He walked out slowly, with the slight stiffness in his gait of someone who has been drinking since mid-morning, which he had, but who wishes, against all the evidence, to appear sober. Tillie, who had sat throughout the meal in silence, stood up and followed him out.

I said, "He didn't like me asking him about *Dora's Room*. Or about my father."

Paula broke off a bunch of grapes and put one in her mouth. "There's been so much pain in his life. You can't blame him if he hates to be reminded of it."

"It's more than that, Paula. I know he remembers why my father wrote those postcards but he refuses to tell me."

"Then he must be protecting him, like you said he

would. Your dad screwed up somehow and the family managed to hush it up and pack him off to South America. You can't blame Archie if he doesn't want to bring it up now."

"I'd rather know the worst about my father than nothing at all."

"Why? What's the point? Look, Archie could be right, you know. You are getting a bit morbid about all of this. Maybe you should forget the whole thing. I mean, you insist on sleeping in his old room even though you practically need a snow plough to get in there, it's so cold. Aren't you getting just a tiny bit Oedipal about all this? It won't bring him back, you know."

"I'm not stupid, Paula, of course I know that. But you don't understand what it's like. You've got both your parents, even though you might not always like them much, at least they're around, you know who they are, what they're like. What do I know about mine? Only that my mother was insane and my father had to go to South America for some mysterious reason that Archie won't talk about, and that he was killed in an air crash."

"At least you know it wasn't suicide."

"But what about Dora? The postcard said— "

"And then again, maybe it didn't. Archie's right, it must have been some private joke they had. You can hardly expect him to remember after so long. It's no big deal, Mary, really it's not. You keep seeing intrigue and suicide everywhere. It's not like you. You're supposed to be the cool, calm and collected one, remember? Look, come back to Bristol with me tomorrow. It must be pretty depressing here on your own."

"On the contrary," I said firmly, "I'm just beginning to enjoy myself."

The next morning I chanced to go into the smoking-room to find a book that I had left there. Elsa, with cold and mottled fingers, was cleaning the ashes of the previous day's fire. Among the greyness something white and angular was sticking out. I swooped, startling poor Elsa, and picked it up . . . all that remained of my father's second postcard: the bottom right-hand corner. A patch of gaudy flowers and on the back:

—ire,
—gland.

Elsa was all concern. "Is that something important?"

"Yes. No. It doesn't matter."

I pushed the fragment back among the still-warm ashes. I like to have something to remember him by, Archie had said. Liar.

This time I said nothing to Paula.

The following afternoon as I drove her to the station, she repeated her belief that I should return to Bristol.

"Don't tell me you're having doubts about my family," I teased, "you're the one who always said they were so wonderful."

"Well, Archie's still great, but as for your creepo cousin . . . do you know he made a pass at me last night?"

"Gerald?"

"After you'd gone back to your igloo. He returned from wherever it is he goes to get smashed on a Saturday evening and came rolling into my room. Not even any sweet talk of camshafts or carburettors. He launched straight into his 'how about it' routine. I told him if he didn't leave I'd break his head open with the silver candlestick."

"Whatever happened to aristocratic romance?"

"Are you joking? After the way he treated those poor dogs I couldn't bear to have him touch me, not if he was a goddam duke. And I always used to think you British were supposed to be so soft on animals. Anyway, I've never known anyone so slow to catch on. He just kept trying so I told him the next time I wanted a screw with a Grade A sadist with commendation in dog abuse he'd be the first to know. He still didn't get the message."

"So what did convince him?"

"A kick in the shins. Lucky for him it wasn't higher. And do you know what Prince Charming said then? He said he'd known all along that you and I were a couple of dykes and that people like us were disgusting perverts who had no business troubling decent folk like him. That was the gist of his argument, anyway, and I didn't see much point in denying it since he was on the point of leaving. I reckoned I should tell you though, just in case it crops up again."

"Thank you, Paula."

"What a creep. And Tillie makes my skin crawl. Don't you think she should be in some kind of a home? Listen, Mary, you can still change your mind and come home. Maybe you're right about that place. There is something odd about it. I had horrific dreams there and, as you know, I'm not usually given to nightmares."

"I'll be all right."

"I get a sinking feeling every time I hear you say that. Why do you have to stay there anyway? You won't find out any more about your father; it was all too long ago."

"Maybe you're right but— " I broke off. We had reached the station and I was relieved not to have to explain to Paula what I barely understood myself.

I only knew that I had glimpsed, on the morning that Dring was manhandled into the ambulance, what it means to drown in a sea of insanity.

My grandfather's bleak mansion seemed to offer me at least the possibility of a lifeline: that golden voice I had heard on the window-seat, stray secrets from my father's past, were enough to make me hope that here I might, one day, discover some bedrock of my father's strength and so escape my mother's cruel legacy.

Chapter 6

I was disappointed, annoyed even, by Paula's lack of interest in my discovery of the postcards; I was cross with myself for having allowed them to fall into Archie's hands. And yet . . . and yet . . . surely Archie's behaviour, first siezing them, then burning them before anyone else had a chance to read what my father had written, proved that he did remember much more than he admitted. It was the reference to Dora that had unsettled him, that he had been at pains to deny. Surely his action added weight to the theory that she was based on a real person?

Suddenly I remembered Adam's rueful, half-exasperated words, "There's a story there, a real story, if only I could dig it out," and a huge longing to see him again washed over me. Several times that morning after Paula's departure I went to the telephone under the crossed pikestaffs in the hall and began to dial his number, but each time my courage failed me. After the catastrophe at Alderly Drive that night I could hardly expect him to respond with his former enthusiasm – and I cringed at the thought that I might hear boredom or coldness in his voice. In the end I spent all afternoon labouring over a letter telling him about the postcards and Archie's reaction to my discovery. I was struggling for a casual "just thought you might be interested" tone – but even I could tell that the finished result sounded hopelessly insincere, like a jolly entry in a girls' school magazine, but I decided to post it anyway.

You don't have that much to lose, I told myself cruelly as I walked down to the post. The village, mellow stone walls washed in late afternoon sunshine, was prettier than I had ever seen it: children were coming home from school, an old man was pruning his roses, a woman reached stout arms to haul down her washing. I longed to be a part of such well-ordered lives. As I shoved the letter into the post box I wondered how Adam would respond. I felt a bit like a shipwrecked mariner putting a note in a bottle and tossing it to the waves. Marooned, somehow, and not even sure there would be a reply.

I continued my search in the attics over the next few days, but with ever less hope of finding anything. The quest had settled into a kind of habit, a way of filling time.

It was a morning of torrential rain: the sky was so dark I had to switch on the overhead light and the usual bird-scuffling noises were joined by the plink-plink of water dripping through the roof into the flowered chamber pot beneath and I was on the point of giving up when I noticed something poking out from between a dressmaker's dummy and a pair of tattered camp beds. A bulky object, mostly obscured by a paisley bedspread.

I pulled it out. A theatre. About a metre in height, its proscenium arch was cut from a single sheet of plywood and the curtains were painted in lavish red and gold. The stage had been broken long ago but there were still the spaces in the wings where the backdrops could be slotted into place.

Not much help in my search for clues about my father – but nevertheless, a good treasure to find on a rainy morning.

It didn't take long to discover the rest of the equipment: several scenes painted on stiff cardboard – a Norman castle, a Red Indian encampment, a moonscape, a deserted island – and the puppets themselves. The scenery was the work of a childish hand: crude brushstrokes and clumsily applied paint, but the puppets had been fashioned by a professional. Like all neglected puppets they had become hopelessly entangled: the maiden/princess/heroine was twined sinuously round the figure of the witch/wicked stepmother/bad queen while the youthful hero was locked in a grotesque embrace with a

163

strange-looking old man with white hair and a gaunt, fierce face.

By now the cold and the damp of the attics seemed to have soaked right through to my bones and I carried my treasure down to the kitchen where the Aga was always warm and where, at this time of the morning, Mrs Viney could be relied upon to be brewing coffee.

She had been baking. The elaborate scales, with their chipped red paint and their array of graduated weights, stood with packets of flour and sugar and raisins on the scrubbed pine table. She threw up white hands in mock horror as I came into the kitchen.

"Heavens above, whatever have you got there?" she exclaimed. "You've been up in the attics again, I can tell by the state you're in. Don't blame me if you catch your death of cold, and careful where you put that down – it looks filthy."

"Yes, but look, Mrs Viney, it's a theatre – and I'm sure some hot coffee will save me from pneumonia."

"I've just put some on. A theatre, eh? So it is, a proper little theatre, well I never. It looks like . . . why, I do believe it is!"

She had been reaching cups down from the dresser but now she came over to examine the theatre more closely and her face grew pink with excitement. "Yes, look, and there's the puppets too! I thought it had all been destroyed long ago and now look . . . well, *won't* he be pleased!"

"Who?"

"Why, Dad, of course. This was *his* theatre."

"Tom's?" My surprise was understandable. Nothing that I had so far learned of the old gardener hinted that he harboured a secret obsession for model theatres. "But if it belonged to your father then what was it doing in the attic here?"

"He made it for the boys, of course, for your father and Mr Archie."

"He *made* it? And the puppets too? But they're brilliant, I thought they must have been bought."

"Dad made them all right. Wonderful with his hands, he was, until the arthritis got to him, can't hardly lift a stick now. Used to make things for charity sometimes. I remember when he made this." She had got down on her hands and knees and was examining the theatre with childlike pleasure. "It was the summer I first came to work here, must have been the year your grandmother died. I reckon Dad thought a theatre might cheer the boys up a bit, what with their mother being so ill and all. Got quite carried away, he did, called it his masterpiece."

"And so it is. But I'm sure Archie told me they weren't allowed these kinds of toys, nothing imaginative like a theatre."

"That was the whole trouble of it. I don't reckon your grandfather knew about the theatre, not while his wife was ill and all the rest of it. The house was so full of nurses and relatives and so on that the boys were pretty well forgotten. It was later that the trouble came. Furious he was, I can remember the row, it went on for days. And of course, the puppets had to go. Near broke Mr Clancy's heart, poor little mite."

"What about Archie?"

"Oh, he never played with it much. Too old for that sort of thing and anyway he was away at school most of the time. It was Clancy always . . . I'm going to fetch Dad now and show him. He'll be pleased as punch about this. He's around here somewhere this morning, potting shed most like."

She hurried out. Above the noise of the rain drumming on the kitchen roof I could hear her calling to her father. I poured myself some coffee, wrapped cold fingers around the cup. Looked down at the red and yellow theatre and the tangled ball of puppets.

My father's theatre. Did the ghost of a small boy still linger in the wings? I smiled. This was the moment when I should stumble on a secret hiding place beneath the stage and find a cache of letters, tiny diaries that would begin to tell me what I wanted to know.

165

But there was no secret hiding place. I knew because I had looked already.

Tom Page hurried into the kitchen. He was drenched to the skin. Despite the rain he wore nothing but a thin jacket: one would have thought him impervious to the cold but for the chronic cough with which he was plagued. He had a face that in old age was returning to boyishness: bright blue eyes, jug-handle ears and a smile which was roguish, an apple-scrumping grin. He was grinning now as he contemplated the theatre.

"Didn't I tell you it was around here somewhere? In the attic, eh? I thought you said you'd looked there, bet you never even bothered. Just look at it! I'd forgotten all the . . . pretty good work for an amateur, eh?"

"It's beautiful." My compliment was sincere.

"Did it all myself too. No one to teach me. Just picked up a piece of wood and worked away at it until I'd got what I wanted. Must have been a natural skill, eh? Not many have that kind of skill these days. Craftsmanship. Takes patience. Can't rush it. And none of the youngsters have any patience, they want to learn it all straight away but it can't be done. Oh no. Look at these faces, no short cuts there. Each one's real, isn't it? Those faces look right at you."

"They're wonderfully lifelike."

"It's a gift, carving. Pity about the stage, though. Still, all it wants is a bit of fixing up. I could do that, still have the tools around somewhere. A spot of glue and some paint. I could have it as good as new again."

"Dad, you haven't got the— "

He ignored her. "I'll sort the puppets out too. Shame to let them go to ruin."

"Can you really repair it all? I'd love to see how it used to look."

Ted had been carrying out his inspection crouched painfully on one knee, but now he stood up and stared at me and his gaze was very direct. "Are you interested in puppets, then?"

"I've always been fascinated by them."

166

"Just like your dad. He thought this was wonderful. Said it was the best present he could have. You should have seen his face when he sat behind the theatre. Magic. Good little hands he had too. You should have seen him."

"Did he paint the backdrops?"

He nodded. "Spent hours on them."

"He must have hated having them taken away."

"A bad business altogether. It was the only time I stood up to old Mr Miller, first and last, I was that angry. It's not right, I told him, where's the harm in a theatre, you tell me that if you can. But it was no use, and he docked me a week's pay for good measure."

I was appalled. "Why did he do that?"

"Said I wasted *his* time making it. Well, most was done in my own time. You'd think any normal father would've been glad to see his boy so cheered up at a time like that. But no. There was no arguing with him, not once his wife had died – and he'd been bad enough before. Shades of the prison house about the growing boy. That's the truth."

"I didn't know you liked poetry too," I said. There seemed no end to the range of Tom's interests.

"Your dad told me that. Must have been about then. Sitting on a bucket he was, watching me while I budded the chrysanths. Never mind, Tom, he said, shades of the prison house . . . Proper little philosopher I thought he was. I can remember his face now as he said it. Sort of old-looking for a child."

"Did he spend a lot of time with you?"

"Fair bit, then. But that was before he went to school, proper boarding school I mean. Must have been in the September for his mother died in August and he was packed off after. Of course it all changed once he'd been away. Sad, really, but I'd seen the same thing happen with Mr Archie. Now then, Susan," he turned to his daughter, "I'll take the theatre with me now and you can bring the other bits when you come down this afternoon. It'll be a fine thing to get them all smartened up again."

Mrs Viney sniffed her disapproval. "You'll never do it, not with your bad hands."

"You keep to your job and I'll do mine."

I managed to persuade him to borrow a raincoat – but I was quickly thwarted when he used it to cover the theatre, not himself. We could hear him coughing as he staggered out into the rain.

"Aren't you afraid he's the one will catch pneumonia in all this bad weather?"

Mrs Viney went to the sink, one of those old-fashioned glazed sinks the size of a small bathtub. She began work on a mound of potatoes, the peel falling from her knife in long elegant whorls. "He's contrary by nature," she said phlegmatically, "it's what's kept him going so long."

That afternoon I went to the library. No books of poetry there, as I had suspected, but there was a dictionary of quotations.

> Shades of the prison-house begin to close
>   Upon the growing boy,
> But he beholds the light, and whence it flows,
>   He sees it in his joy.

The light must have seemed pretty dim, I thought, to the young lad so swiftly packed off to boarding school after the death of his mother. His theatre and precious puppets banished to the attic.

It was a couple of days later that I found myself alone, one lunchtime, with Archie. Tillie had retired to her room that morning with a headache and a singularly gory-looking video. Gerald was simply "out". He never told anyone where he went and grew hostile and angry at the most conventional of questions. ("Did you have a good day?" "None of your bloody business." One learnt, as he would have said, not to ask.)

We sat in silence while Mrs Viney wheeled in the trolley and served out portions of baked fish and buttered carrots. The vast table with our two lonely place-settings marooned at one polished end and the single-bar electric fire placed behind our chairs to wage a hopeless war against the cold seemed to represent all the grandiose discomfort of Chatton Heights.

Mrs Viney paused before returning to the kitchen. She sniffed loudly. I knew that she had been troubled with a cold but the sniff implied more than that. "Do you want me to take *her* some as well?" she demanded of Archie.

"You might as well."

She wheeled the trolley out again, still sniffing her disapproval. I had quickly realised that the relationship between Tillie and Mrs Viney did not reflect their relative status as the master's widow and the cook. Mrs Viney made no secret of her contempt for Tillie, while Tillie avoided Mrs Viney as much as she could. No one ever called Tillie "Mrs Miller" just as Mrs Viney was never addressed by her Christian name by anyone except her father. It was all very puzzling.

Archie began to eat his meal without a word. As though he had forgotten I was there. When not dispersing exaggerated *bonhomie* he often lapsed into a cocoon of silence. It was only my nervous awareness of this unexpected tête-à-tête that drove me to begin a conversation. "Why is Mrs Viney always so down on poor Tillie?" I asked.

Still wrapped in his cocoon, Archie stared at his plate. Then he began to speak, and as he did so it was as if the layers of caterpillar silk in which he had been swathed were being unravelled slowly. "Tillie?" he asked, glancing up as though surprised to see me sitting there. "Oh yes, I see what you mean. Well, Mrs Viney has been with us a long time, pretty well all her life. Tillie on the other hand is a relatively recent visitor to the scene. At first she was a general purpose dogsbody and no one paid her much attention. Mrs Viney was about the only person who was kind to her in those days. Then Tillie moved upstairs, so to speak, committed the unforgivable sin of becoming first the mistress, then the wife of the lord and master – or however my father was construed. I daresay that in Mrs Viney's fairly rudimentary view of things Tillie quite simply got above herself and she has no doubt been endeavouring to remind the unfortunate Tillie of her right and proper station in life ever since. Thus do the labouring classes reward any hapless member of their group who presumes to raise his or her sights above that humble level of aspiration to which they were born."

"I see."

When Archie began to answer my question his words were simple, his manner unaffected, but by the time he finished he was once again the genial master of the extravagant phrase that others saw. I almost felt I was supposed to burst into applause and demand an encore.

Instead I said, "Poor Tillie. It must be so lonely for her."

Archie shrugged. "Tillie's been alone so long she doesn't know any more what loneliness is." And he continued eating placidly. There was a coldness in his words, a desolation. I wished I had not disturbed his reverie but now, having been aroused, he had grown convivial.

"And how is the worthy Madame de Rhin? What is the most recent report from her resting place in the bosom of the National Health?"

I was surprised. He had never referred to Dring before and I had been unaware that he knew of her existence. "Much the same," I replied. "I telephoned the ward sister yesterday afternoon and she said it was too soon to say when she would be well enough to come home." (Or if she would ever come home – but I didn't tell him that.) "But I shall see her myself in a couple of days. She sounds in good spirits. The rest, and all the attention, do her as much good as anything else."

"Good, good. I'm glad to hear it. And I must say, your loyalty to the old lady is most gratifying to me."

Again I was startled. "It is?"

"Certainly. It proves my original analysis of the situation was correct. It was, you must agree, a considerable risk to allow you to remain in her care – hardly a conventional choice of guardian. But at the time I considered further disruption of your environment was to be avoided at all cost. And, of course, the cost was considerable."

I set down my knife and fork. All appetite vanished. "I never thought you had anything to do with it."

"Who else? I was your next of kin."

"I didn't know . . ."

"Once I saw how your mother was deteriorating I persuaded her to make me your guardian in case of her death or – or other incapacity. It saved a god-awful mess, as things turned out."

"And my grandfather?"

"Not in the least bit interested. He was busy winding up his business affairs. By then even he had accepted that I had to follow my literary career and with your father dead there was no one left to take over from him. He was only too grateful when I volunteered to make provision for your welfare, especially as there was the added complication of your mother. Madame de Rhin was not keen to take on the burden of looking after her as well."

The fear came over me again, that fear I had known when I first heard his voice, that fear of the small child standing at the top of the stairs while a man comes to stop her seeing what will happen to her mother.

I said, "You were there, weren't you, when they took my mother away?"

Archie passed his hand over his eyes. "I suppose I must have been. The events of that summer are not ones I care to dwell on. Your mother, I believe, was admitted to hospital shortly before my own wife's death."

This time I had no urge to applaud: there was no denying the strength of his emotion. A tiny muscle flickered, just below his left eye. He poured himself a drink.

"Dring always said it was best to forget."

"Obviously a woman of great good sense."

"Yes."

Silence again, but this time it was a silence that was almost companionable. Just a glimpse of genuine emotion but it was enough to make me wonder if my instinctive distrust had been wrong.

He finished his drink, poured another, and said, "So

you're telling me I did the right thing, are you? That poor old Madame D.R. with her funny hats and her moustache was the best of a bad bargain? I must say you're a credit to her now, my dear. Beauty reared by the ludicrous Beast." He smiled at me then but there was something not quite avuncular in his smile and I glanced away quickly.

I said, "She took good care of me, yes."

"So she should, the amount I paid her."

"*You* paid her?"

"Where else do you suppose the money came from? Dr Bloody Barnado's?"

"I knew that we received money from the solicitors each month but I never thought . . . I always assumed my father had made some kind of provision for us before he left."

"Your poor dear papa was always too woolly-minded to make provision for anyone. He could hardly buy himself a train ticket without screwing up. I had to sort out his finances after he died – bloody chaos they were too – and arrange things so that you and that old lady could survive together."

"So it was you who planned this with the solicitors – and with Dring."

"Initially, yes."

"I never knew you had anything to do with her."

"Didn't she tell you? I daresay she had her reasons for keeping quiet. Once I'd persuaded her to carry on looking after you – bullied and bribed her more like – I had as little to do with the whole business as possible. Hardly the kind of female I'd climb mountains for. And you'll appreciate that I had problems of my own at the time. We were obliged to meet each year to assess the situation. The solicitor and I would try to find out how you were getting on and she'd do her utmost to wheedle more money out of us. The crafty old witch must have a merry fortune stacked away by now. When you were about twelve or thereabouts I thought you should go to boarding school, but our Madame Rhino wouldn't hear of it. She said you needed the stability only she could

172

give you. And in view of your mother's weakness I did not consider it right to press the point. Would you have liked to go away to school?"

"I would have hated it."

"Good. I'm glad to think we acted for the best after all. There was always the possibility she was feathering her own nest and not thinking of you at all. Still, it was all worth the expense if, as you say, you were happy."

"No need to worry about that."

"And here you are, a credit to – but Fern, are you feeling all right?" His heavy-lidded eyes searched my face. Something told me it was important not to betray weakness.

"I'm fine." I forced myself to eat a mouthful of the food which now tasted about as appetising as shredded cardboard. The chewing seemed to take for ever. Then I said, "There's just one thing that has always puzzled me."

"Yes?"

"Why did you and my grandfather never want me to visit here before? It's not as if it was far to come."

"Distance had nothing to do with it. No, you've your female guard dog to thank yet again. I thought you should maintain contact with your family, what was left of it anyway, but she made it impossible. Time after time we sent the car but the driver always came back alone. Either you had a cold or had mistaken the day and gone out or somehow it wasn't convenient. When I did finally manage to pin her down she said you didn't want to see us, that contact with the family only upset you. So we had to leave it at that."

"She never told me."

"No? Devious old crone; maybe she was afraid you'd want to move back here and then she'd lose her sinecure."

Silence. Block out the thought of Dring. Only staying for the money. Too horrible to think of.

Archie continued eating, his florid cheeks moving rhythmically as he chewed his food. A flake of fish remaining in the corner of his mouth. A man I had imagined to be a stranger. And yet he had been in my life from

173

the beginning, always just out of sight. Controller of my childhood.

Don't let him see the hurt.

I laid down my knife and fork, pushed the plate forward slightly. Easy, casual. Looked up and asked, "So why *did* my grandfather leave so much to me? Do you know?"

In a mirror image of my movements Archie too laid down his knife and fork, pushed his plate forward slightly, leaned back in his chair. He emptied his glass with relish and smiled as he poured himself another measure of wine. But this time his smile was inward, secret, as though he and the bottle shared an insight known only to them.

"Who can tell?" he asked, and now he was no longer the jovial public figure but a private man, alone, hardly even aware that I was listening. "Reparation perhaps, atonement for past neglect. An image of how things might have been. Or a sense that you had somehow managed to evade the family net and must therefore be scooped back, returned to the fold. You must not be allowed to go free. Or perhaps, quite simply, there was no one else."

He looked at me and smiled.

"Or maybe he too was mad," he said.

I had intended to spend that afternoon in the attics but, just for the moment, the heart had gone out of my search.

I walked in the garden.

It was a cold day. It seems now that it was always cold that winter at Chatton Heights – but perhaps that was the coldness within. The sun shone low in a sky of milky blue. Bare branches stirred in the wind.

I daresay it is possible to feel more desolate, more utterly alone, than I did then – but if so I can't imagine it.

Wandering idly. Nowhere in particular to go. Paths coated with the slime of autumn's old leaves. Paths that I knew with a stranger's eye, that should have been coloured with the memory of holidays and childish games.

174

I took the path through the laurel to the old summer house. Once, I was told, this had looked out across the lawn towards the house. Now, like Sleeping Beauty's palace, it was grown around with brambles and young saplings. Gloomy here beneath the holm oak.

Too cold – keep moving. The path divides, one way to the orchard, the other to the sunken rose garden. Follow that one. Bushes that were planted when the war ended, their stems as thick as my wrist, moss hanging from the branches.

Oh Dring, wasn't it enough that I needed you? Couldn't you have stayed simply because you loved me? Bullied and bribed . . . how long did it take, what threats were needed, to force her to agree? How much money? Bullied and bribed – a grotesque basis for the only ties of love I could remember in my life. But what had I expected? I had never analysed her position in the house; she was, quite simply, *there* – and that was all that mattered. Just as the cheque arrived each month from the solicitors: a hard fact, sufficient in itself, like spring sunshine or the delivery of milk. A fact. I suppose if I had bothered to think of it at all I imagined that she had been as lost and lonely as I was, that she needed a child to love as much as I desperately needed her.

Not so. To this day I don't know if it was malice or simple thoughtlessness that caused Archie to lay bare the bones of our relationship like that – but whatever his motive the effect was devastating.

Leave the sunken rose garden. Wide steps upwards to a gravel path. Borders on either side overgrown with a thick tangle of weeds. Questions thick as weeds in my head.

Why me? Why leave everything to me? In all those years he never bothered to see me once – why not? Was it still shame at the scandal that had driven my father to South America? Why had Clancy left us when he did, when he must have known that we needed him, my mother and I, more than ever? Leaving us with an old woman who cared so little that she had to be "bullied and bribed" to remain when tragedy struck. And then those other questions, the ones that would not go away: why the mystery about Dora's identity, the Dora my father also knew? And why did Frances take her own life? Was there perhaps a connection between the mysterious Dora and my poor aunt's suicide?

No answers anywhere. My family might have been Sicilians so closely did they adhere to the principle of omerta. I had tried Tillie but her answers were more confused than my questions: "Always meant well, I think . . . but sometimes misunderstood . . . couldn't swim, well, could swim but not strong enough, no one could be . . . your grandfather sometimes too strong but . . ." I knew that Gerald thought his grandfather deranged and was seeing lawyers about his chances of getting the will altered in his favour. Even Mrs Viney: "I'm sure he knew what he was doing but these old ones can be headstrong as children." And now Archie: reparation, atonement, a glimpse of how things might have been.

Money. He threw money at me after he was dead to ease his guilty conscience after years of neglect. No need to worry about *her*, she'll be all right. She's getting all the money. That's settled then. And the money for Dring.

That hurt the worst of all.

Walking beside the empty vegetable beds. A few umbrellas of rhubarb amongst the docks and dandelions.

Poor little rich girl.

Imagine if you can that you discover suddenly that the man you are in love with, the man you have built your life and hopes around, has all along been paid to court you by an over-anxious parent. Every touch of love, every murmur of endearment, measured out in cold cash.

Rooks flying overhead. Ragged. Trailing black harsh cries.

It makes you feel like nothing, let me tell you. Worse than nothing.

I interrupted Tillie and her video long enough to give her some garbled story of the hospital wanting to see me about Dring. Mistress of the garbled story, she accepted it without comment.

Only when I was crossing the court to the old coach house which served as a garage, did I notice Gerald returning from the fields with his two black puppies. Usually when he saw me he ostentatiously changed direction so that our paths wouldn't cross. Perversely, on the one occasion when all I wanted was to leave with as little fuss as possible, he halted me with what passed, for him, as a friendly greeting: "Sneaking off, are you?"

"The hospital phoned and asked that I see them urgently about Dring."

"Must mean she's about to snuff it, eh?"

He stood in front of me. He was wearing the waxed jacket and wellington boots of a countryman. The two dogs no longer gambolled at his feet: they crawled towards me on their bellies and cringed. Gerald was carrying a heavy wooden stick and his face was flushed with exercise.

I said, "What have you been doing to those poor dogs?"

"Not for squeamish little girls to know about," he grinned. "Are you away for long?"

"That depends."

"You'll be back."

"What do you mean?"

"It's got to you already, I can tell. This house, the place, everything." He spoke with a certain relish, like a macabre doctor who delights in telling the patient his illness is incurable. "And once that happens, you can't break away, not ever."

"What nonsense you talk, Gerald."

"You think so? Just wait and see. You'll be back soon enough, just like the rest of us. Do you think we like it here any better than you do? You think I wouldn't rather be anywhere than this dump with Tillie batting around like an evil fairy and my father grinding on about what a bloody genius he is and how he can still pull any girl he wants?"

"So why don't you leave? No one is stopping you."

Gerald stared at me for a moment, and there was a weird mixture of stupidity and cunning in his small, pale eyes. "You want to know why the old man left it all to you, don't you? Don't bother to deny it, I've heard you whining on to everybody. Well, I could tell you . . ."

He was such a child. If I showed any interest in what he had to say he'd never yield the information. "I'm going to be late." I tried to pass him but Gerald caught my arm.

"He wasn't really crazy, you know, not court-of-law crazy anyway, though I'll prove he was if that's what is needed to get me what should by rights be mine."

"What you choose to do is no concern of— "

"Control. That's what he wanted. You'd escaped the trap all alone and he hated that. He wanted you here, with us, suffering just like we all suffer. That bloody stupid will of his was just a great big expensive net to trap you in and it worked. Here you are now, wriggling and twisting and you think you're free to leave but you can't, not any more. Not ever."

I pulled my arm free. "If he was so hellfire keen to see me here then how come he never even invited me to visit? How come he never came to see me, never even sent a card?"

"Maybe he tried to, I don't know. Pa and Tillie were always dead against it. They didn't want you here at all."

"But your father said— "

"Yeah?" A mocking query.

"He always said he wanted me to visit but that Dring stood in the way."

"Shit, I don't know. And I don't much care, either. My dad's the biggest liar around. Almost as bad as I am."

And he began to laugh.

I could still hear his laughter as I reversed my car out of the coach house and drove away as fast as the potholes and my shaking hands would allow.

When I arrived in the ward Dring was conducting a

one-sided conversation with her neighbour, a white-haired wisp of a lady who looked as if all she wanted was to be left in peace to sleep – or even to die. Her greeting to me was typically abrupt. "You've taken your time to visit, haven't you? I've been here weeks."

"Ten days, Dring. And I came to see you before."

"Feels like bloody months."

I unloaded fruit and magazines. "You're looking well." The ward sister had told me that Madame de Rhin was unfortunately an extremely difficult patient – which I found encouraging. A co-operative Dring would have been a contradiction in terms, offering small prospect of recovery.

"It's more than I feel. You'd think if they can put men on the moon they could sort this leg out for me."

"Is it no better?"

"Worse, much worse, though the buggers are too mealy-mouthed to admit it. Well, where are they then? You did bring some, didn't you?"

"Two packets, but I don't think you should— "

She pulled a face. "Better than nothing, I suppose. Quick then, pass them over before the bloody Gestapo see you."

Two packets of cigarettes slid beneath the bedclothes and into Dring's copious handbag. She smiled then, as pleased by the subterfuge as by the prospect of a smoke. "That's better." She settled back on the pillows, already satisfied. Dressed in a cerise nightgown I had bought for her when she first went into hospital she looked a grotesque caricature of old age, mutton dressed up as pink-beribboned lamb.

"Dring, there's something . . . I've been talking to Archie. I never knew you used to meet him each year."

"You never asked." She fussed irritably with the frilled cuff of her nightgown. "You know," she hissed conspira-torially, "that woman in the next bed, she's on the way out. After a week in here you can tell, it becomes an instinct."

I ignored this, only hoping that the old lady Dring was

179

referring to had not heard her diagnosis. I said, "I'm asking you now. How often did you and Archie meet?"

"Every year in November, regular as clockwork. At the solicitor's office."

"What did you talk about?"

"Money. Never anything else. Just money."

"Money?"

"Oh, he'd ask if you were all right, just to be polite. Fat lot he cared. Fine, I'd say. Good, he'd say. But we need more money, I'd say. Oh yes? he'd say. Then we'd bargain for a bit and the solicitor would agree a sum for the coming year and off I'd go. A bit like those union people really – except we never went on strike."

"But when you asked for the money, was it your wages or the money that we had to live off?"

"It was all the same, wasn't it? Your money, my money – we both had to live in that house and eat and pay the bills. And your uncle had no more idea than a child what it all cost, always lived in someone else's house. That was his trouble."

"Didn't you save any money, then?"

"Certainly, put some by every month. Well, I never knew how long he'd keep paying up, did I – and where would we have been if he stopped, eh? I wasn't to know your grandfather would up and leave the bloody lot to you. And you never know when a little bit put by will come in handy. That's where the money came from for that car of yours."

"I wish I'd asked you about all of this before." I shuddered to think of the malice that lingered in the shadows at Chatton Heights, malice in the very air that had made me suddenly suspicious even of Dring. I took her hand, the skin so leathery with age it was grown smooth as a reptile's hide. Dring, never given to demonstrations of affection, shifted uneasily. I said, "It all seems so obvious now. But why did you stop me from going to Chatton Heights when my grandfather wanted to see me?"

"I told you before, didn't I, you went there once and that was enough. Just after your mother went into hospital, before your aunt died. Once was more than enough."

"Why?"

"Different reasons. It upset you. All the nightmares began again. And the not-eating. I'm not sure why. There was your cousin for a start – if ever a child needed strangling at birth it was that one. Your grandfather didn't see you anyway, too busy with his business. All over the place. And as for your uncle, a nastier piece of work I never met. He was the one pushed your mother over the edge."

"What? How? What do you mean?"

"Just that. Don't ask me. But he did."

"How?"

"I told you, don't ask me."

I fought down my frustration. When Dring's face assumed that closed expression there was no reward or threat I knew of that would make her talk. Do not trespass. Do not ask.

I said, "I know she hated him." ("The devil wrote *Dora's Room*.") "She thought he was a devil."

Dring chuckled. "I'm sure she had her reasons. And if you want my advice you won't go spending too much time there now either, even if you do own it all. The place isn't healthy. I thought so then and I can see now by the look in your eyes that it's getting you down. You come back to Bristol and then you can bring me ciggies every day and one in the eye to the bloody nurses."

"Just one more question, Dring. Do you know why my father had to go off to South America when he did?"

"Business. It was business, wasn't it? Something to do with closing down an office."

"But there was another reason too, a personal one. He wrote to Archie about it, said he 'had to' get away. When I asked Archie he said he'd forgotten – but I know that's not true. Did my father do something wrong?"

"How should I know? You and all your questions – I'm not a bloody encyclopaedia, you know."

"Did he ever mention someone called Dora?"

181

Dring closed her eyes, pursed her mouth shut like a child refusing food. She did look very tired. An old faded mongrel face above a torrent of bright nylon.

"I'm sorry, Dring. I didn't mean to wear you out. It's just that there's so much I need to know, so many puzzles I can't untangle."

"Leave them, Mary." Her eyes were still closed, her voice so soft I had to lean forward to catch the words. "Your parents are dead, love, they've gone. Get on with your own life. You can't go back."

"I must understand."

"Why?"

The single word was barely a breath on the hospital air. There was no clear answer. The frail old lady whose imminent death Dring had prophesied was mumbling, singing really, in her sleep. Her words sounded faintly familiar, like a half-remembered nursery rhyme.

"I'll come and visit again as soon as I can."

Drifting into sleep she murmured, "Don't forget the ciggies."

How small the house in Alderly Drive looked now. There were cupboards at Chatton Heights bigger than these rooms. Reluctant though I was ever to see anything from Gerald's point of view, I understood now how hard he would find it to adjust to life in an ordinary-sized house, having grown up amid such vast spaces. I felt that I had grown larger in the ten days since I went away, like Alice, or that the house had shrunk. Poky and dingy, poor little house.

It was a house for newlyweds, I saw that now for the first time. If my father had lived, if my mother had not been declared insane, then surely we'd have moved to a smarter, larger house by now. Maybe even out into the country; I might have had a pony and gone to gymkhanas. The image made me smile; somehow I couldn't imagine that.

Paula, returning from the library, was pleased. "Great to see you again. It's been lonely this past week without

182

you. And I was beginning to worry." She was wearing a yellow tracksuit and her flame-coloured hair was caught back with an orange scarf. From time to time, especially when her love life was on the wane, Paula became dedicated to physical fitness and jogged to the university instead of taking the bus.

"Then you'd better make the most of me because I don't think I'll stay long. How's the Prof?"

She grimaced. "Don't even ask. He's indulging himself in a major guilt trip; even when I try to talk about my thesis he grinds on about how he loves his wife really. As if I cared. By the way, your friend Adam called a couple of times. I gave him the number at Chatton Heights but he said he'd already tried."

"I didn't know he'd called."

"No? He said he had some news that would interest you, something to do with some painter. So how is life in Griselda's castle?"

"Much the same. Archie drinks, Tillie drifts around like some mad ghost and Gerald plays mechanic and mistreats his dogs."

"Sounds a picnic. I still can't get over Gerald. He ought to come with some kind of health warning attached. 'Sensitive souls beware: behind this aristocratic exterior lurks a card-carrying psychotic.' How could I have been so wrong about him?"

"I did warn you."

"I never used to be such a bad judge of character back home. There's something about a masculine voice speaking to me in a smooth English accent that causes my critical faculties to disintegrate. But Gerald! Your uncle, now, is much more my type."

"Isn't he a bit old for you?"

"Well, at least he doesn't have some stupid wife lurking in the background."

"There's Aunt Frances," I teased her. "Never try to compete with the dead. You always said you thought she was his muse and her death is the reason he's never written again. The brokenhearted genius."

"Broken hearts can mend. Maybe it's time he found himself another muse."

It was a flippant conversation. I didn't think much of it at the time – and what followed put all thought of it right out of my mind.

"By the way," said Paula, "I was going to ring you this evening anyway. When I was trying to clear some more space in the cupboard in my bedroom last night I found an old handbag. I think it must have been your mother's. There's some stuff inside it. D'you want to have a look?"

"I thought the cupboard was empty when you moved in." Dring and I had scrupulously cleaned the front room before Paula's arrival. Until then it had stood empty for years. Fifteen years. Empty, spotless, waiting. "Keeping it nice for when Mummy gets better" had been a deeply engrained habit, and hard to break.

"This was in a box right at the back. There were a couple of pairs of old shoes as well but I didn't think you'd be interested in them so I slung them out. I'll fetch the bag now."

It was one of those woven shoulder bags with a sort of fringe at the bottom. Very ethnic. I tipped the contents on the kitchen table: some kind of pocket book, a wallet, a make-up pouch and a few paper handkerchiefs.

"If we were detectives we'd put each one in a polythene bag and label it," I said.

"The diary's the most interesting."

"You mean you've looked through this already?"

"Sure. How else could I know it's your mother's?"

As I had spent a good part of the previous ten days looking through other people's discarded possessions I realised I had no legitimate cause to be annoyed with Paula.

The diary, one of those little pocket-sized ones, was for the year my father had died, the year my mother was admitted to hospital. There was no trace of the traumatic events of those months in the tiny spaces allotted to each day. "2 p.m. Fern dentist. 10.30 Hair." It was something, I supposed, to know that on the day my father was killed my mother had an appointment at the family planning clinic. I pointed out the irony to Paula and we both smiled. Uncomfortably.

He died at the end of May. The entries continued until 18th July – "Lunch Deb" was the last one, and after that – nothing. Empty blank pages. A blank life. Had she made that final lunch date with Deb, whoever she was? I would probably never know. Somehow those white white days were more eloquent than any other testimony could have been. From then on all her days were desolate white.

I looked at the back for addresses, notes, but found none. It was a very unrevealing diary. "A shame she never had a Filofax," I said lightly, "I bet that would have given us more to go on."

The make-up bag contained a stumpy black eyeliner pencil, some long-lash mascara, a very pale lipstick and an almost empty blusher. And a little bottle of patchouli. I opened the bottle, sniffed – and sat back in my chair, suddenly winded.

"What is it, Mary, what's the matter?"

"That smell . . . it suddenly reminded me . . ."

"Of what?"

"I don't know. So many things, feelings – I can't describe them."

"Good or bad?"

"Neither. Both. I don't know."

Paula reached over and put the stopper back on the bottle hastily. "Jesus, Mary, don't scare me like that. I thought a damned genie must have popped out or something. Maybe I shouldn't have shown you all this stuff. Maybe I should have just chucked it out with the shoes."

"I'm glad you showed me, truly I am. But you know how evocative scents can be. What's in the wallet?"

She laid out the contents carefully. A disappointing trawl. A library card, a few coins, a banker's card, a couple of used train tickets (Bristol and London), a few till receipts – and a photograph.

"Is that your dad?"

"It must be."

"Kinda spooky, isn't it?"

It was a studio portrait. The stamp on the back showed it to have been taken at the Las Vegas Photographic Studios, Buenos Aires. The cheap colour had faded into silvery blue. Against a backdrop of painted palm trees and snow-capped mountains stood a serious young man, thoughtful. Smiling as one does for a stranger, a smile for the family back home.

Altogether an ordinary enough photograph for a young husband to send his absent wife.

Except that someone had defaced it. Angrily. Hard jagged lines in red biro: two crescents curving out from his head like a Viking helmet, an oversized garden fork in his hand, squirly shapes in the background.

"Why do you suppose she did that?" Paula asked.

"Who?"

"Your mother, of course. She must have drawn those shapes in. I reckon she was wild – why did she put those horns on him?"

"I don't know. Cuckolds have horns, maybe she had been unfaithful to him."

Paula was unconvinced. She had obviously given the matter much thought since first finding the handbag. "It looks more like the devil to me."

"The devil?"

"Sure. Horns, the pitchfork . . . and those squiggly bits in the background are the flames of hell. A pretty freaky way to dress your dead husband."

"Oh Paula, why should she want to turn him into a devil? And anyway, we don't know for sure that she did it. Maybe it was me. You know what a menace kids can be with a red biro in their hands."

"I thought of that. But you were five years old, right? A five-year-old might have given him a moustache and glasses, but not horns and a pitchfork."

"Didn't I tell you I was precocious? It looks pretty childish to me."

"Angry, that's what it is. Whoever drew that on was burning up with rage. There's real hatred there."

"I always thought she loved him. That's what Dring told me . . ."

"Love and hate are very close, you know. And people often react to bereavement with rage. It's all part of the normal sequence of grieving." (Paula had done a credit in psychology, as I had already learned to my cost.) "I'll lay odds she was angry with him for abandoning her."

"Because he went to South America?"

"Because he died."

"But he died in an accident," I protested. "He was a passenger on an aeroplane. He could hardly help what happened, could he? It just doesn't make sense to be angry with someone over an accident."

"Try telling that to the person who is bereaved. Look at you for instance. Don't you remember ever feeling furious with them for abandoning you, rejecting you the way they did?"

"What's the point? Heaven help us, Paula, sometimes you sound exactly like Dr Phelps. It's a waste of time. It's not as if they did it deliberately. I wasn't found wrapped in newspaper on the church porch or anything like that."

"I'll bet it sure as hell felt like that sometimes."

I had always disliked Paula when she stepped into the role of amateur psychiatrist. Not that I minded when she dissected mutual acquaintances or her colleagues at the university. It was when she started on my family – and me especially – that I drew the line.

"This is stupid," I said, "here we are trying to work out why my mother did something the way she did when . . . well, looking for the logic when she was about to be committed to a mental hospital doesn't make a lot of sense. We'll only tie ourselves in knots." And I began to stuff the objects back into the shoulder bag.

"Okay, I guess you're right. Who listens to a crazy woman? Let's fix something to eat. I'm ravenous and you look half starved. There's eggs in the fridge."

While Paula began to prepare food I took the bag up to my room. Something had been bothering me, nagging at the corner of my brain, ever since I first saw the defaced photograph of my father.

And then I remembered . . .

And sat down on the edge of the bed.

My mother had clearly had an obsession with devils; she believed my uncle to be one. "The devil wrote *Dora's Room*." And now here she was decorating my father with the attributes of devilhood.

She saw devils everywhere. Both the brothers.

Unless . . .

I groaned aloud. Oh, my poor mother. There was room for only one devil in her life and that one devil was my father. And the devil wrote *Dora's Room*. That was what she had been trying to tell me that day at the hospital when her dull eyes stared into my face and she leaned forward and told me the secret that was burdening her. She was telling me my father had written *Dora's Room*.

My God, it was terrifying how a crazy mind can distort reality. No wonder she was committed to an asylum along with all the hopeless cases who believed themselves to be Joan of Arc or the Virgin Mary or the Queen Mother. Along with the woman who thought she was an electric appliance and refused to move in the mornings until she had been plugged in. Ha ha ha, let's all laugh.

I pulled the photograph from the wallet and stared at it once more, only this time the photo shook like a leaf with the trembling of my hand. There was such rage in the crude red lines with the biro, red horns, red pitchfork, red flames in the background against the bland scenery of painted palm trees and the snow-capped South American mountains. I could hear the hiss of her breathing as the red biro dug into the paper, could see her green eyes glitter with hatred.

But why such hatred? For leaving us? For dying?

No – it was the wild unreasoning hatred of a crazy woman.

I suppose all along I had nursed some hope, kept secret even from myself, that my mother had been normal underneath, just like any other mother, the victim of a medical misunderstanding. Highly strung, perhaps, even a bit unstable or neurotic – but then, if all such mothers were incarcerated for their neuroses the hospitals would be full and overflowing and the number of children growing up motherless would be legion.

But here in my hand was the proof that her tenuous grasp on reality had been finally broken and she had stepped across some hidden boundary into that other twilight world where no one could ever reach her, the world of the psychotic.

All those words came back to me, those half-over-heard whisperings of children huddled in the corner of a wintry playground, of messages murmured in the restless silence of the classroom, bolder taunts shouted on the journey home:

Mary Mary, quite contrary, how did your mother go?
With screams and yells and electric bells
And nurses all in a row, a row.

Her mum's mad, bonkers, everyone knows, off to a funny farm, off her rocker, out of her mind, nutty as a fruit cake, mental, crazy. No wonder she's . . .

And I had always thought: they're wrong. They don't really know. She's just in hospital for a bit. Sometimes I'd lie and tell people she had died in the plane crash with my father. My God, I wish she had. A clean tragedy, over, finished, no muddle to tangle me in for ever, not this mud of confusion in which I'm floundering now. If only she had died with my father then I wouldn't be sitting here now with this proof of her madness in my hands, the red biro lines that spelled out her warped vision that Archie was not, after all, the author of *Dora's Room*.

In what delirium had she constructed her crazy version of events? What had driven her to claim the brother's achievement for her dead husband? Only a lunatic would expect anyone to listen: all the world knew Archie had

189

written *Dora's Room*; there must be proof everywhere. "A. Miller, author of *Dora's Room*", and his smiling handsome face beamed from the back cover of every copy of the book ever printed. There must be a manuscript, people had probably watched him write it, there could be no possibility of doubt.

And even if there was, even if, just supposing for a moment that the incredible could be true and my father, not Archie, had written *Dora's Room*, even if she was right, what possible chance was there that anyone would ever listen to the ramblings of a woman who was insane?

The seeds of doubt, once planted in my mind, refused to go away.

I did everything possible to distract myself from the crazy notions that were storming my brain. I became the most diligent of hospital visitors, so that the nurses were first impressed by my compassion, then irritated by my constant presence. I scoured the shops for the most outrageously frilled and coloured nightdresses I could find and since there was room for only two or three of them to be kept at the hospital I had to keep most of them at home. I devised increasingly cunning ways to smuggle in her beloved cigarettes (none of which she was able to smoke but the growing hoard gave her some satisfaction). I became a hardworking heiress: having only communicated by letter before, I now went to London and had long meetings with stockbrokers and made them explain the details of my grandfather's investments. I spent time with the agent, with the solicitors, with anyone, in fact, who could distract me from the growing doubt that blossomed like some hideous fungus in my mind.

Suppose my mother had been right all along, suppose it was my father, not Archie, who had written *Dora's Room*?

Given the evidence I had so far it was just possible. Not probable, of course, but still, just possible. Although the book was not published until the year following my father's death it must have been written while he was still alive – my father's postcards told me that much. And if my father was the author then other, subsequent mysteries became clear. It explained, for instance, Archie's long silence. The silence that had been traditionally ascribed to the death of his wife (Paula's death of the muse) might actually have been caused by the death of the author himself. Archie had never really had a hope of writing a sequel, a successor to the book he had usurped. (There was *Maiden Voyage* of course, but that was a work that was generally agreed to be so vastly inferior to *Dora's Room* that it was quickly forgotten. I had even heard rumours that Archie had tried to have existing copies suppressed. Was that his one attempt, a dismal failure, to emulate the creation of his dead brother?) And weren't people always commenting on the contrast between a novel of such sensitivity that some passages were almost unbearably painful to read, and the figure of Archie, self-indulgent and genial, but with a cold, almost cruel side to him? It was natural that the changes in him should be attributed to the tragedies he had suffered in early life: it was possible that the novel had been written by the introspective young man with the eyes of a dreamer and not by the extrovert Archie.

Time and again I told myself that the direction of my thoughts was futile, leading nowhere. Or, worse still, if it did lead anywhere it led only down the dangerous road my mother had followed all those years ago. Wasn't her madness warning enough? If she had maintained my father had painted the ceiling of the Sistine Chapel would I have listened? Maybe it just flattered my vanity to think that it had been *my* father, not Gerald's, who had poured the tension and heartache of adolescence into a novel that had a steady readership until this day. (My daddy's cleverer than your daddy – No, he's not, and I can prove it.) Just as my mother had channelled her jealousy of Archie's achievement into a fantasy that claimed it for her husband. Of course Archie wrote the book. Everyone knew he wrote it. He did lecture tours to talk about it. He talked about it with an author's pride.

No he didn't. Not really. He hated to talk about it. Well, that was understandable, lots of authors prefer to let their work speak for itself. But wait a moment, what was it I had said to Paula? If you want to get rid of Archie, just start talking about *Dora's Room*. Ask him about the central figure of Dora, the mystery that was never explained, the mythic bird, the anima, Athena's messenger, companion of the way, Dora whose name was an anagram of road.

There had been a Dora, a real person, I was sure of it. Someone whom both Archie and my father knew. What was it exactly my father had written on the postcard Archie had been so eager to destroy? Something about wondering where Dora was now? Not the sort of words you use about a mythic bird or anima or companion of the way . . . more the words you use when talking about someone real, someone concrete.

So why did Archie never reveal her identity? Once my father died, did Dora still have to be protected? (I thought briefly of my mother, then dismissed the idea. Having left us both at Alderly Drive in the care of the recently hired Madame de Rhin he would have been in no doubt as to his wife's whereabouts.) Perhaps the real Dora had lost touch with the brothers. Perhaps she had always been more important to Clancy. After his brother's death Archie had no recollection who she was.

A solution so simple it had the power to take my breath away. The reason Archie had never revealed the identity of the true Dora was so obvious a child could see it: he didn't know who she was. Why had he never written anything since *Dora's Room*? Because he had never written anything before, that's why.

And then, no sooner had all the details fallen neatly into place than I drew back, afraid. Terrified. Scalp crawling with horror at the craziness of the very idea. Of course Archie had written the book. Archie Miller, well-known author of *Dora's Room*. People didn't just go around pinching their brother's masterpiece and then passing it off as their own. How could he have got away with it for so long? Only a lunatic would contemplate the idea.

My mother had contemplated the idea and she had been a lunatic. Signed, sealed and delivered. Drugged, doped and shocked until there was nothing left at all, not a ghost of the wild-eyed woman who had spoken to me in the ward that day and scared me so much that the snowdrops I had brought for her were scattered all across the polished floor.

My poor mother. Was mad.

And I was not. Would not be. Forget the madness, the fantasies, the incoherent creation of devils and geniuses. Stick to the facts.

A man died in a plane crash. His brother wrote a bestseller. A madwoman drew horns on her husband's head, placed a pitchfork in his hand, made a devil of his smiling photograph.

That much was fact. But why? Was her grief so immoderate, her rage so uncontrolled that she really hated him for what she saw as his betrayal through death? I tried to ask Dring but she quickly grew irritable and repeated her opinion that I should leave the past alone.

But the past, their past, had become my only present and I no longer had any choice, if indeed I'd had any before, but to continue my search. Not only was I searching now for information about my father, I was searching for Dora too. For some proof that my father could not possibly have been the author of *Dora's Room*. There was no one in Bristol who could help me.

This time I knew I could say nothing to Adam.

Only the house was my partner in this quest, that huge, monstrous, yellow house on the hill with its secrets and its teasing memories, which was compelling me to return.

Like the swallows who gather in the autumn for a journey so long and arduous that many will die before they achieve their destination, I began to prepare for the inevitable return to Chatton Heights.

Chapter 7

Not much had changed. A few green shoots were poking up between the shrubs but spring still seemed a lifetime away. The house remained bleak, dark and empty. Tom Page said he was busy restoring the puppets and the theatre – and Mrs Viney said that with his arthritis he'd never finish the job. Tillie flitted from room to room like some ageing and breathless doll and her disjointed phrases were as impossible to disentangle as ever. I still forced myself to spend some time with her each day in an attempt to win her confidence and try to learn the secrets hidden behind those blank blue eyes, but more and more my instinct was to avoid her. She gave off an odour of strangeness, of insanity almost – and that frightened me. Gerald's dogs no longer played at his heels but cringed on the ends of their leashes and kept anxious eyes on his marching boots and the heavy stick he always carried. Archie was entombed in his study by day, emerging only to eat and to drink . . .

Paula visited at the weekend and Archie drank less, was more animated. On the first evening Paula herself steered the conversation around to literary topics and it was comparatively easy to weave in the questions I had been wanting to ask. Was there a manuscript of *Dora's Room* surviving? No, he always worked directly on to a typewriter and only the finished draft existed. Had anyone seen the manuscript before he sent it to the publishers? No – with the possible exception of his wife. In fact he had kept the whole business secret until to his amazement it was accepted for publication: people might laugh at his stupidity but in those days he had entertained serious doubts about its merits (warm smile of appreciation for his modesty from Paula). But surely, I persisted, my father must have read it before that, since on the postcard from South America he was recommending possible publishers.

It was after supper and we were seated in the drawing-room. Tillie was hovering around the coffee trolley: for some reason she appeared reluctant to follow her usual habit of retiring to her stuffy little sitting-room and the noisy companionship of her television. She fussed by Archie's chair, refilling his coffee cup (he had paused in his alcohol consumption) every time he took a sip. At the mention of the postcards Archie's previously benign smile vanished.

"Good God, Fern, don't be so bloody boring."

Tillie darted forward with the coffee pot and splashed some more of the dark liquid into his already full cup. "For Christ's sake, woman," he snarled, "can't you find something useful to do, like flying off and turning your neighbour's milk green or however it is you normally amuse yourself on long winter evenings?"

Tillie snatched back the coffee pot and clasped it to her cardigan-wrapped bosom. "But coffee is always . . . and at this time of night especially . . . though also of course chocolate . . ." And she sat down, still hugging the coffee pot to her as if it was a hot-water bottle.

His discomfort only spurred me on, and I could not resist repeating, "From the postcard I assumed my father had in fact read *Dora's Room*. Since he died before publication that means he must have— "

Archie interrupted. Speaking not to me but to Paula, who listened to everything he said with an expression of disciple-like respect. "It never ceases to amaze me how the petty mind delights in meaningless detail. Unable to comprehend the breadth of genuine artistic achievement, they scrabble around on the lower slopes in the desperate hope of stumbling on something their feeble minds are capable of encompassing. Do you like marmalade or jam at breakfast, Mr Miller? Do you prefer the shiny smoothness of a ballpoint pen or the soft and yielding texture of a double B pencil? When your brother wrote to you in the month before he died, had he in fact read *Dora's Room* or had you merely told him of the book's existence? Well, m'lud, beg pardon, your honour, but the truth is I bloody well can't remember. Contrary to what some pettifogging minds seem to imagine, the past is not packaged like some neat little video inside my skull that I can fast forward and reverse at will each time I'm asked some damn silly question by some damn silly interfering female," and here, for the first time, he looked directly at me and his dark eyes were smouldering with rage, "who has nothing better to do than poke around in other people's cast-off rubbish."

I returned his stare without blinking. "Who are you trying to protect, Archie? My father . . . or Dora?"

"Don't be bloody ridiculous." Only that barely perceptible muscle under the eye flickering to betray his unease. "One is dead and the other never existed. Why should I waste my time protecting either?"

"But my father said that Dora— "

"No. He didn't. He never mentioned a person called Dora, only the book. You read in that postcard what you wanted to believe was there. Get a grip on yourself, girl. This obsession with the identity of a fictional character is doing you no good at all. In fact I think it's in danger of doing you a great deal of harm. If there had ever been a person don't you think I would have revealed her identity by now? Don't you think she herself would have been flattered to claim her role in inspiring the book?"

"But the first edition was dedicated to Dora, that's why people always wonder who— "

"And if I'd known the trouble it was going to cause then, believe me, I'd have changed the dedication right away. But you have to remember the circumstances: my wife had just died, I was distracted, I couldn't focus on anything so trivial as the book's dedication. Who do you want this dedicated to? they asked. I don't care, I told them, anyone, you choose, dedicate it to bloody Dora if you want . . . And they did. So you see, for everything there is a simple explanation; the only trouble is that your too fertile imagination likes to make dramas where none exist. It's only fair to warn you, Fern, that your mother had the same fatal weakness. We did not know, with her, how hopelessly vulnerable she was until too late. And Fern, I don't want to make the same mistake again."

It was clever, the threat disguised as avuncular concern. And it hit its intended target. While I was still staring at him in appalled silence, Archie seized the opportunity to make a dignified exit, followed a moment or two later by Tillie, still clutching her coffee pot.

Paula, who had seen only the concern, not the menace that lay beneath it, was at once reproachful. "Why do you have to keep on at him about those stupid post-cards? You know it only upsets him to remember that dreadful time."

I said nothing. Impossible to explain that it was the very ferocity of his reaction that spurred me on. She stood up and put another log on the fire, poking it thoughtfully with the toe of her boot. "I'll tell you one thing, though. He's bloody sexy when he gets angry like that. I only wish I'd known him when he was younger."

If Paula was critical of my attempts to cross-examine Archie, she was more amenable to the search for the original site of Dora's room. On the afternoon before she was due to leave she said, "I've been thinking it over, Fern, and I'm sure Dora's room is somewhere in this house. It has to be."

"Have you asked Archie about this?"

"Sort of . . . he says it is everywhere – and nowhere."

"And you don't believe him?"

"Not altogether but— " She was impatient. "You want everything to be so literal, so black and white. What he says is true in its literary and artistic sense: Dora's room is for everyone and so cannot be tied to a particular location. But Dora's room as it existed for Archie when he was creating that novel, that place has to be here somewhere."

It was a puzzle that others had grappled with before without success, but even so it was impossible not to try for ourselves. The clues to the room's identity were scattered throughout the book. From this room that was everywhere and nowhere one could see the square tower of the church, the horsechestnut that overhung the village pond, the camel-shaped hill in the distance. So far there was no problem, since each of these could be seen from any of the front bedrooms at Chatton Heights. But from Dora's imaginary room more could be seen than that: the horse-pond itself was visible, and the white ducks that swam there. Whereas even from the attics only the uppermost branches of horsechestnut could be seen and the pond itself was quite hidden. Still, Paula was eager to explore so together we climbed the winding stairs to the attics and pushed trunks and packing cases under one of the tiny windows and wrenched it open. We took turns to poke our heads out, like gophers reporting on the outside world. The view was spectacular, vertiginous – the bare sheep-cropped sweep of Cotswold hills, black lines and smudges of winter hedgerows and little copses, occasional clusters of yellow houses and farms, a view that surely had not changed much in hundreds of years – but for all its beauty the view was, for us, disappointing, as I knew it must be. The shelter belt of trees which had been planted to protect the orchard from the north and east effectively blocked the view of the lower part of the horsechestnut and the whole of the duck-swum pond.

Paula was loath to be so easily defeated. "Perhaps when Archie was a boy the trees were not so high and then he could see further."

"But even if the trees weren't there at all I don't believe one could see over the curve of the hill. And anyway, some of those trees are over a hundred years old – that evergreen for instance, the holm oak, that was there before the house was built." I helped her down from the packing case. "I don't see how this mythical room can possibly be anywhere in the house itself, because according to the book you can see the house from the room."

"What makes you say that?"

"The description of the needle-eyed vault, stone tomb of childhood – that must be this house. The windows are unusually tall and thin, even if needle-eyed is an exaggeration."

So we trekked to the outbuildings. It was a long time since there had been horses in the stables, or coaches in the coach house.

"Jesus, look at all those cars," said Paula in amazement. And indeed, for a family of three or four, there was a surprising number of vehicles. Apart from my own small Renault there was a Mini which Archie and Tillie used for local trips and a Rover Archie kept for longer journeys (as far as I knew Tillie never ventured further afield than the village). There were also a Riley, a Morgan, an old Daimler and a couple of Prefects, all in various stages of rehabilitation.

"Most of these belong to Gerald," I explained, "restoring old cars is what he likes best."

"More than beating up his dogs?"

"Hm. Let's see what is visible from the loft," I said, "I think the chauffeur used to lodge up there."

We climbed a rickety ladder and squinted out through the gaps in the wooden door. We were obliged to admit defeat at once. From here nothing at all could be seen but the rear of the house: no church spire, no horsechestnut, not even a glimpse of the far distant camel-shaped hill.

Paula turned to me. "Is there nowhere else?"

"No. I've looked everywhere."

"There could have been another building which was destroyed."

"I've already asked Tom, who's been gardener here since before Archie was born, and he says there never were any more buildings than these. I did think perhaps there might have been something near where the summer house is now— "

"The summer house?"

"Don't raise your hopes, Paula. You can't see anything at all from there."

"Let's look anyway."

So we did. About eight foot square, windows on either side, a door and two windows at the front, the summer house's wood had long ago been painted white and was now faded and flaked to a dark streaked silver. The door was locked but even Paula had to admit there was little point in trying to force an entry: nothing could possibly be visible from these cobweb-hung windows but a tangle of undergrowth.

"It's mysterious here." My voice broke the silence. "I always feel I'm close . . . to something."

"Not Dora's room, that's for sure," said Paula abruptly, "even if all the shrubs and brambles were cleared away we might be able to see the house but we'd never be high enough to see the church spire, let alone the horse-pond. It's impossible. Archie must be right after all and Dora's room exists only in our hearts."

This last statement was made with an air of profound reverence for Archie's genius – and suddenly I found myself longing to hear Adam's refreshingly sceptical "hrmph". That evening Paula returned to Bristol. To my surprise, I was relieved to see her go: since I could not share with her my real suspicions concerning Dora and her mysterious room, it was easier by far to be left alone.

It was a dead end. I had searched the attics so thoroughly I was beginning to recognise the individual spiders who scurried for safety as I disturbed yet another precious cobweb. I had searched, on a morning when I had the house to myself, the drawers and filing cabinets in my grandfather's study. I had talked at length to anyone who had been in the village while my father was still alive but no one had much to offer beyond the traditional "What a pleasant young man and such a tragedy when he died." No one seemed to have known him well – but then he and Archie were the boys from the big house and so played no real part in the everyday life of the village. Once their mother died there was no more entertaining done at Chatton Heights. It was as if my father had been a shadow, without any real substance, whose thirty years of life had left no ripple in the world to mark the place where he had been.

It was all very disheartening. I felt a fog of defeat beginning to descend on me, as though I was becoming as insubstantial and shadowy as my father had been. I could never find out more about him and there was no longer any reason to stay at Chatton Heights. Nor was there much point in returning to Bristol: Dring did not need me except to smuggle in cigarettes she'd never have the opportunity to smoke. No one needed me anywhere. What was I supposed to do now? I had money and freedom and time to do exactly as I wanted, all the things people strive for all their lives. I could learn the violin, travel all over the world, devote myself to charitable causes, socialise all through the night and never have to get up in the morning for work. My freedom was an illusion. I knew I could do none of these things. Not now, not yet. Not until I had gone some way to fleshing out the shadow that was my father, the shadow that I myself was fast becoming.

So I stayed at Chatton Heights and remembered what Gerald had said about being trapped, being unable to go away. I can always leave tomorrow, I told myself . . . and only half believed it was true.

I was in the village one morning, having just had yet another meeting with Mr Markham, when I heard a man's voice calling my name.

It was Adam. At the sight of him, long overcoat flapping in the wind, eyes creased in a warm smile, I felt a sudden lifting of the spirits.

"Adam, what a surprise, why didn't you tell me you were here?"

"I was planning to come up to the Heights this afternoon. I telephoned a couple of times but they always said you were out."

"Who did?"

"Gerald, Tillie— "

"The creeps. They're too lazy to come and find me, that's all. They never even passed on a message."

202

"And Paula?"

"Oh yes, she did say you'd been trying to get in touch but— " But I had forgotten. In the horror of my discovery that my poor brain-tattered mother believed her husband had written *Dora's Room* I had forgotten even Adam.

"Did you get my letter?" I asked.

"Yes. More evidence for the Dora-as-a-real-person theory – though it doesn't get us any closer to knowing who she was. Or why Archie should want to cover up her identity, does it?"

Unless he never knew, I thought; unless he never even wrote the book.

I said swiftly, "How's Ben?"

"Fine. He came down with me. He and Elsa are busy making cakes and driving my father up the wall. Why don't you come back and see him? Or are you doing something else this morning?"

"I don't have much time," I began to say, but it dawned on me as I spoke that since I had a whole lifetime I did not seem to know what to do with, this lie was too monumental even for me. So I said, "Are you sure your father won't mind?"

"He'd be delighted."

Delight was not the emotion that appeared strongest on Ted Bury's face when we went into the Old Rectory. Elsa and Ben's aimless singing and shrieks of glee could be heard all over the house and Ted had retreated to the comparative quiet of his study.

"How can such a very small person cause such total disruption?" he complained. "Elsa barely qualifies as an adult at the best of times; when your son is around, Adam, she regresses to complete infancy. Work becomes impossible, it will be a miracle if lunch is ever cooked, let alone on time. Chaos, total chaos."

Adam was annoyed. "I thought you said you wanted to see him? Do you want me to take him out for the day?"

"Don't be ridiculous. But must they make such a noise?"

"I'll tell them to tone it down – which you could have done yourself. By the way, where did you put that windowsill picture you were showing me? I thought Fern would like to see it."

"It's hanging in my bedroom."

"What picture?" I asked, when Adam had sufficiently repressed Ben and Elsa's high spirits and was leading the way up the stairs.

"See if you recognise it," was all Adam's reply as he pushed open the door.

I had never seen the picture before: a vase of overblown tulips with a view of trees and sky behind, the warm colour of the flowers contrasting brilliantly with the chilly scene behind the window – but I knew who the artist was even before I read the signature.

"D. Brewster," I said at once. "I never realised your father knew him too."

"Not him. Her."

"Her?"

"Yes. That's what I wanted to tell you. Do you remember when we asked Gerald the name of the artist, he had to look at the signature to tell us? And that's the strange part, because D. Brewster is Gerald's aunt, Frances Miller's older sister."

A thought occurred to me then, a thought so wonderful in its implications that for a few moments I felt I was floating about six inches above the grey carpet of Ted Bury's bedroom.

"You've left out the most important thing of all, Adam. What does the D stand for?"

"What does . . .? Oh yes, he did tell me. Deborah, I think, but we can check with my father."

"Oh." My glorious floating ended with an abrupt thud of disillusion. "Are you sure?"

Adam was examining me keenly. "Yes. What did you expect?"

"I thought perhaps . . . but it doesn't matter. I wonder if it would be possible to meet her. Is she still alive?"

"I think so. You need to ask Ted the details. Stay to

204

lunch and you can pump him for information about the past and do me a favour at the same time. It will cheer him up and help keep his mind off the tribulations of grandparenthood."

"I'm sure he adores Ben."

Adam merely "hrmph"ed.

We took Ben out for a walk to the duck pond by the old horsechestnut tree while Elsa concentrated on finishing lunch; the combination of a prompt meal and my curiosity about the past went some way towards reconciling Ted to sharing his dining table with a relative who still preferred to eat apple crumble with his fists.

Ted told me what he knew and it was little enough. When he had moved from Long Chatton to Portsmouth, Frances Brewster was just one of the many girls who visited the brothers. She and Archie were married a year later.

"I was invited to their wedding. I suppose Deborah must have been there but I'm ashamed to say that I was so delighted to be among old friends again that I didn't notice her family at all."

"So she and Archie were married here at Long Chatton as well?"

"Yes. I don't think there were many Brewsters about – in fact now I come to think about it their side of the church was distinctly thin on the ground; people notice these details in a small village. Apparently their father had been a regular soldier but something went wrong, can't remember exactly what, and the story is that Deborah pretty well brought Frances up on her own."

"Were there any other brothers or sisters?" asked Adam.

Ted shook his head.

"But why doesn't Gerald know about her," I wondered, "she's his only aunt, yet he didn't even know that she was the person who had painted the portraits. Do you think Archie had some reason to keep them apart?"

"You'll have to ask him that. Or her."

Adam wanted to know if it was possible to get in touch with her.

"No problem there," said Ted, "she lives with a woman called Molly Dyer whose father has retired near here. One of those minor scandals that keep the village gossips humming."

Having exhausted Ted's knowledge of Deborah Brewster, I tried to steer the conversation towards Archie's authorship of *Dora's Room* without arousing their suspicions. Did Ted, for instance, know of any reasons other than those of practical business necessity which had driven my father to leave for South America when he did? No, but he had always considered it strange that Clancy had decided to go at precisely the time my mother's illness was becoming apparent. Was there any kind of quarrel between him and Archie? Here I noticed that Ted hesitated for the briefest of moments before saying, no, none that he was aware of. Had my father ever shown any artistic – or literary – inclinations? No, but then neither had Archie. The arrival of *Dora's Room* had come as a complete surprise: Archie had been enormously secretive about the whole thing, but that was hardly surprising since his father was so fiercely opposed to the creation of anything except wealth.

"My grandfather wielded tremendous power over his sons, didn't he? After all, Archie was in his mid thirties by then, so why should his father's opinion be so all-important?"

"Money." Ted pronounced the word with great emphasis, as though the two syllables were in themselves sufficient explanation. "Old Everett had the money. He reared his sons with expensive tastes but without the expectation that they'd ever have to go out and work for a living. And he only gave them money when he felt like it. So they remained in his power. Clancy finally managed to escape, but Archie never did completely – he was always too eager for the status and pleasures that money can buy."

"That sounds like young Gerald," said Adam.

"Everything comes down to money, in that household," I reflected ruefully. "I used to think of it as just something you used to buy what you needed – but there it's the only thing that counts, has a value all its own."

"Ah yes. I used to preach on the pitfalls of building up treasures on earth but I'm not so deluded in my ministry that I suppose your grandfather ever paid a blind bit of notice. I think I could have understood his obsession more easily if he had used his wealth in some way – to buy paintings or keep racehorses, to travel – or even to have kept a few mistresses. But that wasn't his style. He just stayed at Chatton Heights spinning a web of money with which to keep all those around him totally trapped in his power."

"They say that money is the root of all evil," I said.

"Frequently. And as usual they're wrong. Money is an entirely neutral substance, like energy or strength. It's the way it is used that can be either good or evil. Saint Paul blamed the *love* of money – though in your grandfather's case the two had become distinctly confused."

"Maybe it's Fern's turn to be corrupted now," suggested Adam.

"Quite possibly."

"Maybe that was what Everett Miller intended."

"Gerald did say my grandfather only left me all the money because he was angry that I had escaped his orbit. He said the will was a huge net to snare me with. Some kind of posthumous control."

Ted's tufty eyebrows lifted with amusement. "And is he right?"

"In a way – I'm not sure – not yet. I only wish I knew why he had singled me out after so many years of not bothering to see me at all. Archie said he thought it was some kind of reparation, an attempt to make amends."

"Maybe," but Ted still looked unconvinced. "It's also

perfectly likely that the old man was motivated by simple spite. I've too often seen a last will and testament used as a means of inflicting punishment on the departed's nearest and dearest. And if your grandfather Everett had wanted to punish Archie and the others for their failings, real or imagined, then he could have thought of no better instrument."

I recoiled from the thought. "It's wretched to feel yourself used as a means of inflicting pain. Especially by a dead man you can't even remember."

"So why remain at Chatton Heights?"

It was the question I had been asking myself all morning. Because there is nowhere else to go . . . But no, that wasn't the answer, not any more. Because there is a chance that my mother was right, that the devil did write *Dora's Room*, not the devil who had claimed the honour, but the devil who had been my father. I had wanted to find an image of Clancy, an image of a sane, wise parent to balance the spectre of my crazy mother and now, instead of my previous blank of ignorance, I was tormented by a question, a huge question which I could share with no one. Because until I knew the truth I could never find out who I was, would never be free to leave and live out my own, independent life.

"I need to know the truth," I muttered, half hoping no one would hear.

Ted smiled, almost kindly. "Ah yes, the truth. Hardly a very modest ambition, Fern. A lifetime's quest, you'll find. But is it necessary to remain at Chatton Heights in order to find it? I've seen such great suffering at that house."

Adam had been watching me with concern. He said lightly, "You make it sound as if there's a curse on the place."

"Tut, Adam. You know I've no time for curses. But I do know that some people destroy those who come into their orbit. Everett was one. I rather believe Archie might be another."

"So you think I should leave the Heights?"

"That is for you to decide. 'The truth shall make you free' after all. John eight, verse thirty-two." I couldn't help smiling at his professional habit of attributing his quotations and I half expected a full-blown sermon to follow, but he contented himself with a simple, "Admirable sentiment, that. It's a pity people don't reflect on it more."

Ben did not allow much time for reflection that afternoon: his buoyant high spirits were such a welcome contrast to the gloom and introspection of my relatives that once or twice I even thought of kidnapping him and keeping him by my side as a kind of bumptious talisman. There was no time to think, no space for worry, no opportunity even to talk to Adam until they were about to leave for Bristol.

"I'll get in touch with Deborah Brewster if you like," he said, "we could drive over and see her next weekend."

I agreed without hesitation. The prospect of seeing Adam again so soon was as appealing as the thought of meeting the painter of the portraits.

It was growing dark by the time I returned to Chatton Heights. Perhaps I imagined it, perhaps my knowledge of subsequent events has coloured my memory, but it seemed, as I went in through the garden room, that the house was wrapped in an unnatural silence. Not a sound anywhere. Outside, the wind, trees moving against the evening sky. Inside . . . nothing.

I was already on my guard as I went up the wide main stairs and through the connecting door to the freezing passageway that led to Gracie's room. My father's room, my room. And I knew the moment I pushed the door open, even before I looked inside, that it was not as I had left it that morning.

The room was so bare, with its crude pine desk and dark Windsor chair, oak wardrobe, narrow bed and the cumbersome gas heater which Archie had found for me in the stables, that the slightest alteration would have been immediately apparent.

And this alteration was anything but slight.

My bed, which had been neatly made, was in disarray. My clothes were scattered over the floor. The empty grate was full of broken glass and tiny scraps of coloured paper.

I knelt down to pick them up and an icy sweat formed between my shoulder blades. A broken smile – a shimmer of dark hair – a baby's tight fist torn off at the wrist. It was, had been, the photograph of my parents and their new baby.

I sat back on my heels, hugged my chest. Rocking. Who . . .?

My first thought was that it must have been burglars. I almost hoped it had been burglars. But I think I knew, deep down, that it wasn't. And a search of the room soon revealed that nothing was missing.

I sat down on the edge of the bed. Tried to think.

Such a mindless thing to do. Stupid. Pointless. Why should anyone want to rip up a photograph. Who . . .?

And then a pageant began to unfold in my head. I saw Gerald push open my bedroom door. His red lips were sulky and his cheeks were suffused with a dull rage. He kicked my suitcase with all the savagery I had seen in the orchard that day when he beat his dogs. He laughed as my belongings tumbled over the floor. Then he took the picture and hurled it with all his vicious strength at the grate. Then . . . but behind him came Tillie. Her eyes were glassy, staring at nothing in particular as, with little gasps and grunts of satisfaction, she began tossing my possessions around the room. And then followed Archie.

I could no more stop the sequence of images than I could stop the violent shivering that gripped me. Archie walked slowly across the room and picked up the photograph, removed it from the frame. He tossed the glass into the fireplace where it shattered into a thousand fragments. He contemplated the image of his brother,

of his brother's wife, his brother's child. He smiled.
He tore the photograph in two. Slowly, deliberately,
as a warning. Then he continued tearing for a long
time and the scraps of paper fell like confetti at his
feet.

I stood up and began to pace the room. My cheeks
were burning but my body was cold as death.

Just a photograph, I told myself. No real damage done.
Why be so upset by it? But it was the stupid vindictiveness
of the action that was so unnerving. That – and not
knowing who was responsible.

My instinct was to blame Archie. He was trying to
warn me off, to frighten me away from my search and
whatever it was about my father he was so desperate
to hide.

But equally I knew it could be Gerald. He still made
no secret of his resentment towards me. This destruction bore all the hallmarks of a child's tantrum and
Gerald's rage was always just under the surface, barely
controlled.

Or Tillie. The least known. Oh, she always appeared
friendly enough, so far as I could tell, but what of her
thoughts? Her real feelings? I knew her no better now
than I had done on the day of my arrival.

Worst of all was the fact that it could have been any
one of them. There wasn't a single person in this house
I could trust. I was quite alone.

At dinner that evening I waited until Tillie, Gerald and
Archie were all present. Mrs Viney had left cold chicken
and potato salad and Tillie had washed out some rather
sad lettuce leaves and put them in a bowl. Among the
pewter plates and tankards on the sideboard stood a glass
bowl of blackberry and apple mousse.

I had brought the scraps of the photograph, every last
one meticulously picked up from among the splinters
of glass and placed in a brown envelope. As soon as
everyone was sitting down, had just begun to eat, I
stood up slowly and held the envelope at arm's length,

211

over the centre of the dining table. Then, when I was certain that all three were watching, I emptied the contents of the envelope. I searched their three faces as the pieces fell like ash from a bonfire on to the polished wood. Even the jolly seaside children in the pictures seemed momentarily to pause in their activity to watch.

Tillie merely stared. Archie raised a single eyebrow and poured himself another drink. Gerald was contemptuous.

He said, "What a bloody stupid mess."

"Do you know what this is?"

"Oh good," drawled Archie, "guessing games already and Sundays are usually so lacklustre *chez nous*. Thank you so much, dear Fern, for thus brightening our drab lives."

Tillie fluttered nervously. "Never very good . . . games aren't especially . . . but always tried . . ."

"Christ," said Gerald, "the bloody stuff's got into my potato."

"It's a photograph of my parents." My voice was shaking but I managed to carry on. "The one you gave me, Archie. I kept it in my room."

Archie said, "Dear girl, don't fret. I'm sure I can find you another picture of them."

"But *who* did it?"

"What the bloody hell is going on?" asked Gerald, biting the blunt tip of his thumb.

"Such a pleasant young couple," said Tillie. Her most coherent phrase of the evening.

"Someone came into my room while I was out today. They threw my things around and tore up this photograph."

"Bully for them," said Gerald.

"Someone?" queried Archie. "Do you want me to call the police?"

"It wasn't burglars, there's nothing missing. No obvious motive . . ."

"Ah, rays of light begin to pierce the darkness." Archie's

florid phrases no longer sounded genial; did I imagine it, or was there menace behind his lazy sarcasm? "You are obviously labouring under the apprehension that someone in this house is responsible. Is that right? Yes, I see. You believe that one of us, driven to a positive frenzy of jealous rage, has penetrated your inner sanctum and – what was it? – scattered your possessions. Might I suggest that this does appear a somewhat pusillanimous form of revenge? Hardly the work of a homicidal maniac."

Gerald sniggered. "I can think of better ways."

"I'm sure you can, dear boy. Such a talent for petty cruelties. But don't laugh, this is serious. Can't you see your poor cousin is upset? She thinks someone has been nasty to her. More precisely, if I'm not very much mistaken, she thinks one of *us* has been nasty to her. Isn't that right, Fern? I thought so. It only remains, therefore, to identify the culprit. I'm sure Fern is studying our faces at this very moment for those telltale signs that betray guilt. Gerald, did you go into Fern's room and mess up her things? No? Tillie, then? No, apparently it wasn't Tillie either. Was it by any chance me? Now, how did I occupy myself today? 'After lunch tore up photograph' . . . no, snoozed over crossword is more likely. So who does that leave? Mrs Viney? Elsa? A half-witted poltergeist perhaps? The ghost of your poor dead papa begging you to leave him in peace?"

I shivered, made myself look around the table at each in turn. Gerald was still smothering his giggles like a naughty schoolboy. Tillie appeared torn between sharing his mirth and commiserating with my distress but I had the impression that both were incomprehensible to her. Archie was calmly pouring himself another drink.

When I spoke my voice was level, apparently unaffected by my fear. "Someone here is trying to force me to leave," I said. "Who, or why, I can't be sure, but I won't. No one can make me go until I'm ready. No one."

Archie picked up a drumstick in his fingers. "I am

delirious with joy at this happy news. Now, would you be so kind as to remove this unusual table decoration from our midst?"

We all finished our meal in uncomfortable silence.

Chapter 8

Adam telephoned in the middle of the week to say he had persuaded Deborah Brewster to see us and, towards noon the following Sunday, I saw his old estate car pull to a halt on the gravel driveway.

As soon as I had greeted him I took him into the drawing-room which, that morning, I had made almost welcoming. I had found several large vases in a room behind the kitchen and had filled them with daffodils from Long Chatton and greenery from the garden. A log fire was already burning in the grate. Best of all, on a low table near the fireplace, stood the theatre I had found in the attic. Tom Page had carried it in wheezing triumph from his cottage the previous day – and he had every reason to be proud of his achievement. The wooden frame and proscenium arch had been repainted in jewel-bright colours. The four puppets, clothes mended, hair glued back and brushed, faces touched up, were hanging with miraculously untangled strings from a little stand at the back.

"I thought Archie might like to see it," I explained, "apparently he was originally part-owner."

"And was he interested?"

"Not really." ("Ah, dear Clancy's thespian era. What a charming addition to your meagre store of paternal memorabilia, Fern. Your fingers can move the limbs that his childish hands once also manipulated. Do you care for the stage? I thought you probably would. I regret that I am unable to share your enthusiasm. I have always found the theatre too close to the artifice of life to be wholly comfortable with it.")

I had had the feeling that Archie's remarks on the

theatre were intended as the kind of pithy epigram that I was supposed to race off and jot down on paper. I offered them now to Adam, just in case he wished to do another article on Archie but he shook his head. "One is quite enough. Besides, that sounds suspiciously like the paraphrase of someone else's quotation."

Adam crouched over the theatre, examining every detail. "What wonderfully vivid faces they have; it hardly seems fair to call them wooden."

The old man puppet, the tyrant/wizard, glared up at him, as if even this personal reference was an insult. Adam lifted one of the puppets from its stand and the young hero, now smartly dressed in green felt doublet and breeches, took a few hesitant steps across the stage.

"A young prince," Adam began, "set out one morning to seek his fortune in the world . . ." He sat back on his haunches and ran his fingers through his hair as though perplexed. "How reassuringly simple these stories always were. As if all you have to do is make friends with the ants and a few other useful creatures, perform a few improbable tasks and all would be well for the rest of your life."

"Would you like to live happily ever after?"

"Wouldn't you?"

"Right now I'd be content with the answers to a few simple questions."

Adam grinned. "You have all the instincts of a born sleuth. Let's hope the elusive Ms Brewster can answer a few."

"Oh— " I laid my finger across my lips, advising silence. "It's time we left," I said quickly, "we don't want to be late."

Although the heating system on Adam's car had been partially mended so that it no longer alternated between extremes of heat and cold but merely oozed a steady draught of tepid air, the old estate had found new means of irritation. At the first smattering of rain the windscreen wipers flung themselves into a violent arc with a good deal of noise but to no obvious purpose. Adam, however, did not appear to notice.

As soon as the potholes and laurels of Chatton Heights were behind us he said, "Why all the secrecy about Deborah Brewster? You don't think anyone was listening back there, do you?"

"Maybe. You know that phrase, the walls have ears? Whoever coined that one must have lived at Chatton Heights. Most of the time it is just about the loneliest place in the whole world and then, just when you want privacy, someone bobs up out of nowhere. Tillie usually, but it can be Gerald, or Archie. And Archie hates my interest in my father, though he pretends not to. And I know he'd mind if he knew where we were going today."

"Why? Do you think he's still afraid the suicide story might get out?"

"Partly, though if she's kept quiet all this time then I don't see why she should suddenly spill the beans in public now. I think it's to do with Dora."

"Dora? Ah yes, you said in your letter that you were more than ever certain she really did exist."

Did he believe me? As we drove through the wintry countryside, the gentle hills and honeyed Cotswold stone villages gradually giving way to the red brick and open spaces of the Vale of Evesham, I told Adam in detail all that had happened between Archie and me since my discovery of the postcards in the attic. "If you'd seen the expression in his eyes, Adam, when he saw the mention of Dora on the postcard, you'd have known he was hiding something."

Adam was silent for a moment before saying thoughtfully, "It's a shame he burnt them, though, I'd have loved to read them."

"He's tried to make out I imagined it, but I know that's not true."

"That explains why you wanted to know what the 'D' stood for; you thought it might be Dora."

Did this mean he believed me? "It might still fit," I said. "Remove a few letters from Deborah and you're left with Dora."

"But why should Archie dedicate a book to his wife's sister? Unless . . . Fern, you don't think Archie and this Brewster woman were having some kind of affair, do you? It is possible – just think. They fell for each other, a brief fling, wife finds out, kills herself, lovers part in a frenzy of remorse never to see each other again . . . but Archie had already dedicated the book to her and added 'wherever she may be'."

"I hadn't thought of that." (If Archie *did* write the book. Or was it "the devil"? My secret weighed heavily inside me, dulling spontaneity.)

"It's more than possible, you have to admit." Adam, never happier than in pursuit of a new idea, was in his element. "Brokenhearted by the separation, the betrayal, an overwhelming guilt caused by his wife's tragic death, he was never able to write again. It explains too why he never allowed the truth about Dora to leak out. If it was known that he had been having an affair with his sister-in-law then people might begin to look into the circumstances of Frances' death and the whole suicide thing would be much harder to hush up."

"If it *was* suicide. You can't be sure."

"You'll just have to ask D. Brewster."

"Me? I thought you were going to ask the questions. It's your job after all. You're the one with the experience."

"And that is precisely why it has to be you. My role in the expedition is strictly limited to that of chauffeur with elegant limousine— " Loud shrieks of denial from the windscreen wipers. "Well, maybe not so elegant. But all these questions are going to come much better from you – you're family. You have a right to know."

"Do I?" The notion that my position in my family conferred any kind of rights was so novel that I paused to savour it for a moment. "But not everyone would agree with you." I hesitated, and then plunged on. "I think someone at Chatton Heights is trying to scare me off."

"What?"

I told him about the disruption of my room, the shredded photograph, my family's unconcern. His reaction was gratifyingly protective.

"Christ, Fern, how dreadful for you. And what a bloody pointless thing to do. Who do you suspect?"

"That's the worst part of it, it could have been any one of them. It might have been Gerald or Tillie, but my guess is Archie, some kind of warped way of telling me to stop meddling in the past."

"I'd put my money on Gerald, it sounds more like his style, the kind of childish tantrum he'd throw."

"Perhaps . . ." I had spoken to Gerald only the day before. He had cheerfully denied the assault on my room and, as if to emphasise his innocence, had explained that if he had wanted to frighten me, he had a most useful collection of antique swords and knives, even a couple of working guns, so had no need to resort to mere photograph shredding.

"That sounds more like our Gerald," said Adam when I had told him of our conversation, "acquitted by his own admission of loathsomeness."

"There was more. When I asked him if he knew his mother had a sister living he said he'd heard she was some kind of arty-farty dyke and that he, personally, had no time for weirdos. He assumes she wears men's suits and smokes a pipe and that, anyway, in his opinion painting is a mug's game."

I had never seen Adam shocked before but for a moment his jaw actually dropped. "He really said that?"

I nodded. Sometimes, after what passed for a conversation with my cousin, I was left wondering if he was unique in the world or whether he was actually representative of a whole genus and it was only by extreme good fortune that I had never stumbled across anyone like him before. For the sake of mankind in general I sincerely hoped he was unique.

After a pub lunch of flat beer and even flatter sandwiches

we arrived at our destination at about two thirty. It was a small red-brick house surrounded by empty fields.

Adam parked by the edge of the road.

"Nervous?" he asked as we got out of the car. When I didn't reply he grinned. "Remember, each person is their own favourite topic of conversation."

He pushed open the gate and we walked down the short path to the front door which, after a few moments, was opened by a stout, upright woman in her fifties with greying hair and features that had never been pretty but would always be attractive. Her manner achieved an uneasy combination of nervousness and welcome.

"Come in, do," the woman said, and her voice retained traces of a Warwickshire accent, "we heard the car."

"Miss Brewster?"

"No. Deb's in the sitting-room. I'm Molly – Mildred actually but for obvious reasons I'm always called Molly. Come straight through. We've been expecting you."

We followed her inside and I was aware of brief disappointment. My vision of a painter's house was nothing like this. I had been imagining something unusual: a whitewashed studio room, perhaps, scrubbed boards or quarry tiles on the floor, something eccentric, sparse, ascetic. What greeted us as Molly led the way into the sitting-room was the kind of environment of which Dring most approved: a celebration of cosiness – shaggy rugs, a blazing coal fire, chintz-covered sofa and chairs and gleaming brass on the walls. Over the mantelpiece was an oil painting of June flowers which I recognised at once as being Deborah's work. Beyond the window was a view of bare fields and a sky that looked as though it would be grey for ever. A solitary hawthorn waved its black arms in the wind at the end of a patch of rough grass.

"Deb, this is Fern. And Adam – Bury, isn't it? Do make yourselves comfortable. I'll make some tea in a little while." She spoke in the jolly, somewhat anxious tones of a party hostess who fears the children in her care may fail to join in with the proper spirit.

Deborah Brewster was seated in a straight-backed chair

near the window and she acknowledged our arrival by the barest movement of her lips. There was no immediate similarity to the image I had of her sister. Her hair was fair – a kind of indeterminate colour somewhere between blonde and grey – and wispy as smoke. She was angular and bony where Aunt Frances had been soft and rounded. The girl in the portrait had possessed the sensible face of a school prefect, plain, but dependable and kind, while Deborah's, or what one could see of it, was soured. A thin mouth dragged downwards by lines of perpetual disapproval. But her real expression was impossible to gauge since her eyes were hidden behind unseasonal dark glasses.

Adam and I sat down on the sofa. He seemed suddenly very long and masculine in this tiny room crammed full of pink frilled lampshades, trinkets and patchwork cushions. He had to arrange his legs carefully to avoid a tiny table on which stood an elaborate arrangement of dried flowers.

"Poor Deb is a martyr to migraine," said Molly, laughing incongruously as she said the word "migraine". "We're going on a cruise in ten days. One does so long for some sunshine at this time of year."

"Oh I am sorry," I said automatically, "I do hope this isn't a bad time to come."

Somewhere behind the dark glasses two eyes were staring at me, but Deborah said nothing. What little confidence I had was beginning to drain away. I decided to plunge straight in.

"I don't know where to begin," I said feebly, "you see, I was hoping . . . I don't really know all that much about my family. My father died when I was about five." I found myself addressing Molly Dyer who was at least listening with an expression of polite attention. "My mother never recovered from his death and she spent the rest of her life in a mental hospital. She didn't have any relatives and I only really met my father's family for the first time about a month ago."

Molly made a vaguely sympathetic tutting noise. "How dreadful for you, dear," she said.

"Oh no," I had yet to find a way of recounting the circumstances of my childhood that did not sound like a plea for sympathy, "I was brought up by a wonderful woman and so I was always perfectly happy."

"Sissy de Rhin." The thin lips moved and Deborah Brewster spoke for the first time. Her voice was totally without expression.

"You knew her, then?"

She inclined her head briefly to acknowledge the fact. It occurred to me then that I had never before heard anyone refer to Dring by her Christian name. I waited for Deborah to elaborate but she remained silent, razor-thin mouth tightly closed once more.

"I went to Chatton Heights for the first time a few weeks ago. My grandfather died just after Christmas and for some reason I haven't been able to work out yet, he left almost all his money to me. And the house."

"Bully for you," said Deborah drily. "Does that mean Archie is dead?"

"No. He— "

"Pity." She turned away in what might have been disgust and gazed out of the window. A handful of raindrops rattled against the glass.

"He and Gerald both have legacies."

"Ah yes, Gerald. Tell me, Fern Miller, did your uncle send you here?"

"Certainly not. I think he'd hate it if he knew I was coming."

"Are you trying to provoke him, then?"

Her questions seemed a deliberate attempt to needle me but I was determined not to rise to the bait. Besides, I was both comforted and spurred on by my awareness of Adam's shrewd eyes watching our awkward exchange. "There are things about my father I need to know," I said. "I was hoping you might be able to help."

"Why the hell should I want to do that?"

Her challenge was so direct that I didn't know what to answer, merely stared at her helplessly. Perhaps sensing that she had gone too far she began plucking at the arm of her chair with thin, nervous fingers. "I loathe and detest every single member of your family," she said.

Adam broke in coldly. "Fern hasn't even had the chance to know them until now."

Still plucking at the arm of her chair. "I can't help that."

I decided to try a different tack. "Since I first went to Chatton Heights I've spent a good deal of time looking at that portrait you did of my parents. Gerald said you did it in a great hurry, that you hadn't really bothered with it, but I love it. Although it isn't finished, not so polished as the other, it has enormous vitality."

"It's only one of the best I ever did." She was silent for a moment, thinking, then, "Usually I had to do that detailed boardroom stuff, like the one of Archie and my sister, but I knew that with Lou and Clancy I could be more adventurous. *Had* to be more adventurous. It wouldn't have been them otherwise. I enjoyed doing that painting, although, God knows, your mother made it difficult enough."

"In what way?"

"Every way she could." Her voice was petulant, as though I was in some way to blame for my mother's behaviour. "She was impossible, never settled to anything. First she was too hot so we'd open all the windows. Then she'd complain of the draught. Then she was bored so Clancy brought a radio along but there was never a programme she would listen to. And the trouble we had with her appearance, her clothes, her hair, her make-up – she found fault with everything. And of course she was quite incapable of sitting still. I've never been so close to hitting one of my sitters, never."

"So you weren't surprised when you heard she'd gone . . . into hospital?"

She shrugged. "I didn't expect . . . but in that house anything was possible."

"What about my father? His expression in the painting looks – anxious somehow. Did he always look like that?"

"Is this the inquisition?" She turned to Adam. "Shouldn't you be taking notes or do you have a tape recorder hidden in your pocket? You told Molly you were a journalist."

"This is what we call off the record. Purely for my own interest – and Fern's." How did Adam manage to sound soothing and determined all at the same time?

I struggled on, trying to ignore the downward tug of her lips. "I thought perhaps he was worried already about my mother, or maybe he was habitually anxious, lacking in confidence, since he felt himself to be overshadowed by his brother."

"Overshadowed? Whatever gave you that idea?"

"Someone suggested— "

"Then you've been talking with bloody fools. If anything . . . and anyway, your father would not have noticed even if Archie did cast a long shadow, which he didn't. Clancy was always much too vague to bother with things like that."

Molly chipped in brightly, "I always understood it to be the other way around. You told me, Deb dear, that Archie was always the jealous one, especially— "

"Molly!" Deborah's warning was more of a hiss.

"Sorry, dear, I forgot."

"Archie tried hard," Deborah continued swiftly, as though to ensure that her friend remained silent. "In those days I sometimes felt sorry for him though, God knows, I was wasting my time. He's one man can look after himself come hell or high water."

"Why sorry for him?"

She sighed, in a manner that implied my question was particularly stupid. "People were drawn to your father. He never went out of his way to be charming, not like Archie, but even so, people cared about him." She sounded exasperated, more as if she was describing his faults than his appeal. "Like a grown-up little-boy-lost. Women especially found him irresistible. Half the time he was so wrapped up in his own private dream world that he never even noticed the effect he produced but . . . that was why he became tangled in such messy relationships.

Beware the charming helpless dreamer. In his sweet and innocent way your father was every bit as dangerous as Archie."

"I see." (I didn't.) "Was there any particular reason why he had to go to South America when he did? I think there must have been but when I asked Archie he said he couldn't remember."

She laughed contemptuously. "If he won't remember then I don't see why I should."

It was as though I was trying to grasp a prize that was dangled temptingly close, only to be snatched from my reach just as I stretched out my hand. "Then there *was* a reason," I said, "something my father was ashamed of. Archie must be trying to protect me from the truth but— "

"The only person Archie is trying to protect is Archie."

"How do you mean?"

"Never mind."

Silence. A blank. Deborah Brewster knew the answers but she refused to share them.

Molly put her hands on stout knees and stared around, beaming. "Well, now, how about a spot of tea? No no, Fern, don't bother to help. I can manage."

Adam stood up. "I'll give you a hand," he said, and it was a statement rather than an offer of help. He followed Molly from the room, throwing me a quick smile as he left.

The silence they left behind them was uncomfortable, prickly. I forced myself to speak before it grew too huge to break. "While I was looking in the attic I found some postcards that my father had sent to Archie. He seemed to be apologising for something but when I asked Archie he refused to talk about it."

"He probably doesn't like people reading through his private correspondence."

Silence again, impenetrable and cold. Deborah Brewster's thin fingers continued to pluck at the arm of her chair; it was a wonder there was any fabric left. At length she said, "Tell me, Fern, daughter of Clancy and Louise, have you nothing better to do with your time than poke around in the detritus of ruined lives?"

"And what is wrong with that?" Her question stung me. "Why should I be the only person who's not supposed to know about my parents? Surely it's natural to want to know where you fit in? My grandfather left me his house and most of his money but he never even bothered to see me when he was alive, I never went to Chatton Heights, never saw any of them for fifteen years. And now that I want to know . . ."

I paused. As my irritation faded I despaired of ever convincing that hostile, sunglass-shielded face but, to my amazement, the cold thin mouth was almost smiling.

She said at length, "So, Fern, it seems I have misjudged you. I took you for one of them but you've suffered the Miller treatment as badly as anyone else."

"I don't know . . ."

"You should put all this behind you. Think of your own future, not other people's past."

"It's hard to explain but . . . it's almost as if, until I know more about *them* I won't know who *I* am."

"Well . . . maybe so . . ." She removed her glasses and rubbed her closed eyes with her fingertips. There were dark shadows like bruises under her eyes and her thin eyebrows were drawn together like an indelible frown. "I nearly went crazy when Fran died," she said in a low voice, barely audible, "I hated your family so much for what they had done to her. The only thing that kept me alive was my hate, that and my determination that Archie wouldn't have the satisfaction of destroying me too."

"So it was suicide?"

The merest hesitation and then, "Oh yes, it was suicide."

"And the letter?"

"The bastard made me give it to him, may he forever rot in hell."

"But how could he force you?"

226

"He had Gerald, the hostage."

"Did he threaten— ?"

"Not directly. There was no need. Old Everett Miller and his son were a powerful team when they set their minds on a course and . . . it was what Fran would have wanted, that was their trump card and they knew how to use it."

"So you agreed to the accidental verdict?"

"I kept quiet, which suited them. There were bound to be rumours but . . . Archie still had his precious smokescreen of respectability."

"But what could have made her so unhappy as to take her own life? She always seemed so kind and gentle. She adored Gerald. I can remember her a little and I simply can't imagine how— "

"Mental cruelty. Archie drove her to it." Amazing that such a soft voice could be so taut with venom. "He made her life a living hell. Sounds melodramatic, doesn't it, but believe me it's the truth. He convinced her that if she left him she'd never see Gerald again. She couldn't leave and she couldn't stay – she was trapped. She was no match for him. And she knew he would go on punishing her for the rest of her life."

"Why? Everyone says they adored each other."

"Who says? Archie?" She laughed bitterly. "He drove her to kill herself and if that's true love you can stuff it."

She was still plucking at the arm of her chair. Her expression was infinitely weary. Was it the weariness of remorse, I wondered. Had her ill-considered affair driven her sister to suicide? Had this woman with the migraines and the sour mouth once been Archie's mysterious Dora?

She replaced her dark glasses, lifting them as though they were an intolerable weight. I could sense her gaze on my face. "You really do want to know, don't you, Fern? I can see it in your eyes . . . but you know what they say, don't you, a little knowledge is a dangerous thing. I can tell you what happened but will that bring

227

you any closer to the truth, the real truth, which is untidy and painful?"

"I think Archie once said something like that."

"He ought to know – about the mess and the pain at least."

I thought for a moment, then said, "I do need to know. I can't be free of it until I do."

"Oh well . . . the whole muddle screwed up one generation, no reason why . . . you see, oh Christ, if Archie was to blame entirely, then – it might have been tolerable. She couldn't go on living with him but – she might even have grown accustomed to losing Gerald. What she could never endure was the guilt. She blamed herself for everything – and you can be sure Archie did everything in his power to exploit that. He couldn't forgive her for ceasing to love him."

"But I still don't understand."

The dark glasses turned to face me and a warm flush of emotion was beginning to spread across her throat. "Of course you don't, you fool. How could you? You see, it was . . . Fran and your father were lovers." She paused and, then, sitting very still, nervous fingers at last motionless, she went on quickly, "Looking back I suppose it was inevitable. Louise was impossible: jealous and bad-tempered and hysterical one day and then the next she'd lie in bed, refusing to eat or speak or do anything. Sometimes she stayed in bed for days on end. Clancy wanted to help: he did his best but he was out of his depth, he just didn't understand what was happening. And all the time there was Frances, good old dependable Frances, warm and affectionate and – oh, all the things poor Lou would never be in a million years. He most likely turned to her for sympathy at first. When they were both at Chatton Heights they went for long walks together and talked endlessly. Archie had always been chronically unfaithful and Fran was alone a good deal – and she was never able to resist anyone in trouble. She told me once that she could talk to your father much more freely than to Archie. Perhaps I should have seen the danger signs then but I didn't, nor did she. Nor did Clancy. They carried on enjoying each other's company, being together whenever they could without thinking of what might . . . and then it was too late. They were in love. Totally and absolutely. Sounds corny, doesn't it, but there you are. Pathetic really. Bloody pathetic."

"But why couldn't they just be together?"

"That was all they wanted. They came to see me once. I was living in London at the time, I had a flat in Belsize Park – and we talked. All night long, going round and round and always coming back to the same stumbling blocks. Clancy was appalled at what Louise's reaction was sure to be, knew he couldn't leave you with her alone. And Archie had told Fran that if she left she'd never see Gerald again. They were in such a fog of love – and neither could understand how their wonderful passion for each other could cause only pain and misunderstanding."

"Archie knew already?"

"By then, yes. They kept it secret for as long as they could but my poor sister was hardly an accomplished liar. When he first discovered the truth he nearly went out of his mind with rage and jealousy. He did love Fran, you see, in his egotistical way. He sure as hell depended on her always to love him. And I think he must have cared for your father too, so that for him it must have been a double betrayal."

"Is that why my father decided to go to South America?"

"The decision was pretty well made for him. Old Everett was brought in and Clancy was given an ultimatum: either he stopped seeing Fran or Archie would tell your mother everything."

"She didn't know?"

"Never. Clancy was desperate to protect her. Of course, he knew that if he and Fran were to make a life for themselves then she'd have to know eventually but . . . not yet. So he and Fran agreed to a trial separation:

as much to prove to themselves as to anyone else that they couldn't stay apart, no matter how high the cost. Clancy agreed to move his family out to South America for a year."

"But my mother and I didn't go."

"You were supposed to. At the last moment your mother refused to leave. When she first heard the plan she was wildly enthusiastic, more optimistic than she'd been for years and she started to learn Portuguese – but in secret. The poor thing had some ridiculous fantasy about amazing Clancy with her fluency when they stepped from the aeroplane. Then she discovered she'd been learning the wrong language, they speak Spanish in Argentina, not Portuguese. That was it. She took it as a personal affront by the entire South American continent. But by then it was too late for Clancy to back out. He got hold of Sissy de Rhin to look after you both and then he left. I went with Fran to see him off and it was the saddest bloody thing I ever did. Five weeks later he was dead."

I was silent, immobile. What could I say? Poor Fran, how dreadful, I'm so sorry. Insulting words.

After a pause Deborah went on, her voice now barely reaching above a whisper. "She always believed he'd come back to her. At first she refused to accept that he was dead, that all she had to remember him by was a few snatched hours. Even so, she would have pulled through, I'm sure, if your mother hadn't broken down."

"Why?"

"Fran blamed herself, of course. Not that your mother ever knew about her and Clancy but still, if Clancy hadn't been in love with her then he wouldn't have gone to South America, there would have been no plane crash, no death. Perhaps it was a hint of the intolerable price they'd have had to pay for their love. Poor Fran was the most honourable person in the world – she had never let anyone down in her life. She was thrown into misery if she was five minutes late for an appointment and now, suddenly, she had destroyed, as she saw it, two people whom she had loved. She could no longer live with herself."

"So she killed herself?"

"In her letter to me she said she thought Gerald was going to be better off without her. That she had only ever brought misery to those she loved. She truly believed that." Her voice trailed away.

The silence was filled with the sound of rain falling gently against the window, the fire wheezing, in need of attention. When Adam and Molly came in with the cakes and tea we were sitting without speaking; Adam glanced at me anxiously as though afraid we had been sitting like that all the time. Tea cups were distributed and tiny tables adjusted. Molly poured tea and bustled around and put cakes on flowered plates with gold rims.

I said, "You mentioned Sissy de Rhin. How did you know her?"

"Fran knew her. Fran was always finding rest for lost souls."

"Then why— ?"

"No more questions, Fern Miller." She was crumbling a piece of sponge cake between thin fingers. I knew she would never eat it. "You've had enough answers for one day. Perhaps another time. The past is only tolerable in small doses. Now talk about the weather."

But when we were about to leave I said, "Thank you. This must have been painful for you but it means a great deal to me."

The dark lenses tilted up to face me. "Does it? And you're not shocked?"

"No. Well – maybe. Just a bit."

"It doesn't hurt to be shocked occasionally. You must come back and tell me about yourself. You have your father's way with you, Fern, though I daresay that like him you are unaware of the fact. Those same eyes. The dreamer who gets what they want. It's lucky for you you've turned out so much like him. And not like your mother."

"Do you not think I'm like her at all?"

"No. It's your father to the life."

I could feel my face relaxing into a smile. "I rather think," I said, "that is all I ever wanted to discover."

Chapter 9

We drove back through a landscape of fierce contrasts: the relentless grey of the sky had begun to break up into clumps and from time to time the sun shone through, a harsh storm yellow. As it grew colder the inadequacies of the car's heating system became more apparent and I was soon huddling under the old tartan rug that Adam kept in the back of the car.

As we set off from Deborah Brewster's house Adam had asked simply, "Did she talk?"

And I replied, "Yes, she talked."

Adam did not question me further and we drove in silence. I needed that silence, retreated into it like a wounded animal. The imagined landscape of my early years, bleak though it was, had been at least familiar. Now all that was swept away, dissolved, disrupted, and the few facts I had clung to, landmarks of a bleak certainty, were certain no longer.

There was an ache buried deep within me. I desperately wanted Dring. Wanted to hear her say, "No point in fretting over what can't be helped." Wanted to hear her say, "Stop moping about nothing and do something useful for a change. It's hours since you made me a cup of tea." Wanted . . . but I knew I wanted someone more than Dring, someone who had never been there and whom I knew now could never be found.

"On Dora's wise wings I myself found freedom." My father's words? His voice reaching down the wasted empty years to comfort me now? Too late, I thought, you followed your own tragedy and left me nothing but its ruins, pain and muddle.

After about half an hour Adam said gently, "You've

had your silence, Fern. What did Deborah tell you back there?" And then I told him: about my father and Aunt Frances, the ultimatum that had driven him to South America, her grief and self-reproach when he died. When I had finished he said nothing for a while, then glanced across as though waiting for me to carry on. "Is that all?"

"Isn't it enough?"

"That depends. It certainly explains much that never made sense before but I'm still left with the feeling that you're holding something back. And that whatever it is, is important."

The temptation then was almost overwhelming: to unburden myself of my huge secret, to turn to him and say, "Yes, Adam, there is more. Archie may not have written *Dora's Room* after all . . ." Would he believe it was possible or would he look at me and think, poor girl, the burden of the past is too much for her. First of all we had those hallucinations on the motorway and today this impossible fantasy. It's a pity, really, we could have got along. And I cowered from his scorn, his terrible pity.

"That's all," I said.

We drove in silence for a while until at length he turned to me. "You know, when I'm with you I find myself envying my son, an entirely novel experience. You're different when you're with him – more spontaneous, natural."

I laughed awkwardly. "But he's just a child," I said.

"It must be that I thrive on challenge," he muttered, almost to himself.

And now the silence between us was uncomfortable, almost antagonistic. I imagined how it might be otherwise, how he might hesitate, then say, "You're probably going to laugh at this, Fern, but I've always had the oddest hunch that it was your father who wrote *Dora's Room* . . ." and we could join hands across the common ground of my search. I knew that he was losing sympathy with me, losing patience – and that there was nothing I could do. Although I passionately wanted him to be my friend, to cling to the possibility that he might grow to be more than a friend, there seemed nothing I could do or say to hold him.

By the time we reached Chatton Heights it was raining steadily in the darkness. Adam pulled to a halt in front of the fortress façade of the building.

"I feel as though I'm depositing you back at some ghoulish boarding school," he said, glancing up towards the unlit windows. "Are you sure there isn't somewhere else you'd rather be?"

"I shall be fine."

"Hmm. I wonder why my heart sinks every time you speak like that." I could just make out his features in the darkness and his expression was sombre. "You're such a peculiar mixture of vulnerability and strength, Fern, that I never know which is uppermost. Still . . . I must take your word for it."

"Do you want to come in?"

"I'd like to but . . . I'm supposed to look in and see Ben on my way back to London."

"Oh well . . ." I was surprised at the strength of my disappointment.

He hesitated. "It's been a useful afternoon."

"Yes. Thank you for arranging everything."

"Don't mention it. And keep me posted if you discover anything else."

"Yes. You too."

"Of course."

The memory of that night at Alderly Drive lay between us, a warning of further disaster. There seemed no way across the huge divide of our politeness. So much of me was held back by my fear of sharing my crazy speculations about my father and *Dora's Room*, there hardly seemed anything left over to offer Adam.

He took my face between his hands and kissed me gently on the mouth. "Good night, Fern," and added ruefully, just as I was about to slide from the car, "and spare a thought for the poor sod of a prince who hacks his way through all the brambles and forests only to discover the lady in question preferred being asleep all the time."

I almost turned back to him then and told him everything – but the habit of secrecy and shame is a hard one to break.

As I ran across the rain-wet gravel towards the dim light of the side door I could hear his car driving away into the darkness.

I went straight to the portraits and contemplated them once more. Archie and Frances, Clancy and Louise. Frances and Clancy. A note of vulnerability had crept in; they looked younger, somehow, more fragile. Or maybe I was the one who was changing. They were fixed in a frame of everlasting youthfulness, while I alone was growing older.

As I went along the passageway to the drawing-room I could hear the sound of women's voices. It was such a rarity for Tillie to have visitors – in fact I could not remember seeing a friend of hers in all the time I had been at Chatton Heights – that I wondered if perhaps Archie was entertaining a new influx of female admirers. But drawing closer I realised there was something odd about these voices – as well as a couple of female ones there was a weird-sounding man's voice, a growly voice, the kind a large animal might have in a Christmas pantomime. A bear perhaps. Something phoney.

I pushed open the door. The room was empty. A single table lamp cast long shadows against the dark wallpaper, the darker curtains. The oak sideboards and bureaux, the leather sofas and chairs, seemed to loom even larger than usual in this dusky half-light. Then there was a flicker of movement and I saw a puppet spring to life and walk with bouncing steps across the stage of the little theatre.

It was a sickening moment, a second or two that hurtled through my mind into an endless falling. So this is what happens, the falling shrieked across my head, puppets dance. And you spin downwards into madness.

"That's better," said a voice – and Tillie straightened herself behind the low table and her hands jigged inexpertly at the strings, "now you are dancing to *my* tune . . ."

"Oh Tillie!" In my relief my voice bubbled over enthusiastically. "You've found the theatre. Tom Page brought it in this morning. Isn't it wonderful?"

She ignored me completely. All her attention was focused on the puppet whose strings were in her hands. I realised then that I had never seen Tillie actually concentrate on anything before: normally her china-doll eyes were gazing somewhere into the middle distance but now they were focused on the puppet with an intensity so fierce it was frightening.

It was the old man doll who had been chosen to dance across the stage. The magician.

She was making him speak. That growly, pantomime bear voice again: "I'm tired. Let me rest. I'm too old to dance."

Her own voice now, but not as I had ever heard it before. Coaxing, but relentless too: "No no, not tired. Not yet, not ever. Can't be tired. Up the stairs and down. That's right. In my lady's chamber. Dance, I say. Can't be tired. Your turn now."

"Tillie— " She didn't hear me. Couldn't hear me. I was an intruder on a most private scene, almost as though I was invading the secret places of her mind. I wanted to creep away and hope she never realised I had been there but at the same time I was unable to move. Rooted to the spot.

So I stayed. Watched and listened.

The growly voice: "So tired, please don't. You're killing me. Must stop now."

Tillie again with her forceful voice: "Oh no, not yet. Not ever. Now you dance to my tune, I'm pulling the strings. See how you like it. There you go. Dance away, dance away. Oh look, who's this, Miss Pretty-pretty. Now, what shall we do with her?"

Even before she stepped out from the wings I knew that this second puppet was going to be the young girl, the heroine, the princess. And I knew that just as for Tillie the old magician had become my grandfather, so I knew that this second puppet was myself.

She was talking to the second puppet. "And where have you been all this time, pretty little maid? Can you dance too? No? Then let me teach you some steps. You'll have to learn, you know. In this place everybody has to dance."

Now both the puppets were jerking up and down on the stage. I could see Tillie's hands moving with odd little stabbing movements and the cobweb wrinkles around her mouth were crumpled into a grin of vengeance. Above her head was the painting of the stag being dragged to a bloody death by the hounds.

"Jig, jig, my little pig. Let's see you dance, your turn now." Her voice began to rise, like a wind getting up on a winter's night, a long thin stream of hate. "Up and down, in and out, skippety skip, how do *you* like it, eh? Now I'm in charge and you can't escape and— "

A man's voice behind me, a real one this time.

"Christ. Now she's really gone."

It was Archie. Like Tillie I had been so absorbed in watching the scene on the stage that I never heard his footsteps behind me.

I turned to him with relief. "Oh Archie, I— "

But he pushed past me. "Right ho, Tillie," he said loudly, "fun time is over. Time to put the toys away and get back to normal. I said Tillie, Tillie! Listen to me!"

But even though Archie was by now standing right beside her, Tillie's trance was unbroken. Still she crouched over the stage, still the puppets danced their jerky little steps, arms flapping as if for flight.

"Tillie – oh hell."

Archie struck her then, quite hard, on the side of the face. She did not even flinch, only turned slowly to look at him while the red blotch appeared on her cheek. Then, focusing on him briefly, she turned once again to look away into the familiar middle distance.

"I didn't know . . ." she said, "I never saw . . ."

"That's all right, Tillie." Archie's voice was brisk, matter-of-fact even. Just as the blow had been. Violence quite devoid of all emotion, almost routine. "No one will be cross with you. You just got a bit carried away with your game, that's all. No need to be upset now."

"Yes . . ." she murmured, "no . . ."

"Now, put these silly dolls away and go and make yourself useful. It must be time to lay the table for supper, eh?" He was speaking to her almost kindly now, the first time I had ever heard him talk to her in quite that tone.

She was shivering. I could tell because the puppets were rattling slightly. Then she glanced down and an expression of surprise crossed her face, a look that said quite plainly: how did I come to be holding these?

The old man took a tentative step.

"Tillie, put them down at once."

She relaxed her grip suddenly and both the puppets collapsed in a heap. She straightened slowly.

"I must . . ." She began to look about her anxiously.

"That's right. You run along now."

She didn't run, exactly, but she left the room, brushing past me as she did so. That familiar odour of neglect . . . and yet although the sleeve of her green cardigan brushed against my hand I could have sworn she never even noticed I was there.

As she vanished from sight I let out a long breath.

"Care for a drink?" asked Archie. "I'll get you one anyway, though God knows you don't deserve it. If you hadn't left that bloody stupid theatre lying around none of this would have happened. Here, drink up. Tillie can be pretty ghoulish at times."

"Does she often— ? I mean, has she ever— ?"

"Steady on," he smiled cruelly, "you're beginning to mimic her uncanny grasp of sentence structure. If you mean does she have these odd turns from time to time then the answer is yes. Though I must say I've never seen a performance quite so bad – or as good – as that. I must have a word with Bob Collins about her medication."

"I didn't know— " I began.

Archie broke in harshly, "There's a hell of a lot you don't know." And this was so obviously the truth that I said no more.

"Drink up," he said, "Tillie in full spate is bad enough when you're used to it but first time around . . . mind you, she's getting worse."

"Since my grandfather died?"

He stared at me levelly. "No. His death was an unmitigated relief for us all, her included. It was hearing the will that did it."

I sat down on the edge of the sofa. "Then it's my fault."

"Sob sob. My heart bleeds for you. Please excuse me if I refrain from breaking down in public."

I looked up. He was watching me with an expression of triumph and this time there was no attempt to disguise his malice with his usual veneer of geniality.

I said, "But I don't understand. Why should he have treated her so badly?"

"What a fatuous question. He treated everyone badly, haven't you even realised that much yet? It was the way he was. Some people like gambling or collecting stamps – my dear papa liked making people suffer. A kind of hobby, you could call it. At any rate, it kept him amused."

He stooped and picked up the strings of the old man puppet.

"She thought that was him," I said, "and the other one was— "

"You, of course. Well, what do you expect? You're the one who was mad keen to get Daddy's little theatre back in working order. I could have told you to leave well alone."

"I never imagined there'd be any harm in an old toy theatre."

"Then your imagination is sorely lacking."

240

I sat for a few moments, sipping the sherry. An image formed itself in my mind: I saw Tillie come into my bedroom, Gracie's room, the one that had belonged to my father. Her face had that intent, concentrated expression that I had seen just now while she manipulated the puppets, a kind of serene malice as, slowly and deliberately, she began scattering my belongings around the room. And then turned her attention to the photograph in its wooden frame.

"Archie," I said, "I want you to tell me about Tillie."

"I thought you picked up that kind of gossip from the servants."

He poured himself another drink. "Hmm, what can I add? Strangely enough she was rather charming when she came here first. Big blue eyes, very shy, and attractive in a washed-out, spinsterish sort of way. She was employed to nurse my father when he contracted pneumonia, oh, ages ago. Before Clancy died."

"I didn't know she was a nurse."

"Not qualified, you understand. She'd looked after her ghastly geriatric father for years before he died and that was thought to be some kind of recommendation. She ought to have quit once Everett recovered but she didn't. I don't suppose she had anywhere much to go by then. And she'd become useful to my father."

"Is that why he married her?"

"Christ no, not until he had to." Archie sat in an armchair and leaned his head back and beamed for no apparent reason at the ceiling. "One remarkable day Romance swept into poor Tillie's abject life. Mr Right on his white charger in the person of a balding and overweight civil servant whose ambition was to retire and run a newsagent's in Devon. He swept our poor heroine off her feet with promises of paper rounds and a seven-day week. When Everett contemplated the prospect of losing his handmaiden he married her. Mr Balding Newsagent didn't stand a chance. And ever after, my father considered he had been blackmailed into this rash act, so devoted his twilight years to punishing her for gross presumption."

"And is doing so still, through me."

Archie ignored me. "Their wedding was quite the most loathsome farce I have ever seen and God knows I've seen a few. Tillie held out for a proper ceremony. I think she even managed to exhume some moribund female relative who obligingly sobbed into her hankie throughout. And Tillie dressed up in all the white lace and frills she could lay her greedy paws on – she looked like a vision from Transylvania, one of the risen dead come to prey on the tranquil folk of Long Chatton."

I shuddered. "Poor Tillie."

"A lamb to the slaughter." He had stood up to refill his glass but paused, watching me closely. "A bit like you, Fern, in some respects. Tell me, how are you progressing in your quest for Daddy-dear?"

I glanced up at him. Had he found out about my visit to Deborah Brewster? But surely that was impossible. "I've given up," I said, "it was becoming a waste of time."

"Sensible girl," he nodded his head approvingly, "I was becoming somewhat anxious for your well-being. You often strike me as so— " and here his hand rested lightly on my hair, "so – vulnerable, my dear." And his hand trailed down to touch my shoulder. Like snail slime, his corruption sticking to me. I shifted uneasily out of reach.

There was a movement in the doorway. Tillie had come to announce supper and was staring at us with huge blank eyes. Eyes as big as saucers, I thought, as I followed her from the room.

That night when I fell asleep I dreamed that I was driving my car along an unfamiliar stretch of road. Or rather, I was attempting to drive it. For every time I tried to steer or change gear, an invisible something tugged at my wrist and made me do the opposite to what I had intended. At first I was annoyed, then frightened. A lorry was approaching and I knew that the strange tugging would make me steer towards it, not away . . . and I had lost control. And then I realised that my arms and legs were attached at the joints to lengths of twine, almost impossible to see but very, very strong. And that above me an unseen presence was tugging at the strings. And manipulating my every move.

I awoke in a cold terror and switched on the light, waiting for the fear to pass. As I slowly adjusted to waking reality, there was no problem in seeing what had caused the nightmare: the experience with Tillie and the puppets and what I was learning about my grandfather was all the explanation I needed. Yet even as the fear rolled away and I was able to think clearly again I understood that there was truth in the dream. It was stupid to imagine that my grandfather was controlling us still, from beyond the grave: he was dead and his power had died with him. What was true was that we were all of us contriving to act as though he did still control us – perhaps Tillie and Gerald and Archie were too demoralised by years of his tyranny to do anything about it, but that did not mean I had to remain passive as well. And I was the one best placed to break the stranglehold he had on his family.

No sooner had I thought this through than the solution announced itself to me clear as a banner headline. Why had I not seen the answer before? Now I was all impatience for the slow night hours to pass and morning to arrive so I could begin to put my brilliant plan into practice.

At our first meeting the solicitor, Mr Markham, had told me in his hearty way that he was available whenever I needed him and I now discovered he was as good as his word. By eleven o'clock I was seated in his comfortable office above one of Long Chatton's innumerable antique shops explaining my idea.

He did not share my opinion of its brilliance. Far from it. In fact his vision of a neatly ordered world was definitely offended. His expression gradually changed from that of a well-fed eighteenth-century squire to that of a huntin' shootin' and fishin' gentleman who has just discovered his son and heir to be an anti-blood-sports vegetarian. He said I should consider carefully before doing anything rash. He then went on to make a good many avuncular remarks about youthful idealism and being pragmatic and Life in the Real World (which is always "out there" of course, never where you are now) but eventually he was forced to admit that yes, what I was proposing was a technical possibility. Not until the coming August, of course, when I would be twenty-one – and in the meantime he hoped . . . but I was no longer paying him any attention. He had given me all the information I needed.

I returned to Chatton Heights, parking my car as usual in the huge coach house at the back. As usual Gerald was there, large feet poking out from under the engine of the Daimler.

"I hope you're coming to lunch," I said to the pair of boots which twitched irritably in response, "I've something to tell you all which you're sure to find most interesting."

Pale winter sunlight was filtering through the magnolia leaves that overhung the dining-room window and shining on to the huge dining table, polished that morning by Elsa until it glowed like a mirror. In one of the back pantries I had found an elaborate porcelain bowl encrusted with hundreds of tiny flowers and this now stood in the centre of the table, filled with winter greenery. My efforts to brighten my grandfather's house sometimes seemed futile as sweeping sand off a beach with a dustpan and brush, but nonetheless I was determined to persevere.

Mrs Viney had brought in a steaming apple pie but today, knowing that the moment had come to announce my decision, I found my appetite had vanished.

"I went to see Mr Markham this morning," I said, "that's what I wanted to talk about."

I was half expecting one of Archie's sarcastic comments or Gerald's rudeness, but they said nothing, only waited. Archie briefly touched his cravat, an especially opulent one in shades of purple, green and pink. Tillie looked more doll-like than ever: she had smeared blusher on her cheeks, perhaps to hide the mark left by Archie's blow. Gerald was looking as though nothing I said could possibly be of interest to him.

I carried on. "Since the terms of my grandfather's will are so obviously unfair – not in a legal sense, you understand, legally it is completely watertight, but as a way of sharing what belonged to him – then the obvious course of action is to make our own arrangements. It's the only way to free ourselves from this muddle he has us all caught up in."

Gerald's eyes had that slightly squinty look that they always got when he was concentrating hard. "What are you getting at?" he asked.

"It's so simple, don't you see. All we have to do is get together and agree to draw up a document called a deed of family arrangement, something like that. We can *agree* to share out the inheritance absolutely equally, four exact quarters. Everybody the same."

Archie spoke. "Do you mean to sell the house?"

"If that is what we all agree, yes. But the money and the house are separate issues: we can divide up the money fairly and there'd still be enough income from the estate, the tenancies and so on, to keep the house going as it is now. The whole point of what I'm proposing is that *we* are the ones who decide what happens. We can break this mythical power you all seem to imagine my grandfather still wields."

"Hmm. Mythical, eh?" It was Archie again, a question not really expecting an answer. He still fingered the silk at his throat.

Tillie chimed in suddenly, "Always a bully . . . but of course we never really . . ." I had no idea if she had comprehended my words.

Gerald said, "So we're all supposed to get handouts from you instead." But even his statement was strangely without rancour. I had expected my plan to be met initially with scorn, delight, disbelief, some strong emotion. This stunned acquiescence took me by surprise. It was only then, as I watched their blank faces, that I understood the full extent of my grandfather's control over them.

Even Archie, who had the ability to fill me with such fear, even he was in many ways as childish as Gerald: they were both passive, saw themselves as victims, dependent on the whims of others. As I absorbed their suspicious silence I felt as if I had opened the door of a cage in which a group of animals had long been imprisoned. And instead of kicking their heels and making a gleeful dash for the open spaces while they still could, they sniffed around the inside of the doorway and glanced over their shoulders with timid eyes. Suspicious. Wary of a trap. Fearing freedom above all things.

"If you consider it, you'll see what a good plan it is."

"Oh yes, it's a good plan, all right," commented Archie, neither enthusiasm nor disapproval colouring his normally expressive voice.

"The whole thing can't be finalised until after my birthday in the summer but— "

"Oh, I see," Gerald's sneer sounded almost like relief, "leaving Lady Bountiful plenty of time to change her mind."

I said calmly, "I won't change my mind. But you'll have to trust me for the time being."

Gerald snorted. I suppose I should have realised that nothing in his upbringing had taught him to trust anyone.

"Well, I think . . ." Tillie was frowning slightly and the thousand tiny lines around her mouth worked vigorously as she sucked on her imaginary peppermint. "A very good . . . of course, if it works . . . so often disappointment . . ."

I looked at her curiously as she struggled to pin down the wayward thought. Last night when she was playing with the puppets she had seemed an object of terror: today I could see her as she was, a pathetic and lonely woman whose life had been blasted by the selfishness and cruelty of others. How would she choose to use her money? A little flat in London? A bungalow by the sea? Who knows, her freedom might signal the start of a new phase of her life, some of the hurt might be eased away.

Or she might be unable to leave. Maybe she had grown so used to her dreary life at Chatton Heights that she would be quite incapable of breaking away.

Perhaps, for Tillie, freedom was coming too late.

That evening I telephoned Adam and told him of my decision. He responded with enthusiasm and said I must explain the details to him properly when next we met. I could hear voices in the background, voices from his London life in which I played no part. As I put the phone down I couldn't help wondering wistfully if his approval of my scheme had been simply an attempt to keep our conversation as brief as possible.

Chapter 10

Three days later I was on the motorway heading for London. On the way to meet Archie's publisher.

I was still giddy from my newfound boldness. Was this really timid Mary Miller, the human camouflage expert whose one ambition in life had always been to blend into the background, who had calmly arranged a meeting with a total stranger? Exploited her parents' tragedy to gain what she wanted? ("You remember Clancy, the brother who died in the plane crash. I'm his daughter." Paul Sobey's voice had changed from boredom to a warm, "Oh yes, Fern, wasn't it? How about lunch some time this week?")

I was sure Paula would have disapproved. She would have told me I was becoming obsessed and maybe she was right. Unlike Adam she had been thoroughly scornful when I told her of my plan to change the will.

"Mary Fern," her voice on the end of the telephone had been almost hushed with disbelief, "I do believe that's the stupidest thing you've done yet. If you don't want the money yourself surely you can find a good cause to support."

"You don't understand," I tried to explain, "even if I give all the money away to a home for stray dogs, I'm still helping my grandfather punish the others. The only way to break free of him is to do what he should have done in the first place and share the money equally."

"You're such an innocent it breaks my heart. How do you know they didn't plan this from the outset and you've tumbled straight into their trap? Who says your grandfather has used you to punish them all? Why, *they* do. And bully for him if he did. Maybe they only got what they deserved. If you want my opinion I don't think Tillie is half as batty as she makes out. I think there's been some cold hard calculation going on in that house and now they must all be rubbing their hands with glee because it's paid off so easily."

"You surely don't think they actually worked all this out between them, do you?" I protested. "But Paula, they never even speak to each other!"

"Not in front of you, maybe. But you don't have the first idea what they get up to behind your back. They're all still living there together, aren't they? If they all hated each other as much as you say, well, one of them would have moved out by now, surely."

At the time I laughed at her suggestion, told her it was ridiculous. And it *was* ridiculous. Yet even now the scene kept forming in my mind: Tillie, Archie and Gerald, gathered around the hearth in the drawing-room, firelight glinting on their faces and giving them the appearance of conspirators in an old film. Gerald speaks first: "She's decided to stay here for a bit. That's a point in our favour." And Archie says, "The poor half-wit is so gullible she'll swallow any bait. All we have to do now is make her believe she's playing into Everett's hands by keeping the money." Tillie adds, "And I can pretend to be crazy, that my disappointment has totally unhinged me." Gerald again, "Yes, you'd be good at that." And they all laugh. In harmony.

The very idea of it was grotesque. Oh yes? And what about this present mission, this idea that my father might have written his brother's book? Surely it was every bit as ludicrous to chase around the countryside and all because of the babblings of a madwoman. If my mother had claimed to be heir to the throne would I now be frantically searching for proofs of swapped babies, mistaken identities, no idea too outrageous so long as it restored my faith in my crazy mother? Did I really expect Mr Sobey to say suddenly, "By the way, it was your father who sent in the manuscript of *Dora's Room*. It was only after he died in the plane crash that Archie told me he had written it."

Several times on that journey I was on the point of turning around, turning back, giving up the search. It was growing too dangerous. Yet something made me carry on. My obsession. Those others were right, I was becoming obsessed and there was nothing in the world I could do about it.

I caught sight of my face in the mirror as I parked the car in a wildly expensive car park in central London. There was an expression on my face I'd never seen before. A kind of determination, I suppose. A growing strength and refusal to admit defeat. Or perhaps . . . I looked again. Yes, see there, wasn't that stubborn set of the mouth just a little bit *too* determined, that cold, closed look in the eyes just a little *too* uncompromising? Something out of touch with ordinary everyday reality that I'd seen once before?

Oh God, I prayed, as I collected my ticket from the attendant, make Paul Sobey give me proof positive that Archie must have written *Dora's Room*, that my father could not possibly be the author. Let him free me from this maze of delusions. Oh please.

"Your father was a very private man, you know. I can't say that I ever really knew him well." Paul Sobey smiled suddenly, as if apologising in advance for his limitations as an informant.

I had taken to him at once. He was tall and thin with lank, fair hair and meagre, studious features. He exuded a steady kindness which was quite different from the routine empathy of the likes of Dr Phelps. When we met I had the impression that he was wondering just how he had let himself in for a lunch appointment with the niece of one of his authors but he was far too courteous to say so, or to give me less than all of his attention.

We had arranged to meet in an Italian restaurant not far from his office. Since I had never heard of most of the items on the menu I ordered an avocado, with sole to follow. "How wise," he agreed, ordering the same.

While we waited for the first course to arrive I asked, "Did you meet my father through Archie?"

"Not at all. It was the other way around. Your father and I were at Merton together. We didn't have much contact to begin with: he was reading Law, which he hated by the way, and I was a historian. We only became friends towards the end of our second year."

"Why did he choose Law if he hated it?"

"Family pressure. People get pushed into doing all sorts of things for the wrong reasons. But he didn't work at all, barely scraped home with a third. He spent all his time acting and trying to get some new magazine off the ground."

"Was that how you got to know him?"

"Over the acting, not the magazine. We were in one of those summer plays together. Oddly enough, although Clancy was one of those people who don't put themselves forward much – the kind of person you'd expect to run a mile from any sort of public performance – the moment he walked out in front of an audience he was transformed. You know the way some actors seem not to have much personality of their own until they step into a role and then it's as if the role fills them, makes them grow into someone totally different. I've only seen it happen once or twice since but each time it reminds me of Clancy."

"I know he always liked the theatre. He was given a toy one as a child."

"Not that I'm saying he was lacking in personality, far from it. Only it wasn't until he walked on stage that first night that I realised how much of himself he'd kept hidden away. Oh dear, I'm not putting this very well."

"Why do you say hidden?"

"I'm wondering myself. I hadn't thought of it in quite those terms before." He frowned at his avocado and thoughtfully scooped out a mouthful. "I know of course that his father was something of a tyrant, the kind of 'These are my footsteps now make sure you follow them' type of parent. Pretty well an extinct breed these

251

days but they were commoner than you'd think back then. But you must have known your grandfather well."

"I don't remember him at all. After my father died I had no further contact with my family until a month or so ago."

"Hm. That's strange . . ." He waited for me to elaborate but when I didn't he went on, "I only met old Everett a couple of times. Once was at Clancy's wedding when he was clearly enraged by the whole situation – but by then Clancy had broken free."

"Broken free?"

"He never really managed it at Oxford. For instance, he didn't have the courage to change from Law to a more sympathetic school, English for instance. His rebellion was still of the passive kind, not working, making sure he got a lousy degree. After Oxford he inevitably went to work for the family firm – and of course he loathed every minute of it."

"So why didn't he leave?"

"Hard to say, exactly. It wasn't through weakness because Clancy was not a weak person – far from it. A weaker man might have quit sooner."

"I don't follow you— "

"He believed, you see, that he could force himself to do anything, to *be* anything, that it was all a question of will. And I suppose too there was a part of him that still longed to be the kind of son his father had tried to mould. He'd probably have stayed in the firm for ever if his health hadn't broken down and the doctors said he needed a holiday, a complete break. That was when he made the overland trip to Nepal and met your mother. After that there was no going back to the family."

"Wouldn't they accept her?"

"Probably not, but that wasn't the point. There was a kind of wildness, a freedom about Louise, that must have attracted him right from the start. She didn't so much try to flout the conventions, she simply had no idea conventions existed. She 'did her own thing' long before that became fashionable. Later on, of course, that got her into all sorts of difficulties . . . but you know all of that."

"Yes."

"Well. Anyway. Once he had teamed up with Louise there was no chance of ever being father's dutiful son again. They drifted for a while, but gradually I lost touch . . . by then your mother was becoming pretty difficult."

"My father did work for the family again. He went to South America to close down an office."

"So I heard. I never did understand the reason for that trip."

I was silent. The avocado shells had been removed and the waiters were bringing the main course and salad. Paul Sobey smiled at me, an encouraging smile. Tempting, in that moment, to tell him of my real concern . . .

I said, "It was my father who suggested Archie bring the manuscript of *Dora's Room* to you."

"Was it indeed?" His interest was no more than polite.

"Yes. Just before my father died he wrote to Archie from South America and gave him your name. That must have been some time in May. Can you remember if Archie had already sent *Dora's Room* to you before that or was it some time afterwards? The first edition didn't come out until the following year."

"Hm. It was a long time ago. I could check the file but— " he was frowning, "I remember it was very hot so I would guess it must have been July or August, though without checking I can't be precise."

"But it was some time during that summer?"

"When I first discussed it with Archie, yes. So I'd imagine he'd already sent the manuscript off – at Clancy's suggestion as you say – and I'd had a chance to look through it. I wish I could say I'd spotted a winner right away but I didn't. I was enormously excited by its originality but I feared it might suffer from being so impossible to categorise."

"Did he make any alterations to the manuscript?"

He laughed. "You're not some PhD student in disguise, are you? Trying to wheedle out of me information that Archie refuses? No, of course not, though if you didn't look so exactly like your father I might wonder. As a matter of fact he made no changes whatsoever which is most unusual. He pretty well said that if we were satisfied with it then that was good enough for him."

"How fascinating." My throat was beginning to burn with the pressure of the words I could not speak.

"Your uncle is remarkable in all sorts of ways. You'd never think, for instance, that he's essentially a highly *modest* man, now would you?"

I thought of Archie. "Not really, no."

"And yet he is."

"In what way?"

"Well, not changing the manuscript for one thing. He always listens to advice, usually takes it too. I don't suppose he told you this, but when he sent the typescript to us first he said it was the work of a friend. I say, Fern, is there something wrong?"

Recovering myself as quickly as I could. "Oh yes, of course, it's just so stuffy in here I felt . . . but please, do tell me about his friend."

"I can ask the waiter to open a window."

"No, don't bother. I'm fine now. Please go on."

"If you're sure you're all right . . . it's a common enough ploy. Testing the water, so to speak. You know the kind of thing – 'My friend thinks she's pregnant, what should *I* do?' Archie must have been so anxious that *Dora's Room* was no good that he decided to hide behind the familiar 'my friend' smokescreen."

"You're quite sure he said it was a friend. Not— ?"

"Quite sure. Who else?"

"I just wondered."

"I guessed at once what he was up to. You see, I'd been to Chatton Heights once or twice so I could see the location of the story. But I played along with him anyway. I invited him – and his friend – to come and have lunch and talk things over. That was when we had the meeting in the restaurant near here, the day it was so hot. Of course, no friend appeared. It wasn't until I'd convinced him that the book had genuine artistic merit that he admitted to being the author. I don't know when I've come across someone with so little confidence in their achievement."

"And yet he always seems so sure of himself."

"Superficially. He was still working with his father then. Unlike Clancy he'd always seemed quite happy to fit into the family mould, but the pretence must have placed him under enormous strain."

"But why the secrecy?"

"You should ask him. Fear of failure, fear of alienating old Everett . . . it's easy to imagine how torn he was."

"Yes." Again that constriction of the throat as I spoke. The constriction of a lie. "Tell me, one of the most fascinating problems is the dedication on the first edition."

"Ah yes, the mysterious Dora."

"When did you suggest adding that on? Was it during your first meeting?"

He looked puzzled. "Added on? I don't believe it was. I'm pretty well certain the dedication was already in place on the original typescript. I do remember thinking it was a bit odd."

"You're sure it wasn't suggested by you? Or by someone in your office?"

"Absolutely. If we *were* helping with the dedication we'd never come up with a fictional character. My own theory is that Dora was a private name for his wife and that once she had died he simply decided to revert to her public name. He went to pieces after her death, you know, they adored each other."

"Do you believe she was his muse?"

He smiled. "I've never been quite sure what a real-life muse looks like, have you? Some kind of baroque-looking female in diaphanous garments stepping through a mist-shrouded Arcadia. A lady who belongs in a silvan glade. I never met Frances but she never sounded especially silvan or baroque. Still, something happened to Archie

255

when he lost her. I always ask him if he's writing again, but only for form's sake. He's a one-book man, I fear." He paused. "And what a book." The expected tribute.

The conversation shifted to memories of my father, but he told me nothing new, nothing that helped to pin down that strange and insubstantial character.

"Thank you for your help," I said as we parted.

"A pleasure." He smiled, his thin, wispy features warming with kindness. "Your father was a good friend and I . . . and he . . . well, remember me to Archie."

"Yes," I said. Knowing I would not.

For a while I simply walked. I hardly knew whether to be elated or worried by what I had learned. If I had really been hoping for some proof that my father could not possibly have written *Dora's Room* then I had been disappointed. Everything Paul Sobey told me was consistent with a sequence of events that began with Clancy sitting down at his desk, pen in hand, to write a book called *Dora's Room*. But there was no indication that it had not been Archie. Only the word of a madwoman and his own long silence.

A fine sleet had begun to fall but I hardly noticed it. Just walked.

I remember once when I was quite small, eight or nine, Dring and I went for a few days to the seaside. There was a scruffy little shingle beach near the guest house and one day, when the sea was rough, too rough for swimming, I went and stood in the shallows anyway. It was fascinating, the waves were pushing onwards to the beach with all the weight of the Atlantic rollers behind them and then the fierce pull of the undertow as the water was sucked out over the pebbles. Both pressures existed simultaneously, towards the beach and back into the ocean. And that was how I felt now. One part of me was sorry that I had not been pushed back on the firm dry land where everybody else, all those people who knew Archie to be the author of *Dora's Room*, were calmly going about their normal everyday affairs. Paul Sobey might have said, "Oh yes, I remember Archie approaching me when he first had the idea for *Dora's Room* and I like to think I was able to provide constructive criticism while he was working on it too. I saw all the rough drafts." No more questions. Mystery solved. Firm ground beneath my feet once more. But there was another part, equally strong, which rejoiced that the search had not led to such a dead end. Not yet. The strong undertow, the current pulling me back towards the deep black waters far out to sea where nothing was as it seemed on the surface, that current was terrifying. But there is exhilaration even in fear.

Think calmly, I told myself. Reconstruct how it might have been. My father went to South America in an attempt to end an affair with his brother's wife. It was hardly likely, was it, that he would leave his precious manuscript with the brother whom he had just betrayed. And yet, if he was indeed the author of *Dora's Room*, then that was precisely what he must have done.

From what I had learned so far of my father's character – unworldly, unrealistic about relationships – it seemed entirely possible. After all, he couldn't leave it with his wife, nor his sister-in-law, nor his father. And he left in a hurry.

So he set off to South America, having deposited the manuscript with Archie. Why did Archie then say that it was the work of "a friend", rather than of his brother – or himself? Had Clancy asked him to do this? Or was he simply testing the water, genuinely unsure of the merit of the work which he, or his brother, had produced? By the time Archie and Paul Sobey did meet, Clancy was dead. The revelation that the book was a fine one came as a complete surprise to Archie – that famous modesty? or was the truth perhaps that he hadn't even read it? – and it must have been still more surprising to Archie when Paul Sobey said, "And of course, Archie, there's not much point in denying it now. You wrote it, didn't you?" Did Archie start to protest? "No, actually . . . it was— " And maybe Paul Sobey interrupted him, "This book will make your name, you know. It might even make you rich." And then the temptation had been too strong. After all, he only had to agree. Clancy was dead and the book's success made no difference to him now.

And then? The deception grew. Perhaps Archie even began to believe the part he was being called upon to play. And there was little danger of being found out. After all, the only person who knew the truth had been certified insane. Who would listen to her?

My head was bursting with possibilities and conjecture. I went to a telephone box, dialled Adam's number. I needed to talk to him. I would even risk his disbelief for the chance of unburdening myself of the jumble of questions and doubts that were humming inside my head.

There was no reply at his home. His office said he was out on an assignment and was not expected back that afternoon. My voice speaking to the receptionist had been tinny and unreal. I tried his home again, just in case. I emerged from the call box and looked around – but I had walked for so long I had not the faintest idea where I was. I hailed a taxi to take me back to my car.

As I drove away from London through the grey pall of sleet the need to touch base again increased. To make contact with something solid and unchanging. Instead of turning off for Long Chatton I continued into Bristol and drove to the hospital.

The bed at the end of the ward which Dring had occupied since her admission had been taken over by an elderly lady with grotesquely peroxided hair.

"Dring?" I mumbled stupidly. Staring at the unfamiliar face, my arms full of flowers and well-disguised cigarettes.

The peroxided lady beamed at me toothlessly. "Are you looking for someone, love?" she queried.

Dring is dead, was the first thought that leaped into my mind. She died in the night and they haven't told me and now it's too late. A moment of headlong panic before, "Are you looking for Mrs de Rhin?" A trainee nurse was standing in front of me. "She's been a bit

258

poorly recently so we moved her into a side ward. Just for now."

My relief at seeing Dring alive was so intense that it was a few moments before I realised how desperately unwell she was looking. Her skin had turned an odd yellowish-grey colour and seemed to be sinking round the bones of her face. When I spoke her name it was a long time before she dragged her eyelids back and focused on my face.

"Mary?" she said, and smiled.

"Hello, Dring." All the strength had drained from my legs and I sank down on to the bed. "I brought you some flowers. And this box of chocolates. And there's two packs of cigarettes hidden under the top layer."

"That's nice," said to please me. Knowing she would not smoke them.

"Are you feeling dreadful?"

"Just a bit. But the nurses are very kind."

"Oh Dring!"

It was all I could do to stop myself from getting up then and there and fleeing the hospital. So passive, so beaten, this gentle, compliant Dring. What had happened to the grumbling and the cursing and the determination never to give in? Once again those anonymous ranks of white-dressed professionals with their bright smiles and smell of antiseptic were destroying the person I cared for most in the world.

"You'll feel all right in a day or so," I said stupidly, "I know you will. And then we can plan how to get you out of here. I've been enquiring about nursing homes."

Anxiety puckered her brow. "I don't want to move, dear. It's comfortable here. Only my leg hurts so."

"Has it been that bad?"

She closed her eyes. "Tell me what you've been doing."

"Talking to people. Finding out about my parents. I know you don't approve but right now it's what I have to do. I went to see Aunt Frances' sister. Deborah Brewster, the painter."

"Oh yes," she said, no tremor of recognition.

"Do you remember her? She knew you. Or at least, she knew who you were."

"No." Her eyes were still closed. "Can't say I remember her."

"Dring, listen. You once told me that Archie had somehow harmed my mother. I think you said he was the one who pushed her over the edge, something like that. Why did you say that? What did he do to her? I know you hate to talk about the past but please try, for my sake. It is important."

She was too weak to resist my questions. "He came to the house. Your mother was still there. They talked. I don't know what they said. You and I went out to the park, I think. When I came back she was . . . different."

"Did she give you any idea what he said, or did?"

"And he took away some stuff."

"What?"

Plaintive now: "How should I know? Boxes of it, papers, that sort of thing. Nothing valuable, I would have cleared it out anyway. But *she* was upset."

"What sort of papers?"

"I told you, I don't know. I never saw them."

"Were they to do with my father?"

"I don't know. They might have been."

"Did she try to stop him?"

"I don't know. He was gone by the time we came back."

"But you said she was different. How?"

"I told you already. She sort of . . . gave up. Stopped fighting. I can't explain."

"And Archie was the one who arranged for her to go into hospital, wasn't he? How soon was that after he— ?"

"Excuse me." It was the trainee nurse again. No longer helpful and jolly-looking but containing righteous anger with difficulty. "Mrs de Rhin tires very easily. It is important she isn't stressed. She needs to rest now."

"Oh yes, of course, I'm sorry. I didn't mean . . ."

Appalled by my clumsiness. From beneath Dring's closed

eyelids tears were oozing. Tears of exhaustion and defeat. "I'll come back tomorrow. Another day. I didn't realise. I'm sorry . . ."

"Mary, wait." Dring opened her eyes, which were suddenly urgent. "Be careful, Mary. Keep away from your uncle. It's not worth it. Believe me . . ."

I bent down to kiss her forehead. "I'll be careful. And you must take care and get better soon too."

Such a stupid thing to say, I thought, as I left the hospital ward. As if she was any longer in control of what was happening. As if she wasn't entirely at the mercy of that great lump of her body and of the doctors and nurses who cared for it. As if getting better was something she could just choose to do.

For my sake.

Still seeking some kind of reassurance, some familiar territory, I drove from the hospital to Alderly Drive . . . yet there my sense of unreality only increased as I moved through the tiny and oh-so-familiar rooms. It was not so much that I now felt myself to be a guest in my own home, although that was a part of it. Paula was out but her books and papers and clothes were spread all over the sitting-room which no longer even smelled of Dring's lavender water and Silk Cuts. No, it was more like the feeling a snake might get were he to return to an old skin he had cast off some weeks before, a sense of "did this place ever fit me?" Was this ever home, this empty assortment of rooms and furniture which now has less than nothing to do with me? Except, of course, that a snake would never think in those terms. But I did.

I spent the next hour or so making telephone calls which required privacy and which could not therefore be made on the old-fashioned black telephone beneath the crossed pikestaffs in the hall at Chatton Heights.

I tried Adam's number again – and this time he was at home.

"Oh Fern . . . it's you— " I think if I had heard even a trace of enthusiasm in his voice I would probably have dashed back to London right then, so urgent was my need to talk to him, but his "Listen, I'm just on my way out and I'm late already. Can I get back to you tomorrow?" only made me feel a fool and ask myself how I had ever hoped to confide in him.

As I set down the receiver I wondered if it was always this difficult to reach out to another person. Was that why my mother had given up the attempt, retreated into silence and solitude?

Suppressing my disappointment I made a series of long and increasingly frustrating calls to the hospital in which my mother had been confined. Finally I discovered that the psychiatrist who had been responsible for her admission to hospital had died about three years earlier and that her medical records remained confidential and the property of the hospital. Even to elicit this much information I had to invent an imaginary psychiatrist of my own who "considered it important for my own treatment that the details of my mother's psychosis be revealed". I noticed how the voice at the other end of the line altered perceptibly at the mention of "my own psychiatrist". More helpful in some ways, but also guarded, careful, as though all the information given from now on must be scrupulously edited. "I'll see what I can do for you, Miss Miller," the voice (which could have been either male or female) said kindly. "I'll have to raise it with Mr Jeevons. Your mother was under his supervision at the end. But I don't hold out too much hope."

"Thank you anyway." I gave him/her my telephone number at Alderly Drive. "Maybe I could arrange to see him."

"He's more likely to pass the information on to your own doctor directly," said the androgynous voice.

"Thanks anyway."

I made myself a cup of tea, watered the plants, but after that there seemed nothing more for me to do at Alderly Drive. I left a note for Paula saying I was sorry to have missed her and then, as it was beginning to grow dark, headed back towards Long Chatton.

262

My brain still teemed with questions and possibilities, noisy and demanding as a troop of starlings. If I abandoned the search now, after all I had learned, with so much still to discover, I knew I would stand condemned of cowardice in my own eyes for the rest of my life. Proof, I needed proof.

A light was shining in the Old Rectory as I drove past and I was reminded of Ted Bury's words: the truth shall make you free.

Will it? I wondered, as I turned off between the eagle-topped gate-posts. The truth hadn't done much for my mother. And right now, as I felt myself being sucked back into the strange and secret world of Chatton Heights, the search for the truth seemed to be a trap, closing me in.

Chapter 11

The next morning there was a letter for me addressed in a strong italic hand.

Dear Fern,

It would be quite wrong to say that your visit gave me pleasure – but neither was it the ordeal I had been anticipating. I was prepared to dislike you – wanted to, in fact – but found it impossible. And so I could no longer entirely blame your family for all that had happened. Frances was not a pawn: she made choices and had to live with her decisions . . . and I must live with the knowledge of her last decision, however painful.

But this is my part in the story – yours is different. You say you are trying to discover all you can about your parents. I believe that I have told you the most important facts and you should now be able to put their tragedy behind you. If you choose not to do this – well, that is up to you.

You asked me about Sissy de Rhin. I can't remember her story exactly. She was one of the many waifs and strays that Fran collected. (Tillie was another – distressed gentlewoman. I hear she married your grandfather but that sounds impossible – can it be true?) It was a common joke in the village that you had only to be alcoholic or ex-criminal or mentally retarded for Fran to find you a job with one of her friends or relatives. Not that Sissy was any of those, merely rather tragic. Some story about losing her husband and children in the war, but as I say I can't remember the details. And I think she'd been some kind of housekeeper or lady's maid before her marriage but presumably she has told you all about that. I remember Clancy's horror when he met the "treasure" Fran had found for him and he was all for going to a proper agency but Fran promised to keep an eye on things. And no doubt intended to do so.

Perhaps I gave a rather one-sided impression of Louise, if so let me correct that now. True, she was neurotic and impossible, but that wasn't the whole picture. When she was on form – which I must say was less and less often during the last two or three years – she had a kind of vitality, an energy, that was almost electric. Quite literally, she dazzled you. But she'd had a classically messed-up childhood: her mother was never around and I can't remember mention of her father at all – she was farmed out with all sorts of horrendous-sounding relatives. She always gave the impression that she was a woman living on the edge of something – of disaster or great discovery or complete breakdown. After you left I remembered suddenly the last time the two of us had lunch together. It was about a week before she was admitted to hospital. I'm sure of that now because I can remember being so surprised when I heard the news. She had appeared to be coping so well following Clancy's death. In lots of ways she seemed stronger and saner than before he went away. But a psychiatrist friend of mine says that sequence of events is fairly common. Someone on the verge of mental illness can be temporarily lifted out of their own neuroses and appear quite normal under the pressure of some outside catastrophe – mental hospitals empty at the outbreak of war, he said – but as often as not the remission is short-lived. This must have been the case with Louise. The same psychiatrist said it sounded as if part of her trouble might have been some kind of untreated post-natal depression though I'm sure Fran told me she had a history of problems since her late teens. We'll never know, now.

Tomorrow Molly and I are leaving for the Canaries. I'm writing to you now because I want to be able to put all this behind me while I'm away. The Millers have taken up too much of my life. Don't get in touch again. I've told you all I know,

Deborah Brewster

While I was engrossed in my reading a subtle change had begun to take place, though not until I had finished the letter and folded it away in the pocket of my coat did the change become apparent. The voice had returned. The voice I had heard for the first time while I sat on the window-seat in the drawing-room and watched Tom Page wheel his barrow across the gravel, the voice that promised so much but which had always eluded me just when I was about to pin it down. Only now it was different. Now the voice seemed to emanate from the walls, the floor, the ceiling, from every carpet and painting and piece of furniture. As if the entire house and everything in it was talking to me, whispering, murmuring, a whole beehive hum of voices all speaking to me in urgent tones. It was desperately important to hear what they were saying but in their eagerness, in the rush of voices, the words became jumbled and garbled and though I strained every nerve to make sense of the weird cacophony of sound, the individual words remained tantalisingly indistinct.

I should have been afraid. I think there was a rational, thinking part of me that did feel afraid, that said, "Take care, these voices are not normal. They will only lead you down the road your mother took." And that part of me wanted to run away and hide and find a place where there were no voices, where everything was just as it had always been in the days when I lived with Dring at Alderly Drive and was an ordinary girl who only heard what was clearly audible to everyone else. But that sensible part of me was no match for the yearning that the voice aroused, a longing so fierce that I would have risked everything to be able to pin it down and hear it clearly.

266

There was a summer enchantment in its murmur, a comfort too strong to allow space for fear; warmth and content; the gold at the foot of the rainbow and waking up on Christmas morning and everything I had ever yearned for all rolled into one. I could feel myself being drawn into the luminous heart of the mystery and I surrendered myself to it gladly.

Follow me, the voice seemed to be saying, follow me and the truth will make you free.

Yes, my heart answered, I know that now.

"What in hell have you been playing at?"

Archie's tone, his words, were so horribly out of tune with the secret world in which I had been submerged since morning that it was a moment or two before I could comprehend that he was fully real. And when I did, I more than wished he wasn't.

He was standing just inside the doorway of the drawing-room; he leaned against a glass-fronted cabinet in the attitude of a stout man who has just climbed too fast up a steep hill. His face was pale and the veins on his cheeks stood out quite clearly. He had been drinking, although, as it was still only late morning, he was relatively sober.

"What is it?" I asked.

"You – interfering – bitch!"

It occurred to me then that he must somehow have guessed the contents of my letter from Deborah Brewster, recognised the postmark, the handwriting. Had he steamed it open? I should have checked the envelope. I fingered the folded paper in my pocket guiltily.

"What is it?" I asked again. My mouth was suddenly very dry.

"Paul Sobey, that's what."

"Oh. I see."

"That was him on the telephone just now. He said you visited him yesterday and that you'd had lunch together."

"Yes."

The crude reality of Archie's presence had quietened my

inner voice to a faint murmur. Like the distant breaking of waves on a gravel beach it was dimmed, but had not been reduced completely to silence. I felt myself embarked on an infinitely risky balancing act, that I had become a tightrope walker picking my way between his harsh rage and my inner secret, my talisman.

I said, "Perhaps I should have told you first."

"He was phoning with some information you wanted. Something to do with dates." Archie's breathing was still rapid. He put his hand on his chest as though to steady himself.

"Did he tell you what the dates were?"

"He might have but I've forgotten already. I told him that if he had any further dealing with you then my association with him was terminated. Forthwith. For ever."

"Didn't he consider you were over-reacting?"

"We creative types are allowed our eccentricities. It is expected. What the hell were you snooping around there for?"

"To find out more about my father. They were friends together at Oxford, you know."

"Of course I bloody know. Was that all?"

"Yes, he was most helpful."

"Just about Clancy. Well, that's . . . no harm really." He was muttering now, more to himself than to me as he walked across to the sideboard and poured himself a drink. I let out a sigh of relief: I don't think I had realised until that moment how apprehensive I had been. And then, as I watched him raise the glass to his lips and drink greedily, I thought, he is as relieved as I am. He too was afraid, panic-stricken . . . and with far more reason.

Without pausing to consider, for I knew that if I thought about it my instinctive nervousness would prevail, I said, "Naturally *you* were bound to crop up a good deal."

"Really?"

"He was most informative." I had drawn my lips back into what was intended to be a smile of sweet innocence but which probably looked more like a grimace. "It didn't occur to me that you might mind."

His eyes narrowed. He was weighing me up, trying to decide exactly how much sweetness and innocence lay behind my smile. "What the hell d'you want to talk about me for?" he growled.

"He was interested to know that you contacted him originally because of my father's recommendation."

"What makes you think— ?"

"Don't you remember, Archie?" My voice remained surprisingly calm, considering the violence with which my heart was bumping against my ribs. "He mentioned it in that postcard he sent you from South America. He said, 'How are you getting on with *Dora's Room*? Why not try Paul Sobey.'"

"I don't remember that."

"Don't you? We could check the postcard just to make sure. Except that you burnt it. That was the one where he mentioned Dora. 'I wonder where she is now,' he said. Something like that. Surely you remember."

All the colour had drained from his face. He took a step towards me and the expression in his eyes was murderous, as if he would like to kill me right there. He stared, breathing heavily, and I could see his inner turmoil as I held my breath, waiting . . . and then it seemed that the need to maintain an appearance of normality triumphed. He half smiled, turned and went to the drinks cupboard and poured himself a long measure. Then, as though making a mental note that it was important to remain as sober as possible, he replaced the glass and took a few slow breaths before turning to me and saying with measured calm, "My dear Fern, I've told you before, I really can't think why you allow yourself to become so embroiled in these old tired details. Good heavens, child, it was all such a long time ago, do you really imagine that someone as busy as Paul is going to be any help to you whatsoever? All these dates and petty facts – you have the mind of a filing clerk. It's what comes of being reared by a comatose geriatric in an urban terrace slum. I can tell you about your father, everything you need to know. I can tell you about the living breathing man."

269

"But you never do. You never tell me about him at all. It's as if he never existed for you."

"Your gift for melodrama is most unfortunate. What do you want to know? Let me think . . . he smoked pot, liked bad music, couldn't get along with his father – but then nor could anyone else. He was lousy at sports. Liked almond macaroons and Mrs Viney's kedgeree. Called himself a socialist. Refused to wear a morning suit to his wedding. There, see how you malign me, I'm a positive mine of information. For Christ's sake, girl, he was my brother – why do you have to go behind my back to ask other people about him?"

"But I never for a moment thought you'd mind me talking to Paul Sobey." It did occur to me that I might be over-playing the sweet innocence card, but I could tell by the muscles that leaped on the left-hand side of his face, almost closing his eye, that this was effective. "I merely wanted to chat with him. He was kind enough to ask me to have lunch with him. He was a very close friend of my father's, knew him well."

"He told you that, did he? You have to take Paul with a pinch of salt. He likes to pretend he's on intimate terms with everyone. Has a positive mania for friendship which I, as a cheerful recluse, have never had any time for. But why have you been pestering the poor fellow for dates?"

Let's try honesty, I thought. I said, "Because I was curious to know whether he received the manuscript for *Dora's Room* before or after my father's death. To test a hypothesis."

Instantly I regretted my honesty. I had never seen Archie move fast before. All his movements were slow, measured. The movements of a man who prefers his comforts to any form of exercise. But now it was like watching one of those big cats who lie motionless one moment, only a gently flicking tail to show that they are awake, and the next there is a spring and a leap and the creature is on its feet, alert, savage and very very dangerous. That's how it was with Archie. Before

I had time to think or move he had slammed his glass down on the glass-fronted cabinet and covered the short distance between us in two long strides.

His face was livid with rage, an ugly purple, and with his right hand he grabbed my throat.

"Archie – no!" And then I could not speak because his thumb, the round soft ball of his manicured thumb, was pressing into my throat and I could only grab his wrist with my hands and try to pull him off but my strength was nothing compared with his.

"You— !" he said. "You— !" And then, in the midst of my shock and fear there was a sudden spurt of joy, of revelation. He was powerless to say more, this man who usually possessed a whole armoury of sarcasm and cruel words. Powerless because anything he said would only give him away. And as the realisation sank home I was suddenly reminded of the phrase, "Anything you say will be taken down and used in evidence against you" and I had to fight an overwhelming urge to giggle at the incongruousness of it all. And my hysteria was only partly due to my fear of his murderous hand around my throat but more, much more, to the fact that in this moment of uncontrolled rage, Archie had finally and irrevocably betrayed himself to me.

He stared at me incredulously. "You – you're laughing!" he said. "You must be crazy," and he released his grip slightly, enough to let me breathe again.

And I gasped and said, "No, not crazy, only— "

But he had not let me go. As I twisted to escape his grasp his hand caught hold of my hair and wrenched my head back so that I was forced to look up into his face which was moving closer as he said, "You *are* crazy," and for one moment of horror that was worse even than his murderous attack, I thought he was going to kiss me.

There was a glimmer of movement in the doorway.

I looked over Archie's shoulder and said, "Oh Tillie, did you want— ?"

But Archie did not release his grip. Without even

bothering to look towards her he said, "Get out of here, you interfering harpy."

"But here . . . someone friend . . . expecting anyway . . . says Ella . . ." Her words were, if anything, more disjointed than ever but her insect-dry whisperings had never sounded so welcome.

"You have a visitor, Archie," I gasped, trying to prise my head free but his grip remained strong.

His face was very close. I could see the tiny red threads on his cheeks, the bluish dots of stubble, a glimmer of spittle in the corner of his mouth. I could see his fear. And our mutual fear which neither of us could account for in words was become our common secret, binding us in reluctant intimacy.

The muscles in my neck were so taut with loathing I could scarcely breathe.

"Archie . . . Your visitor . . ."

As if to demonstrate his greater strength he gave a last, vicious tug on my hair, before releasing his grip. His hands, as they fell to his side, brushed my neck, my breasts, almost as if by accident.

"Take care, Fern." His warning was a gentle murmur, audible to no one but us. "Your mother also tried . . ."

And then he turned, laughed himself back into his public self again, smoothed his cravat, touched his hair and strode to the sideboard where he emptied his glass with one swift gulp.

"What an enchanting sense of timing dear Ella has always possessed," he said, and without another glance at either me or Tillie, he walked swiftly from the room.

I stood for a few moments without moving. In the hallway Archie was greeting his guest: Ella, my dear, how long is it since you visited? Our lives have been an empty desert without you. Here, sling your coat at Tillie, she makes a useful coat hook . . . I was only half listening. The show must go on, I thought. Archie the great showman.

Still trembling, I forced myself to go over to the window and seated myself on the cushion whose faded fabric of leaves and twisted flowers had first awoken the murmuring summer voice which was even now crooning a low and steady refrain in my head.

Archie entered the room and went to the sideboard, pouring drinks for himself and his friend: a tall woman whose jet-black hair was cropped short, hugging her small head like a bathing cap. She had an anxious, wary expression. As he introduced us his voice purred like a satisfied cat's and his expression was that of an impeccably genial host, just as on the day of my first visit. I looked at his face and for the first time saw this was nothing but a mask, a coarse and discoloured mask, deceiving all the world but me. I was glad when they moved back towards the warmth of the fire and left me to my solitary contemplation by the window.

I know the truth, I thought. The guessing is over and now I know. The truth.

A blue tit was pecking at the windowframe in search of food. I smiled at him. The truth, I wanted to tell him, I know the truth. My father did write *Dora's Room*. I saw it in the panic in Archie's eyes when all he could say was "You . . . you . . .!" for fear of giving himself away. He knew that I had stumbled on his secret. Even now he must be wondering what other documents I had found in the attic.

I watched him covertly as he sustained a performance that must have cost him dearer even than normal. Imagine him now, as he puts his hand on the black-haired Ella's knee and tells her yes, he's only too delighted to look at her latest manuscript and offer some suggestions, imagine how desperately he must be grappling with the problem: how much did I know, and how much proof had I uncovered?

I almost laughed. Poor Archie, he could never ask me what I knew since to do so would be to betray the very secret he hoped to preserve. The teeth of the steel trap had snapped shut long ago – he could never escape from it.

Well, he needn't worry too much. Not yet. For the

time being his monstrous secret was safe with me. My proof was enough to satisfy me but there was nothing, so far, that would convince anyone else. So far. Surely it was only a matter of time. Either some other evidence would come to light (Dora, if only I could trace her) or perhaps Archie, now that he was rattled, would give himself away.

I conjured up the scene, like ones I'd watched a hundred times on television and in films. All I had to do was convince him that I had some proof and he would be tricked into giving himself away. "Show me the proof," he'd say. "Okay, you're right, I admit I never wrote the book, but how can you ever prove it?" And all the time my hidden tape recorder was preserving every word. Oh! If only it was that simple.

While the others were at lunch I began to read *Dora's Room* again. And luxuriated in the warm flow of words. Clancy's words. My father's words. The presence of Dora herself was strong throughout the book, strong and yet intangible. Each time I reached out to grasp the character she eluded me, just as the voice always did.

I will find her, I said to myself, devouring the book with a sense of elation. I must.

And I shall find her room. It was here at Chatton Heights. The book described it so clearly: light filtering through leaves on the windows, the smell of wood floors and age. Somewhere high up and remote, secret and secure, from which a young boy looked down on all his little world. Perhaps there was another attic, one I had not yet found. I had looked so many times already but now I must look again. Keep on looking until I found the answer.

Some time around four o'clock, when I had finished the book for the second time, my restlessness drove me out into the garden. It was a fine, clear day. Large white clouds bannered across a blue sky. In the shrubbery a few small snowdrops were beginning to flower. I crouched down to examine them closely, admiring the delicate pale green veining on their petals. When I was a child the sight of snowdrops had been enough to send a jarring chill of fear up my spine and I had always wondered why . . . now I knew. A memory persisted: white flowers scattered across a floor made smooth by the shuffling of endless slippered feet and my mother's voice pursued me with her cry, "The devil . . ." I shuddered even now, remembering. Then forced myself to pick a tiny bunch and sniffed their faint scent. My mother's flower. She was not a force for destruction only. Unstable, yes. Wild, yes. But she had freed her man from his father's tyranny and that was an achievement to take pride in.

I was wandering with no particular sense of direction when I found myself at the summer house and experienced that strange sense of dislocation of the internal compass when a familiar place has undergone a subtle transformation and you can't, just for the moment, see why. This little house of wood and glass had been dark, enclosed beneath the green umbrella of the holm oak but now there was a sense of light, and air . . .

A neatly stacked pile of logs gave me the answer. Looking upwards into the dense mass of branches I saw the white gash of the wound where a branch had been torn away. It must have broken off in the storm wind a week or so ago and someone, Tom Page probably, had already sawn the timber into logs. I smiled. He reminded me suddenly of one of those beetles that live in the forest, the ones whose purpose is to clear away the dead wood and leaves.

My attention was caught by something incongruously grey which seemed also to have fallen, crushing a tentative growth of snowdrops. A rectangular piece of metal, a semi-circle worn smooth as though – yes, it was the seat of a swing.

Childish delight in the discovery of a new toy was thrust aside by a burst of excitement so powerful that for a moment I was giddy with it and the greenery all around me seemed to tip and sway.

Not just any swing. *The* swing.

When those first stirrings of memory began to feather

beneath my scalp on the day of my first visit to Chatton Heights, when I heard for the first time the murmuring summer voice that promised so much of warmth and love, there had been a memory too of movement. A gentle, rocking, cradling movement as if I was curled up in the cabin of a ship at anchor. Or on a swing.

It was important, no doubt about that. I could tell by the whirr of anticipation that shivered through my body. The certainty that another piece of the pattern was sliding into place. The whole picture was far from clear, but it was beginning to emerge.

If only I could find Dora. The Dora my father had known. Perhaps I had sat here with her on a summer's afternoon all those years ago, while insects hummed in the flower beds and a wood pigeon called to his mate in the orchard. Scent of honeysuckle and roses and new-mown lawns. The voice of high summer.

Perhaps that voice was Dora's.

The black-haired Ella stayed for supper. And I could tell from the way Gerald scowled and chewed his thumb and talked too loudly that this woman with the sharp, tired face that might once have been beautiful had either been, was now, or hoped to be in the future, a mistress of Archie's.

"Your uncle is so brilliant," she said to me in the brief moment we spent alone together in the drawing-room before the meal, "*Dora's Room* has provided some of my finest inspiration. Archie's looking over a draft of my new work now. I must tell you that I value his opinion above all others."

"I'm sure he's most helpful," I said stiffly.

She peered at me over wire spectacles and I could see she attributed my lack of enthusiasm to ignorance. The philistine niece of the lonely genius. She must have decided that I was too stupid to appreciate the full glory of his achievement. A vast chasm opened up between her belief and my certainty. A vast chasm into which I could so easily pitch headlong.

That evening I experienced for the first time the lonely burden of knowing a truth that was shared by no one else. Her picture of reality was wrong and I knew it was wrong but had to pretend to subscribe to the common view.

Throughout that long and painful evening my sense of unreality grew stronger. Ella contrived to keep the conversation firmly on Archie's and her own literary achievements. And every time Archie muttered something like, "Some of the descriptive passages seem rather overwritten," she cocked her head on one side and said with a worried frown, "Yes yes, of course you're right. I see that now." And I wanted to shout out, "Don't listen to him! Can't you see he's a fraud?" But I remained silent and my silence was a thick weight of lies, suffocating me.

And then it no longer seemed to be such a fine thing to know the truth. Not in a world of lies. It was lonely and hard and I yearned more than ever to be able to share my secret.

I was suddenly reminded of the story I had heard about the woman who watched the soldiers marching past and who said with maternal pride, "Look, they're all out of step except my Johnnie." Only this time I was Johnnie and the world was out of step and suddenly it didn't seem such a funny story any more.

On my way to bed that night I overheard Archie and Ella talking in the hallway.

"Stay tonight," Archie was saying in his smokiest of Havana cigar voices, "you must know how I've missed you."

And she replied, with more than a trace of sadness, "If I thought for a moment that you meant it – but it's been good to see you, Archie."

"How good?" And there was a long silence. I heard no more because I gently closed the door that led to my lonely corridor.

A long time I stayed awake, listening to the wind in the trees and the rustle of ivy near my window. I heard tyres crunch on the gravel beside the house and the noise of a car's engine fade as it travelled down the long driveway. Archie's admirer was leaving after all. Far off I heard the ragged bark of a vixen and then, quite close to the house, the haunting call of an owl. A pale light was shining through the gap between my curtains.

When I heard the church clock strike midnight I climbed out of bed and pulled on my dressing-gown. If sleep was impossible then there were other, more useful ways to spend this midnight hour.

The whole house was awash with moonlight. As I paused, briefly, on the landing above the hallway I could see the moon through the glass-domed skylight above the stairs. It was still a few days short of the full but even so, as my eyes grew used to the watery light, pictures and furniture, the polished curve of the banisters and the rugs lying like shimmering pools on the floor of the hall, were revealed with unexpected clarity.

My bare feet made no noise as I trod softly past Archie's door, then Gerald's, and on down the stairs. As I moved, stealthy as a burglar, around the huge house, I knew for the first time that this all belonged to me.

The exhilaration of the moment. Exhilaration, not fear. Without having consciously decided where to go, I found my footsteps took me down the moonlit corridor and only halted when I stood outside Archie's study.

The round handle was smooth beneath my palm. I turned it silently. The door swung open.

The first thing I saw were two dark eyes, staring into mine from a moon-pale face. Terror shivered down my spine like a ripple of wind. Then I saw it was only a painting that had alarmed me: Archie's portrait, smiling and proud, looked down from over the mantelpiece.

Sweat was trickling between my shoulder blades as I took a deep breath and stepped into the middle of the room, closing the door behind me. There was a large desk with a brass table lamp on it which I switched on before preparing to search through every drawer and file and envelope in the room.

I knew now what I was looking for and it did not take

long for me to realise that my search was useless. The room was sterile: no letters, no papers, no manuscripts – nothing. There were copies of *Dora's Room* in plenty, hardback and paperback and translated into a multitude of languages. There was a file of correspondence with Paul Sobey but none of it more than five years old, some documents of interest to Archie's accountant, a file of press cuttings . . . but no breath of my father.

I forgot to be afraid. Exhilaration turned to despondency. Surely here, if anywhere, I might have hoped to find some evidence of Archie's fraud, but there was nothing. Dring had said that after my father's death Archie came to Alderly Drive and took away a mass of papers. He must have destroyed the lot.

It's not fair, I thought, to come so close, to learn so much – and then to be thwarted of the final proof.

The floorboards above my head creaked and I heard voices. In a sudden panic I flew to the lamp and switched it off, cursing myself for having been so careless as to leave the window uncovered when Archie himself slept over this room.

I let myself out and sped along the corridor and back towards the hall, but there I stopped and listened, horrified and yet fascinated by the voices I could hear that drifted down the stairs.

Archie's voice, rough and angry, "Get out of here, you old hag. I'm not drunk enough to put up with you, not tonight."

And then a woman, anguished and pleading, "Let me stay, Archie, I'm sorry, I promise, only let me stay— "

Archie again, "Don't be so bloody boring. I've had enough, can't you see?"

The woman, "Don't turn me out, oh please, I won't— "

At first I thought I had been wrong when I heard the car leaving earlier. His devoted authoress had decided to stay after all. A few words more revealed the owner of the female voice as Tillie.

I already knew Archie had a swift way of dealing with

her excesses so I don't know why the sound of the blow should have been so horrifying. I heard her cry out and then Archie's brutal, "Does *that* convince you? Now, get out!" And the next moment Tillie herself appeared on the landing.

With her hair glowing like a halo around her head and wearing nothing but a filmy nightgown she might have been a ghost as she jerked with her odd, awkward movements and came to a halt at the head of the stairs. If I thought she looked like a ghost then she must have been convinced that I was one for, with an oddly theatrical gesture, she clapped her hand to her mouth and screamed, a little high-pitched scream like a child at play, not very loud at all.

"What the hell are you bawling at now?" said Archie.

I said, "It's only me. I couldn't sleep and I've been in the kitchen."

As I climbed the stairs towards her I remember thinking how enormous her eyes were as they stared at me with a kind of hypnotised disbelief. She stood absolutely still, not saying a single word or flinching a muscle until I had reached the top step, then she turned suddenly and vanished in the direction of her own room.

Archie was standing in his bedroom doorway. There was a table light shining somewhere behind him, he was wearing a loose-fitting nightshirt and his face was in shadow so that I could not see his expression but when he spoke his voice was smooth as oil.

"Gruesome, eh? And now here comes the bad penny looking enchanting in her little dressing-gown. Couldn't you sleep either? Don't look so downcast, Fern. If it's company you need, then my bed is still warm."

"Don't be disgusting!" I stepped backwards.

"Go to hell, then," he said thickly, and, as if suddenly weary, he slumped against the door. "Christ, but I need a drink. And there's no need for you to stand there looking so bloody superior."

To reach the green door that led through to my own corridor and room I would have to walk past Archie, and just then, to make any kind of movement towards him was impossible.

He raised one hand to cover his eyes, then let it fall loosely to his side. "Damn you, girl, you have your father's eyes. What in God's name did you expect? You should have known our family has always had a penchant for necrophilia and Tillie has always been a most obliging corpse . . . oh hell. Get out of here, Fern. It wasn't always like this. Not that you care, smug little bitch . . . go back to Bristol before you're as trapped and hopeless as . . . oh, what's the use, you won't listen. Bloody well find out the hard way, follow your own sweet route to damnation."

And with that he turned and went back into his room, slamming the door shut behind him.

Dring had always been a firm believer in the avoidance of all forms of excitement. "No good over-stimulating yourself," she grumbled, "your type only gets fussed and then you can't sleep and the next you know you're off your food as well."

Fussed. I pondered her wisdom, though the word "fussed" grossly understated my present condition as I returned to my room knowing that sleep was impossible that night.

The final certainty of Archie's fraud, this sudden glimpse of the hidden liaisons of my family and then his self-loathing and despair had combined to create a potent cocktail of which Dring would surely have disapproved entirely. I wasted no sympathy on my uncle: he was my enemy. I turned away from his suffering and self-pity and despised him for it.

He was my enemy. And now he knew that too.

As I lay in bed that night and still could not sleep, all the night-time sounds of a lonely old house marooned in country stillness were magnified to a threatening loudness. There was menace in the low wind that idled through the chimney pots, danger in the scuffles of birds and mice; each creak and groan of the old timbers sleeping was enough to make the hairs on the back of my neck tingle with panic.

So many possibilities . . . Archie inhabited an ivory tower constructed entirely of lies. A huge and monstrous lie. And now that I had discovered the false core of his life, how far was he prepared to go to protect himself?

How far had he gone in the past? My mother had known his secret and she had been destroyed. Tipped over the edge as Dring had so graphically described it. Who else had known? Aunt Frances? Surely Clancy would have shared his creation with the woman he loved. My body was encased by sweat like an icy shroud. Perhaps her death had not, after all, been suicide. Perhaps Archie feared that more than negligence, or mental cruelty, would be revealed by any thorough investigation of her "accident". Easy enough to engineer a catastrophe at sea when one sailor is not so strong, not so ruthless as the other.

Long ago Archie had drowned the truth, had it labelled mad and committed to an asylum. He had stayed safe in his web of lies until now, until the moment when the terms of my grandfather's will brought me back to Chatton Heights. He had destroyed before. Surely he would try anything to protect his vicious fraud.

By the time the sparrows in the ivy around my window cheeped the first note of their most unmusical dawn chorus I knew that I must share my secret with someone. If anything were to happen to me . . . at least there must be one other person who had known the truth.

At once I thought of Adam. In my mind's eye I could see the grave expression on his face as he heard me out, could hear the caress in his voice as he said, "I believe you, Fern," could feel his arms around me, no longer any barriers of silence between us. But if he did not believe? If he thought . . . But he *would* believe me. He must.

I telephoned his home. No reply. Tried his office; not expected in that day. He should have called me back the previous day but had not done so – or had he tried to get through only to be told by Tillie or Archie or Gerald that I was unavailable? In desperation I phoned Jane's flat in

Bristol. She had no idea where he might be. I spoke to Ted Bury; no, he hadn't heard from him. "If you speak to him," I said, "please tell him I need to talk, really talk. He'll know what I mean."

I replaced the telephone. Would Adam hear my message? Would he even be interested? I had thrown a lifeline to an uncertain shore. All day I wandered the house, my head bursting with the need to talk. Several times I thought of telephoning Paula, but each time I started towards the telephone a dozen hesitations entered my mind: on her first visit I had seen how the grandeur of Chatton Heights and Archie's fame had combined to sabotage her critical faculties. She had an annoying habit of never accepting anything at face value and always placed some weighty psychological interpretation on the most straightforward statement. I was groggy and confused from lack of sleep. Adam would surely get in touch. The truth felt too monstrous, too incredible to be spoken out loud. Later, I told myself, do nothing in a hurry.

So when, some time in the afternoon, the telephone rang and I heard Paula's cheerful voice saying, "Hello, Mary, how are you today? I was thinking of paying you a flying visit," it seemed like the answer to a prayer.

"I dreamed about you last night," she confessed, "and you were in some kind of trouble. And anyway, I could do with some country air in my poor lungs."

I was grinning with relief. It all seemed wonderfully obvious. Fate had caused her to ring. I glanced at my watch and asked only, "How soon can you get down here?"

Chapter 12

The sight of Paula's cockatoo plume of red hair, her purple fingernails and her general air of transient fashion, so out of place after the timeless ugliness of Chatton Heights, was like touching home base after long travels in a foreign land. Even her brand of flattery was reassuringly similar to Dring's.

"You look like shit," she said cheerfully, as I greeted her at the station, "what on earth have you been doing to yourself?"

"It's only lack of sleep," I explained.

"Has your randy cousin been making a nuisance of himself again?"

"Gerald? No – it's . . . but not now. I'll tell you everything later."

Paula was only half listening. Her arrival at this placid station with the regular Friday evening commuters had caused a barely discernible ripple of interest. She had a gift, which I had noticed before, of somehow absorbing the admiration of strangers as though through her pores, without ever having to look properly in their direction.

"We have all weekend to talk," she said, pitching her voice fractionally higher than was necessary, "you can tell me everything at Chatton Heights."

But in fact I did not confide in her that evening, nor the following day. The mere fact of her presence at Chatton Heights was enough to dissolve the web of tension which was entangling me. The breath of outside air which accompanied her reduced my relatives to more manageable proportions. She did an impersonation of Tillie's vacant stare and still more vacant speech that was sufficiently accurate to be funny, sufficiently exaggerated to render my grandfather's widow completely ridiculous. Gerald she treated with such blatant contempt that I was almost sorry for him, but only almost; at any rate I was relieved that he chose to avoid us. Archie she alternately flattered and teased; warmed by her attention he became positively benign, a good-hearted Victorian uncle with a weakness for the bottle and a pretty face but a genial old buffer nonetheless. As I sat down at the dinner table on Saturday night I marvelled that Paula had so swiftly transformed my relatives into little more than the cardboard characters who are wheeled out each Christmas season for the pantomimes: surely there could be nothing to fear from that agreeable literary gent with the greying hair and the self-indulgent paunch and a weakness for silk cravats? In the daylight world inhabited by people like Paula, middle-aged men did not drown their wives nor render their sisters-in-law insane – though nothing, now, would make me swerve from my certainty that he had stolen his dead brother's masterpiece and claimed it for his own.

So thorough was her taming of my unruly family that by the time Sunday morning arrived my secret inner voice had faded to a barely audible whisper: and for that loss I resented her, was almost glad when she announced after lunch was over that she must return to Bristol that evening.

"Then I shall drive you," said Archie, "I have business to attend to there and the journey always seems shorter with company."

We were sitting in the drawing-room, the coffee trolley in position as it had been on the day of my first visit. Gerald was absent; we had not seen him all day. Tillie was present in body only. She poured the coffee, handed cups around but made no contribution to the conversation; one could almost have forgotten she was there at all but for her faint yet persistent aroma of dust and neglect.

Forgetting to remain on guard, I allowed myself to study Archie's face, the downward tug of his mouth that was, I noticed now, like Gerald's, his heavily lidded eyes that were like no one else's. When Paula left the room briefly to fetch cigarettes from her room Archie looked up, and, since I had been staring at him, our eyes met. He raised one eyebrow in sardonic query.

He mimicked a child's teasing voice, "Oh Grandmama," he said, "what big eyes you have," and then, more harshly, "what in hell do you find to stare at?"

I said nothing. I want to look into your soul, I thought, I want to read your mind.

He shifted irritably, all trace of the genial uncle, that veneer constructed entirely for Paula's benefit, vanished without trace. "Damn your eyes, girl, stop gawping at me."

Forcing myself still to meet his gaze. "My father's eyes, that's what you told me once," I said.

He laughed at that. "Poor Clancy. His beautiful brown eyes didn't do him much good, did they?" And then, as an afterthought, as the sound of Paula's heels echoed on the stairs and in a voice so faint that later I wondered if I had really heard him or whether my imagination had conjured menace from the whispering of the wind in the trees beyond the house, he murmured, "The only one left." And he paused, pondering, before caressing the air with the words just as Paula came into the room, "I'm a survivor, Fern. Are you?"

After a few initial questions Paula, to my amazement, heard me out in silence. Wrapped in coats and scarves we were sitting on a bank at the top of the orchard. Below us Long Chatton lay wreathed in the stillness of a winter Sunday afternoon. A straight plume of smoke rose from a tidy gardener's fire; children's voices rose from the area of the huge horsechestnut and the pond; a robin was singing from a bare branch of one of the old apple trees. I knew I could only talk freely to Paula away from the house – but against a backdrop of such serenity I feared my story would be even harder to believe. Yet Archie's warning had hit home and I forced myself to begin.

She already knew about the postcards. I told her about

Paul Sobey, about Archie's murderous rage when he learned that he had been discussed during our meeting. About the visit to Deborah Brewster and the story of my father's affair with Aunt Frances. "Was Adam with you when she talked about that?" she asked, and when I said no, that he had been in the kitchen with Molly, she merely nodded and told me to go on. I did not tell her about my inner voice or the swing, nor about the scene I had witnessed between Archie and Tillie, nor did I tell her my suspicions about Aunt Frances' death, nor my mother's final breakdown. I did tell her that Archie was not the author of *Dora's Room*, that he had stolen his brother's book and claimed it for his own.

There was a sensation almost of giddiness as I released my secret into the calm air of the orchard, that no-going-back feeling a diver must have as he arches forwards to spring from the safety of the highest board. And then relief, huge and wonderful relief. The facts that I had locked away inside myself for so long, the facts that had only existed within my brain, now grew solid and strong and assumed their separate substance somewhere in the cold still air between us. And I knew the facts were true.

There was silence when I finished speaking, only the distant drone of a car ascending the hill from the village and the robin still singing on his high branch. Paula was snapping stalks of dead grass between long, pale fingers.

"Is it— " Now that I had unburdened myself I hardly had the courage to ask. "Is it so very difficult to believe?"

She turned to face me and her warm smile was all the answer I needed. "Your family is so bizarre," she said, "I don't think anything you told me about them could surprise me."

"Once you accept that Archie never wrote *Dora's Room* then everything else, the lack of any further books, his reticence about the identity of Dora, all begins to make sense."

"Yes. I can see that."

(So why was she so subdued?)

I leaned back on my elbow. The landscape lay before us, the whole Cotswold stone landscape of Long Chatton set amongst a panorama of little copses and rolling hills, so many landmarks that would be familiar to any reader of *Dora's Room*, this view that was so similar to the one my father had looked out over from his secret room. And yet the panorama was misleading since so much that was important remained hidden from sight.

"If only I could find Dora," I said fiercely, "then I could understand it all."

"Yes," Paula was chewing thoughtfully on a grass stalk, "that would help."

And then she spat the grass out and scrambled to her feet. "Why on earth do people in films eat grass? It tastes disgusting!"

Before she left I made Paula promise that she would tell my secret to no one. She clearly accepted what I had told her and emphasised that my burden was safe with her. Once again she affirmed that nothing I could tell her about my family would surprise her; she regarded them all as alien as creatures from a distant galaxy. I suspected that I might have told her my suspicions about Archie and his wife's "suicide" and she would have accepted that as well with no problem.

"Come back to Bristol with me this evening," she said. "These people are not healthy."

I murmured something non-committal (would I be able to hear the inner voice in Bristol?) and she hugged me impetuously. "You take care of yourself, Mary Fern. I might come down again in a day or so, but there are a few things I must do first."

When she and Archie had driven away in the winter dusk I went back into the empty house. (Tillie was probably there, but her presence no longer stopped the house from being empty, or so it seemed.) I found myself humming peaceably as I stoked up the fire in the drawing-room. Paula's knowledge had relieved me of much of the burden of my secret. And Archie was away for the rest of the evening, perhaps longer.

It was enough to make me almost content.

Going to bed early that night, I fell into the deep sleep of someone in whom painful tensions have been eased. So I must have been sleeping too soundly to hear the footsteps outside my door, the creak of a hinge swinging open slowly. I was still dreaming without fear.

In my dream I was walking along a shingle beach; the sea was calm and shining but gave off a strangely noxious smell. Reluctantly I was forced to take shelter in a cave, but here the smell only grew stronger. I knew I must escape from the acrid fumes that enveloped me. I found a narrow passageway, but still I could not escape the nauseous gas which all the time was growing denser . . . Now it was burning my throat, now stinging my eyes. A huge sickness swelled my stomach. I put out my hands to touch the sides of the passageway but they were pressed back. The very walls were closing in on me, thrusting against my shoulders. I dropped to all fours and began to crawl but soon I was on my stomach, squirming like a worm and still the cold walls crushed me, squeezed out the life, rammed against my skull like granite. And now the rocky surfaces of the passageway were a stone vice filled with stench and my skull was being crushed and I could go no further.

"Let me out," I groaned, "let me out— "

And the sound of my own voice dragged me from the dream.

Which was real.

I rolled over and reached for the light but my head screamed with pain and all around was a noxious smell and a steady hissing sound . . . Gas.

Terror burned inside me, terror as fierce and real as the burning pain in my lungs.

I tried to sit up but as I did so the room ballooned around me and the moment I put my feet down the floor arced up and struck me on the face.

For a while I lay there, the coarse pile of the carpet against my cheek, too stunned to move. My lungs were on fire. I had to reach the door.

It might have been an endless expanse of desert, the short distance between bed and door. Only my terror of the monstrous thing hissing poison into my face gave me the strength to struggle across. Heaven knows how long it took to reach the handle of the door – seconds, maybe, certainly not more than a few minutes – but time no longer had any meaning. Time had become a spectator to my struggle.

I reached the door, grasped the handle, turned it and pulled the door open. Choking and retching I half fell into the corridor. I tried to cry out for help but my voice made only a strangled sound. When I attempted to stand, the pain in my skull exploded like a bolt of lightning and I collapsed on to all fours. Beaten and terrified, like an animal that dare not give in, I crawled on hands and knees along the corridor and only after what seemed like a lifetime of pain and effort did I feel the green baize of the door against my palm.

Pushed it open and struggled the last few inches into the main part of the house. The door swung shut behind me and the murderous hiss of the gas was silent. My head felt it might split in two pieces.

"Help!" I tried to cry out but the only sound that emerged was a whisper. Someone must find me, don't leave me here, please find me.

The silence of the house was awesome. A silence awash with pale moonlight.

A tall vase stood on a table in a recess. I caught hold of the table leg, pulled it . . . and the crashing splintering sound that followed was the sound of my own frail eggshell skull breaking into a thousand fragments.

My face on the carpet, fire burning in my lungs. A door opened, and another. Voices swooping and diving like bats on a summer's night.

Did you hear . . . burglars, here's a stick . . . something is broken . . . no, look, here, someone . . . my God, it's

290

Fern . . . what the hell is she trying . . . Christ, stinking drunk . . . what a way to . . . hang on a minute, can you smell gas?

The nausea had swelled so huge it blocked my mouth and I could not speak. Heavy footsteps, Archie's, and I heard him say, "What the bloody hell is going on here? Don't you know what time it is?" And then, as the questions and explanations followed he took command. "Stop twittering, Tillie. Gerald, run through and shut off the gas. Tillie, is there a bed made in the end room? Okay, okay, can you walk? Here, I'll help you."

Too weak to struggle against him, I tried to stand as his arm circled my waist. My whole body cringed from his touch, cringed with fear and disgust.

And as he half carried, half steered me to a nearby bedroom he said, "If you must kipper yourself, Fern, for Christ's sake do a proper job of it next time. And don't wake us all in the middle of the night."

Surfacing in an unknown room. The unfamiliarity. Light filtering through different curtains; the door in the wrong place; the unaccustomed shape and feel of a strange bed.

Surely that had all been a dream, a nightmare? That struggle along the passageway, the breaking vase, the anxious voices circling my head?

Open my eyes again and surely I would see . . . but no. The dry noxious feel of my mouth, the dull pain in my head, these were only too real.

What had happened? Only one answer – but I shied away from it, told myself it couldn't be true. Someone had come into my room and turned on the gas. Someone had wanted me dead. Who . . .? Who had brought the old gas heater for me in the first place? Who wanted— ? Archie, always Archie. Only Archie, it must be him.

I tried to gather my thoughts, my strength – but they slid away from me like a gust of wind. I slept.

I dragged my eyelids back: they were heavy as those thick

velvet curtains in theatres. Through my half-opened eyes I could see a strange man sitting on the edge of the bed, staring at me. He had the face of a melancholy walrus. I closed my eyes: it must be a mistake; opened them again. He was still there.

"I'm Dr Collins." He smiled kindly. (Was I ill? I must be for my whole body ached with disease.) "How are you feeling now?"

I considered for a moment, then, "Grim," I replied. My throat felt rusty, as though no one had bothered to use it much during the last ten years. Still he sat there and smiled at me, that kind, slightly lugubrious droopy-jowled smile. It occurred to me that he must be a very dedicated doctor, just to sit there like that with a new patient. A good bedside manner. He made me feel safe.

"You had a narrow escape," he said.

I frowned. Escape? From what? And then the memory came back to me like a suffocating cloud. Archie . . . the gas . . . and with the realisation that someone had actually wanted me dead, had tried to kill me, I felt such a wind of horror it was like falling over the edge of a cliff, falling for ever . . .

"There now, don't excite yourself." He reached forward and took my hand.

"I could have— " But I could not bring myself to say the word "died".

"I know." His reassurance was swift and the pressure of his hand holding mine was firm; his professional strength flowing from him to me through the contact of our hands. "But you've been lucky in one respect; at least there is no lasting damage."

I stared at him. How did he know what had happened? Had Archie perhaps confessed everything to him? (Professional confidentiality: did that apply to murder?) Oh, if it was true that he knew and I did not have to explain . . . the vision of relief was almost overwhelming.

"Did he tell you?" I ventured.

"Your uncle telephoned me at once. This morning he has told me as much as he could. You gave him a bad fright. Your uncle is more concerned about you than you know."

I gave *him* a fright? I closed my eyes, tried to think. There was something wrong here, something that did not fit. I opened my eyes and his smile, which was still in place, did not look as kindly as I had thought at first. Now it was tinged with slyness.

"What did he tell you?" I asked.

"I'd rather hear it from you."

The mirage of the all-seeing kindly doctor dissolved, and I groaned aloud. "Oh my God, you think I did that deliberately!"

"Would it make you happier if we agreed to call it an accident?"

I turned my head away, no longer able to stand the sight of that too-kind smile, the too-sympathetic sadness in his eyes.

"It was not an accident," I said in a low voice.

"No, I didn't really suppose it was. I only thought that— "

"If I told you what happened you'd never believe me. So you see, there's no point in talking." I pulled my hand away.

He allowed the silence to hover in the air between us for a while before saying gently, "In a day or two, I very much hope you will come to see that talking about it is just what you need to do. For the time being I suggest you rest as much as possible. Let Mrs Miller" (it was a moment or two before I registered that he was referring to Tillie) "and your uncle take care of you. I shall call again tomorrow to see how you are getting on. And try not to dwell too much on unpleasant subjects."

Like attempted murder? I wanted to ask him. But all I said was, "Can you give me anything to stop my headache? It feels as though my skull is splitting in two."

But Dr Collins wanted to probe the secrets of my soul and therefore had scant interest in mere bodily discomforts. He suggested, with a nonchalance which indicated that the hammer blows crashing against the sides of my head were of little interest to medical science, that Tillie could fetch me aspirins or paracetamol. And then, with a final sad, almost reproachful smile, he lumbered heavily from the room.

There must have been someone waiting for him in the corridor, because I could hear their low voices murmuring in a conspiratorial way. Talking about me. I strained my ears but was unable to distinguish what they were saying, nor recognise the second voice. And if I asked, I thought, no one would tell me. I was ill. My status in the household had become that of a cosseted second-class citizen. The story was I had tried to kill myself, thus forfeiting my right to be treated as a responsible adult.

Footsteps retreated down the main stairs. Silence. Only the cheep and squabble of sparrows beyond the window.

My whole body ached and the smell of nausea, its bitter taste in my mouth, lingered still. I had never felt so dirty. An overwhelming sense of grubbiness, of squalor, was in my hair and in my clothes and in my skin. It seemed to have worked its way into my very bones. An image of the bathroom at Alderly Drive floated into my mind like a half-forgotten dream of safety and comfort. Lovingly I remembered its white tiles and coloured soaps and the brown stain under the tap and the spider plant on the windowsill. If I could only lie in that tub of hot deep water and know that I was far away from Chatton Heights and my uncle, far away and safe, then I might scour this odour of filth from my skin.

Slowly I sat up in bed, lowered my feet to the floor. There was a cup of cold tea on the table beside my bed, an earlier offering from Tillie no doubt, and I forced myself to drink it down. A moment's nausea and then, to my relief, my head began to clear. It still ached as though someone were driving a nail into my skull, but my eyes were able to focus on objects almost steadily. I stood up.

By the time I had reached my own bedroom and dressed I was shaking with exhaustion as though I had

294

just achieved some amazing feat of mountaineering. I rested for a few moments, or maybe it was a long time, not thinking of anything at all, before going down the stairs to the kitchen where I made a cup of coffee. This normally simple task now required a superhuman effort of will; every nerve concentrated on the single purpose of making myself sufficiently strong to escape this lethal house.

So intent was I on the effort of pouring the coffee into a mug that at first I did not notice Gerald come into the kitchen. I looked up; he was wearing a green waxed jacket and his eyes were watching me with that slightly squinty expression that indicated he was grappling with a thought.

"Do you need help?" he asked awkwardly. "You look pretty shaky, Fern. Are you sure you shouldn't still be in bed?"

"I shall be okay once I've drunk this. Can I get you a cup?"

"No thanks, but . . . well, about last night— "

"Yes?"

He was evidently struggling to overcome his embarrassment and at that particular moment I had neither the energy nor the inclination to help him out. After a further moment of hesitation during which his cheeks turned a brighter-than-usual shade of pink, he said, "I thought at first when I heard the crash and saw you lying on the landing, well, I obviously thought you'd gone and got yourself quietly plastered, but when I found the gas, well . . . I mean, I know it's sometimes been hard for you here, Fern, and I suppose I haven't always been exactly . . . but, oh hell, I just wanted you to know that I'm glad you didn't manage it last night, I mean, I'm glad you're okay and not . . . you know . . ."

By the time he had limped to the end of this amazing speech he was staring furiously at the toes of his shoes and his cheeks had flushed a worrying shade of purple.

I said steadily, "I didn't try to kill myself last night, Gerald."

But this was too much for him to accept. "Well," he said, "whatever— " and then, turning to more practical subjects with enormous relief, he said, "By the way, there were a couple of phone calls for you earlier. Adam Someone-or-other. And the hospital."

"The hospital? Why?"

"They didn't say. I think they've been trying to contact you for a couple of days or so. Tillie took the calls. Didn't she tell you?"

Damn Tillie and her stupid forgetfulness, I thought as I hurried to the hallway and picked up the phone. The warm coffee had combined with Gerald's totally unexpected but apparently genuine concern to make me feel less like the zombie who had woken in a strange bed that morning and more like a normally functioning human being.

To my frustration the hospital switchboard was in chaos. First I was put through to gynaecology, then to X-ray, then the line went dead. Suppressing my concern for Dring as best I could I tried Adam's work number – and wonder of wonders, it was his voice, reassuring and brisk, which answered.

"Fern," he said at once, "thank God you called. I've been so worried about you."

My head swam. "Worried? About me? But why?"

"Where are you now?"

"I'm at Chatton Heights but— "

"I'll drive down this afternoon. Did you get my message?"

"What message?"

"Hell, I spoke to Tillie and she promised— "

"I haven't even seen her yet today."

There was silence at the other end of the phone.

"Adam, there's not much point in coming here. I'm about to leave for Bristol."

"Then I'll see you there. I'll be at Alderly Drive as soon as I can get away. There's so much we must talk about."

"But why? Did Archie tell you— "

"Archie? Good God, no. I haven't spoken to him. Are you sure you'll be able to manage the drive?"

I frowned. Why should I not be able to manage? Who had he been speaking to? My brain was still stalling over the enigma of Adam's sudden concern as I tried once again to reach Dring's ward. This time, just for variety, the switchboard put me through to physiotherapy. Physiotherapy tried to put me through to the switchboard but instead I was caught up in a crossed line, two harassed voices complaining about a shortage of artificial limbs. I tried again. This time the phone rang in Dring's ward (but how could I be sure it was her ward?) but there was no reply.

"Do you want to try again later?" asked the girl on the switchboard. "Or would you rather hold?"

But there was no time.

The effort of telephoning had exhausted me. I tried not to think of the long drive that stretched ahead and focused instead on the safe harbour of Dring's solid bulk, her tired and crumpled face, her rough laugh. "Never mind about your uncle," she would say, "didn't I tell you he was a dangerous bugger? Put it all behind you, Mary. Forget it all."

And surely, if only I could reach Dring and Adam and Alderly Drive, I would indeed be able to forget.

The day was overcast, threatening rain. As I went out to my car I monitored the condition of my body: my legs were a bit gluey, my head throbbed painfully and every now and then a film of sweat would cover my shoulders but otherwise I felt reassuringly normal. I focused all my efforts on managing my little car, guiding it through the narrow country roads, staying in the slow lane on the motorway and hardly noticing the huge lorries that thundered past. I seemed to be journeying between two lonely fears; the fear of Archie and the gas that I was leaving behind me at Chatton Heights and the wordless dread of what I might find when I reached the hospital and Dring . . .

And yet it is not solitude or fear that I remember

when I think back to that desperate drive to Bristol, for I did not feel myself to be alone: my summer voice travelled with me, that crooning inner voice that spoke of security and love and wrapped me in a magician's fine cloak, protecting me from danger.

It was only as I began to climb the wide stairs leading to Dring's ward that my protective mantle fell away, exposing me for the first time to the chill blast of fear. The hospital had called several times, had wanted to speak to me urgently, surely there could be only one explanation: Dring was dead.

I groaned. "Oh dear God, no!"

A bearded man who was following glanced at me curiously. "Is anything the matter?"

I stared at him blindly, shook my head, walked slowly the rest of the way, bracing myself for the inevitable moment, the horrendous moment, when a nurse (or maybe it would be a doctor?) would walk towards me and say, "Miss Miller, we tried to contact you last night. Bad news, I'm afraid . . ."

It was all I could do to drag myself into the side ward where I had seen her last. The ward seemed to be lit by a dazzlingly bright light and the pain pulsing inside my head made it hard to see clearly. It was several moments before I was truly convinced that the more than solid flesh in the bed by the window was my beloved Dring.

"Oh Dring, you're here . . . you . . ." There was a burning sensation at the base of my throat and, just for the moment, speech had become impossible.

Above the puce froth of her nightdress, the old face looked immeasurably weary. Slowly, very slowly, the creases round her eyes deepened and her eyelids fluttered open. She stared at me.

The pain in my throat was almost unbearable. "Do you feel so very bad?" I asked gently.

She frowned. Her wrinkled hands scrabbled at the bedclothes. "Where's Tom?" she muttered petulantly. "What are you doing here?"

I faltered. "Don't be cross, Dring. I never knew the hospital had been trying to get in touch. I came as soon as I could— "

Her eyes shifted from side to side, not fixing on me at all. "Mr Tom ought to be here. Who sent you? I didn't want strangers."

"But— "

"My leg hurts. Can you do something for my leg?"

"Yes, of course, I'll try— "

"Not you. I don't know you."

The ground was sliding away beneath me. "Dring, dear Dring, what is it? Can't you even see who I am? I'm Mary, you must know me."

"She told me Mr Tom would come. Where is he? What have you done with him? Is he still playing cricket?"

"But Dring !"

A tall woman, whom I had noticed vaguely before but had assumed was visiting the patient in the nextdoor bed, loomed over us both. "There there, Sissy, no need to make a fuss. No one is trying to deceive you. This is Mary Miller. I'm sure you remember her really. You used to look after her, can you remember that?"

The woman's voice was managerial and sure. I looked up at her: a big, middle-aged woman, tweedy and square-cut. Her face was blonde and open. She did not smile.

"Who are you?" I asked, though I knew already. Her young face had smiled down from Dring's mantelpiece for as long as I could remember. Even now it looked out with supreme confidence from the picture on her bedside table.

"Lucy Price," she introduced herself briskly, "Sissy was my nanny for years and years." She leaned over Dring and boomed at her, "This is Mary, she's come to visit. Isn't that nice? Say hello to Mary, there's a dear Sissy."

Dring stared at her, still frowning, darted me a stranger's glance. She turned plaintively to the big woman. "Where's Mr Tom? You told me Mr Tom would come."

"I said he'd try, Sissy, only that he'd try!" Why was she shouting? Dring wasn't deaf. "He's got lots of staff off sick right now and it's hard for him to get away. But I'm here and now your friend Mary has come too."

"Lucy, my leg hurts too much. I want to go home."

Dring never even looked at me. I was shrinking to a vanishing point while this woman, this stranger, loomed ever larger and robbed me of my childhood.

"All in good time, Sissy dear. We've got to get you well first."

She straightened herself and gestured to me with a jerk of her head and, too stunned to argue, I followed her out into the corridor. Some seats covered in dark green plastic were arranged along the wall and she indicated to me to sit down.

I moved slowly, as though through some opaque substance of dream, and did as she suggested. I was too numbed to protest, too numbed even to think.

She addressed me as if I were a small meeting. "This is bound to be a shock for the poor old thing, only to be expected, though. Amputation at her age and in her state of health is a pretty serious business, though the doctors seem to think that there's about a fifty-fifty chance of her regaining her memory completely."

Her words seemed to be travelling across a huge distance, to be slurred as though we were talking together under water.

"Amputation?"

"Heavens, surely they told you? They had to take the leg off a couple of days ago. The surgeon did·tell me the technical name for the problem but it sounded pretty much like good old-fashioned gangrene to me. Not a pleasant operation at any age and she seems to be coming through it all remarkably well."

"But I never knew. No one ever told me."

"I know they tried. I did think it was a bit rum that you didn't turn up sooner, I must say."

"No one told me." No one told me. No one told me. No one had ever told me.

"Well, it can't be helped now. The main thing is to get her well again."

"She didn't even know who I was." Again I had that feeling of sliding off the edge, fading to the merest dot, far away: in a few moments I might disappear altogether . . . I forced myself to focus on this sturdy woman's words.

"All her recent memory has gone," she was saying, "at least thirty years. I was trying her out earlier and she couldn't even remember her husband."

"Who?"

"You knew she was married, surely?" I shook my head. "What a dark horse she's been. We all thought it was a bit of a joke at the time. She eloped with this funny little Frenchman with a moustache and pigeon toes. But my parents didn't see the funny side of it, I can tell you, because they were left nannyless, but we all thought it was a hoot. Poor old Sissy, struck by Cupid's dart at last!"

Poor old Sissy. Where had Dring gone? I said with deliberate casualness, "What happened to him?"

"Oh, it was all jolly sad. He was killed in a car accident after about six months. She wanted her old job back but my father always said if someone had let you down once you could never trust them again. She rather went to pieces after that. I did keep in touch when I could but she was pretty well down and out until I managed to get her that job with you."

"*You* did?"

"Indirectly. An old friend of mine, Deb Brewster, put me in touch with her sister. Said she was very soft-hearted and always found a niche for lost souls somewhere. Which turned out to be the case."

"Then you always knew about me?" My childhood was become a kaleidoscope which even a stranger like this loud-voiced woman could twist at will, destroying with a casual phrase, a sentence she was barely aware of, the pattern I had been familiar with all my life, reassembling the fragments for her own convenience. Why should she notice my discomfort? A kaleidoscope is only a toy, after all.

"Heavens, yes. I used to come and visit Alderly Drive at least once every year – but always when you were at

301

school. She liked to keep things separate, Sissy, always had done. She was jolly fond of you, no doubt about that whatsoever. You know, you don't look at all well. Would you like me to ask one of the nurses to fetch you something?"

"No, no thank you."

"Well, if you're sure— " She looked doubtful but, "I'd best get back and see what I can do for her. The nurses are wonderful but they simply don't have enough time. I'm going to move her to a private home just as soon as possible. There's a terribly good one in our village."

"But – I— "

"Why not come back tomorrow? She might even recognise you then. But don't worry about me; I like this kind of project, stops me moping about the place, and I'm sure you've got your own life to lead."

Her arms swung by her side as she strode back towards the ward in a jaunty, purposeful way; the door banged closed behind her, leaving me alone on my green plastic seat, staring at the wide stairs and the huge grey sky beyond the window.

It would have been easier to bear, I thought fiercely, if Dring had died.

And in a way, that was what she had done. This decrepit widow, this Sissy, was no part of my life. Not the old Dring.

As I walked down the stairs the walls seemed to bend and sway like parachute silk and my legs felt as though the bones had turned to elastic. One or two people glanced at me as I passed and I wondered if secret strangeness showed in my eyes. I wanted to hide my face away from their too-perceptive gaze. Was it possible that I already looked different?

In the car park the cold air was temporarily reviving; it brought me sufficiently to my senses to realise that I was no longer capable of driving through city traffic. I remembered with relief that there was a bus that went from here nearly to the house.

Standing in the bus queue near the hospital I was amazed by how grotesque were the other people around me. The woman nearest had wiry black hair like a dog and a pale doughy face that formed lumps in all the wrong places. Another woman had features so sharply pointed she reminded me suddenly of an army penknife with all the blades exposed. The man in front of her was thin and droopy as though the essence of him had shrunk and no longer filled his baggily hanging flesh. At the very front of the queue a girl with make-up caked across her face was holding an enormous baby with the gross cheeks of a trumpeter, who was banging his forehead against her shoulder. The baby was going to grow up into another grotesque specimen, just like all the others. I could tell.

When the bus arrived it made such a terrifying noise that for a moment I was afraid to enter but a woman behind me jabbed me in the back with her shopping bag and I stumbled up the steps.

The driver looked at me expectantly, but I found to my dismay that I could not remember the name of my bus stop even though I must have stopped there many thousands of times before. I stared at him hopelessly. His teeth were bright yellow and hideously misshapen and the whites of his eyes were yellow too. He asked me a question and without hearing what he said I nodded and he took some money from my hand. I sat down beside an enormous black woman whose body had oozed over three-quarters of the seat. I looked through the window. All the streets looked the same, all the houses. An endless maze with no sense in it anywhere. It was tempting to lean back, close my eyes, stay on this magic bus for ever.

"This here is your stop."

It could have been the black woman beside me who spoke but I wasn't sure. I stood up and wobbled down the aisle which had suddenly stretched to a great length. "Take your time," said a voice. Nastily, I suspected, but it was hard to be certain. I stepped off the bus just as it began to move away, and nearly fell.

For a few moments I stood motionless while the buildings tipped and swayed and rearranged themselves around me. It seemed that they had fitted back together again in a different order from the one I had always been used to, but I couldn't be sure. I couldn't be sure of anything any more.

I began to walk in what I thought was the direction of Alderly Drive. Windows leered at me.

Where was my home? I stood on the pavement and searched for it. Had it gone, vanished already, just as Dring had vanished? Taken over and painted and given a different name, a new owner, so that there was nowhere left for me to hide, no safety anywhere. Perhaps Lucy of the photo lived there now and if I looked closely I would see her loathsome jolly face beaming at me from behind new net curtains in the downstairs window.

The wind had grown colder. I stood alone in the street and thought the wind would blow for ever.

"Mary, come inside. You're freezing."

A pale face looked down at me, a pale face fringed with orange hair. Paula slipped her arm through mine and led me up the steps to our blue-painted front door. (It must have been there all the time.)

The narrow hallway greeted me like an old friend. There was the familiar wallpaper, the oval mirror over the little table, the worn stair carpet with the stain on the third step where I had spilled a bottle of ink, years ago.

"Come and sit down." Very gently, Paula shoved me towards the sitting-room. "You look washed out – and no wonder."

I sank into my old and favourite armchair and it seemed as though it folded me in steady arms, shutting out the terror of the streets.

"Oh Paula," I breathed, "you don't know how good it is to be home."

She smiled. "I can guess. What would you like to revive you properly?"

"I wouldn't mind a cup of tea – but you don't have to wait on me, I'm perfectly able to— "

But she wouldn't hear of it. "I'm only glad you've turned up safe and sound – heavens, now I'm beginning to sound like my own mother. You should know, Mary Fern, that you had me worried sick when I heard you'd left the house on your own like that."

"Who told you?"

"I telephoned this morning and spoke to Archie— "

I frowned. Why was she talking about Archie when he was the very person I was running from? And there was something else, something that was wrong, though I couldn't put my finger on it. I had that niggling sense of unease that you get when you leave the house knowing you've forgotten some important item, but are quite unable to remember what that item is.

I said, "Archie drove you back here last night, didn't he?"

Paula was on the way out to the kitchen but she paused in the doorway. "No such luck," she said bitterly, "I had assumed, in my naïve North American way, that his offer to drive me back to Bristol constituted a door-to-door service, but I had omitted to read the fine print. He was going to Park Street and lo and behold that was where I fetched up as well. I might just as well have caught the train."

"The rotten swine. But didn't his sparkling conversation on the journey make it all worthwhile?"

"No conversation is worth a two-mile walk in high heels *and* carrying a suitcase."

I couldn't help laughing at her obvious chagrin. Poor Paula; in their different ways the men in my newfound family had both failed to match up to her expectations.

With the laughter some of my tension began to ease; I leaned my head back in the chair and closed my eyes . . . and yet still I could not relax. I was home and I was safe and I could hear Paula singing tunelessly in the kitchen as she put on the kettle for tea and yet still I was alert, sensing danger.

Stop fussing, I told myself. It's over, you're home. You can stop being afraid, stop trying so hard to . . . what? To keep going, that was it, just to keep going.

But still I could not settle. There was something out of joint, something that did not fit. That smell – I opened my eyes and sniffed cautiously – that smell belonged elsewhere, not here in Alderly Drive. But perhaps it was me. My hair and clothes, my skin, were grubby with fear and exhaustion.

Paula brought me a tray set with cup and saucer and a plate of biscuits. "You've become suddenly very domestic," I smiled. "Lord, but I need a bath."

"And plenty of rest."

Rest, yes. But what was it about the house that felt so different? "Paula, does this room smell odd to you?"

She wrinkled her nose. "No, you must be imagining it. You've been through a lot recently."

It was then that I decided to tell her just how much I had been through. "When you spoke to Archie this morning did he tell you that he tried to kill me last night? He came into my room and turned on the gas and now he's telling people that I did it myself. Even the doctor believes it was attempted suicide."

She tutted sympathetically. Paula as mother hen was a new phenomenon. "You must be feeling like hell," she said.

"He's done it before. Somehow he tipped my mother into madness and I think he may have killed Aunt Frances and made it look like an accident – or suicide. All that to protect his secret. And now it is my turn."

"Try not to think about that now. Don't dwell on it until you are strong again."

"Yes," I said, "forget . . ." It could have been Dring talking. Forget the bad things, pretend they never happened. And now Dring had followed her own advice so thoroughly that she had erased the whole of her life with me from her mind, wiped me clean away like chalk from a dusty slate. In her mind I no longer existed.

Forget . . .

Suddenly afraid and no longer wanting to remain in this timelessly familiar room which had changed in a way so subtle that the exact nature of the alteration still eluded me, "I shall run myself a bath," I said.

In the little crowded bathroom I at last experienced the healing reassurance of familiar things: the spider plant (which needed watering), the white tiles, the brown stain under the hot tap and the way the water roared into the bath as if in a terrible hurry.

I put liberal quantities of flower scents into the steaming water and allowed myself the luxury of a long hot soak. Paula had told me once that baths are so relaxing because they revive memories of the warm waters of our mother's womb and I wondered foolishly if I could have spent my first nine months floating in amniotic fluid that was drenched in the scent of rose geranium. It was a conundrum which I felt just about capable of dealing with; and all those other, impossible puzzles with which my mind had been grappling could wait until another day, the next day, when my head had stopped throbbing, when I had eaten and had spent a night in my safe little bed right here at Alderly Drive.

I lay so long in the bath that my fingers and toes began to pucker and I only climbed out when the water had gone tepid and Paula poked her head around the door to make sure I hadn't fallen asleep and drowned.

"I'm making pasta," she called back as she ran down the stairs. "Carbohydrates are the essential antidote to any kind of stress or shock."

Being cared for had never felt so sweet. I reached across to the rail for the old towel with roses on it which was one of a pair Dring had bought in the sales while I was still at school and as I did so something shiny and coloured as bright as stained glass slipped to the floor.

I turned away, not wanting to see it. I dried myself with exquisite care and then padded along to my bedroom, found fresh clothes and put them on.

Then there was nothing for it but to go back to the bathroom and pick up the jewel-bright thing that lay, venomous as a snake, beside the bath.

Nausea circled in my stomach as I carried the deadly scrap of material down the stairs – but this time the nausea was not caused by the inhalation of gas, it was the nausea of reluctant revelation.

Now I knew why the house no longer smelled of home; now I knew the cause of the unease which had nagged me since the moment Paula took me by the arm and led me into the hall.

Still holding the shimmering silk in my hand I walked on trembling legs into the kitchen where Paula was stirring a pan of spaghetti sauce.

She glanced up. "Do you feel better now?" And then, seeing my face, "Mary, what in God's name is wrong?"

The words forced themselves out of me, tight and hard. "Why did you lie to me?"

Her gaze fell to the silk cravat in my hand and she swore softly.

I spoke. "He came here last night. That smell I couldn't put my finger on, it was one of Archie's cigars. You told me he dropped you in town because . . . you've lied to me all along. Did you go to bed with him?"

She laid down her wooden spoon and took a step towards me, then thinking better of it she stayed where she was and said, "Listen, Mary, let's keep some kind of proportion here. You're upset right now and I can see how this must look but if you just calm down and look at it all sensibly then— "

"Did you go to bed with him?"

"What the hell does it have to do with you anyway? And I'm sick of your bloody English euphemisms. No, I didn't go to bed with him but I did screw him. On the couch as a matter of fact and then— "

"You lied to me." (Didn't she know the truth was all I had to hold on to now?)

"It wasn't a lie, Mary, not really. I mean, I was going to tell you eventually. But right now I knew you'd take it

308

wrong and be upset. You've been overwrought recently and I was trying to protect you, that's all. Just calm down for a change."

Calm? Where was that? The pain clanging in my head, the floor sliding away, the cold wind which now had entered even here and would never cease to blow . . . "You were pretending all along. You never believed me."

"We want to help you, Mary."

"Did you tell Archie?"

"He's worried about you too, you know. I only told him I thought you'd been under pressure recently, that it was getting on top of you."

"But did you tell him?"

"And when he learned that you'd been seeing a psychiatrist without telling anyone— "

"What?"

"There's no reason to be ashamed of it. The man telephoned here last week, asking to speak to you. I thought it was great. Knowing when and where to seek help is an entirely . . ." I'm sure she carried on talking because I could see the way her mouth kept opening and closing but her words became tangled with the pain and the endless pounding that boomed in my ears. I tried to speak but my mouth had grown huge and the words emerged clumsy and ill-formed, like monstrous children.

"Did – you – tell – him?" But I could not go on. The thunderous noise which roared within my skull seemed to be coming out of her mouth, her wide red ugly mouth with the white and grey teeth and the tongue bouncing up and down stupidly to shape the sounds and the saliva gleaming like foam . . .

I put my hands over my ears. The din had become one with the pain in my head. The voice was there too, my secret voice, but now it was barely audible above the hurricane roar inside my head.

I turned and went through the hall to the front door. Paula was the cause of the hideous din and I had to escape her. She followed me to the front door, tried to hold me back. I think I heard her say, "You can't go, Mary, I promised them I'd keep you here." But I was stronger than her. In the doorway she opened her mouth again and the sound that came out was a high-pitched whine like a mad wind in winter trees.

I plunged out into the street. Her voice followed me like a dying scream. Cold biting my face, my hands.

I walked.

No room for thought, or questions, or fears. No room for images of Archie or Paula or Dring. No room for anything but the huge effort of placing one foot in front of another and moving myself along the pavement, one foot after the other, getting as far away from that evil house, that evil noise, away and gone for ever.

Over the hills and far away. (But who was the piper's son?) Some of the streets had a vaguely familiar appearance, others were unknown. It was all the same anyway. The streetlights were beginning to come on: lollipop-red suns that gradually turned to orange. A sky filled with slowly changing suns. Red suns, orange suns. I watched them, fascinated. Why had I never noticed them before? Fur crushed against my face and above the fur a woman's eyes were furious, her mouth spat out angry words but I couldn't make out what she was saying. I had an idea that the fur she was wearing was an old family pet and I was sorry if I had hurt it . . . but it was cruel to keep it over her shoulders in that way.

I walked on.

The pain still thumped in my head but it no longer hurt my eyes and I could see things clearly. I was part of the street, yet also suspended above it. People were scurrying everywhere like ants. The street and the houses surrounding it was a huge termite colony, crowded with frantically busy dots of life, each one with their own smell, their own worries, their own urgency. Each wrapped in their own cocoon. Each one identical to all the others. Pale faces in the winter dusk. And then I saw quite clearly that they weren't human at all, they were maggots, and the whole city was a festering corpse and they were swarming over its rotten flesh, sucking out the juice.

I was cold. But it was no longer the coldness of the outside air. The cold had entered my bones, my blood, my inmost soul. Cold and dead and laid to rest. Except that there was no rest, not here or ever in the future. Only this endless cold and the throbbing in my head and the wind of fear which would never cease to blow.

Something smooth and metal rammed against my leg. A car stopped. The driver leaned out of his window and his eyes were angry but from his rapidly opening and closing mouth came only the gentle swish swish of a sea-shell held to the ear.

Maggot faces staring. Dark eyes in pale pale faces. Someone tries to catch my arm. Turn and run away.

Railings, grass beneath my feet, look up and see the high clear vault of the sky, ribbed with the black lines of trees, their branches an irregular veining. Look up, leap high and free above the earth. Such a fragile beauty, that intricate pattern of black against the deep blue of a clear winter's evening. Why had I never noticed before how perfect, how painful are those winter trees? Turn slowly and take in every detail. Remember this.

Remember another . . . branches above my head and a gentle rocking motion. The warm summer voice holds me tight in an infinitely careful grasp. I am safe. Not cold any more. Sunlight warms my face. There is a smell of honeysuckle and mock orange. But then the voice stops, falls silent and lets me go, lets me drop. I am falling, forever falling, the black branches sway and spin. They are grown pointed fingers reaching down to claw me apart.

Grass and earth against my cheek. Smell of dampness.

Words, hands.

No, leave me.

Fern, can you hear me?

No, no. Leave me alone.

And then words that pierce the hard shell of my terror: "Fern, don't be frightened. It's me, Adam, and I believe you. I know you are telling the truth."

Chapter 13

Memories blur and dissolve, re-form and crystallise and then once more evaporate in the unending dream of that night. I was aware of cold blue walls, a room so impersonal it could have been a hotel but was, I found out later, the spare bedroom belonging to one of Adam's many Bristol friends. He must have known I could not return to Alderly Drive, could not be exposed to Paula's treacherous care. "I promised them I'd keep you here." Promised whom? Archie . . . Paula and the house were mine no longer. Archie possessed them both.

I remember that for a long time I was unable to stop shivering; that the pain still crashed its hammer blows against my skull. I remember Adam cradling me, rubbing my hands, my arms, my back, as though to warm me, to return me to living warmth. I think he must have fed me, morsels of soft food as though I were a sick child. And all the time his voice wove around my head, promising me that he believed me, that I was not and never would be mad. My skull felt as though it was going to crack open with the pain and he wanted to call a doctor but I would not let him. No more doctors. Never. He fed me aspirins and stroked my hair and slowly coaxed me towards the safety of the real world's shore.

All night long I clung to him, like a drowning swimmer who finds at last a life raft in the heavy seas. His flesh was warm and sure and nourished me. Some time in the stillness of that night we made love. He was all around me and inside me and the gentle movement of his body was the caress of a wave, cleansing me of fear. And afterwards I slept, a different kind of sleep.

*   *   *

313

When I awoke in the morning I was at once aware, even before opening my eyes, of Adam's arms encircling me, the feel of his skin pressed against mine. Instinctively I tensed; how had I let him break down the fortress of my solitude?

His eyes opened, very close to my own, and they creased into a smile. "Fern?" he murmured. "Good morning, Fern."

I turned away, too confused even to return his greeting. Beside me I could feel him shift himself to prop his head on his hand.

"Don't slip away from me now," I heard him say softly, while his finger traced a delicate spiral on my bare shoulder, "not when it has taken me so long to find you." But still I could summon up no words to share with him. He said, "Never forget, Fern, that I believe you, every single word of it. I believe that Archie is a fraud; I believe that he's gone to terrible lengths to protect his secret. I believe you, Fern."

"But how can you?"

His mouth gently brushed the curve of my cheek. "It's easy," he said, and then he kissed my forehead, my eyes, the tip of my nose, all the compass points of my face, and his kisses were light and magical as fireflies, and where his lips had touched, the surface of my skin glowed with a lingering warmth, like the aftermath of sunshine. I turned back to face him, and what I saw in those gold-flecked grey eyes staring down at me spurred me on to name at last the terror that had hounded me for so long.

"Adam, you don't know . . . I thought I was falling . . . like my mother. I thought I was insane."

"Hush, Fern," he said gently, "I know. Don't torment yourself any longer, you're safe."

"Safe, yes . . ." He was not to know, and how could I ever explain, that for me the events of the previous day could never be erased from my mind entirely. When I plunged from the house at Alderly Drive into the hostile city streets, I had caught a glimpse of the endless abyss of howling darkness where my mother's fragile grasp on life had been swallowed up and destroyed – and as a result my world had been forever altered.

If Adam had not believed me . . . but Adam *did* believe me.

And, finally convinced, I put my arms around his neck and pulled him to me and returned his loving, suddenly aware of every detail of our two bodies. I felt like a child who has lived all her life on a cold and lonely street, occasionally glimpsing through the windows of a house where people laugh together and find pleasure. Since that morning in the unfamiliar bed in the blue-painted bedroom I have become acquainted with many different rooms inside the house of love, learned to savour its many delights, but as long as I live I shall never forget those first tentative and miraculous steps within its walls.

When we were finished we lay in silence for a while. Adam may have slept but I remained awake, every nerve and muscle alert yet fully relaxed. I thought of what had passed and what yet remained to do.

At length Adam said, "I always knew it was right for us, Fern. Why couldn't you trust me before? If only you had told me sooner."

"I did want to, Adam. I tried phoning you several times. I was planning to tell you everything then but when I couldn't get hold of you and Paula showed up at the house, I told her instead."

"The all-knowing disciple of Freud."

"You never liked her, did you?"

"Not much. Not my type, really. I think she reminds me uncomfortably of Jane."

In the ambling, leisurely pace peculiar to conversations between two people lying in sweaty contentment in each other's arms we pieced together the events of the previous twenty-four hours. It turned out that Paula had phoned him late the previous evening. She and Archie must have reached Alderly Drive soon after six and Archie had probably left again some time around ten, which was when she phoned Adam. At first he was unable to understand why she was calling. "She can be maddeningly incoherent, your friend. It took an age to extract the information that she thought you had finally snapped under all the strain and had concocted some incredible fantasy about your father and *Dora's Room*."

"But it *is* incredible, Adam. Why did you believe me?"

He grinned. "Instinct, I suppose, true love, a sixth sense . . . what Paula was saying, all her devious psychobabble about trauma and projection and God knows what else, simply didn't sound like you at all."

"What *did* she tell you?"

I almost wished I hadn't asked. The gospel according to Paula: because of the traumas of my early life I had always experienced problems with reality boundaries (or some such phrase), and my mother's recent death, annihilating all possibility that she would ever recover and *be* a mother to me, followed so swiftly by coming face to face with the evidence of my uncle's success and my father's failure, caused me to create a version of events which shifted the balance in my father's favour – and thus also in my own. In my warped view of events my father gained not only his brother's masterpiece but his wife's love as well. Archie had thus become the convenient scapegoat for all that was negative in my life, so that I even projected on to him my self-destructive impulses, deftly transforming the occasion of the gas-filled room from failed suicide to attempted murder.

"Stop please!" If I heard any more I thought I probably would go mad after all. "Did she say all this to Archie?"

"She swears not. She claims that all she told him was that she thought you had been under terrible pressure and she was worried about your mental state. And, as it happens, I believe she was telling me the truth. A vague concern for you was more than enough for her purposes."

"Which were?"

"To get Archie, of course. 'I think we should talk about Fern' is at least a variation on the etchings ploy."

I groaned. "Oh Adam, I trusted her!" There was a dull ache at the base of my throat.

"I know." He kissed me gently. "And if it's any

consolation I'm sure Paula was convinced she had your best interests at heart. Netting Archie was a bonus."

A shudder of pure horror passed through me and Adam pulled me close to him again and told me I was safe. But already the cold wind from the outside world was beginning to blow around our hidden bed; that old sense of urgency, the need to discover the truth, was pursuing me again.

"I wonder if I shall ever find Dora," I murmured.

Adam frowned. With the awareness that intimacy was bringing in its wake I could sense his caution, his protectiveness. "You have to accept that's not very likely any more, Fern. Even if she *was* a real person, she might have died, or emigrated, or changed her name. You must stop tormenting yourself, try to put the past behind you."

But the search had been a lifeline, an obsession, for so long that it was impossible to relinquish it now. "I could have asked my mother," I persisted, "I think maybe she knew and that's why . . . Dring said it was Archie who pushed her over the edge . . ."

My voice trailed into silence; since yesterday I knew only too vividly the aptness of that lethal little phrase: "Over the edge".

But how?

Random words, half-remembered fragments of the puzzle . . . and when the truth washed through my brain like an ice-green wave, I groaned aloud and clung to Adam. "Oh no!"

"What is it, Fern? Are you crying?"

"I never cry."

"Never?"

I was shivering violently. "That's it, that's what he did, don't you see now – oh! How could he be so cruel?" I was trying hard to be calm but, "My mother was coping, you see, that's what everybody has told me. She was upset by my father's death obviously but somehow she was managing. Her world didn't collapse then, it didn't collapse until the day Archie came to clear out my father's papers – and obviously by then he needed to remove all the evidence for *Dora's Room*. And then, while Dring and I were out of the way, he told her – everything."

"But what?"

"About my father's affair with Aunt Frances. She never knew of it until then, but from that moment onwards she was stripped even of memory, of everything she had been able to believe in. A different person, a more flexible person, someone more secure, perhaps, might have found a way to come to terms with it but for my mother it was, quite simply, too much to bear."

"Do you really think Archie did that deliberately?"

I nodded my head. "Oh yes, can't you just hear his reasoning? 'Why should Louise be left in blissful ignorance when I have suffered so much pain?' I'm sure he told her."

Adam held me tightly but still the shivering did not stop. "He destroyed her, Adam, he destroyed her. And then he murdered his own wife too."

Adam's comfort was grim. "Maybe he didn't need to," he said. "If he told Frances what it was that had finally driven her sister-in-law to madness then no wonder the poor woman blamed herself for everything. Like your father, she had always endeavoured to protect Louise— "

We clung to each other without speaking, but the earlier warmth, the sense of being two parts of a whole, had been corroded. Archie's influence reached even here.

"Come to London with me," said Adam as he dressed.

Yes, I said, then no. To leave Chatton Heights was essential, I knew that now, but with dignity, not running away . . . Today I must return and collect my things – that photograph of my father as a boy standing in front of the window with the full-blown roses, that must never fall into Archie's hands. I must say a proper goodbye, not to the people, parasites every one, but to the house, monstrous and unique, to the house I must say farewell. I tried to explain, failed miserably.

Adam only smiled. "That place draws you like a magnet. What is its secret?"

I hesitated. He was gazing down at me with a strange

expression, half laughter, more than half loving, in those intensely grey eyes. I took the risk. "There's a voice I hear," and then, glimpsing his eyebrows flickering with disbelief, I hastened to explain, "It's a memory voice, Adam, not a mad, Joan-of-Arc-type voice. I heard it first at Chatton Heights on that afternoon you interviewed Archie. I believe it's to do with my father – and with Dora. Can you believe that? I sometimes think I must have heard it when I was small, but over the years while I was cut off from my family it became buried. Buried, but never completely forgotten. And just recently it has been growing stronger all the time."

"What does it say?"

"That's just the problem, I can't distinguish the words. Adam, when I first heard it I thought it was a – a symptom, a sign that I was a crazy person just like my mother. But now I'm sure it is a memory, too precious to fear but always just out of reach."

"And can you hear it now?"

"Faintly. It's always strongest at the Heights."

He had been listening attentively; now he smiled and drew me close to him, cupping my face between his warm hands. "I never imagined," he said, "that such an ugly house could sing a siren song. Come to London with me. I've an interview with an American biographer this afternoon that was scheduled weeks ago. But tomorrow I can come with you to collect your things."

"I can go alone, Adam. If I go today then it's over and done with."

He sighed. "You've that steely look in your eyes again. I know better than to waste my time trying to make you change your mind. Do you want me to cancel my interview and come with you?"

Of course I didn't. But, when the moment came to part and he put his arms around me for the last time, I wanted to cling to him, say stay with me, come with me today, never let me go.

He pushed me away almost roughly. "Are you sure you won't change your mind?"

319

I shook my head.

"Then for God's sake, go. The way you switch from grim determination to waif-like vulnerability is more than I can bear. I shall never get used to it."

"I'll come to London this evening."

"You'd better," he said grimly, "and if you change your mind again I shall come down to Long Chatton tomorrow and drag you away by force, and a hundred mysterious voices won't be enough to keep you there."

As I drove towards Long Chatton I remembered Adam's words. "The siren song of Chatton Heights," he had called it . . . and the music of that siren song grew sweeter and louder as I drove through the narrow lanes that led from the motorway to the village. Despite my fear at the memory of danger, there was a skip of anticipation as the familiar landmarks of the journey told me I was drawing nearer to my grandfather's house. I caught a glimpse first of the camel-shaped hill, then the church tower rising above the assorted russet roofs and chimney pots of Long Chatton, and I knew once again that tantalising sense of impending revelation . . . something about to happen. And now the voice was billowing as though on a warm summer wind, sometimes faint, sometimes so clear that I could almost reach out and grasp the separate words.

At first I thought I was imagining the change that was occurring as I rounded the corner that led down the hill and into Long Chatton. The sky was the colour of pewter yet held a strange light, all its own. Everywhere trees and animals were very still, not a breath of wind. Waiting. And then, as I turned off between the two stone eagles and plunged into the laurel-sided ravine of the driveway, the first delicate flakes of snow drifted idly on to my windscreen.

In the hall I nearly collided with Mrs Viney as she wheeled a trolley through to the dining-room: cheese and biscuits and an aromatically steaming apple crumble. I told her I had already eaten but said I would join her in the kitchen for a cup of coffee later, to say goodbye.

My suitcase was quickly packed. Even if I had been inclined to linger over the task, the foul smell of gas which still permeated the room would have soon deterred me. I looked around the spartan bedroom for the last time: Gracie's room, my father's room . . . as impersonal and remote now as it had ever been. It had told me nothing.

Regret is a pointless emotion and one I knew Dring would have had no patience with at all. And yet it was impossible not to feel an almost overwhelming sense of waste and failure as I went down the wide stairs to the hallway and looked around at the still ugly but now familiar scene. I knew that there was much I could be proud of: I had uncovered many truths about my family; I had survived all that Archie and Paula could throw at me; I had even survived the loss of Dring; I had been able to accept and return the riches Adam was offering; all that I could do, I had done.

But it was not enough. I was leaving Chatton Heights with many questions still unanswered, and with Archie still safely swaddled in his lie.

In many ways the search for Dora had led nowhere . . . I decided then to go just once more to the part of the garden where my secret voice had often seemed strongest, to the summer house and the clearing in the shrubbery where the swing had hung down from the old holm oak.

Snow was still falling in an absent-minded sort of way, not bothering to settle but dissolving into nothingness when it touched the ground, as I crossed the gravel and the wide lawns that led to the shrubbery.

Secret as Sleeping Beauty's castle and every bit as boxed in from the outside world, the summer house stared out with cobweb-blinded eyes. Yet years ago, when my father was a boy and before the surrounding trees and shrubs soared upwards, there must have been no more delightful spot in which to dream away a sleepy summer's afternoon.

I turned the handle of the door and tried to open it, but either the door was locked or it had been so warped by the weather that it was jammed tight. I hesitated only for a moment before throwing all my weight against the door.

And the summer house shifted.

I leaped back, as startled as if the summer house had suddenly found a voice and spoken to me. Had I imagined it? For a brief moment a giddy fear wavered through me: were shock and defeat finally driving me to hallucinate? Cautiously, a second time, I leaned my whole weight against the corner of the summer house – and pushed . . .

With a groan of long disuse it turned a few degrees on its axis.

I was so relieved to discover that my senses were not playing tricks on me after all that I was laughing as I found its secret. Beneath each corner of the summer house there was a wheel and these wheels were set on a circular track. Originally, before tree roots and ivy had clawed their way over the metal, it would have been possible to turn the summer house in a full circle according to the direction of the sun.

And still the door refused to open. I reflected that it was no great loss after all; surely nothing could be visible from the dust-veiled windows but a tangle of undergrowth and green leaves. If I wished to know what had been visible from this point in my father's lifetime then I would do best to climb on the roof.

Why had I never thought of this before? Suddenly excited I looked around for some means of ascent. Two large branches brushed against its side and, as I used them to hoist myself up on the sloping roof, I registered, vaguely, that they were the lowest limbs of the holm oak.

The next moment I was on the roof and everything was forgotten in the burst of pleasure that thrilled through me. From here I could see so much: the camel-humped hill and quite a bit of the church tower; a sizeable portion of the chestnut tree that stood beside the village pond.

Perhaps if I climbed just a little higher I would be able to see the pond itself.

Very carefully, and wishing that I had thought to wear gloves since my fingers were already numb with cold, I crawled on to the central ridge and looked around. Even here I lacked sufficient height. Perhaps if I stood . . .

There was a branch that reached almost across the width of the summer house and, catching hold of it, I cautiously pulled myself into a standing position.

Surely from here . . .

A movement in the shrubbery below distracted my attention for a fleeting moment; the next I felt the branch wrenched from my hands as though the tree itself was rearing away from me, the whole roof on which I was so precariously balanced seemed to bucket under my feet, the sky tipped and the branches all around soared suddenly over my head as I plunged down towards the ground. I heard my own sharp cry of fear pierce the silence and a blackbird, startled, called back, mimicking my alarm.

I remember clutching frantically at anything that might slow my fall – the roof, twigs, branches, leaves . . . then there was nothing but empty space and the ground reared up and pounded against my side.

I must have been temporarily winded by my fall. Perhaps I passed out but I don't think so. The snow-dampened ground was very cold, pressed against my cheeks, numbing my scratched and bleeding fingers.

I sat up slowly. Thank heavens, I thought, as I looked around me and the trees, the summer house and the sky all returned to their proper positions, that was lucky, no harm done. Suddenly, probably as a result of the shock, I discovered that I was very cold. I stood up – and then fell over again with a howl of pain. It was as though someone had sliced through my ankle with a red-hot knife.

Don't be foolish, I told myself, it's bound to be only a sprain. But when I tried to stand for a second time I took care to put all the weight on my left foot. Despite my caution, the pain, as I hobbled down the path that led out of the shrubbery, was so acute that I soon forgot the cold altogether and by the time I emerged on to the lawn I was sweating with the sheer effort of forcing myself to keep going.

"Help!" I shouted, but hearing my voice echo feebly in the huge and empty garden I had scant hope of being heard.

I had managed only a few steps across the lawn when a rescuer did appear in the unlikely shape of my cousin and his two dogs.

"Christ, Fern, whatever have you done to yourself now?"

I explained as best I could while Gerald put his arm around my waist and took my weight, and I hopped a little way before he said with a grin, "You're so skinny we'll get along faster if I carry you; just tell me when it hurts."

It was at that moment, as Gerald scooped me into his arms, that I happened to glance across at the driveway just in time to see Archie's Rover disappear between the snow-speckled laurels.

Gerald set me down on one of the huge leather sofas in the drawing-room, fussed the fire to a warming blaze, sent Mrs Viney to make me a pot of tea and then left me while he went to telephone the doctor. I wondered if he had a passing weakness for females with damaged ankles or whether it could really be the case that his good mood of the previous day had lasted.

On his return he said cheerfully, "The doctor is out on call but if I drive you down to the surgery in an hour he'll see you then."

"Dr Collins?"

"No. Apparently this is his day at the hospital. His partner, Dr Fletcher."

"Where is Archie?"

Gerald chewed his thumb. "Not due back until tomorrow morning. Off after some new female who's thrown herself at him. Bloody middle-aged pervert – I hope he gets AIDS."

Mrs Viney brought me tea and beautifully cut sandwiches and tutted over my throbbing ankle. She arranged the cushions under my shoulder and fetched me aspirins to alleviate the pain. When she and Gerald had left I lay back on the sofa, stared at the fire and tried to collect my thoughts . . . collect for once was an entirely appropriate expression: it felt as though they had been scattered far and wide by the buffetings of the past few days. Weariness . . . it was so tiring to have to think clearly. A series of images presented themselves in my mind, like a picture book falling open on random pages: Archie's car vanishing between the laurels; Archie's exquisitely manicured hand caressing Paula's flaming mass of hair, that feline smile of his whiskering the corners of his mouth in pleased anticipation; that moment when I crouched on the roof of the summer house and the blackbird flew out of the bushes, its call signifying danger . . . Archie's car vanishing between the laurels.

It was so obvious now that I even smiled. He must have followed me into the shrubbery, seen his chance, thrown his weight against the corner of the summer house to turn it on its axis, vanished as silently as he had come . . . driven off to Bristol.

I had been lucky to escape with nothing more serious than a sprained or broken ankle. Falling from such a height I could have . . . but my brain stalled and refused to spell out what might have happened.

There was a bitter taste of failure in my mouth. Archie had not killed me but he had triumphed all the same. I was leaving Chatton Heights, the secret of Dora and her hidden room still undiscovered.

Few things as wearying as defeat.

Flames curled around the logs in the grate, my ankle pulsed with pain, the secret voice circled my head, whispering a message as wordless and soothing as a summer wind . . . if only I could sleep, forget the pain, forget defeat. Forget.

Gerald roused me when it was time to visit the surgery.

With his arm around my waist I was able to hobble with passable skill to the back door where the cream-coloured Daimler he had been working on for so long stood waiting.

"Isn't she a beauty?" Gerald's voice had a tone almost of awe as he surveyed his finished handiwork. "And she runs so smoothly you'd hardly even know she was moving."

I have never been any kind of expert on cars but even I could tell that there was something special about this one. The moment I sat down I felt myself enveloped in luxury: walnut fascia, pale leather seats, space and comfort – this car evoked an era when "motoring" was the exclusive pastime of a wealthy few. I was so impressed by the car itself that it was a few moments before I gave any attention to Gerald. If anyone had asked me I would probably have said he was an aggressive driver, chewing his nails and blasting his fellow road-users with curses. Nothing could have been further from the truth. He drove with such care he might have been carrying a consignment of rare birds' eggs. He was in harmony with his car in the way top-class riders are at one with their horses. For the first time since I had met him he appeared almost serene.

I was still marvelling at this startling side-light on Gerald while the doctor prodded my ankle and announced it to be sprained merely, not broken. He bandaged it and advised pain killers as necessary. His manner was brisk and efficient and I guessed he had not read his colleague's notes on my "suicide bid".

When I stepped outside into the flurrying snow, Gerald was waiting for me. He was leaning against the bonnet of his car, one foot crossed in front of the other in the attitude of a patient chauffeur. I half expected him to tip his cap (except that he wasn't wearing one) as he handed me back into the car.

"What's the verdict?" he asked.

"Only a sprain, thank heavens."

We drove back to Chatton Heights in an almost companionable silence. I sensed he was reluctant for the journey to end and when we had glided to a halt under the high roof of the old coach house I said, "Thank you, Gerald, I enjoyed that."

He ran his fingers lovingly round the steering wheel. "Cars are beautiful machines," he murmured, "they never let you down."

Unlike people . . .

For a moment I almost felt sorry for him. "You drive with real skill," I said.

"Yes, I know." And then he smiled, something, I realised, that I had never really seen him do before. "It's a gift . . ." Still he sat there, that tentative, half-fearful smile lightening his features. "Miller's Vintage Cars," he said, "a special vehicle for that special occasion. One could build up a fleet gradually, really make something of it. A Morgan, a Bentley. Only hand-picked drivers. White uniforms in summer."

"That's a fine idea," I said. "As soon as our grandfather's money is properly shared, there's no reason why you shouldn't do it."

He shrugged. "A bit bloody pathetic though, isn't it? 'My son the taxi driver.'" He mimicked Archie's biting sarcasm. "'My son the motor mechanic.' Any dumb peasant can drive a car, for God's sake, not much of an achievement, is it? Bit of a let-down for the son of a bloody genius, don't you think?"

"When you get your share of the money you must decide how you want to use it without worrying about what Archie – or anyone else – thinks. It will be yours, after all."

He examined me carefully, and this time his anxious, squinty expression was almost friendly. "You really do mean to rewrite his will, don't you? I didn't believe it at first but . . . you're different from the rest of the family. It takes a bit of getting used to." And then he laughed. "You must be mad."

And, perhaps for the first time in my life, that joking accusation had no effect on me whatsoever.

A low wind had begun to blow, sending the snowflakes

in agitated flurries and spirals through dusk made early by the heavy canopy of cloud.

I pondered my next move. I could not drive my car (could not even fit a shoe over my heavily bandaged ankle). Archie was away, not expected back that night. Tillie brought me tea and freshly baked scones and, in answer to my query, said that yes, my grandfather's bedroom could be locked from the inside.

It made sense, after all, to stay at Chatton Heights for one more night.

Several attempts to reach Adam ended in failure. His American biographer must be taking up more time than he had anticipated; perhaps they had decided to have supper together.

I dined with Tillie. Which is to say, I dined alone. She did not answer my questions and when she spoke her words seemed to seep up from some subterranean stream of thought which flowed without regard for outside reality. I wondered by what strange logic my mother had been incarcerated while Tillie was free to flit in harmless lunacy around this sad old house in which she must once have been younger and more beautiful.

We ate in the kitchen, having moved our chairs closer to the Aga for warmth. Beyond the window the snow was blowing in mysterious gusts, random flurries. I panicked briefly at the thought that I might become trapped at Chatton Heights by the snowstorm (an echo of that panic I had experienced on the occasion of my first visit) but reason reassured me: in the morning I could walk into the village if necessary, and it would take a fiercer blizzard than this was expected to be to block the roads there.

In the morning . . . the voice remained, elusive as the snowflakes that were settling now on the ivy leaves beyond the window. That familiar buzz of anticipation. Somewhere deep in the core of me was a part that did not want to leave. Not yet . . . not without Dora.

Towards ten o'clock Adam phoned. His gentle bullying was mixed with exasperation which changed rapidly to concern when I told him I had slipped and sprained my ankle. "But I promise I'll leave in the morning," I assured him and I could almost hear the grin on his face as he said, "You're damn right you will, Fern Miller, and just to make good and sure I intend to drive down first thing in the morning and collect you. Make sure you're ready."

His voice was so reassuring that I felt myself wrapped in the certainty of our reunion as I went up the wide stairs to my grandfather's bedroom. The wind and the snow had combined to make the whole house bitterly cold, and this room was no exception. Tillie found me a fan heater and a hot-water bottle before retreating to her cosy room and her ever-playing television.

I was to spend a night in my grandfather's bedroom and this fact no longer made me uneasy. I sat on the huge bow-fronted chest at the foot of the bed and looked around me: now this was just another large and ugly room, one in which an old man had died. And his influence, I was sure, had died with him.

I was undressed and ready for bed when I heard the car approaching down the drive. The snow made it impossible to distinguish its outline in the darkness. Was it Gerald returning from the pub? Or Archie . . .? Suddenly my heart was pounding against my ribs as I turned the key in the lock.

The car turned behind the house, the sound of its engine faded. No human sound remained, only the primeval whine of the wind through the trees, the advancing snow. The stillness of the house was more menacing than any noise could be.

Then footsteps on the stairs. I climbed into the massive bed and wished I was asleep already. Don't make dramas, I told myself, whoever it is will surely walk straight past.

Heavy footsteps, a man's footsteps, they paused outside my door.

"Fern?" It was Archie's voice.

"What is it?" My throat was suddenly parched.

"Can I come in?"

"No. I was almost asleep."

I heard the handle turn, the rattle of the door against its frame.

"You've locked the door."

"Are you surprised?"

Silence; then, from beyond the door a strange sound. It was a moment or two before I realised that eerie noise was Archie's laughter.

"So, you really do believe you have a homicidal uncle on your trail. What do you suppose I'm armed with this time? A knife or a gun? A machete? One of those fine pikestaffs from the hallway, perhaps?" That laugh again. "A pikestaff is perhaps the most dramatic choice. I should compliment you on the fertility of your imagination. Your sick and fevered imagination."

"Go away!" My command sounded hopelessly childish and futile. For one ludicrous moment I remembered a story book I had had as a child: a frightened piglet in scarlet breeches sat inside his little house while the big bad wolf, tongue slavering with hunger, prowled outside his door. But was my grandfather's locked bedroom a house made of bricks or straw?

I heard him draw up one of the ornamental chairs that stood on the landing and settle himself comfortably just beyond my door. "Tillie has just been entertaining me with the story of your failed attempt to fly from the roof of the summer house. I daresay in your pathetically deluded mind you hold wicked Uncle Archie responsible for that calamity as well as all the others." He paused, waiting perhaps for me to speak, and then continued in that tone of casual menace that was more frightening than shouting or anger could have been. "I can guess what you were doing there too . . . you won't tell me? You were looking for Dora's room, weren't you? Poor bloody simple-minded fool that you are, do you honestly believe that with all the rooms in the house to choose from I'd have elected to freeze my pubescent balls off on the roof of some crappy summer house?" More laughter, and this time his amusement sounded chillingly genuine.

"Oh, Fern, poor bloody Fern, whatever are we going to do with you? You're maybe not yet a top-notch loony like Louise but you're moving that way fast. I have great hopes for you in the future. You really ought to let me in, you know, so that we can discuss this in a civilised manner."

"There's nothing at all to discuss."

"Borderline psychosis, that's what your dear friend Paula calls it."

Paula?

"She thinks that with proper treatment you could be almost normal again one day but I'm not so optimistic. I've seen it all before, you know. The dear girl was most informative this evening. Did you know she has made a study of psychology?"

"What did she tell you?"

"Everything, dear Fern, absolutely everything. All your wicked slanders against your poor uncle. I honestly believe the earth moved for your friend Paula today, at all events, her tongue was loosened in a most informative manner. Vastly entertaining, the whole thing."

I said nothing, only sat there, rigid with the effort of willing him to leave me alone.

After a moment's pause he went on, "Dr Collins will be around in the morning to look at that ankle of yours. He's an old friend and I fully intend to describe your hopeless delusions to him. Or maybe you'd rather tell him yourself? I'm sure he will be fascinated by the whole business – as I remember, he was intrigued by your mother's ramblings as well."

"How dare you talk about my mother like that after the way you treated her!" I had climbed out of bed and padded across the room to the door.

His voice moved closer, as if his cheek were pressed against the thin panel of wood that separated us. "Let me in, Fern."

"Go away!"

"I can still help you, Fern. I wanted to look after your mother, you know, I tried to take care of her but the stupid cow missed her chance. Poor Louise was frigid, did you know that? A bit like you, Fern. Now, be a good girl and open— "

"You're wasting your breath!" My voice was shaking with disgust. "Get away from here and leave me in peace."

"Hysterical now, eh?" At last the cruelty in his voice was undisguised. "What are you going to do now, throw a fit? foam at the mouth? All right, I'll go, for now. But remember, you poor deluded half-witted bitch, I'll give you just enough rope to hang yourself with, no more."

And with that, I heard the scrape of his chair leg against the floor, his departing footsteps melting into the endless silence of the house.

I pulled the eiderdown from the bed and wrapped it around my shoulders, and prepared to wait for the night to pass. All possibility of sleep had vanished. As I sat huddled beneath my quilt on the chair by the window, the drama that unfolded outside was as fierce and vivid as the turmoil I was experiencing within.

The wind was blowing in ever stronger gusts and the trees that bordered the garden were thrashing in the gale. The snow had almost ceased and the dense mass of clouds was breaking up – and then the torn clouds parted to reveal the moon, full and pure and untouched, and I gazed on it with wonder and something that was close to fear.

The moon had long been a symbol both of wisdom and madness. But which of the two, wisdom or madness, had brought me to this locked and lonely room? Or were the two perhaps more closely linked than I had known? From my grandfather's window the view, silvered now by snow and moonlight, was so beautiful it was almost painful. Moon shadows faded and were clear again on the snow-blurred gravel and lawns; then the wind howled the clouds across the moon once more, blotting out its light.

And I found myself thinking, not of Archie, not of my mother, not even of the coming day and my departure with

Adam, but of my grandfather. If it is true that something of the inhabitants of a house remains and colours it with their personality after their leaving, then this room, so lonely and desolate despite its grandeur, made me wonder what had lain behind old Everett's tyranny. I would never know, for sure, but on that night alone in his room, with the wind and the snow and the moonlight making strange magic beyond the window, I felt myself come close to his lonely secret.

At some point I must have fallen into a disjointed kind of sleep. I dreamed that I was all in white in a huge crowd of people, familiar faces all of them, and they were branding my ankle with a white-hot iron, branding me with a symbol of madness.

The tumult that aroused me was so loud that I thought at first the roof must have caved in, or that Archie had smashed down my door and burst into my room . . . I pulled the eiderdown more tightly around my shoulders and was just about to hobble over to switch on the light when I glanced through the window. And stared.

The night sky was grown larger.

This is it, I thought. Archie is right and I am mad. How can the sky grow larger?

Clouds peeled away from the moon and the air was so clear and bright I could see every detail as if it were day. Then I saw an object white and angular and out of place in the midst of the shrubbery. Like a ship beached in a gale, the summer house had reared up amongst the trees.

And the holm oak was no longer there.

Chapter 14

When the sun rose over the brow of the camel-shaped hill on the far horizon it revealed a landscape doubly transformed. The view from my grandfather's bedroom window seemed to have stretched while the world was sleeping: with the falling of the holm oak the sky had grown larger and the immediate prospect had shrunk. The summer house, tipped on its axis by the uprooting of the huge tree, looked for all the world as if it had been tossed away by some bored giant-child. Laurels and lawns, fields and woods beyond and the geometric roofs of Long Chatton were stippled a dazzling white by the brief dusting of snow.

Wasting no time I unlocked the door of my room and went silently down the stairs. To my relief, my ankle, although still painful, no longer prevented me from walking and I guessed I could drive a car as well. My foot was still too painful to be fitted inside a shoe, but wellington boots were a perfectly good substitute.

I hobbled out into the garden.

It struck me then that the aftermath of a storm is always exhilarating, however sincere one's regret at the destruction it has caused. Like a fallen Goliath the holm oak had smashed through a huge area of the shrubbery and the base of the summer house had been so entwined with its roots that it too had been dragged to its ruin. Above the sea of laurels I could see the tree's massive roots which had been torn from the ground yet still clung to the metal track on which the summer house had stood.

I approached slowly, not only because of the throbbing pain in my ankle but because of a growing sense of awe that a single night, a gust of wind blowing more strongly than the rest, could have effected such a huge and irreparable change. As I drew nearer I paused. I had not expected anyone else to have ventured out so early but the sound of a muttering voice informed me of my mistake.

My brief annoyance at what seemed like an intrusion passed as soon as I saw that it was Tom Page who had preceded me. As usual the old man was woefully ill-clad, a shrunken scarecrow in a thin and flapping jacket, nose and ears tipped pink by the morning cold. He acknowledged my arrival with the briefest nod of his head before continuing with the muttering lament, "I told them this would happen but they never listened. Weighed down by the snow, it was, didn't stand a chance in that wind . . ."

I broke in. "Wasn't the holm oak the oldest tree in the garden?"

He was poking among the tangle of leaves and branches with the tip of a walking stick and he made no sign that he had heard my question. "Like watching someone die," he grumbled, "just like a death, losing an old friend. Climbed this as a boy I did, right to the top. And now it's gone." And I wondered as I watched him if the rheumy film in his old blue eyes might even have been tears.

He continued to prod the ground with his walking stick. Almost, I thought curiously, as if he were looking for something.

I ran my fingers over the rough surface of a fallen branch and then looked up at the sky, vast and empty where the holm oak had been for so long. "It changes everything, doesn't it, now that the tree is down."

He wasn't attending to me. His stick had banged against something hard and smooth. "Ha!" he exclaimed, with every sign of satisfaction. "I thought as much."

I peered at the patch of ground that was providing him with so much interest but all I could see were a few shattered lengths of timber. It didn't occur to me then to wonder how they came to be there.

"That's right," I said, "the swing was here."

And I experienced a tremor of recognition, a flutter of anticipation: something about to happen.

His stick twanged against metal and he gave a little grunt of eagerness. Reaching into the tangle of branches he hauled out something that was rusty and square and might once upon a time have been a festive red.

I said, "Good heavens, Tom, that looks like an old biscuit tin."

"And so it is." He was grinning like a schoolboy as he offered the aged and battered tin to me as if it were a precious gift. "And by rights I reckon it's yours now. Cream they were and some had jam in too. Present from the wife's sister in Evesham one Christmas."

I took half a step backwards, suddenly afraid that his reason had been uprooted in the night like the holm oak. "You'd better throw it away, Tom. I don't want it."

But still he grinned, insisting. "Open it. You'll see right enough."

To humour him, I took the biscuit tin. The metal was so cold it burned my hands; the picture on the lid had long since been obliterated by rust and scratches. I began to think longingly of the warm kitchen but I hugged the tin to my chest and pulled at the lid with numbed fingers.

I was smiling at him ruefully as I offered it to him once again. "There you are, Tom, no hidden treasure."

And yet I discovered that I was startled by the intensity of my disappointment (what, after all, had I expected to find?) but it was obvious that Tom's excitement had been misplaced: the tin contained nothing but a couple of old exercise books, a cheap penknife, one of those plastic charts that swivel to show the night sky at different times of year and a large and oddly shaped piece of wood.

Tom, hopping from one foot to the other like a schoolboy with a vital message to relate, was undeterred. "No, look. See, I always wondered where . . . his old treasure tin. I gave him this. Come on, my beauty." And so saying he lifted the misshapen piece of wood from the tin. Just as the sight of him muttering endearments to an old chunk of wood convinced me that his sanity had been either frozen or blown away in the gale, he began to run his fingers over the surface of the wood. And as he did so I realised the vastness of my mistake. This was no useless lump of wood, but an owl, about ten inches long and carved with exquisite skill.

"There you are." A blissful smile had spread across the old man's features. The owl lay on the palm of his hand and stared back at him with wide and contemptuous eyes. "My lovely." Still smiling, he turned to me. "Laburnum wood, that is, wonderfully hard, the very best for carving. I remember the summer I did that. Fine, hot summers we had then."

"*You* carved it? Then surely, Tom, it's yours and you should keep it for your grandchildren."

"Rubbish, girl." Suddenly irritated, he pushed the wooden owl into my hands. "That's not right. This was your father's when he was a lad and mighty fond of it he was too. I made it for him, to cheer him up. Now she belongs to you and she can cheer you up too. You're always asking about your father. Now you must have his owl."

"It is very beautiful."

"Of course she is, I made her, didn't I?" His irritation had passed and he chuckled. "Something to keep his mind off losing the puppets. You remember I told you they were taken away from him after his mother died. Poor little lad, he took that hard, so I said to him, cheer up, Clancy. We'll make you a fine owl and she'll be better than all the puppets put together. And she was, too."

"Why an owl?"

"Not just any owl, oh no. It had to be a tawny owl. There were a couple of young ones at the back of the coach house that summer. We kept them well hidden until they could fly. Mr Archie would have killed them if he'd known. We used to look for them in the woods after that. Your father loved all the creatures of the night; even when he was a little boy, four or five years old, he used to love the night-time."

"But why keep it in a biscuit tin? Why here?"

"To keep it hidden from his father, and from Archie. So she wouldn't be taken away like the puppets were. This was his secret place, his own secret place where no one could ever find him."

"My father's secret place? But where was that?"

For answer he stabbed at the ground with the point of his stick and eased up one of the shattered planks of wood that I had noticed earlier.

"There, that's part of it. His tree house. I made it for him on my afternoons off. The wife was furious, said it was a waste of time – but it was worth all the trouble. No one else knew about it, see, just him and me. Right in the middle of the holm oak it was, couldn't hardly see it unless you knew what to look for. He'd sit up there for hours, reading, thinking. I don't know what. Said he could see for miles around. Said he felt like a king. Said . . ."

But my knees were folding under me and I sank down on a fallen branch.

There was a strange choking sensation in the base of my throat.

"Oh Tom, Tom! I've found them, don't you see! I searched and searched and they were here all the time!"

And then suddenly I was laughing, laughing until Tom laughed with me, although he did not, could not, know the reason for my joy.

And that was how, on the morning when it was destroyed for ever, I found Dora's room.

My father's secret eyrie, his hidden bower, the room from which he could gaze out and see – everything. The whole panorama of the surrounding countryside must have been spread out around him like a rippling patchwork quilt: the sturdy tower of the village church, the huge horsechestnut tree and the pond with the ducks and children playing; the camel-shaped hill in the distance and the grim needle-eyed fortress of a house from which he was always so eager to escape. And the vast canopy of the sky above him and the ever-changing patterns of light. Yes, and the leaf-dappled windows and the smell of old wood.

Why, oh why had I not thought of it before? The holm oak, that tree I had identified on that first morning, before I had ever seen the house, that had been the place of his hidden room after all. And now it was too late – the room was shattered, destroyed and gone for ever. No one could ever again look out and see the world that he had gazed on with his child's fresh vision. I had been so close to the truth all the time; when I had stood on the roof of the summer house the previous day I had been just below it and not known . . . I could have reached up, climbed higher . . .

But still, I had his owl.

I looked down at the beautifully carved wood lying in the palm of my hand.

"Tom, did my father have a special name for her?"

He thought for a moment, then, "Can't say as I remember one."

"How about Dora? Did he ever call her Dora?"

Memory flooded across his features and he beamed at me, delighted. "Yes, that's it! Dora, how did you guess? Funny name for an owl, I thought, but – 'I'll call her Dora because I adore her.' That's what he said. Hang on a minute, though, isn't that something to do with Mr Archie's book?"

Later, I thought, you can explain everything later. "Yes, well – it's not that simple."

"I reckon Mr Archie must have remembered the name and liked it."

"Did my uncle ever use the tree house?"

"Not him, he would have hated it." Tom chuckled at the memory. "Afraid of heights, see, but much too proud to admit it. I reckon that's one of the reasons Mr Clancy was so partial to it, gave him a chance to get away from his big brother. He loved to be on his own, your father did, not like other children."

"When was the last time he went up there?"

"I couldn't say. I don't believe anyone else ever discovered it, not Gerald or any of his friends. I'd forgotten about it myself until this morning."

Forgotten all these years. Dora's room.

I examined the other contents of the tin. The writing in the exercise books was for the most part illegible with age but on one or two pages a few faint traces of ink remained: a childish drawing of an owl, a huge owl with a small child seated between its outstretched wings; clouds around them and a crescent moon above and below them a crudely drawn landscape of trees and hills.

And written below that, and barely legible on the crumbling paper, I was able to make out the words, "Dora and I go flying. Adventure the 4th."

The writing, though childish and unformed, was still recognisable as that of the adult postcards from my father's Indian trip which were still in my possession.

Proof, all the proof I had ever wanted.

"Thank you, Tom," I said, "I shall treasure these for the rest of my life. You don't know how much all this means to me."

Embarrassed, yet pleased all the same, Tom looked away from me and poked at a branch with the point of his stick. "Don't you mention it, I reckon your dad would have wanted you to have his treasures."

I was hugging the precious tin to my chest and laughing as I hobbled back towards the house. Dora, I repeated to myself over and over again, I've found Dora. I was so excited that I barely noticed the burning pain in my ankle. I honestly think that if my whole foot had caught fire at that moment I would have been only mildly interested.

Then, as I reached the edge of the shrubbery, I saw something that made me hesitate. A strange car was parked in front of the house and a man was getting out whom I had seen before: Dr Collins. I grimaced. No doubt the dutiful doctor had come to visit his suicidal patient, his friend's unfortunate niece with the paranoid delusions. No, I told myself, don't go back. Don't risk precious Dora's safety.

I realised that I should have warned Tom not to speak of our discovery to anyone. But when I returned to the fallen holm oak there was no longer any sign of him. It was too late: he had gone already. I sat down on the fallen branch to think.

The little owl, resting on my knee, stared up at me pensively.

"Well then, little Dora," I said, "now that we have found you, where can we keep you safely, eh? We must never let Archie get his hands on you, never."

A shadow of concern seemed to pass across the owl's features and I laughed. She had one of those haughty, rather aristocratic expressions that are sometimes the result of short-sightedness. Slightly spinsterish and genteel – but wise, of course, as all proper owls are wise.

"Did my father use to talk to you like this? I wonder – if only wooden owls could speak but . . . never mind. I've found you, that's the main thing. Perhaps I should hide you in the summer house. What? Are you frowning? You're right, that is definitely not a good idea since people are bound to come from the house sooner or later to inspect the damage. But who can be trusted to keep you safe until Adam arrives?"

I could have sworn Dora frowned slightly, as if to say, how could I be so stupid . . .

"Ted Bury, yes, I should have thought of him myself."

I ran my fingers lovingly over the smooth surface of the wood. The little owl sat so comfortably in my palm, as if she had always belonged there. Just as she must have rested in my father's hand all those years ago.

The pattern, the story, that I had struggled so long to understand was now revealed in all its wondrous simplicity. It was so easy, now, to imagine my father, that sensitive and desperately lonely boy still grieving for the loss of his mother; a boy who found no solace in his father's grim house and who escaped instead into his own special room high in the old holm oak – a room he shared

341

with no one but the little owl carved to console him for the loss of his favourite puppets.

I was sure he had spoken to her, just as I was speaking to her now. Her indignant little face invited conversation; the smooth texture of the wood was resonant with the patina of many whispered confidences. He had shared with her his sorrows and his dreams, his fears and secret hopes. And then he escaped from unhappiness on wings of fantasy and created magical adventures of the mind which he shared with the only person he could really trust – Dora.

How old had my father been when he climbed down from the tree house for the last time and left his Dora in the biscuit tin with his other childhood treasures? Certainly, by the time he went to South America he could no longer remember where the little owl had got to. "I wonder where Dora is now." But Archie could not even remember (had never known?) who she was.

Yet my father never entirely forgot those wondrous fantasies of childhood and early adolescence. Perhaps they only resurfaced when his already unhappy marriage became intolerable and he escaped once again into the daydreams which had sustained him as a boy. Only this time the adult refashioned them into a work of art – *Dora's Room.*

Or perhaps he did not turn to the memory of Dora until the time when he was confronted with the impossible agony of falling in love with his brother's wife. Dora then became both an interpreter to help him understand the complexities of adult life but also, as before, a means of escape. Perhaps it was only through writing the book that my father, in many ways still so immature, had finally come of age. It was this process of growing up, worked through in the novel, which had surely given *Dora's Room* its universal appeal.

I must have looked a complete idiot then, sitting on a branch in the middle of the shrubbery, grinning at the little wooden owl, stroking it, talking to it . . . delight in

342

my discovery was a huge bubble of pleasure, welling up inside me.

Then I heard voices beyond the shrubbery, men's voices and they were coming closer. Instantly I was on my feet again – heaven forbid that Archie should find me here, talking with the elusive Dora. (Would he recognise her? Maybe, maybe not . . . but I had no intention of finding out, not yet.)

Too late now, to go back to the house.

There was a path, one of many, that ran almost parallel to the drive and emerged just before the eagle-topped gate-posts. I set off as fast as my sprained ankle would allow and within five minutes I was on the road and looking down over Long Chatton which still lay, bridal and unreal-looking, beneath its white dusting of snow.

When I had walked a little way down the road I could no longer ignore the pain in my ankle and was forced to pause. I sat down on a boulder on the grass verge and put the biscuit tin down beside me, laying Dora on top. "Rest there, little owl," I said, "you've been cooped up in darkness for far too long." Then I shook off my boot, pulled down my sock and rubbed snow on my ankle which by now seemed to have swollen to twice its normal size. There was a robin sitting on a high branch in the hedge beside me and his song was sharp and clear as the morning air.

The snow did not do much for my already frozen hands but it did ease the pain in my ankle and after a few minutes more I felt able to continue walking towards the village.

I had just eased the boot back over my misshapen ankle when I heard the car.

There is nothing all that unusual about the sound of an approaching car when you are sitting on a boulder beside a quiet country road so I don't know why the sound of that particular car filled me with such unease. The engine was unusually quiet. Stealthy almost, or so it seemed to me, and it was coming from the direction of Chatton Heights.

I had just stood up and tested my weight on the still-painful ankle, when the Daimler appeared around the bend. It must have been instinct, some premonition of danger, that told me this was wrong. The car was not properly following the direction of the road.

I took a step towards the deeper snow of the verge but still the car did not swerve, only continued towards me, straight towards me, that was what was wrong as panic exploded within my skull – the car was aiming straight at me.

In that moment of horrified recognition of danger, the curved façade of the Daimler resembled an evil snarl and I flung myself towards the hedge, plunging into the deeper snow of the ditch, struggling to scramble for safety. But there was no way through the hedge; I was trapped and still the car was roaring straight towards me. Stupidly I put my hands over my face as if somehow by not seeing I could blot out the danger and save myself . . . and then I heard a smashing splintering sound and the noise of gears being crunched and a smell of exhaust and I lowered my hands and saw the rear of the cream-coloured car disappear round the bend in the road that led towards Long Chatton.

Shaking with shock I stumbled out of the ditch and back on to the road.

The snow, although churned up and messy on the road, made it easy enough to trace the car's path. Here were the tracks which showed where it had diverged from the normal route of traffic, here was the point where it had struck the boulder which had perhaps saved my life and here—

"Oh no!" My voice rang out helplessly in the cold still air. "Oh no! Not Dora!"

The biscuit tin was unharmed, a bit dented maybe, but that hardly mattered. Among the fragments of glass where the car's headlights had struck stone were other fragments, fragments of wood. Laburnum wood.

Dora.

"No!"

I fell to my knees and began to search frantically for the precious scraps of wood. This piece could have been a wing tip, this perhaps a tufty ear, and this . . . all at once I could no longer distinguish them. The snowy ground, the gravel and the broken glass, the shattered splinters of wood, had become blurred. My eyes were brimming with tears, huge tears, warm and overflowing and running down my cheeks.

"No!" I wailed again, stupidly, uncontrollably. "Oh no, not Dora too!"

And then my words were engulfed by racking sobs of grief and pain.

To cry for the first time after nearly sixteen years dry-eyed is an agonising and ugly experience. That hurt feeling in my throat, deep down, that I had experienced so many times before, came back now, only ten times stronger than ever before. There was a pressure in my chest as though the grief that was inside me was so strong it must surely burst its way free.

I could hear strange, animal noises and knew they were the sound of my own weeping, but any kind of restraint was impossible. The loss of Dora after I had searched for her for so long – my father's talisman and friend and she would have been my friend too, my talisman – and now she was gone, ripped from me leaving my heart crushed and bleeding.

Everything gone, everything. They couldn't even leave me a little wooden owl, a harmless owl, no use to anyone but it meant everything to me. And now Dora was gone, just as Dring had gone and Paula betrayed me. Why should I have expected anything different? Hadn't I learned long ago that's what always happens – it makes you vulnerable and tears you apart, heart from body, limb from limb until you go nearly crazy with the pain?

Didn't my father once take me on his knee and tell me he would be home again soon and not to cry because he would return before the summer was over? And he never did, he never did. It was lies, all lies. And then my mother changed and slipped away between my fingers and I couldn't hold her. She left me for a different kind of country and there was never any way to come back from that far place either.

I hadn't cried. I had been a good girl like they wanted but although I waited and waited, now everything was gone, even harmless little Dora. And there was nothing left for me to love, not ever.

I suppose I must have been hysterical. Did any cars pass by as I sobbed beside the snowy road? If they did then the drivers no doubt gathered speed and hurried from the sight of a stranger's grief. I don't remember seeing anyone but then I don't suppose I would have noticed if a convoy of trucks had passed within inches. I've never cried that way before and I pray God I never cry that way again.

Harsh, painful sobs. I thought they would tear me apart.

I cried for all the painful loneliness of my childhood, for the secret fear that I had driven my parents away, that I had not been good enough to hold their love, that no one could ever love me. And I cried in a tangle of misery and hurt for all the might-have-beens of my childhood, a childhood that was over, gone for ever with no chance to get it right next time.

Gradually, slowly, my weeping began to change. No longer the awkward, painful sobbing that seemed to be wrenching the heart from my body but a gentler kind of grief. For everything and for nothing in particular. There was comfort now in this sorrow, an easing of pain.

And as the pain lessened there was a new flame that began to burn, white and cold and hard. A strong fire of anger, of rage which I had denied so long. I pounded the earth with my fists and roared my fury at the sky. "How dare they!" I stormed. "How dare they do those things to me!"

And at that moment I hated my father. No wonder my mother had called him a devil, it was nothing less than the truth. He should have known better, he should have thought of his family, of his daughter, me, who needed him and he should never have taken that plane. How could he have abandoned me when I clung to him so desperately, when I was still too young to understand? Why go to South America? Why take that plane? Didn't he know we needed him with us? Hadn't he loved me even enough to stay?

And my mother was no better. She escaped into illness, she had betrayed me, worse even than dying she had left me alone to battle with the stigma, with the awful terror of an insane mother. You were supposed to take care of me but instead you poisoned my life with fear. Fear of the void, that endless black void of panic and craziness.

But no more.

Never again. I was done with all those fears for ever. No one could ever touch me again. I knew the truth, I had discovered it at last. I was whole and I was strong – no, not strong, more than strong, I was invincible. Now I could show them all, tell them all what they had never thought to hear.

Goodness knows how long it took before my weeping died down. All the physical strength had been wrung from me along with my tears. I was exhausted.

Slowly I stood up. Gathered up the shattered fragments of what had once been Dora. Rubbed snow on my cheeks and eyes which were hot and swollen with weeping. Gazed at the snowy scene.

All was just as it had been. Brown tracks on the road, drifts of snow in the ditches. The same robin was singing his bright song in the hedge and in the valley below, somewhere in the village, a dog was barking.

But I was different. Something had happened, something had broken or been built – I could not tell which – and I would never be the same again.

Deep within me a flame of anger had been kindled, a pure fire of rage, and I knew it was going to burn for a long long time.

Chapter 15

By the time I reached the Old Rectory I was so exhausted I could barely stand. The combined effects of my sleepless night, the shock of being nearly run over and my outpouring of grief on the lonely road had left me drained of all emotion. I was aware that my ankle was still throbbing painfully, that my legs were weak as water and that my head ached; most important of all I was aware that I still held the precious biscuit tin; but beyond these basic facts I was aware of very little.

Ted Bury ushered me into his home with the practised calm of someone who has devoted a lifetime to picking up the pieces after other people's catastrophes. As he opened the door I had caught a brief glance of surprise in his face at my dishevelled appearance but he was far too wise to make any comment, enquiring merely if I had breakfasted that morning.

The thought of such a normal activity on this most abnormal of days was so bizarre that I almost laughed, but he seemed to consider it a good idea. "Tea or coffee?" he asked, adding casually, "And while the kettle is boiling you might like to . . . um, freshen up?"

One glance in the bathroom mirror was enough to show what had prompted his suggestion: never in my life before or since have I so closely resembled one of Macbeth's three hags. My hair was tangled with twigs and leaves from my attempt to find safety in the hedge; my hands were scratched and stained with earth and my face was almost unrecognisable, red and puffy from long weeping. The sight of my abject reflection staring back at me over Ted's old-fashioned shaving equipment was almost enough to set me off again, but I splashed cold water on my face until the dangerous moment had passed and then set about patching together some attempt at normality.

Ted had made me a pot of tea and some toast and we sat together in his spacious kitchen; he seemed to be absorbed in his morning paper while I first picked at the toast and then, discovering that I was, after all, quite hungry, ate two pieces.

At length he glanced up. "Would you care for anything else?"

I shook my head and then, after only the briefest moment of hesitation, I pushed my battered and rusted treasure tin across the table towards him.

"I brought this to you for safe keeping," I said, and then, "I found Dora's room this morning – all the evidence that is necessary to disprove Archie's long lie is in that tin."

His white eyebrows swooped closer together into a pair of questioning "S"s, but all he said was, "Do you want to tell me about it?"

And his enquiry was so gentle that I found that yes, I did. I told him about the holm oak and Tom Page and Dora's room; I told him about the puppets and the postcards, the faded exercise books and the little wooden owl called Dora; about the gas-filled room and the summer house and the Daimler coming towards me down the snowy road. This time I did not hesitate in the telling of my tale, no longer dreaded the pitying look that said, as clear as words could have done, "Poor girl, the strain has been too much for her." This time, supported by the evidence of the holm oak and the contents of the tin, I expected to be believed – and Ted's quietly attentive expression and his occasional grunts of understanding or amusement told me that I was believed. And, while I was describing to him all the separate pieces of the puzzle that had baffled me for so long, some of my former emotion began to revive, and I realised, with a kind of grim resignation, that my work at Chatton Heights was not yet complete.

I set my mug down on the scrubbed kitchen table. "And

now I want to ask you one more favour," I said. "Could you give me a lift back to the Heights? Adam will be expecting to find me there and— "

"And?"

"And I want to talk to Archie."

"Under present circumstances," he said, "that seems an altogether strange inclination. Are you sure it would be wise?"

I grinned. "I don't know if wise has anything to do with it."

"Then why?"

I thought for a moment. "I don't know, exactly. I suppose I want to show him I'm not afraid of him any more. Or to show *myself* maybe. To let him know that his secret has been uncovered and that whatever he does to me he can never again stay safe behind his lies. To see his face when he learns the truth about Dora."

"All of them perfectly good reasons," said Ted with one of his rare smiles. "Very well, then, we'll find a safe hiding place here for Clancy's old treasure tin and then, if you are quite sure that's what you want to do, I shall of course drive you up to Chatton Heights." I stood up and was about to thank him for his kindness when he interrupted me, saying sternly, "But only on condition that I stay there with you until Adam arrives. I wouldn't want to have to face that son of mine if anything happened to you now."

We found Adam already waiting for us when we arrived at Chatton Heights. His car was parked on the gravel outside the house and I could see him pacing anxiously in the direction of the shrubbery. Ted sounded his horn to attract his attention, saying as he did so, "A vulgar practice, and one which normally I abhor." Adam turned and, seeing me emerge from his father's car, ran back across the lawns and wrapped me in a warm embrace which can have left his father in no doubt as to how things had changed between us.

"Where the hell have you been?" he muttered fiercely

to the top of my head. "When they told me no one had seen you all morning and that your car hadn't been used I was worried sick."

Suddenly, safe at last in the protection of his embrace, I felt my determination to confront Archie begin to fade. I kissed him gently before pushing him away. "Oh Adam, you can't imagine how much there is to tell you. I found Dora and I found her secret room."

He was staring at me, an expression of amazement spreading across his face. "But Fern," he said, "you're crying . . ."

Angrily I wiped my tears away. "It's all different now. It's – but I can tell you everything later. First I must go and say – say goodbye to Archie."

Adam was about to protest but his father gave him a warning frown. "While you take Fern's belongings to your car," he told his son firmly, "I'll stay in the house, just to keep an eye on things." Adam was clearly irritated by the way he had assumed command but Ted added a gruff, "Don't fret now, Adam. Let her do what she must and there'll be time enough later for explanations."

Just as we were about to enter the house I turned and looking back across the garden I marvelled afresh at the changed outline of the trees, still somehow naked-looking, now that they had lost the huge sheltering umbrella of the holm oak. It was at that moment that I realised I had an unseen companion, my hidden voice, weaving like a silken thread through the tired fabric of my thoughts. I think it had been with me all that morning but, over the past few days, it had become so familiar that often now I only noticed it by its absence.

My ankle was still throbbing, causing me to hobble as we passed through the garden room and down the passageway that led to the hall. Waves of pain pulsed through my leg but I gritted my teeth; let truth and anger make me strong.

In the hallway Ted stopped and pulled out a tapestry-covered chair near the crossed pikestaffs at the foot of the stairs. "I propose to establish a strategic position at the nerve centre of the household," he said, and touched my shoulder briefly. "Go on, then, my dear, go and do what you must."

Adam regarded his father with a kind of baffled annoyance. "You're really relishing all this, aren't you?" he complained.

His father waved him airily away. "Fetch the suitcases, Adam. Do try to make yourself useful for once."

Adam "hrmph"ed irritably as he started up the stairs.

Just as I was crossing the hallway to the corridor leading to Archie's study, Gerald burst in from the direction of the kitchen with such an explosion of fury that we all but collided.

"Bloody bitch!" he exclaimed, and for a moment I thought he had reverted to his original hostility and was referring to me but then he added, "Do you know what she's bloody done now?"

"Who?"

"Tillie. She's— " But I was no longer listening. I caught hold of his arm and pulled him towards the smoking-room. "Don't waste time ranting on about poor Tillie," I said. "Whatever she's done can't be all that important. I'm leaving here in about five minutes and I don't suppose I'll be back for a while but before I go there's something I want to tell you. It will be public knowledge soon enough but it's only fair that you should be one of the first to know."

Once inside the smoking-room he shook himself free of my restraining hand. "I knew it all along," he said sullenly, "you've changed your mind and now you aren't going to rewrite the will after all. I bet you never even intended— "

"Oh Gerald, shut *up*. Of course I'm still going to change the stupid will. I said I would, didn't I, and I'm not about to go back on my word after all that has happened. Now sit down and pay attention."

And, so stunned was he by my sudden air of determination, that he did sit down and he did pay attention. It was so easy that I wondered why on earth I had let myself put up with his boorish behaviour at the beginning. And then I thought: but of course, this is what my family have been waiting for all along. My grandfather's death created a vacuum which only I could fill and over the weeks I had been beginning to fill it, even without knowing that I was doing so. And now *I* was the puppet-master in this house and all I need do was gently manipulate the right string . . .

Firmly banishing this thought from my mind I said, "You've never let yourself do the things you wanted, Gerald, because you've always felt yourself to be in Archie's shadow, that somehow, because of *Dora's Room*, he was an impossible act to follow."

He started to protest but I steam-rollered on. "Maybe that's a bit of an over-simplification, but you know well enough what I'm trying to say. The important thing is, Gerald – and I can't go into all the details now, there's not time, but when you hear them you'll know that I'm only telling you the truth – the important thing is that Archie never wrote *Dora's Room*. No – don't interrupt me, you'll have to accept it sooner or later so you might just as well get used to the idea. He never wrote *Dora's Room* and he never wrote anything else either. His whole life has been a fraud. So you see, when the money has been divided properly and you receive your fair share you'll be free, free to do whatever you want with it, free to *be* whatever it is you want to be."

He was staring at me and his expression was gratifyingly slack-jawed. He swallowed, made a conscious effort to return his mouth to the closed position before opening it again to comment, "Oh hell, when the lawyers discover you're barmy they'll never let you alter the will."

"Don't worry about that," I said, "I'm as sane as anyone in this house." I thought of Tillie and added, "And a good deal saner than many. Do you know, Gerald, I think I must have envied you, for years and years I envied you because you were here with the family while I was on the outside. But over the last few weeks I've come to see how much harder it must have been for you. I suppose what

I'm trying to say is that from now on, whatever happens is up to us. You and me. In their different ways our parents have left us with a hopeless muddle – but we don't have to be the same. That's all. Now I want to go and say goodbye to Archie."

In an unexpected burst of protectiveness towards Archie, Gerald said, "Don't you upset my pa."

I almost laughed. "I shall only tell him what he knows already, or what he's always pretended to know."

As I was leaving the room I caught sight of the two double portraits gazing impassively down at me: Archie and Frances, Clancy and Louise. It was curiously satisfying to know that our conversation had taken place under their timeless scrutiny. I was sure that my mother must be applauding my words wholeheartedly. But what of Aunt Frances? What of my father?

I only hoped that they approved as well.

As I emerged into the hallway Adam was just coming down the stairs carrying my suitcase. Ted, still seated on his tapestry chair, nodded his approval.

"Is there anything else you want to take?" asked Adam. And then, at the foot of the stairs, he set the suitcase down, smoothed back my hair and brushed a kiss across my forehead. "Poor Fern. I've never seen you looking so exhausted. Let's leave right away."

"But I haven't seen Archie yet."

"Surely he can wait. You can always say what you want in a letter – or tell him yourself on your next visit."

It was a deliciously tempting prospect, to stop battling on, to allow myself the luxury of wrapping the blanket around me in Adam's most unluxurious car and telling him everything as we drove, drove away from this hateful house. But, "I must talk to him now," I said, "it won't take long and then we'll be free to go."

It was all I could do to hobble down the passageway that led to Archie's study. I knocked briefly, turned the handle and walked straight in. Only once before had I entered this room and that was on the night when I

354

crept in like a burglar, stealthy and afraid. Now I was too exhausted, too drained, for either stealth or fear.

My uncle was seated in a commodious armchair, his morning paper spread untidily on his lap. He looked deceptively tranquil, considering that barely an hour earlier he had tried to run me over.

He glanced up and said testily, "What the hell are you barging in here for? I thought I told you never— "

"You told me many things," I said wearily, "almost all of them lies."

"Don't be bloody tiresome, Fern. And what in God's name have you been doing to yourself? You look like hell."

"You know what happened as well as I do."

"Do I indeed?" He folded his paper, set it down on the floor beside him and folded his hands contentedly across his stomach. "Riddles time again, is it? Dr Collins should be coming back again any moment. I suppose I might as well play along with your little fantasies in the meantime. Anything to keep the poor imbecile smiling until the medicos arrive. Tell me, then, dear Fern, what is it I'm supposed to know?"

His contempt stung me to anger. "You can forget all about Dr Collins for a start. I'm not mad and I never was and never will be. I'm as sane as anyone who ever set foot in this house – and a good deal saner than most of them."

"Boasting now, are we? Isn't that a little risky, in your condition?"

"Goad me all you like, Archie, but you'll never destroy me the way you destroyed my mother."

"No? Well, never mind. You appear to be doing an admirable job all on your own. I hate to disillusion you, my dear, but contrary to your somewhat obsessive belief I did not destroy your late lamented mother either. Loath though I am to shatter your pathetic illusions I absolutely refuse to be held responsible for that wretched woman's fate. She was insane."

My earlier exhaustion was now all forgotten, swept

355

away by a burning rage. "Everyone is agreed that she was coping well after my father died, until the day you came to Alderly Drive and told her about him and Aunt Frances."

"Frances? What the hell does my wife have to do with this?"

"No more lies, Archie, no more skeletons hidden away. We both know that Aunt Frances' death was not an accident."

His self-satisfied smile gradually turned into a grimace of undiluted hate. "You bloody interfering bitch. Who the hell have you been talking to?"

"People say that you tried to make her death look like an accident because you didn't want everyone to know she committed suicide, especially not Gerald. But it was worse than that, wasn't it? You were responsible for her death."

He was staring at me, his breathing harsh, his eyes round black stones of rage. He raised himself from his chair, took a step towards me, but I stood my ground.

"You murdered her, didn't you, Archie? The same way you've been trying to kill me and make it look like suicide or an accident."

Slowly his expression relaxed again, his hands loosened at his side. "Don't be bloody pathetic, Fern. You don't seriously believe I'm trying trying to murder you, do you?" And he smiled, that feline, taunting smile, coaxing my denial.

"You know you are," I said quietly, "you turned the gas on in my room, you pushed the summer house, you tried to run me over just now."

Archie's smile was expanding into a regular Cheshire cat's grin. "And at what time do you imagine I performed this miracle of teleportation?"

"Don't try to deny it now, Archie."

"You see, my poor dotty niece, I've been tucked up in here all morning and for most of that time the worthy Elsa has been irritating the shit out of me with her hoover and her bloody dusters. What is commonly known as an alibi. If your past performance is anything to go by then my guess is that you stepped out into the traffic and then kicked up hell when some poor driver nearly ran into you. The sooner you get treatment for your problems the better for everyone."

"It was you, Archie."

"Oh yes, I'm famous as the serial killer of Chatton Heights. Might I ask to what motive you ascribe my homicidal tendencies?"

"You must have realised that sooner or later someone would discover your deception, Archie. Well, now they have. *I* have."

His performance had been so polished until now. Was that a flicker of anxiety that flashed across his face at the word deception? It was gone immediately, the complacent smile once more glued to his face.

"Daddy's book, eh? Your brain is addled by too much television, girl. But since you are so patently deranged I shall suppress my natural anger at your accusations. Now, go away, Fern. You're becoming boring. Go and chew on some Valium, or whatever it is you people keep happy with these days, and leave me in peace."

"Lies, Archie, you've tangled everyone in your lies."

He yawned. "So you keep saying. But don't mind me, rant and rave all you like; my only regret is that John Collins isn't here to admire your performance."

"This is no performance." I paused, then took a deep breath and continued quietly, "You see, I've found Dora."

Silence then, the colour draining from his face.

And when he spoke again it was in a voice I had never heard before. "There is no such person as Dora. There never was. She was a fiction from start to finish."

"Not a person, but real enough for all that."

He tried to shrug it off, to turn away and dismiss me, but he could not drag his eyes from my face. "You boring bloody maniac. Go to hell and be damned and take your wretched fantasies with you."

My voice was still quiet, controlled. "I found Dora's room too. You never discovered it, did you? My father

357

knew, but then he knew who Dora was too. Of course he did. It was *his* book. *His* book, Archie, not yours. You're an impostor. You destroyed Dora when you tried to run me over but you can't destroy the truth any more."

"Christ Almighty, I wish I *had* run you over just now. I'd have made sure I did a better job than the poor sod who missed you. And good riddance, you ought to be dead. Where the hell do you think this mythical Dora's room is anyway?"

"Do you remember the tree house Tom Page built for my father during the summer after your mother died? You never climbed up there because you were afraid of heights and the tree house in the holm oak was immensely high. My father used to sit there for hours and the view was spectacular: the horsechestnut, the pond, he could see it all."

Archie licked his lips. "And Dora?"

"Tom Page can tell you about her as well. She was a wooden owl that he had carved for my father at about the same time. I expect Clancy confided in her – you know the way children are – sensitive children, imaginative ones. Not the kind of lout who would as soon kill a real owl as look at it. But you don't know anything about imagination, do you, Archie? Only about stealing other people's dreams. Your problem was that you never understood any of it."

"You are definitely raving."

"This is the truth. The cold hard truth. None of that pretentious nonsense about Dora being an anima figure, a mythical being, anagram of Road. Just an owl, a little wooden owl. So simple really, all the time. But you could never see it."

He attempted a smile. "I have thought for some time that the mystery surrounding Dora had outlived its former usefulness. Did Paul Sobey tell you, when you had lunch together, that I intended to include a full explanation of the Dora enigma in the new edition? The tree house, the owl, I expect it was Paul himself who told you this."

"Stop faking, Archie. You never wrote the book."

"I fear I must disappoint you, Fern. Ingenious though you've been, I don't for a moment believe anyone will listen to you, and as someone who has always maintained an avuncular interest in your well-being, I really must advise— "

"You never give up, do you? But listen to this: I'm not the only person who knows your secret. When the holm oak blew down last night, the tree house blew down as well. That's where I found Dora. And with her all the evidence I need to put paid to you and your lies for ever."

"What – evidence?"

"Notebooks, drawings, early pieces of writing. You thought you had destroyed all my father's papers when you came to Alderly Drive after he died. But you never thought of looking in the tree house?"

"What have you done with it all? Show me."

I laughed bitterly. "You don't suppose I'd make that mistake again, do you? You took the postcards, but the evidence about Dora is safe. It is being looked after by someone who believes me, who had guessed all along that you were a fraud."

"Who?"

"You'll find out soon enough. When the whole world has been told your secret, knows that you're a fraud and a crook. I'm going to expose you, Archie, make sure everyone knows what you've done."

At last, at long last, I could see that he believed me. Half choking in his rage he spluttered, "I never tried to kill you before but by Christ I'll see you dead before— "

He broke off. A strange expression had come into his eyes.

"Before what? Go on, Archie, threaten me all you like. But you can't hurt me now, too many people know the truth."

"Bitch," he gasped, "bitch, can't you see— "

But he seemed unable to finish his sentence. I've read old-fashioned books where choleric gentlemen are seized by fits of apoplexy and that seemed to be what was happening to Archie just then. I suppose I should have gone to help him, but at that moment I was so filled with glorious hatred for him that I don't think I'd have lifted a finger if I'd watched him roasting over a slow fire.

I regret that now. But not much.

As I left the room I turned briefly and said, "If Dr Collins does appear I'll tell him you're not feeling very well."

But he only stared at me, with that peculiar and unforgettable expression clouding his face.

So easy, I thought, as I floated back towards the hallway, so easy. Why have I allowed myself to be so put-upon all this time? (In fact my ankle was still so swollen and painful that I must have hobbled, not floated, but at that moment I truly believed myself to be slicing through the evil of the house like an avenging angel of justice, wielding a two-edged sword – and hobbling was therefore completely out of the question.) The voice floated beside me, curled its way around and through my mind like smoke.

In the hallway Ted Bury half rose as I approached. "Are you ready?" I heard him say.

"I'll just check that Adam hasn't missed anything," my voice replied.

Just as I was about to go up the stairs, Tillie bobbed up behind the curve in the banisters. Her eyes looked at me with an odd expression, almost frightened, I thought. How could I have overlooked Tillie, saddest casualty of all?

I turned. "Tillie," I said, "I'm leaving this house now and I don't know when I'll be back. No, don't say anything. There'll be a good many dramas here over the next few days but you mustn't worry, I won't go back on what I said about the will, I promise. You'll receive your share like everyone else."

She was still staring at me and her tiny mouth moved vigorously but no words emerged. Poor creature, I thought, it's probably a kindly nursing home that offers her most hope now.

Halfway up the stairs I paused and turned back to say,

"By the way, Tillie, if Dr Collins does come you might get him to check on Archie. He seems unwell."

And now that all my tasks were accomplished a kind of overwhelming numbness flooded through me, so that I could barely drag my aching limbs down the corridor that led to Gracie's room. I retrieved the photograph I had been above all anxious not to leave behind: there was my father as a small boy standing in front of the narrow window which was garlanded with summer roses. And there, cradled in his arms and unmistakable now that I knew what to look for, was the little wooden owl.

As I walked back towards my grandfather's room to check that nothing had been overlooked I heard sounds of pandemonium rising from the ground-floor rooms. But too much had happened already that morning and I no longer had the energy to wonder at the cause.

Rest – that was all I longed for.

I went to the window of my grandfather's room and eased the weight from my throbbing ankle, leaning my elbows on the narrow sill. I wanted to look for the last time at the view which had grown so familiar, which had been forever altered with the falling of the holm oak.

On the gravel driveway below I could see Adam slam down the boot of his car and the sight of him was enough to rouse me from my lethargy. Wake up, I told myself, get going.

There was a basin in the corner of the room and I turned on the cold tap, crouching to splash the icy water on my face. The enamel rim of the basin closed over my face like an anaesthetist's mask. The noise from the rest of the house seemed distant and unreal: doors banging, a woman's agitated cries, footsteps on the stairs.

What is it, I wondered. What is happening?

A high-pitched scream (was it mine? No, coming from the direction of the landing, outside my room) and the door howled open.

"Tillie! Whatever— ?"

"He's gone he's gone you murdered him you bloody bitch you murdered him!"

"But Tillie— " Sudden fear made me turn too quickly on my weak ankle and I fell, jarring the side of my head on the hard edge of the basin.

Dazed, I struggled to my feet, gripped the basin as if it had the power to save me.

"Tillie, wait— "

She was changed beyond all recognition. No longer did those china-blue eyes gaze blank and unseeing as a wax doll's. Now all their coldness was focused on me in an intensity of hatred that made me gasp with panic. And her voice, that breathy puffball voice that was incapable of finishing a phrase, had been transformed into a high and lethal stream of venom.

"You can sweat and fear and it's all your fault everything since you came here destroyed it all because of you you'll pay in blood for what you've done to me and now him and he might be dead and all because of you— "

"Is it Archie?"

"What if I loved him I looked after him and he loved me too until you came and took it all and the house and the money and wasn't it enough you had to have him too— "

"But Tillie, you know I never wanted . . ."

"And I was watching and I saw the way how he looked and touched and all for you it wasn't fair you had the money that's why he wanted but I had loved he threw me out and wouldn't and now he can't because of you you you— "

"Tillie, please listen— "

I tried to take a step, to pacify her, to stop her foul tirade, do something but the floor was quicksand swallowing me up and as I fell Tillie loomed over me huge and angular as a sculpture in scrap metal, all arms and legs and elbows and something else – a long and razor-sharp knife.

Her tiny mouth amid its ball of cobweb wrinkles was still spitting poison at me. "Now you can't you're weak I tried before you got away not now not ever again . . ."

And as I caught hold of the corner of the bed and gripped the wooden post and dragged myself to my knees a series of images came into my head: Tillie's bony fingers tearing the photograph to shreds, Tillie turning on the gas, Tillie at the summer house, driving the Daimler. Always Tillie . . . And I had thought . . .

"Oh no!" I groaned. "I should have guessed— "

But Tillie was beyond hearing, beyond everything, so tangled in bitterness and a strange twisted love for Archie she could never escape.

Her voice screamed around my head like the cry of a scavenging gull, like the high-pitched scream of metal, like all the banshees in the world and above the noise of the scream I could hear the voice, louder, always louder, but still indistinct and I thought, yes, I am mad, I must be. None of this is actually happening. It is a nightmare and the real me is strapped into a strait-jacket on a metal bed and the world is exploding in craziness inside my skull.

This is madness, this is insanity, this battle of voices in and around my head and the pain in my ankle and the aching of my head and—

Then I saw the blade of the knife above me. One of those long, thin blades. A filleting knife. I'm going to be a fillet, I thought. No, please, I don't want—

"Tillie, you must listen, for God's sake listen to me!"

And then the knife was curving down in a wide arc and behind the gleam of metal Tillie's eyes were very blue and gazing with a strange concentration that was worse than hatred. All hatred had been wiped away. Now all that remained in those doll's blue eyes was a dedication to finishing her gruesome task. But as the knife came down I rolled over and heard her little grunt of exasperation and her fierce muttering as she grasped the knife more firmly and steadied herself for the second attempt . . .

"No, Tillie, don't— "

I raised my arms to protect my face. The blade flashed again and this time a hot ball of fire bolted through my arm, my wrist, my hand and I stared, as if at some other arm, as the red blood jetted out on to my hand and the

363

strange silver thing, the metal blade, swam from my flesh like some beautiful glancing fish.

My scream had become someone else's scream for I was beyond fear.

Beyond Tillie and this room and the warm red blood pouring from my arm and the filthy knife raised to strike once more. I was in another place.

In this place was air warm as a caress, no thought of danger, no violence here. In the trees above my head were singing birds. Smell of roses, old roses, deep and rich in perfume, crumpled petals like old velvet. And lavender and honeysuckle and new-mown lawns and everywhere the pollen-drowsy murmur of bees and unnamed insects hovering in the sleepy summer air.

And I was safe. I was small again, no bigger than a child, and the arms that held me were those of a strong man. I could see his spidery dark hairs against the pale skin of his arms and through the thin material of his shirt I could smell the summer, warm animal smell of my own father.

My father was the man who held me. His was the voice which wrapped me in its gentleness, its tender mocking humour, its infinite loving.

"Tell me again, Daddy, I want another story."

The knife flashed down. I could see it so clearly, so slowly, but I was powerless to move.

Then a sudden rush of air, a body hurtling against the crazy woman with the knife and a familiar voice yelled out, "Get away from her, you murdering bitch!"

Adam, I thought. Quite peacefully. He's come. To rescue me. But it is too late. I am dying and the strangest part of all is that I don't mind in the least. This must be heaven, then, this warm bowl of summer contentment, this peace and glory. I shall be happy to stay here for ever. Here I can sit on the swing and be safe and feel my father's arms around me and he will never go away, never leave, never let me fall into the void. This time the happiness will never fade.

Now that I can make out the words.

364

"Tell me another story, Daddy."

His voice is gentle as the breeze that ripples through the trees. "Which story do you want to hear?"

"One of the Dora stories. I like them the best."

"Very well then."

And we sit together on the swing and the sunlight glimmers and shivers through the leaves of the holm oak above our heads and the birds fall silent and creep closer so that they too can hear the magical words. I look up and see my father's eyes, brown eyes like my own, loving and tender, eyes that look only at me, smiling into my face as he begins, in his sing-song story-teller's voice:

"Long ago, when I was young, not so very much older than you are now, I had a friend, a wonderful friend. A secret friend, for those are often the best kind. And at night-time when all the grown-ups were sleeping and the moon rose over Long Chatton and magic rustled through every breath of wind, we used to steal away together to our secret room in the trees."

"Tell me about your room, Daddy. Tell me, tell me."

"It was a special place, a magic place. And when you are older, Fern, I shall take you there myself. But you must learn how to keep secrets and not to be afraid of heights and you must never stop believing in magic if I am to take you to Dora's room."

"I will, I will!"

"Then I shall take you there very soon, Fern, we shall go to Dora's room together, I promise."

My father's arms hold me tight, hold me safe from all danger. And my belief in him is unending as the summer days and my happiness will endure for ever.

Epilogue

As Adam walked out of the village he left behind the
gaudy reds and blues and manicured greens of the gardens
and walked along the track leading to the orchard at
Chatton Heights. Dog roses and wild campion were
flowering against the hedge; he had not taken this route
since that January day when he had brought Fern here
for the first time. Six months ago . . . so much had
been transformed in the six months that had seen the
ruthless cold of a Cotswold winter give place to bright
midsummer.

At the entrance to the orchard Adam paused. The fine
weather had held for over a week now, a succession of
lazy days which were already gaining the timeless charm of
all those other remembered summer afternoons. His gaze
lingered on the orchard: long rows of apple trees, their
leaves motionless in the late afternoon heat, stretched
over the curve of the hill: they were old and cankered
and would not bear much fruit. But they would be spared
because they were beautiful.

Adam had paid a visit to his father while Fern was
closeted for yet another meeting with the ever-cautious
Mr Markham. Her bold scheme for changing Everett's
will was in real danger of becoming hopelessly bogged
down in a tangle of legal ifs and buts, yet she was sticking
to her original purpose with her usual determination, that
gritty determination which so often came as a surprise
to those foolish enough to be deceived by her apparent
diffidence.

He was smiling as he walked through the long grass
between the apple trees; thoughts of Fern almost always
brought a warm smile to his face. He had known, perhaps

from the day he opened Jane's front door and saw Fern's pale face, her eyes gazing up at him, dark eyes haunted by some secret fear whose cause he could only guess at, that theirs might grow into a relationship different from the others. In the following weeks he had begun to think it must have been the challenge that attracted him: a girl so unlike any he had known before, who seemed so desperate to reach out and yet who held back, a prisoner of inner terrors. He remembered feeling uncomfortably like the hero of those folk tales who must fight their way through the forest of briars before they can win the sleeping princess – and since he was not prone to reflections of such a whimsical nature, he supposed he must have been falling in love with her even then, though he had not known for sure until he burst into her grandfather's bedroom to find Tillie swinging the kitchen knife in a wide arc, aiming with crazed accuracy at Fern's throat.

He had barrelled Tillie to the floor. Her first cut had inflicted a deep wound on Fern's arm which had left a long and ugly scar – except that Fern did not consider it ugly at all. Her "memory scar" she called it. That moment of terror had blown open the last closed door within her mind and she knew now that the golden voice had been her father's. Adam still found it hard to understand the full significance of this discovery to Fern; he only knew that the events of that snowy morning had marked a vital step on the journey that changed Fern from her former reserve to her present state of confidence and enthusiasm. Like someone who has been kept in a dark prison, she revelled now in her liberty and even the simplest pleasures possessed the spice of novelty.

Fern had succeeded in breaking free, but for some of her relatives the chance of freedom had come too late.

Archie's heart attack had kept him in hospital for over five weeks. Apart from a partial numbness, his body was healed but his condition still baffled his doctors. No organic damage could be found, but since that last verbal battle with Fern he had not uttered a single word. The phrase "elective mutism" was being mentioned – and

Adam appreciated the justice of this; since the man could not speak the truth, since he had used words to spin a web of lies around his life, let him remain forever silent now that the lie had been exposed.

Adam had arranged for a friend on a Sunday paper to investigate the story of Clancy's authorship. He had produced a strong piece which argued the case well – and yet events never turn out as one expects and Fern in particular had been stunned by the response. There were plenty who accepted the story, yet there were others, like his publisher and Archie's loyal cohort of female admirers, who had invested too heavily in the myth of his genius to admit they had been duped. Most observers merely sat back and enjoyed the contest: to Fern's bewilderment she was fast becoming a player in an elaborate literary game. A game which Archie, entombed now behind a wall of silence, refused even to acknowledge.

During the course of their research for the first article, Adam and his colleague had confirmed that Archie's wickedness stopped short of murder (though his cruelty to Louise had in all probability been vicious enough). They had checked out the exact circumstances and learned that, on the afternoon of Frances' death, Archie had remained in the yacht club, drinking with friends; high winds were forecast and Archie and others advised her not to go. But she had already posted her sister the letter explaining her actions, and she ignored their warnings.

Tillie was now in her little bungalow by the sea; for her, too, freedom had come too late. At least she had been spared incarceration in a real prison. Quickly sedated by Dr Collins, Tillie had reverted to her usual appearance of frail dottiness. The doctor had assured the police that faulty medication was the cause of her murderous outbreak and Fern, to Adam's dismay, had refused to press charges. Fern was in contact with the warden of Tillie's sheltered accommodation at least once a week and at the last report Tillie was said to be happily occupied making boxes out of shells. Gluing the empty carcasses of dead lives into artificial patterns seemed an appropriate occupation for the woman, Adam thought.

And Gerald? It seemed likely that Gerald was discovering a kind of freedom. At first, with a loyalty that had amazed Adam, he had raged against Fern for what he saw as her scurrilous attack on his father. But Fern, as always, had stood her ground, waiting until his first fury had subsided: gradually she had shown him how he might cast off the chains of self-doubt and envy with which he had always been burdened. She had encouraged him, bolstered his confidence and she had persuaded Adam to do the same. Recently he had been forced to admit that Gerald was becoming almost pleasant, while Miller's Vintage Car Hire showed signs of turning from a dream to reality.

At the top of the orchard Adam paused to look back over the village. Its stone walls glowed in the afternoon sunshine and beyond them were the vistas of cornfields and pastureland stretching towards Clancy's beloved camel-shaped hill. It seemed remarkable that anyone could live in a place of such beauty and remain so obstinately blind to its teachings.

Though he had not spoken of it to Fern, Adam did wonder if there had perhaps been another victim of the Miller tyranny, one whose suffering had been no less acute for having been unobserved and secret. Several times over the past few days he had found himself remembering an afternoon long ago, an afternoon of mellow sunshine just like this one. He had been about nine years old, a young lad intent on the endlessly absorbing game of secret spying. He had crept through the laurels until he reached the clearing beneath the holm oak where, to his amazement, he saw a man seated on a swing. He recognised him instantly and his first thought was to run away . . . but his curiosity was too strong. He stayed. And stared.

All the village knew Everett Miller. He was the school governor whose appearances terrified the teachers almost as much as their pupils; he was the ogre who bullied his tenants and short-changed the tradesmen, the man whose business interests stretched around the world but who still found time to attend to every detail, not only of his own affairs but also those of his family, his staff and his neighbours, a granite-faced tyrant who scowled his disapproval of modern ways and fashions.

The shock of seeing him now was almost as great as if Adam had found him suddenly naked: in fact there was a kind of nakedness in those hopelessly slumped shoulders, those hands, no longer grasping but lying idly on his lap, that face utterly transformed by a weariness beyond despair. It had been a hot day, and doubtless the old man was sweating . . . or could those really be tears that shone on his cheeks? Appalled, yet fascinated too, Adam had watched for a long time before the figure on the swing stood up slowly, sighed and, without once looking round, turned to walk back to the house.

Recently Adam had devoted some time to finding out more about Everett Miller. He had discovered that the man who was regarded with such awe in the village had been, in fact, a second-rate man of business. A poor judge of character, he had trusted where he should have been wary, gambled when he should have been cautious, and hesitated disastrously when times called for a quick decision. But for his mismanagement, Fern's inheritance would have been far larger than it was. Adam could not help wondering what price Everett had paid to maintain, even to himself, the image of the single-minded businessman. Like so many men of that age and class he had been stuck fast in the web he had inherited and never questioned, a web constructed of blind respect for traditional values, of ruthlessness and reserve, a web that allowed no room for poetry or fun.

Adam had mentioned none of this to Fern. It was only conjecture: after such a lapse of time, and with the cast of characters either dead or silenced, it could hardly be anything else.

He could see Fern now as he emerged from the shrubbery and began to walk across the lawns to the house.

She was saying goodbye to Mr Markham, but as soon as she caught sight of him she raised her hand in greeting and hurried towards him. He brushed a kiss against the mass of her dark hair as she exclaimed, "Lord, how I hate all that legal talk! Do they deliberately make everything as complicated as they can just so that people like me will give in and comply with their own pettifogging wishes?"

"I expect so," Adam laughed, "but I don't believe for a moment that you are buckling under the strain."

"Of course not. And poor Mr Markham knows that as soon as I am twenty-one he'll have to do what I want – unless he intends to have me certified insane so that he can hang on to the trusteeship for ever."

"There's precious little chance of that."

"I know," said Fern, with the happy certainty of one who can laugh at old fears; she caught hold of his hand. "I have something to show you. Tom and Elsa's boy have been hard at work all afternoon."

She led him back along the path he had just followed, turning off suddenly to enter the empty patch of ground from which the remains of the holm oak had only recently been cleared away.

"Look," she said, "they've planted a new one."

The little sapling rose with fragile optimism from the newly dug earth. But Adam only glanced at the tree; it was Fern herself who drew his attention. She was wearing a sleeveless dress of a tawny-coloured cotton; her dark hair was pulled back from her face and her skin glowed with the beginnings of a honeyed tan. It was hard to believe that this was the person he had first seen sitting hunched and miserable that afternoon when they had looked through the drawer of old photographs.

"Well," she demanded, "what do you think?"

"I think you're beautiful."

"But the *tree*, Adam."

"It will take an age to grow, that is, if the new owners don't neglect it."

"Tom has promised to keep an eye on it for me."

"In that case it is sure to thrive." He put his arms around

her shoulders and kissed her softly. "We shall come back here together when it is a fine big tree and we are both old and wizened and have been happy together for a long long while. And we'll remember the time it was planted."

"Do you really believe that, Adam?" Suddenly she was serious, the shadow of old doubts appearing in her eyes.

"Yes. And you too must have faith."

She kissed him; they walked back across the lawn in silence. Often it seemed to Adam that Fern's newfound buoyancy was as fragile as the sapling they had just inspected. It had not always been easy for her to give up the old burdens: Dring's recovery had been slow and Adam knew that Fern blamed herself for her long illness. Fern had shuddered as she spoke of it. "I couldn't bear the thought of losing her so I made myself blind," she had said. And was lavish in her tenderness now.

A few days earlier Fern had at last made contact with one of the doctors who had supervised her mother's care. He said her illness had been organic in origin; that external events might have hastened or delayed her ultimate disintegration but they could not have had any major effect on the course of her illness. He had told Fern there was little chance that her mother's malaise was hereditary.

As they approached the house they could hear the decorators packing up for the day, the clang of metal ladders folding, cheery shouts of "See you tomorrow," and footsteps echoing on the back stairs.

They wandered slowly from room to room, noticing the progress, the changes. The smoking-room, where the double portraits always hung, had been stripped of its sombre wallpaper and was in the process of being painted a serene blue-green.

"*Eau de nil*," Fern commented, "the decorators are adamant it's the last word in sophistication."

Draped in dust-covers, the portraits leaned against the rest of the furniture in the middle of the room. Adam lifted a corner of the chequered cloth and four faces stared out at them impassively.

"I wonder if they approve of your innovations?"

Fern pondered. "Heaven knows, they ought to," she said, "but I can't be sure." She was silent for a moment before adding slowly, "And I honestly believe I don't care what they think, not any more. It no longer seems to be any of their business."

She stood for a little while longer, staring at them thoughtfully, before turning to him with a quick smile. She caught hold of his hand. "Let's inspect the bedrooms."

It was in her grandfather's bedroom that the transformation was most dramatic. It was like watching someone who has lingered too long in mourning cast off their funereal black and dress instead in the colours of sunshine.

Fern looked about her and a frown puckered her forehead. "I do believe," she said thoughtfully, "that they might have overdone the yellow. It's like standing in the centre of a giant buttercup."

"The colour will calm down when the furniture is back in place. You did tell them it wanted cheering up."

"Hmm." And then she giggled suddenly. "Oh Adam, wouldn't my grandfather have *hated* it!"

But Adam remained serious. "I'm not so sure. Sometimes I think that in some contrary way these changes were exactly what he did want all along, though he was too trapped to be able to do it for himself. Yet some hidden part of him was hoping for this when he left everything to you."

Evidently Fern thought he was talking nonsense. "All this trouble just to change the colour of his bedroom?" she queried scornfully.

Adam was on the point of trying to explain when Fern went to the window. A white butterfly was battering its wings against the pane.

"Poor thing. Out you go."

She opened the window.

Adam warned, "It will lay eggs all over Tom's cabbages."

"Lay away," she admonished cheerfully, as the butterfly took off in an erratic line from the window.

Summer sounds drifted up from the garden and the village: the distant hum of mowers, children's voices, birdsong and insect drone. Sunlight was pouring into the room as Adam stepped across the bare boards to take Fern in his arms and kiss her once again.

"The workmen have left. We could stay here tonight."

Fern considered for a few moments before answering softly, "No, Adam. There are no ghosts here now but still . . . this place belongs in the past. Better by far to leave it in peace until the new owners take over."

And Adam was too wise to argue.

The driveway was already deep in shadow as they drove slowly over the potholes to the gate. Fern turned to look back at the house, its windows touched with gold by the fading sun, and already it had assumed that blank, impersonal look of empty houses everywhere, closed in its own secret silence.